# Falling for
# MR. BAD

## The Bradens & Montgomerys
### (Pleasant Hill – Oak Falls)

*Love in Bloom Series*

# Melissa Foster

Cover Design: Elizabeth Mackey Designs
Cover Photography: Sara Eirew Photography

WORLD LITERARY PRESS
PRINTED IN THE UNITED STATES OF AMERICA

# A Note to Readers

I don't think I've ever written a couple who was as stubborn and challenging as Sable Montgomery and Kane Bad. They were so much fun to write! These two have full lives, great families, and so much on their shoulders, they don't even realize the weight of it all. It's no wonder neither knew they were missing love in their lives, much less that they were not open to it. Sparks fly all the way through this funny, sexy story. I hope you fall as hard for Sable and Kane as I have. If this is your first Love in Bloom book, all my love stories are written to stand alone, so dive in and enjoy the fun, sexy ride. You will find a Braden family tree included in the front matter of this book.

For my avid fans, I will answer the burning questions. Yes, Kane's sisters will be getting their own stories, and at the end of this book you'll find a preorder for Pepper Montgomery's story, PLAYING MR. PERFECT, the first book in The Bradens at Ridgeport series.

**Be sure to check out my online bookstore for exclusive discounts on bundles, pre-orders, print books, audiobooks, and more.** Shopping direct is quick and easy. Once your digital purchase is complete, you can start reading or listening in minutes by sending your ebook to the e-reader of your choice or listening to your audiobook on the free and easy-to-use Bookfunnel app. Shop my store:
shop.MelissaFoster.com

The best way to keep up to date with new releases, sales, and exclusive content is to sign up for my newsletter and join my fan club on Facebook, where I chat with readers daily.
www.MelissaFoster.com/news
www.Facebook.com/groups/MelissaFosterFans

## About the Love in Bloom Big-Family Romance Collection

The Bradens & Montgomerys is just one of the series in the Love in Bloom big-family romance collection. Each Love in Bloom book is written to be enjoyed as a stand-alone novel or as part of the larger series, and characters from each series make appearances in future books, so you never miss an engagement, wedding, or birth. A complete list of all series titles is included at the end of this book, along with previews of upcoming publications.

### Download Free First-in-Series eBooks
www.MelissaFoster.com/free-ebooks

### See the Entire Love in Bloom Collection
www.MelissaFoster.com/love-bloom-series

### Download Series Checklists, Family Trees, and Publication Schedules
www.MelissaFoster.com/reader-goodies

### Love Audiobooks? I've got you covered
www.MelissaFoster.com/audio-books

# Chapter One

"SHE'S NOT KEEN on the idea? What kind of musician doesn't jump at the chance to open a world tour for one of the hottest rock stars of the decade?" Kane Bad said into his rental car's Bluetooth Friday evening. He should be back in New York City having a stiff drink and deciding which lucky lady would get on her knees for him. Instead, he was in the Podunk town of Oak Falls, Virginia, home to rolling fields, horse farms, and from what he'd heard, the most stubborn small-town musician on the planet—Sable *Fucking* Montgomery. His younger brother, rock star Johnny Bad, had promised his fiancée that her friend, the guitarist and lead singer for the band Surge, could open for his upcoming tour. As Johnny and his band's manager, it was up to Kane to make sure Sable was good enough for the gig. *If* she rocked the stage and *if* her band wasn't shit, he'd close the deal with the woman who *wasn't keen* on accepting the opportunity of a lifetime. She was obviously either a prima donna or an idiot.

His money was on *both*.

"The kind that doesn't want the gig. I don't know why you bothered going to see her play," Victoria "Victory" Braden said. Victory owned Blank Space Entertainment, the label that

1

represented Johnny and his band, Bad Intentions. She was also one of Johnny's fiancée Jillian Braden's many cousins. "I met Sable at my cousin Nick's wedding, and trust me, she has zero interest in making it big. If she did, she'd have ridden her brother's coattails long ago." Axsel Montgomery was the lead guitarist in the group Inferno, and he was nearly as famous as Johnny.

"I'm here to appease my future sister-in-law, whom I adore and John loves more than life itself. I didn't think he was serious about this woman opening for the tour until he called me a little while ago to tell me how excited Jilly was." Kane had been so sure this was a placating trip, he hadn't even ordered a background check on Sable or her bandmates. He'd gone online to try to find something—*anything*—about them but found nothing beyond comments in music forums and a few poorly taken cell-phone videos of the band playing at local festivals. None of which were clear enough to get a handle on their sound or their image.

"You should save your time and go back to New York. Let me do my job instead of being hell-bent on micromanaging Johnny's career."

"Do I need to remind you how we got here?" Kane owned businesses and properties up and down the East Coast. He'd stepped in to manage his brother's career, and his band, after it came to light that Johnny's previous manager had not only spent years paying a groupie hush money to keep quiet about a daughter of Johnny's that his brother hadn't known existed, but he'd also embezzled more than a million dollars. Kane didn't have any experience managing musicians, but for a man who managed billion-dollar businesses for a living, he assumed it couldn't be nearly that complex. He'd take a boardroom over this nonsense any day, but there was nothing he wouldn't do for his family.

"I get it, Kane. You're not leaving anything to chance. But it's the middle of January, and since the tour's been moved up to March to accommodate extra shows in two of the larger venues, we don't have much time. And you *know* how important pre-event publicity is. I'll give you twenty-four hours. If you can't get her to agree to it by then, I'm doing my job and hiring another band to open so Johnny's tour doesn't go up in flames."

Kane scoffed. "If they're good, I won't need that long. I can seal a deal with my eyes closed. And for the record, Johnny could have a piss-poor opening act, and fans would still be clamoring for more of him."

"That's not the point, and you know it. He doesn't need more bad press."

"No shit. That's why I'm here." They'd finally gotten past the media nightmare surrounding Johnny's situation. The embezzling bastard was in prison, Johnny and his fourteen-year-old daughter, Zoey, had settled into a new life in Maryland with Jillian, and they had twins on the way. Kane had never seen his brother happier, and he didn't want to upset their apple cart. But if this Sable woman and her band weren't stellar onstage, he'd give Victoria the go-ahead and find some way to make it up to his future sister-in-law.

He ended the call and pushed the pedal to the metal. The sooner he got the job done, the sooner he could return to civilization. But as he passed rural farmhouses and stark fields, his speed dropped. He pumped the gas, but the car sputtered and stalled.

*Fuck.*

He maneuvered to the side of the road and tried to restart it, but the damn thing was dead. He should have known it was going to be a crappy day when he'd spilled espresso on his Tom Ford suit on the way into his first morning meeting.

He popped the hood and got out to take a look, cursing under his breath as the brisk winter air stung his cheeks. *This* was what he hated about traveling. Relying on other people's subpar things—vehicles, hotels, airlines. He had a private jet and a fleet of pristine cars at his disposal and owned several luxurious hotels and properties. Yet here he was, stuck on the side of the road in this godforsaken town. He rolled up the sleeves of his dress shirt to check the oil and realized he didn't have a rag.

*Par for the fucking course.*

He wasn't about to ruin a six-thousand-dollar suit for a rental car. He reached for his phone to call for a tow just as an old cherry-red pickup truck pulled up behind him. A tall woman climbed out of the driver's seat wearing baggy overalls speckled with paint and a bulky blue jacket. Her dark hair was piled on her head in what his younger sisters referred to as a messy bun, with strands sticking out all over. Their eyes connected, causing an arousing thrum of heat and an unfamiliar clench in his chest, overshadowing the irritation that had consumed him. He was used to women stirring awareness below his belt, but this new sensation threw him for a loop. She sauntered toward him, bringing her full lips, high cheekbones, and slightly upturned nose into focus, her mesmerizing sea-green eyes drawing his full attention.

"Need a hand?" she asked in a voice as sweet and rough as whiskey.

Wasn't she adorable, thinking she could help? She probably

saw the Mercedes, got an eyeful of him, and thought it was her lucky day. Maybe it was his lucky day, too. Not that he had time to entertain the attraction, but for her he might find the time. Sure enough, her gaze drifted down the length of him, interest gleaming in her eyes. At six-plus feet, with jet-black hair, perfectly manicured scruff, a body full of tattoos, and expertly tailored clothes, he was used to getting more than his fair share of female attention.

"Thanks, sweetheart, but I've got it under control." He closed the hood.

She stopped a few feet away and planted a hand on her hip, eyes narrowing, a scowl forming on those plump lips. "You sure? I'm pretty handy with cars."

*Maybe in the back seat, which doesn't seem like such a bad idea at the moment.* "I'm sure you are. But I've got this."

Her brows lifted, eyes sharpening. "I can see that by how well your fancy car is running. Sure you don't want a hand?"

He wasn't much for country girls, but he liked her sass. He raked his gaze down the length of her, imagining what she looked like without those baggy clothes. He'd bet she had smoking curves and long legs that would feel fucking fantastic wrapped around him. He didn't even have to wonder what she looked like without the usual mask of makeup some women wore. She was makeup free and stunning. If he was stuck in this rinky-dink town overnight, he might as well enjoy himself.

"With the *car*," she hissed, bringing his eyes back to hers.

*Damn.* This one had claws *and* breathed fire. A definite plus in his book. Holding her gaze, he closed the distance between them. "You sure that's all you're offering?"

Her eyes narrowed even more, but there was no hiding the hunger in them. "Keep it in your pants, Casanova. I don't share space with arrogant city boys."

"I assure you, I'm no boy, and my arrogance is well earned."

"Not a boy, huh?" She lifted her chin defiantly. "Ever wrangled a steer? Built a barn? Get those tattooed hands dirty with something other than money?" Before he could respond, she said, "You reek of entitlement, and you've already taken up too much of my time. Good luck with your shitmobile." She turned and stalked away.

"Says the woman driving a twenty-year-old truck," he called after her, amused.

She looked over her shoulder with a victorious smile. "Forty-plus years, and she still purrs like a kitten." As she climbed into the driver's seat, she hollered, "Call Charley's Auto over in Rockingham. They'll fix you up."

He watched her drive away and called roadside assistance. When he mentioned Charley's, they said Rockingham was two hours away, and they'd send someone from a local repair shop.

Half an hour later he was still thinking about the way the paint-speckled, sass-mouthed beauty had fucked with him when a flatbed tow truck arrived. He went to meet the driver and was surprised to see the snarky brunette climb out.

"Hello again, sweetheart. You drive for the auto shop? Does your old man own it or something?"

"*I* own it, and if you call me sweetheart again, I'll hook *you* up to this flatbed and drag you down the road." She held out her hand, flecks of gold shimmering in her serious eyes. "Sable Montgomery, and you are?"

*Fucked.* That's what he was.

He'd wanted to fly under the radar until he'd heard her perform, but he couldn't very well do that now. He should have done his homework. Sable owning an auto shop was news to him, and it made her even more intriguing. "Kane Bad. I'm here on behalf of Johnny Bad to listen to your band play."

He reached for her hand, but she pulled it away, eyes shooting daggers. "I already told Jilly I'm not interested." She strode away and began lowering the lift.

"How can you turn down an offer that hasn't been made yet?"

"Pretty freaking easily."

"And here I thought Southern women were supposed to be hospitable."

She didn't bother to respond as she loaded the car onto the lift, tight jawed and furious. She moved with the confidence of an expert and the stealth of a she-panther. Which he found strangely, and insanely, sexy.

On the way back to town, she kept her eyes trained on the road. "The car just sputtered and stopped?" she asked icily.

A safe subject. Smart woman. "That's right. It's probably the transmission. Think your mechanic can get it fixed quickly?"

She gripped the steering wheel tighter. "It's more likely an ECU failure. These cars are known for them."

"ECU?"

"Engine control unit. The brain of the vehicle. It manages and controls various aspects of the engine's performance." She glanced at him, smirking. "Don't tax your pretty-boy head over it. I'll get it taken care of, *sweetheart.*"

He laughed. "So you do have a sense of humor."

"And a short fuse for bullshit, so how about you ride and not talk?"

"Afraid of a little conversation?"

"Just uninterested."

"You didn't look uninterested when you were checking me out back there."

She scoffed. "Dream on, city boy. Men like you are a dime a dozen."

"Yeah? Are there many self-made billionaires out here?" Kane disliked people who threw their status around, but the words were out of his mouth before he could stop them, like a young boy trying to impress a girl instead of a man who needed to impress no one.

"Is that how you win women over? You wave money and they come running to stroke your overinflated ego?"

"Do I look like a man who needs to wave money to get women to stroke my ego? Or anything else?" He leaned closer, lowering his voice. "Before you answer that, remember, I was there. I saw the way your eyes traveled over my body." He sat back. "But if that's how you want to play it, it's cool. It's not like I'd sleep with a woman I'm going to do business with."

"Stop talking."

"I'm just saying—"

She glowered at him. "We're *not* doing business together, and I'm definitely not fucking you."

As amused as he was by her adamance, he was a competitive guy, and he wasn't about to let her have the last word. "Look, I don't like Johnny's decision any more than I like small towns, but this is his last tour, and he made a promise that I intend to help him keep, assuming your band is worthy."

She eyed him again, daggers in full force. "Jilly told me what happened. We both know he made that promise under duress."

She wasn't wrong. The deal was made the morning Johnny's life had imploded. He and his newly discovered disgruntled teenage daughter had both been too freaked out to be left alone, and Zoey had needed a woman she could trust to go with them when they'd been forced to leave town to avoid the media. Johnny would have signed his life away to make that happen for her. Given how things ended up with Johnny and Jillian, he'd made the right decision.

"That doesn't matter. A Bad's word is as good as gold."

"Well, not this time," Sable said with a huff.

"We'll see about that."

"You just can't stand the idea of losing, can you?" she challenged.

He cocked a grin. "I wouldn't know how that feels. I've never lost." It wasn't exactly true. He'd lost *once*, a long time ago, but he ended up winning in the long run.

"I see my initial arrogant-city-boy assessment was spot-on."

He enjoyed pushing her buttons too much to let this one go. "Like I said, I earned every inch of my arrogance."

She rolled her eyes and pulled into Oak Falls Automotive. The two-story, three-bay shop had a balcony on half of the second level, and he could see patio doors up there, too. The entire building was covered in metal signs from GOODYEAR, FIRESTONE, PENNZOIL, and about a dozen other auto-related companies.

"Do you live upstairs?" he asked as he followed her into a tidy office.

Ignoring his question, she grabbed a clipboard and pen from an ancient metal desk and handed them to him. "Fill this out. I've got to change for my gig or I'll be late."

"Okay. Where's the nearest rental car place?"

"Out by the airport." She headed for a door in the rear of the room.

*Great.* He pulled out his phone and searched for a ride service. "There's no Uber or Lyft out here?"

"Sorry, Dorothy, but in case you haven't noticed, you're not in the big city anymore." As she reached for the door, she shot him a warning stare. "*Don't* touch anything."

She shut the door behind her, and he heard her ascending a staircase. He wrote his name and phone number on the form, leaving the rest of it blank. As he set the clipboard on the desk, he looked around the sparse office, wondering what she was worried about him touching. There were photographs of cars and trucks and more of those tacky metal signs on the walls. A water cooler sat in the corner beside a metal file cabinet with parts catalogs stacked on top of it. He scanned the schedules hanging on the wall beside the desk, which had a computer monitor and a plastic in-box piled high with invoices for auto parts, signed by Sable. He studied her wide, sweeping *S* followed by nearly illegible letters, with the exception of the upright loops from the *B* and *L*. Her signature was feminine and strong. *Fitting.*

He tapped the keyboard, but the monitor didn't bloom to life. *Smart.*

His gaze moved over the jar of lollipops on the other side of the desk beside an open notebook and day planner. Was she a sucker for sweets, or was the candy for kids who came in with their parents? He glanced at the notebook and wasn't surprised to see musical notes and lyrics scribbled on it. *Your musical mind never turns off, does it?* He scanned the day planner, reading over penciled-in appointments for oil changes and alignments, and skidded to a halt on Wednesday night, where *DA* was written in black ink. He flipped the pages of the calendar, noticing DA once a week, on different days and times. *Why so mysterious, sassy girl?*

*Why do I fucking care?*

Pushing aside his annoyance with himself, he turned away from the desk, catching sight of a framed photograph on the wall. He stepped closer, studying the image of a lanky teenager with thick, wild dark hair and an unmistakable smirk sitting on the back of the roof of an old truck, playing the guitar. Her brows were drawn together. A much younger boy with a shock of dark hair holding a child-sized guitar sat beside her. Sable had one cowgirl-booted foot tucked beneath her other knee. Her other foot hung above the bed of the truck, where two teen girls lay on their backs reading, one with dark hair, the other with a mix of dark and fairer hair. Beside the truck a blonde was twirling in the grass, and another, younger-looking blonde was playing with a puppy. He studied the picture more closely. Through the windshield, he made out part of a giant red bow on the hood of the truck and what looked like Sable's name painted on the driver's door beneath the window.

He went to the window of the shop and gazed out at Sable's truck, seeing her name painted just below the window. *I'll be damned.*

"You're still here?"

What was it about that whiskey voice that had his temperature rising? And why hadn't he heard the door open? She was snarky and stealthy. "Where did you expect me to—" he said as he turned around, his thoughts stumbling at the sight of her in a clingy black tank top and skintight jeans tucked into worn cowgirl boots, accentuating killer curves that far exceeded his imagination. He caught the tail end of her pulling the clip from her hair and shaking it out, sending a mass of dark waves tumbling over her shoulders and breasts. Her eyes were smoky and seductive, cheekbones accentuated with makeup, fuckable, tempting lips painted dark red. She was like the hottest cowgirl porn come to life, and man, he'd like to make that movie with her.

She cocked a brow, crossing her arms.

Trying to push away the image he'd conjured of those perfect lips wrapped around his cock, her wild waves tangled in his fist, he cleared his throat and said, "Where did you expect me to go? There's no car service in this town, and I'm here to listen to you play."

"So you're expecting me to drive you?"

"More like hoping you wouldn't mind giving me a lift. I'd offer to pay you, but I know how you feel about that." Drawn to her even with her claws ready to strike, he couldn't resist stepping closer, bringing the odd combination of the sweet scent of confidence and youthful recklessness, throwing him back to his college DJ days. Those were good times, but what the hell? He hadn't thought about them in years.

"As if I have a choice? I don't have time to argue. I'm already late." She stalked past him and opened a closet door, pulling out a brown suede jacket.

"I could give you a few grand for your truck, if you prefer, and drive us both."

She looked at him like he'd lost his mind as she put on her jacket. "Fat chance. Now stop looking at me like I'm starring in your favorite porn movie."

"Now you're a mind reader?"

"It's not exactly a big leap. You're practically drooling."

"Because I'm a gentleman, I wasn't going to mention that spittle dripping from the corner of your mouth, but I believe they call what you're doing transference."

She stormed out of the building, and he followed her, enjoying the view of her gorgeous ass.

SABLE HAD ALREADY had a tough day before Kane Bad had appeared on the scene. She'd spent the morning painting Deloris Aiken's house. Deloris was in her eighties, and she was like a grandmother to Sable. Sable had worked for her husband, Lloyd, at Oak Falls Automotive from the time she was fourteen years old, when he'd taken her under his wing and into the fold of his family, teaching her nearly everything she knew about mechanics and many other life skills. He'd passed away when she was twenty-four and left her the shop in his will. That was almost six years ago, and Sable had been caring for Deloris ever since. But Deloris's cognitive abilities were failing fast, and she'd become a danger to herself. Sable had found her wandering in the fields by her house a month ago, and together with Deloris and her sister, Lara, who lived three hours away and didn't travel, they'd decided it was time for Deloris to move to an assisted-care facility. With the writing on the wall, Deloris had signed power of attorney over to Lara. Sable and her brother-in-law Reed Cross, a historic preservation expert, had offered to fix up Deloris's house so she could sell it to help pay for her care. It was heartbreaking even if inevitable—and now she was in an even fouler mood thanks to Mr. Bad.

She threw open the passenger door of her truck and took out her guitar, feeling Kane's eyes on her as she stalked to the other side and stowed it behind the driver's seat. Why was he there, anyway? She'd made it crystal clear to Jillian that she'd never agree to go on tour with Johnny's band. Jillian had begged her to think about it, and she'd finally given in, just to get her off her back, but Jillian *knew* where she stood. That should have been the end of it. She'd watched her brother's life change with his success and had seen the emotional toll the public criticism had taken on him in the early years, when everything he did was dissected. For a guy who had been afraid to come out in his own hometown, it was painful to watch. Sable had no interest in putting herself out there to be scrutinized by strangers.

She climbed into the truck, trying to rein in her frustration as Kane settled his big, athletic body into the passenger seat. His biceps strained against his dress shirt as he put on his seat belt. She was going to murder Jillian for not warning her that he was coming. She never would have stopped to help him if she'd known why he was there.

Even if he was the epitome of her Achilles' heel.

She was a sucker for men with sharp features, thick black hair, and olive skin, but all that and a true alpha attitude? A man who made no bones about what he wanted? *That* was her kind of candy, and those piercing dark eyes and thigh-tickling scruff were killing her. Don't even get her started on the ink covering his muscular forearms and snaking up his neck. God, she loved tattoos.

Now her office *and* her truck smelled like *him*: dark, dangerous, and too damn enticing. But she wasn't a weak-kneed girl who couldn't control herself. She despised city slickers and all they stood for, with their overinflated egos and money-solves-everything attitudes, and Kane Bad was the very definition of them. As she drove through town, she tried to concentrate on the road and not the heat of his stare.

He reached for her cowgirl hat on the bench seat between them.

"*Don't*," she warned.

His hand stilled. "Special hat?"

"Special hand? Or can you live without it?"

He held his hand up in surrender. "Sorry. Did you get it from your boyfriend?"

"Like an ID bracelet? What am I? Fourteen?"

"My guess is twenty-seven or -eight."

"Don't try to flatter me." She turned down the main drag, heading for JJ's pub. "I'm sure Jilly told you more than you need to know about me."

"Actually, she didn't. She raved about your musical ability and said you weren't keen on opening for the tour."

"Then why are you here?"

"We discussed this already, and I don't enjoy repeating myself."

"Neither do I, and I already gave you your answer." She pulled into the pub's parking lot and drove around back to her usual spot, parking beneath the trees. Without so much as a glance in his direction, she put on her hat, climbed out to grab her guitar, and headed around to the front of the pub.

Kane kept pace beside her, eyeing the building with distaste. "This is where you're playing?"

"No," she said sarcastically. "You're just so irresistible, I thought we'd stop for a drink and piss off my band by not showing up." She reached for the door, but he snagged it first, holding it open for her. Why that annoyed her, she had no idea, but she hurried inside, hoping to lose him in the crowd as she made a beeline for the bar.

She forced a smile as friends called out greetings, and noticed her youngest sister, Brindle, cutting through the crowd.

"You're late," Brindle said.

"I'm aware." Sable shrugged off her jacket and put a hand on the bar beside her friend Jeb Jericho as she lifted her chin toward Jeb's brother, the owner of the pub, Justus, aka JJ. She motioned as if she were doing a shot and mouthed, *Whiskey*. He nodded in acknowledgment and headed her way.

"Who's that yummy guy you walked in with?" Brindle eyed Kane, who was watching them from a few feet away. She waggled her brows. "Is he the reason you're late?"

Jeb arched a brow, his interest piqued.

Sable shot them a death glare as JJ set a shot glass in front of her, his deep-set eyes shifting to Kane, then back to her, silently asking the same question. Oak Falls had a close-knit community. Jeb and his brothers, including Brindle's husband, Trace, were as protective of the Montgomery siblings as Sable was. But Sable could handle her own shit.

She downed the shot, meeting Kane's curious gaze as she said, "He's just some jerk who had car trouble."

"Need me to take care of him?" JJ asked.

"Nope." Sable handed him her jacket and headed up to the stage, where the rest of her band—lead guitarist Tuck Wilder, drummer Lee Jenkins, and bassist and keyboardist, brothers JP and Chris Dunn—were waiting. She felt a stab of guilt for turning down Kane when it wasn't solely her decision to make. She and her bandmates had been playing together since high school and had been there for each other through thick and thin. They'd helped Tuck get through the death of his twin sister, had scraped Chris's heart off the floor after his wife's miscarriages, and they put up with JP's and Lee's incessant need to one-up each other. But she couldn't allow that guilt to take hold when the whole damn bar was waiting for her to play.

Shoving it down deep, she took her guitar out of its case and put on her best show-stopping smile as she hit the stage. Cheers and applause rang out, giving that guilt the boot the way only being onstage could.

Tuck turned his back to the crowd and flipped his dark hair out of his eyes, watching her closely. "You cool, Bell?"

She was closest to Tuck and had been since they were kids. Now he worked with her at the auto shop, and he was the only person on earth other than her niece she'd allow to call her a nickname.

"Good as gold." Adrenaline pumping, she addressed the crowd. "Sorry for the holdup. I had to rescue a pretty-boy city slicker from the side of the road. He's here. You can thank him directly."

Laughter rolled through the crowd as everyone looked around, easily spotting Kane with his slicked-back hair and crisp white dress shirt, standing out like the interloper he was among the T-shirts, cowboy hats, and flannels. He appeared unbothered by the attention. He cocked a brow, as if to say, *Is that all you've got?*

*Not even close.*

"This one's for you, *sweetheart*," she said, and began playing "Woman" by Kesha, causing an eruption of squeals and cheers as girls ran to the dance floor, and Kane shook his head, amusement glittering in his eyes.

# Chapter Two

KANE WAS CAPTIVATED by Sable as she strutted across the stage like the music lived in her soul and the lyrics were the very air she breathed. She was a natural performer, with an unexpected, and exceptional, stage presence. She moved with intensity, radiating wild-child energy that had been honed and harnessed and the unflappable confidence he'd already experienced, creating an undefinable and seductive aura. With her raspy voice and legs that went on forever, she was impossible to look away from.

This woman didn't need anyone telling her what to do or how to do it, and he'd bet she was the same way in the bedroom. He lingered on that thought, unable to remember the last time a woman held his rapt attention in that department.

Sable segued into another song, breaking through his thoughts. He needed to get that shit under control, but he was as drawn to her as he was to success. *Fuck.* He needed a drink. *Stat.*

He stepped up to the bar beside a burly dark-haired guy and motioned to the bartender. He'd seen the guy beside him *and* the bartender sizing him up earlier, and he wondered if one of them was involved with Sable.

"How's it going?" the bartender asked, wiping the bar in front of him.

"Pretty well, thanks. Can I get whatever top-shelf whiskey you've got? Neat. Actually, make it a double."

"It's been a day, huh?" the guy beside him asked as the bartender poured Kane's drink.

"You could say that."

The bartender set the glass in front of Kane. "What brings you to town?"

"Just passing through." He took a drink and nodded toward the stage. "They're pretty good. Have they been playing here long?"

The guy beside him was watching him closely. *Too closely.*

"Longer than I've owned the place," the bartender answered. "This was their first paying gig the year Sable and Chris graduated from high school."

"Chris?"

"Chris Dunn, the keyboardist," the guy beside him said.

"Sable put the band together when she and Chris were teenagers. The other guys are younger than them," the bartender explained.

The cute young blonde Kane had seen scoping him out when she was talking with Sable sidled up to the bar beside him, fanning her face. "*Whew.* Sable is on fire tonight. Hey, Jeb." She smiled at the guy beside him.

Jeb nodded. "Brindle."

"JJ, can I get a pineapple martini, please?" she asked.

"Coming right up," JJ said.

As JJ went to make her drink, she turned to Kane. "Hi, City Slicker. What did you do to piss off my sister?"

Mouthiness must run in the family. "What makes you think

I pissed her off?"

Jeb looked amused by the question.

"The song, the callout, the way she's *not* looking at you," Brindle said.

Yeah, he'd noticed that, too. "Your guess is as good as mine." He took a drink.

"It's Sable. It could be anything," she said as the bartender set her drink down.

"Are you harassing the customers, Brin?" the bartender asked.

"Relax. I'm just saying hello to Sable's new friend." She turned to Kane. "I'm Brindle, by the way, and these guys are my husband's brothers, Jeb and Justus Jericho. JJ owns this place."

"Kane Bad. Nice to meet you all."

JJ and Jeb nodded.

"As in Johnny Bad's brother and new manager?" she asked with awe.

"The one and only." He downed his drink, noticing Jeb's curiosity was piqued.

"No wonder she's pissed." Brindle lowered her voice. "You're here to get her to open for his tour, right?"

Jeb's eyes narrowed. "Just passing through, huh?"

"I was hoping to keep a low profile while we work things out." Kane pushed his empty glass across the bar with a nod.

As JJ refilled Kane's drink, Jeb said, "You're barking up the wrong tree with Sable. She's not interested in horse-and-pony shows."

"Got that right." JJ slid the glass across the bar to Kane.

"No, he's *not*," Brindle insisted. "Sable needs to be barked at. She's too good to be playing here for another decade. No offense, JJ, but look at her up there. She belongs on a bigger stage."

"She doesn't want more," JJ said sternly.

"She just doesn't *know* she wants more," Brindle retorted. "Don't you have customers to tend to?"

JJ shook his head and went to help another customer.

"You're playing a dangerous game, Brindle," Jeb warned, and set a serious stare on Kane. "You'd be smart to take Sable's word over hers."

As Jeb walked away, Brindle said, "Don't listen to them. Her talent is wasted here."

"There's no doubt about that." Kane nodded in Jeb's direction. "Is he her boyfriend?"

"No. He's just a friend."

He cocked a brow. "He seems to want to keep her here pretty badly."

"He's just watching out for her. You know how small towns are. We all watch out for each other."

He knew small towns all right. He'd grown up in one that was driven by gossip and good intentions, both of which often went south.

"You're smart to try to keep a low profile about who you are. Half the people here would run you out of town if they knew what you were really here for."

"Why is that?"

"Because they know what she wants, and like Jeb and JJ, they're protective. You must know our brother, Axsel, is a famous musician."

"Yeah. So?"

"Who do you think taught him how to play?" She hiked a thumb at Sable, who was belting out a country song he'd never heard before. "For years, people tried to convince her to get out

21

of here and go to Nashville or LA and make it big, like Axsel, but she wouldn't."

"Why not?"

Brindle shrugged. "Who knows? Sable isn't exactly the type to share her inner thoughts, but she must have her reasons."

"From what I've seen, she doesn't seem to hold much back."

"That's surface stuff. She'll tell you if she thinks you're a dick, and she'll tell you if she wants a piece of it." She giggled and sipped her drink. "But you'll never know what's really going on inside her head."

He had no idea why she was being so open about Sable, but he'd happily arm himself with whatever information she was willing to share. "Has she always been like that?"

"For as long as I can remember. But she's *always* been there for everyone else. She pushed me and my sisters and Axsel to do the things that make us happy, and she's always had our backs. Even when we didn't deserve it."

His own siblings would probably say the same thing about him.

"That's why I'm going to help you. But you can't let anyone know I'm telling you this." She leaned closer, as if sharing a secret. "If you want to get Sable to agree to open for the tour, tell her you don't want her to do it."

"That won't work."

"You don't know Sable."

"I know her well enough to realize she wouldn't believe I found her and the band unworthy of opening. The other flaw in your suggestion is that I'm a businessman, and I don't make deals built on lies." He finished his drink and pushed to his feet. "Thanks for your help, sweetheart, but I've got this. I never lose."

She stood, lifting her chin as defiantly as her sister had. "I can see I was wrong about how you pissed off Sable. Good luck getting her to listen to you at all."

SABLE REFUSED TO look at Kane while she played, but the heat of his stare was inescapable, bringing the kind of thrill she'd want to chase if he were anyone other than an arrogant, citified prick who wanted to rip her away from the life she loved and wouldn't take no for an answer.

Applause rang out as they finished the set. She put her guitar on the back of the stage and headed for the bar.

"Another kick-ass performance," Chris said as he and her other bandmates fell into step with her. He and JP had the same dirty-blond hair, but that was as far as their similarities went. Chris was a thick-bodied math teacher, as methodical and detail oriented as JP, a lanky ranch hand, was impetuous and scatterbrained.

Lee raked a hand through his shaggy brown hair. "Too bad JP fucked up that last song."

Sable rolled her eyes at the troublemaking construction worker.

"Fuck off, Jenkins," JP said.

She stepped up to the opposite end of the bar from where Kane stood as JJ set three beers on the bar for JP, Lee, and Chris.

"You guys were awesome." JJ held up a glass of water in one hand and a shot glass of whiskey in the other for Sable. "What'll it be?"

23

He tipped his head to the right, and Sable looked in that direction. Kane was walking toward them, eyes trained on her. That unwanted thrill vibrated through her again, stronger and hotter with his every step. She grabbed the shot and tossed it back, but she had a feeling she could be drowning in the amber liquid and it wouldn't quell the burn of desire Kane caused.

Kane put a hand on the bar beside her, his proximity making her temperature rise.

How could a man who embodied all the things she despised turn her on like that? She looked away, intentionally breaking their connection, and said, "You haven't bought your way out of town yet?"

"We still have a matter to settle. Care to talk privately?"

"No."

He leaned around her, speaking to her bandmates. "You all sounded great up there."

*Bastard.*

"Thanks, man," JP said.

"We always do," Lee added.

"Have you ever considered taking your music on the road?" Kane asked.

Chris looked up from the text he was thumbing out. Tuck's gaze moved between Kane and Sable, conveying more scrutiny in that one glance than most people could get across in a diatribe.

"That's the dream, man," JP said.

"Excuse us." Sable grabbed Kane by the arm, dragging him through the crowd, into JJ's office. She closed the door behind them, seething, "Who do you think you are, trying to circumvent me with my own band?"

"I know exactly who I am, and I'm doing what I came here

to do."

His frustratingly calm tone further irritated her. "You already got your answer," she snapped.

"From *you*, but the offer is for you and your band." He stepped closer, eyes never wavering from hers, like a lion stalking his prey. "How do you think they'll feel when they find out you turned down their chance at opening the biggest tour of the decade?"

She swallowed hard, guilt and anger tightening like a noose.

"Are you really that selfish?" His voice was low and seductive, the air between them sparking as hot and precarious as clashing metal.

"Keep your judgments to yourself," she fumed.

"It's an observation, not a judgment." His lips quirked. "Save your selfishness for the bedroom. This is business. This opportunity would change your bandmates' lives."

"And you think watching us play for one night qualifies you to decide what's best for any of us? Your arrogance is infuriating." She stormed away, but he moved with her, standing so close his body heat seeped through her clothing, his rugged scent assaulting, *taunting* her senses. She was livid at him for pushing her, at herself for being turned on by him, and at Jillian for putting her in this position.

"Do you have any idea the kind of notoriety and money we're talking about?"

"I don't give a damn about either of those things."

"I bet your bandmates do. We're talking about roughly fifty grand per show," he said vehemently. "Split between the five of you, that's not piss-away money. You can't tell me it wouldn't change your life."

No amount of money was worth giving up her life or her

privacy. "I like my life as it is."

His eyes narrowed. "You sure about that? A woman like you could go far. This would get you the *attention* you deserve."

He said *attention* invitingly, like a double entendre. Silence descended like darkness upon them, broken only by the heat thrumming between them. "Let *them* open the tour and leave me out of it."

"They're good, Sable, but *you're* phenomenal." He leaned closer, bringing his body and those tempting lips a mere inch from hers, dark eyes boring into her. "But you already know that," he said just above a whisper. "So what are you afraid of?"

"Nothing scares me." The lie shot out like a bullet.

His lips quirked. "Lying is unbecoming of a woman as beautiful and strong as you." He leaned in, his chest brushing hers as he rasped in her ear, "Tell me what you're really afraid of."

His hot breath coasted over her skin, and her mouth went dry.

"Let Big Daddy Kane ease your worries," he whispered gruffly as the door opened behind him.

Neither of them moved. She'd never wanted to hit—*and fuck*—anyone so badly.

Tuck's voice cut through the tension. "Sable. We're up."

"We'll see what the band says," Kane said for her ears only. He leaned back, eyes trained on hers. "Tell them tonight, or I will."

As he strode toward the door, the air rushed from Sable's lungs.

Tuck eyed Kane as he walked past, then turned to Sable. "Did I interrupt a *moment?*"

"Hell no." She stalked past him.

Tuck chuckled. "If you say so."

# Chapter Three

"WHAT'S UP WITH you and Mr. Mafia?" JP asked as they put away their equipment later that night.

"He hasn't taken his eyes off you all night," Lee said.

Tuck arched a brow at Sable.

"It's not what you think." Sable closed her guitar case and glanced over her shoulder at Mr. Tall, Dark, and Arrogant, with his perfectly tailored suit that probably cost more than her entire wardrobe. He was watching her from a high-top table where he'd been all night. She'd seen Brindle drag Trace over to talk with him. She could only imagine the trouble, or rather, the gossip Brindle was stirring up.

"Meaning…?" Chris asked.

Her chest tightened as she looked at the guys she'd grown up with, fought with, laughed with, and on rare occasions, shed tears with, and knew that what she said next would forever change their relationships. This wasn't a conversation for the back of a bar. It wasn't a conversation she wanted to have at all. But even if Kane hadn't called her out on it, she'd have told them what was up, because while she might not want anything to change, the fact that *she* knew there was an offer on the table meant it already had.

"He's not watching me. He's watching *us*. That's Kane Bad. He took over managing his brother Johnny's career last year after all that shit went down. He wants us to open for Johnny's tour."

Chris barked out a laugh. "Sure he does."

Tuck's brows knitted, as if he was trying to figure out if she was serious, but before she could confirm, JP said, "Are you serious? Is that why he asked about taking our band on the road?"

She nodded. "Yeah."

The guys exchanged incredulous glances.

"Seriously?" Chris asked.

"Yes, and keep your voices down. We don't need the whole town weighing in on this."

"What is there to weigh in on?" JP asked. "This is *huge*. It's a no-brainer."

"For *you*," Chris said. "I've got a wife and kids and a job that I actually like."

JP stepped closer to his brother. "Are you kidding, bro? This is what we always dreamed about as kids."

"We're not kids anymore," Chris snapped. "I've got a life. I can't just pick up and travel around the country."

"Are you crazy? This is our chance to *be* something," JP seethed.

Chris gritted his teeth. "What part of 'I can't just pick up and leave' don't you understand?"

"Fuck that," JP said. "You're not going to screw this up for us because you're pussy whipped."

Chris got in JP's face. "That's my *wife* you're talking about."

Sable pushed between them. "*Stop it.* Nothing is going to be decided tonight, and fighting isn't going to solve anything. You don't even know the details or what we'll be paid."

"For once I agree with JP," Lee said. "I don't care if they don't pay us a cent. This is too big to pass up."

Chris glowered at him, then turned to Tuck. "What about you?"

Tuck shrugged. "Seems too good to be true."

All eyes turned to Sable.

"Are you in?" JP asked.

*No* was on the tip of her tongue. Especially after seeing how just the idea of going on tour was coming between them. But there were bigger things at play than friendship or what *she* wanted. The money could go a long way for Chris's kids' college funds, and Tuck was too talented to stick around the town where ghosts of his sister lurked around every corner. Lee and JP were solid musicians, but they'd both dabbled in drugs when they were younger, and she worried about what stardom would do to them. Money and a fast-paced lifestyle could lure them back in. But again, this wasn't about *her* worries.

"We should all hear what he has to say before making any decisions." She eyed JP and Chris. "Think you can hold your shit together long enough to sit down with him and listen?"

Half an hour later they were sitting at a table with Kane as he gave them an overview of what would be involved in opening for the tour. He was the picture of professionalism, briefly covering schedules—three months with US shows three to four times a week, starting the third week of March, and another two months overseas in the fall.

"Are those dates set in stone?" Sable asked, despite knowing the answer. The Bad Intentions tour was the biggest industry news in years, but her thirtieth birthday was at the end of June. She and her twin, Pepper, always celebrated together. This tour would prohibit that.

She added that to the long list of reasons she couldn't agree to it.

"The concerts are sold-out. This is an all-or-nothing offer," Kane said. "Why? What's the problem?"

"No problem. Just curious."

With a nod, Kane went over transportation, finances, promotional efforts, and other details, patiently answering their questions and reassuring them that every detail would be outlined in contracts they could have reviewed by their attorneys.

As if they had attorneys.

"Chris, you mentioned your family. How many children do you have?" Kane asked.

"Two, and I've got to be honest, I don't think my wife will like the idea of me taking off and leaving her to handle everything."

"That's understandable. Kids can be a handful." Kane flashed a knowing smile.

"You have kids?" Chris asked.

"No, but I have sisters who are ten and twelve years younger than me, and I'm sure you've heard about my teenage niece. How old are your kids?"

"My son is nine months, and my daughter is two and a half."

"Little ones," Kane said affectionately. "Your family is welcome to come with us. We'll make sure they have proper accommodations..."

Sable noted how smooth he was, gaining Chris's trust and gathering information as if he really cared. The trouble was, it seemed like he did care. He could have gone straight to the band, but he'd been respectful enough to come to her first. It was easy to imagine him schmoozing business associates at fancy dinner parties or commanding a boardroom in a big-city skyscraper, and just as easy to envision him demanding a private performance in a luxurious bedroom. His gruff voice whispered through her mind. *Let Big Daddy Kane ease your worries.* She still couldn't believe he was arrogant enough to call himself that, but there was no denying the way even the thought of that low demand had lust simmering inside her.

"I think we've covered just about everything," Kane said, drawing her from her runaway thoughts. "I assume you'll want to sleep on it and discuss this as a group and with your families. I'll be in touch with Sable tomorrow, and I'm happy to answer any questions that come up."

He stood, and they all followed suit. Sable was relieved the night was finally over. If she had to be near Kane for another minute, she'd lose her mind. JP and Lee shook his hand, thanking him profusely, while Chris and Tuck were cordial but less enthusiastic. She had a feeling Tuck still didn't believe the offer was real.

As the guys walked away, she moved to follow them, but Kane stepped into her path, his dark eyes turning up the heat again. His lips curved into a grin, and he bent his neck forward, rubbing the back of it, his eyes angling up to see her.

Why was that so sexy?

"I just realized I left my things in the trunk of the rental car. Mind if I catch a ride with you to pick it up, and then maybe you can give me a lift to the B and B where I'm staying? The Bramble Inn?"

What had she done to deserve this torture?

"I THINK THAT went well," Kane said as they drove to Sable's shop. She hadn't said two words, much less looked at him, since they left the pub.

"Of course you do."

"I can read a room, Sable. I know Chris and Tuck are on the fence, but they're leaning my way. The question is, why aren't you?"

She shot him a narrow-eyed glance but didn't respond.

"There's clearly something, or someone, holding you back. You might as well get it out in the open."

She didn't spare him another glance and drove the rest of the way in silence, tension thickening with every passing mile.

When they arrived, she threw open her door, hissing, "Stay here."

He watched her strut into the building. Jesus, she was sexy. All legs and attitude, just begging to be taken down a notch. He was itching to get his hands on her and be the one to bring her to her knees, but that could fuck up Johnny's chances at keeping his promise, and Kane had already crossed lines he shouldn't. He wasn't proud of that. He'd never acted inappropriately with a woman he was doing business with. But he'd never felt anything like the chemistry burning between them, drawing them closer with every cutting remark. Sable got under his skin like no one ever had, pissing him off and turning him on in equal measure, igniting something hot and sharp and primal. It made him crave the forbidden fruit and took everything he had to hold back. It was a good thing Tuck had interrupted them in the bar office, because he'd been seconds from kissing her, and he knew they wouldn't have stopped there. Images of Sable bent over that desk, bare-assed and begging for his cock, had been assaulting him ever since.

She stalked out of the building, snapping him from his fantasy. He needed to shut that shit down fast. She didn't look at him as she piled his overnight bag and briefcase on the seat between them like the Great Wall of China.

"Thanks," he said as she climbed behind the wheel. He didn't like being shut out and moved his things to the floor. "You'd think after all these years, the people in your town would be sick of seeing the same band play every week."

"You'd think," she said flatly, eyes trained on the road.

He allowed her a few minutes of peace as they drove to the other side of town. When the Bramble Inn came into view, he said, "It's easy to see why they're not tired of your band."

She glanced at him curiously.

"For a woman who doesn't want to be in the spotlight, you sure owned that stage. I bet you give a hell of a good perfor-mance every time you play."

"You're not going to get what you want by blowing smoke up my ass."

"I don't waste my time blowing smoke up anyone's ass. I'm trying to figure out what your problem is. Are you afraid of success? Afraid you might not measure up? Because you obviously do, or I wouldn't be trying to get you to take the gig."

She didn't respond as she turned into the parking lot.

"If it's not that, is it because you're attracted to me, and you're afraid you won't be able to keep your hands to yourself? Because it's not like I'm not used to that. I mean..." He motioned to his body and splayed his hands.

She pulled up in front of the entrance and threw the truck

into park, glowering at him. "Don't flatter yourself."

"Do you think I can't read you, just like I read your buddies? While we were discussing the contract, you were replaying what I'd said to you in the office. Wondering what it would be like to hear me tell you exactly what to do and when to do it in a more intimate scenario."

Her eyes narrowed, the desire in them betraying her.

"What's the matter, Sable? Don't like feeling quite so seen?"

"You're wrong," she said coyly. "You're easier to take when you don't speak. I was wondering what it would be like to gag you."

"Then I wasn't very far off the mark, was I?" He leaned closer, enjoying the flames burning up her cheeks. *This*, he could work with. "If the situation were different, I wouldn't mind a little silk-tie play with you." He sat back, letting that sink in and reminding himself the situation *wasn't* different. "But you might want to work on your game face. You suck at being an ice queen."

"If I wanted to freeze you out, you'd be a tundra by now," she said coolly.

He knew he should stop walking such a dangerous line, but he couldn't remember the last time a woman gave as good as she got, and he was fucking enjoying it. "So, you're a tease?"

"No, City Boy. I *take* what I want." A sly grin curved her lips. "I just don't want you."

"Your eyes tell me otherwise. But that's okay, sweetheart. I'm not on the auction block."

She clamped her mouth shut, annoyance overtaking the desire he'd seen.

"How about telling me what else is holding you back from taking the offer? Is it your business? Your family? A boyfriend?

All of the above?"

"Have you considered it might be something simpler? Like I can't stand the messenger?"

"I'll add *lying* to the list of things you suck at."

"While you're at it, you can add smarmy ass to your résumé." She lifted her chin. "Now, if you'll kindly get out of my truck, I have things to do."

"Of course, but we're not done with this conversation." He stepped out of the truck and leaned in to grab his things, holding her gaze. "For the record, if we'd met under different circumstances, those silk ties would be put to much better use while I gave you what your farm boys can't. Sweet dreams, cowgirl."

If looks could kill, he'd be bleeding out on the sidewalk instead of heading into the bed-and-breakfast with a chuckle in his throat and a hard-on for a certain witchy brunette.

# Chapter Four

SABLE AWOKE TO continuous knocking on the side entrance to her apartment. She rolled over and put the pillow over her head, sure it was Brindle, since she'd dodged her texts last night and had turned off her phone. She'd been too sexually and emotionally frustrated to think straight and had been up half the night trying to figure out what to do about the offer. She'd tried to work through it by checking out Kane's rental car, but that made her think of *him*. She'd started writing a new song, but it was filled with so much vitriol, it had made her even angrier. She'd finally given in to the sexual frustration, conjuring images of the annoying city slicker as she gave her battery-operated boyfriend a workout. But orgasming to the image of Kane Bad had pissed her off all over again.

"Sable! Open the fucking door. We need to talk."

*Damn it, JP.*

She threw off the pillow and covers, knocking two note-books off the nightstand, and cursed as she climbed out of bed in her nightshirt and underwear. His incessant knocking echoed in her head as she strode out of her bedroom, through the open living room/kitchen, and pulled the door open, glaring at him. "What the hell is wrong with you, coming here at the ass-crack of dawn?" She walked away without waiting for an answer.

"It's seven o'clock," JP said. "We've been texting you, and we brought you coffee."

"We?" She turned around as Lee and Chris came through the door with a tray of coffee and a bag of doughnuts. *Great.* "Where's Tuck?"

"On his way," Chris said, following JP into the living room while she went into her bedroom.

She pulled on the jeans she'd worn last night and grabbed her phone from the charger, turning it on as she went into the bathroom. She brushed her teeth, scanning two missed calls from Tuck and one from her father and several missed texts from Brindle, Chris, JP, Lee, and Tuck, one from her sister Pepper, and one from a number she didn't recognize, but the preview read, *Sable, it's Kane.* How the hell did he get her number?

Bypassing all the other messages, she opened Pepper's. Her brilliant twin was in most ways her total opposite. While Sable was a night owl, Pepper was an early riser, had no musical ability, and preferred research to anything else, including men. She didn't curse, barely drank, and would sooner walk away from an argument than raise her voice. But they agreed on one thing: Sable belonged in Oak Falls, and Pepper didn't.

Pepper: *I heard you had an unwanted visitor last night.*

Sable: *Brindle has a big mouth.*

Pepper: *She said he was gorgeous and sparks were flying between you two.*

Sable: *They were more like knives. He's an arrogant ass.*

Pepper: *You like arrogant men. Did he change your mind about the tour?*

Sable: *No, and the band just showed up at my place. I have to go talk to them.*

Pepper: *Okay, but remember this is YOUR life. I know you don't want any part of that world, despite the fact that you would blow the world away with your talent, so when you're thinking about what everyone else deserves, please make sure you're on top of that list. Don't let your heart get the better of you.*

Sable: *When have I ever let my heart rule my decisions?*

An eye-rolling emoji popped up.

Pepper: *When haven't you?*

Shoving her phone in her pocket, she went to face the music. Tuck was just coming through the door when she walked into the living room.

"Sorry, Bell. I tried to give you a heads-up."

Chris handed her a to-go cup of coffee. "You're lucky. JP and Lee woke me up at six."

"I bet Katie loved that." Katie was Chris's wife. Sable leaned against the TV stand, drinking her coffee. "I take it you've all made your decisions?"

"No," Tuck said, and the other guys shot him confused looks.

"Dude, you said you were in," Lee said.

"The hell I did," Tuck snapped. "I said I *could* be in, but I wanted to talk to Sable first." He looked at her with a conflicted expression. "We all know how you feel about doing something like this, and on top of that, what'll happen to the garage if we do it? Buddy and Eli can't run it alone." Buddy Wilson had worked at the shop for eight years. He was in his late fifties and was an excellent mechanic, but he was slow as molasses, and Eli Norwood was a sixteen-year-old part-timer Sable had taken under her wing last year. Eli was great, but forgetful as shit.

"She'll be so rich, the garage won't matter," JP said.

Sable looked at him incredulously. "You're not stupid enough to think I run the shop for the money." Before he could respond, she turned to Chris, who had uncertainty written all over his face. "What did Katie say?"

"She's worried about groupies. You know our history, and Axsel makes it sound like there are groupies all over him twenty-four-seven."

Chris and Katie had gone through a rough patch right before they'd gotten married, and he'd cheated on her. They'd worked through it, and though marrying a guy who had cheated wasn't something Sable would have done, they'd been solid ever since.

Sable knew she could use this opportunity to sway his decision, but she wasn't that big of a jerk. "You're not Axsel. He gets off on that and encourages it."

"Katie knows that." Chris leaned forward, elbows on his knees. "She's still worried, but we can't walk away from a chance to pay off our debt and save for our kids' college educations. She agreed to take the kids on the road with us, with about a million stipulations, but I guess I don't blame her for that."

Sable had known that Chris would probably convince Katie, but it still hit hard. She looked at Tuck, wanting to talk with him about his decision, but he was a private guy who wouldn't appreciate her doing so in front of the others. She motioned to the balcony, and he pushed to his feet. "We'll be right back."

He followed her out to the balcony, closing the door behind them.

"What are you thinking?" she asked.

"That if we take this, we're screwing you out of what you want."

"Take me out of the equation. Where's your head?"

"All over the place." He paced. "You know I don't like the spotlight any more than you do."

"Yeah, but you need to get away from this town and your parents and all the shit they put you through." His parents had always been rough on him, but ever since his twin sister, Thea, was killed in a tragic accident, they'd been brutal.

He leaned both hands on the railing, gazing out at the road. "Once the media gets wind of my past, it could hurt the band's reputation."

"No, it won't. You were a kid when your sister died, and it screwed you up for a while. There's no shame in that. So you did some things that you're not proud of, and you were in and out of juvie. It's not like you were in prison."

He nodded, going quiet for a minute. "But Thea's here."

Her heart ached. "No, Tuck. Thea's *here*." She put her hand over his heart. "She will always be with you, no matter where you go. But you're twenty-eight. You're not a kid anymore, and we both know Thea would've wanted to see you get the hell out of here and make something of yourself."

He pushed from the railing, pacing again. "What about you, Bell? You don't want this shit."

"You're right, I don't. I've got a lot to figure out. Do you think you can hold down the fort at work this morning? I need to take care of a few things. You can move Kane's rental out of the bay. I already ordered the part."

"No problem. Anything else I can do?"

She shook her head, and they headed inside.

JP and Lee stood up. "Well?" JP asked.

"I need a few hours," Sable said. "I was up half the night. I need to eat breakfast and think this through."

"Come on, Sable," JP said. "You can't seriously be thinking of passing this up."

"I've got a business to think about. It's not an easy decision."

"So, you'd just screw us out of this chance?" JP snapped.

"She said she needs time to think. Let's go." Tuck grabbed JP by the arm, ignoring his complaints as he dragged him out the door behind the others.

Sable wished she could turn back the clock and be so firm with Jillian, she wouldn't dare defy her. Her phone rang as she headed back into her bedroom. She cursed at Kane's number on the screen. *As if I don't have enough pressure already?*

She put the phone to her ear. "How did you get this number?"

"It's surprising how accommodating small-town folks can be, but is that any way to greet the man who's offering you what most people would call the opportunity of a lifetime?"

"I didn't realize this was Johnny Bad. I thought it was his carrier pigeon."

He was quiet for a beat, and she took great pleasure in imagining his irritated expression.

"I'm calling to see if you'd like to meet for breakfast to further discuss the offer before I leave town."

"I don't have time for breakfast. I have a rental car to diagnose."

"Lunch, then?"

"Not likely. What time is your flight?"

"Whatever time I tell my pilot to take off," he said smugly.

She rolled her eyes. "I'll be in touch."

She was about to end the call when Kane said, "The offer expires at one o'clock."

Annoyed, she said, "Typical man, rushing to the finish line."

"One o'clock, Sable. Not a minute later." The line went dead.

*Jerk.* She tossed the phone on the bed and stalked into the bathroom.

SABLE WAS DRIVING to her parents' house when her phone rang with a call from Jillian. Irritation clawed at her as she answered on speakerphone. "I hate you right now."

"You can't hate a pregnant woman."

She pictured her petite mahogany-haired fashion-designer friend with an adorable baby belly and a big-ass grin on her face. "Wanna bet?"

"*Sable*, come on," she pleaded. "You deserve this."

"How could you sic that arrogant ass on me without giving me notice after I told you I wasn't interested?" she fumed.

"I did it because I love you."

"If this is how you love, then I feel sorry for those babies you're carrying."

"*Hey!*" Jillian said in a pouty, offended voice.

"Sorry," she grumbled. "I didn't mean that. But you put me in a shitty position."

"Well, I'm not sorry. And as far as Kane goes, he's not an arrogant ass. I mean, he can be a little cocky, but he has the right to be. The guy's a billionaire with a reputation as a ruthless businessman and a sought-after lover. And get this. Women call him *Big Daddy Kane.* Can you believe that? It's true. When I first met him, before Johnny and I got together, I told him that nickname made me gag, and Kane didn't miss a beat. He said he went down smoothly. No gagging involved." Jillian laughed. "He's definitely got game."

Sable cursed under her breath. She'd known he must've been a player, so why did that proof bother her? "Do you have a point?"

"Don't I always? He was there for Johnny and Zoey, and even for me, every step of the way when all that crap went down last year. He could've just hired another manager for Johnny, but he wasn't taking any chances at his brother getting hurt again. He's a *good* guy, Sable."

"You just like him because you're marrying into his family, and you thought I'd agree to do it because he looks like filthy, wild sex on legs."

Jillian laughed. "That he does, and I don't just like him because he's going to be my brother-in-law. He's smart, honest, and caring, and he gets things done. In fact, speaking of Kane getting things done," she said more playfully, "You two would be hot together. He could do *you*."

"Goodbye, Jilly."

"Wait! Are you going to do it?"

Sable gritted her teeth. "I'm *not* screwing your future brother-in-law."

"Well, that's a shame, but I meant taking the offer to do the tour."

"I'd rather screw the arrogant ass. I've got to go, and in the future, please keep me out of your harebrained ideas." She ended the call and turned down her parents' street, the knots in her chest loosening.

Their old Victorian came into view, with its welcoming

wraparound porch and enormous yard filled with childhood memories. She had such good memories of running around with her six siblings—Grace, Pepper, Amber, Morgyn, Brindle, and Axsel. They all lived nearby except Pepper, who lived in Charlottesville, and Axsel, who basically lived on the road. Usually one or two of her sisters joined them for breakfast a few times each month, but this morning her parents' driveway was full, causing those knots to tighten again.

Sable had read Brindle's texts after she'd showered. Her pushy sister had admitted to wanting to help Kane convince her to open for the tour. Sable had no doubt that Brindle had told her entire family, and probably half the town, exactly why Kane was there. She considered turning around and driving away, but Brindle was relentless when she wanted to be. She might as well get it over with.

She headed up the walk to the kitchen door and heard their muffled voices talking over one another. Steeling herself, she headed inside.

"Finally!" Brindle exclaimed, causing their parents' golden retrievers, Dolly and Reba, to come running.

All eyes turned to Sable as she loved up the dogs. Her mother was plating eggs and bacon at the stove, while her oldest sister, Grace, and her husband, Reed, stood at the island eating muffins. Sable felt a pang in her chest. They had been having trouble getting pregnant and had just undergone their second round of IVF. Reed had opened up to her when they were working at Deloris's house about how hopeful he was, and she'd spoken to Grace the other day about it. She knew her sister was trying to temper her hope so as not to be too disappointed if the procedure didn't work. She needed to be there to support them. She glanced at Morgyn, the bohemian of the family, sitting at the table between Brindle's adorable toddler, Emma Lou, who was busy shoving a fistful of eggs into her mouth and dropping half of it on the floor for the dogs, and her husband, Graham, who happened to be Jillian's brother. *Did you know about this?* Before she could get caught up in that, another thought pushed in. Morgyn and Graham traveled all the time. Sable was lucky to catch them for a few days here and there, but if she went on tour, when would she see them? She glanced at Amber, the quietest of her sisters, sitting beside her husband, Dash, and was hit with another kernel of worry. How many times had Amber stopped by to talk out a problem? Who would she turn to if Sable wasn't there?

Sable struggled to shove those concerns down deep. "I guess Trace and I were the only ones who didn't get an invitation to this morning's party."

"My hubby is fixing his father's barn." Brindle hurried over to Sable, looking as stylish as ever in jeans and a low-cut gray sweater. "And this *party* is for you! Did you agree to open for the tour?"

"Congratulations, Sable. This is huge!" Morgyn popped a piece of bacon into her mouth. She and Brindle were fair haired like their father.

"It sounds like a great opportunity," Grace added, tucking her thick dark hair behind her ear. "You can experience another side of the music industry and you don't even have to relocate. That's a win in my book." She had been a playwright in New York City before reconnecting with Reed and moving back to Oak Falls. Now she wrote and directed plays locally in a theater Reed had renovated.

"*Well?*" Morgyn urged. "Did you take it?"

"Late for your gig, late for breakfast. Did Kane try to convince you *all night long*?" Brindle asked in a singsong voice.

"*Brindle*," Amber chided. "Why do you always assume she's with a guy?"

"Because he's gorgeous, and she's not afraid to go after what she wants," Brindle retorted.

"That is more information than a father needs to know," her father said as he walked into the room.

Graham and Dash chuckled. Sable rolled her eyes and went to grab a muffin from the island.

"It's probably not smart to fool around with the guy who's hiring you," Grace said.

Sable gave her a deadpan look.

"I think Sable's smarter than that. Right, honey?" Her mother held up plates piled high with bacon and eggs. "Shall I make you a plate?" Sable shared her mother's dark hair and emotional strength, but her mother was all warm smiles and hugs and possessed the same ever-present spark of positivity that Morgyn did. In that area, Sable took after her father. She was a slightly skeptical realist.

"No, thanks, but a muzzle for Brindle would be nice."

"Ha ha," Brindle said sarcastically as their mother set the plates on the table and kissed their father.

"It wasn't a joke." Sable bit into her muffin.

"Someone's testy. I guess you didn't get any last night," Brindle teased.

"*Brindle*." Their mother shook her head.

Sable looked at Graham, who was wearing his MIT baseball cap and an amused expression. "Hey, Cracker, did you know your sister sent Kane out here to harass me?"

"I wouldn't call handing you part of a tour that'll go down in history as harassment, but no," Graham answered. "Jilly knows I don't keep secrets from Morgyn, and if I told Morgyn, she'd tell you, so I'm not surprised she kept it from me."

"Well, I for one am elated that the universe has finally stepped in and shined its light on you." Morgyn pushed to her feet, wearing a colorful flowing dress, several long necklaces, and pink cowgirl boots embellished with jewels, all of which were her own creations. She repurposed everything from clothing to lawn mowers and sold them in her store and at craft shows. She hugged Sable. "This is your chance to show the world how great you are."

Sable arched a brow. "Why would I want to do that?"

"Because you deserve to be recognized for your talent," Morgyn said.

Sable knew her sisters meant well, but she was too frustrated to appreciate it at the moment. "I don't play because I want to be *known* for it. I play because I love doing it."

"That's why you should open for the tour!" Brindle exclaimed. "You'll be doing what you love, *and* you'll be able to travel."

"You'll probably get a record deal out of it," Reed said. "And who knows what else. Some opportunities have unexpected rewards." He pulled Grace closer to kiss her temple. He'd reconnected with Grace when he'd come back to town to help his ailing uncle.

"That's right." Grace gazed lovingly at him before turning an excited smile on Sable. "Think about all the things you'll learn about the music industry and the interesting people you'll meet."

"I don't want to push you to do something you don't want to do," Amber said carefully. "But those are all good points."

Her husband, Dash, put his arm around her. "Yes, but we

all know how Sable feels about celebrities and their lifestyles." He winked at Sable.

Sable was protective of all of her siblings, but she was even more so of Amber, who had been diagnosed with epilepsy when she was eight. When Dash, a professional football player turned author, had blown into town with his boyish charm and big personality and had set his sights on Amber, Sable had put him through hell. But he'd pulled out all the stops to win Amber's heart, and in the end he'd won them all over.

"I don't blame her. I could never live in the public eye like that," Amber said. "I don't know how Axsel does it."

"Axsel likes the thrill of it," their father said. "But he's also several years younger than Sable. We'll see how he feels when he turns thirty."

Sable crossed her arms. "Are you calling me old?" She didn't feel old, but with most of her sisters coupled off, she felt...something. She just couldn't place what it was. But it definitely wasn't old.

"I wouldn't dare," her father said. "I'm just saying there's a difference between what people find enjoyable in their early twenties and at thirty."

"Let's not rush her to thirty. She's got a few months before her birthday," their mother pointed out. "Why don't we stop force-feeding opinions and let Sable tell us how *she* feels about the opportunity."

"You already know how I feel about it," Sable said, immediately regretting her sharp tone, which her mother didn't deserve. "Sorry."

"It's okay honey. I take it Kane didn't have anything to say that piqued your interest?" her mother asked.

"Nope." *At least not about music.* She thought about the

dirty things he'd said that *had* piqued her interest, but that just annoyed her anew.

"I don't see what your problem is," Brindle said. "You're already a local celebrity. It wouldn't be that different from playing at festivals."

Sable scoffed, feeling even more twisted up inside than she had when she'd arrived.

"Maybe you'll like it even more," Morgyn suggested.

*I should've left when I had the chance.* "And maybe pigs will fly. Have fun discussing my life. I'll be outside." She pushed through the door, filling her lungs with cold air as she stepped onto the porch and looked out at the yard that held more than its fair share of secrets. She heard the door open behind her, and the dogs barreled into the yard. "Can't I get a minute alone?"

"I'm just bringing you some breakfast, sweetie," her father said.

She turned around, meeting his caring eyes. Her father had always been a stable force in her life. His hair was thinner and graying at the temples, but his patient, thoughtful nature had never changed. Not even while wrangling a gaggle of girls and a rascally boy.

"Sorry, Dad. I guess I'm a little edgy."

"You have a right to be." He handed her a steaming mug of coffee and put a plate of food on the table between the two rocking chairs.

"I'm not hungry, but thanks for the coffee."

"I know. You never eat when you're upset. It was just an excuse to come see you. I told the crew to give you half an hour to eat in peace."

"Thanks. I appreciate that more than you know."

"Let's take a walk." He shifted his gaze to the kitchen window, where Brindle and Morgyn were peering out. "They love you," he said as they descended the porch steps, just as he'd done so many times over the years.

"I know." Sable had never been one to go to her parents when she had problems. Her father had worked full time as a professor of engineering at the local college when she was growing up, and she knew they had their hands full with so many kids and her mother's service dog training business. But her father had always known when she could use a little extra attention, and at those times, he'd ask her to take a walk. They'd usually end up in the barn, where he'd gotten her talking while teaching her how to tinker with riding mowers and tractors, and eventually in the garage, tinkering with her parents' cars. He was heading for the barn now, and she was thankful to have his undivided attention. At least for a little while.

"Brindle's championing you in this endeavor," he said.

"I don't understand *why*. Does she want to live vicariously through me or something? I thought she and Trace were happy."

"She's very happy. In fact, she told your mother they're thinking about trying to have another baby."

"Seriously?" Brindle was an excellent mother and a loving wife, but Sable was a little surprised to hear she wanted more kids already. As the resident secret keeper for all of her siblings, she knew it had been a major adjustment for the sister who had once been even more rebellious than she had, which was no easy feat, to conquer marriage and motherhood.

"That's what she said. She wants Emma Lou to have siblings close in age, but she's going to wait until Grace and Reed find out if this round of IVF worked."

"That's nice of her to wait, but if she's so happy, why is she hounding me?"

"Because you're her idol. You helped her become who she is."

"You mean I kept her out of trouble."

"No, I mean you taught her how to be strong, and you gave her the confidence to live life by her terms, regardless of what anyone else thought about her, and to go to Paris by herself to have bigger experiences so she could figure out what she really wanted. You did for her, and for all the others, what your mother and I could only take so far. Brin just wants to do the same for you."

"I'm already strong and confident. I don't need to get up in front of a hundred thousand people to prove it." The scent of their horses, Sonny and Cher, comforted her as they entered the barn. The horses peered out of their stalls, bobbing their big heads in greeting.

"No, you sure don't." Their father pulled carrots from his coat pocket and handed her two. He petted Sonny as he fed him a carrot. "Do you remember the first time you played onstage?"

"You mean at the pub? How could I ever forget? Being paid to play changed everything. I felt like I was going to throw up before we went on."

"You were pretty nervous that night, but that wasn't the first time you played onstage. Don't you remember the spring you turned eight, when you played at the Jerichos' barn bash?"

She remembered that night well. Her grandmother, who had taught her how to play the guitar, had passed away several months earlier, and she'd been missing her terribly. Her grandmother had been a musician before marrying and having children, and Sable had loved listening to her sing while she did chores, when they took walks, and when they were sitting outside under the stars. She'd shared dozens of stories about her youth, when she'd sung at weddings and other events like the summer music festival in Romance, Virginia, where her grandparents had met. That night at the barn bash, Sable had been singing *to* her grandmother, hoping she'd somehow hear her.

"I don't consider that a stage," she said. "I played while they were setting up. Not at the event."

"Well, I'll never forget what it felt like seeing you standing up there all by yourself. You were a skinny little thing, with your cutoffs and cowgirl boots. Your hair was a tangled mess, and you had dirt on your knees because you'd gotten into a fight with one of the Jericho boys."

"It was Shane. He called Amber a stupid girl."

He laughed softly. "That's right. I remember now. You gave him a heck of a shiner, but he never made that mistake again. When you were up there singing your little heart out and playing your guitar, I swear it was like watching a flower bloom brighter right in front of our eyes. I'd never heard anything so beautiful. It brought tears to your mother's eyes."

She stroked Cher's cheek. "I wasn't that good."

"No? Then why did everyone stop what they were doing to listen? That's when your mother and I knew you'd inherited your grandmother's talent. It was a good thing, too," her father said, bringing her back to the moment. "Because we'd had a hard time figuring you out when you were younger."

"What do you mean?" She fed Cher another carrot.

"While the other girls were playing with dolls or kicking a ball around, reading, playing dress-up, or whatever else kids do, you were taking apart the vacuum, and you were never a talker, so we weren't really sure what was going on in your head. You and Pepper have always marched to a different beat than the others, but when Pep was bothered by something, she'd tell us. You kept yourself busy taking things apart and figuring out how they worked, and you were also the self-appointed protector of our brood."

"Someone had to do it. Even as little kids, Brindle was climbing out windows and Morgyn was stealing stuff out of people's sheds to make things out of them."

He laughed softly. "I never said we didn't appreciate another set of eyes. I'm just pointing out that it was nice to find something else you were passionate about. We could read your mood by the music you played."

"You probably still can."

"For the most part. You know, other kids would've dreamed of becoming a star, but you never looked at it that way. You had a guitar with you every minute, but you were still more interested in taking care of everyone else and fixing anything you could get your hands on than being the center of attention."

"Did that bother you?"

"The fact that you didn't want to be a star? No. That didn't bother me or your mother. And thankfully, when you were ready to learn more about fixing things than I could teach, Lloyd was happy to take you under his wing."

"But I'm still that person, so what are you trying to say?"

He slid a hand into the front pocket of his slacks. "I guess what I'm getting around to is that you don't have to be. We've had some really wonderful men join our family these last few years, and they love your sisters to no end. You don't have to be the one watching out for them anymore. You can follow another dream, and they'll be okay."

She wasn't surprised that he saw what others didn't, but it still made her feel vulnerable. She crossed her arms. "Husbands are not the same as sisters."

"I agree, but, honey, there's a big world out there, and you've barely seen any of it."

"I have a business to run, remember?"

"Yes, and you've got Buddy and Eli to help. I'm sure if you asked Carter Patel, he'd gladly fill in while you're gone. He's bored out of his mind these days."

Carter had worked with Lloyd and had remained on after Sable had taken over. He was an excellent mechanic, but his wife had convinced him to retire two years ago, and he often hung around the shop just to get out of the house.

"And what about Deloris?" she asked, her throat thickening as she thought about their last visit. Deloris had been going in and out of lucidity, and during their last visit, she hadn't recognized Sable.

His brows knitted, compassion warming his gaze. "I think she would want you to explore whatever path makes you the happiest. She might be losing her memory, but a heart never forgets someone they love. You know your mother and the rest of Dash's Darlings will make sure Deloris has plenty of visitors." In addition to creating a workout app, Dash ran a morning exercise group for women, and they dubbed themselves Dash's Darlings. "Talk to me, honey. What do you really want?"

"To keep doing what I'm doing, here in Oak Falls." She paced, getting worked up again. "I'm doing exactly what I've always wanted to do."

"Then there's your answer."

"It's not that easy. How am I supposed to turn it down

knowing I'd be holding the guys back? They deserve this chance."

"Yes, they do. But it sounds like you're against it, so maybe the cost is too high."

She sighed heavily. "This is so hard. I wish Jilly never made that stupid deal."

"And I'm sure Jilly wishes you would take a chance."

She stopped pacing. "Whose side are you on?"

"Yours, always. But being on your side doesn't have to mean agreeing with you."

"So you think I should do it?" she asked incredulously.

"What I think doesn't matter. This is a decision only you can make."

"Well, it sucks. Thanks for the talk, but I'd better get back to work."

"That's where you do your best thinking." He put his arm over her shoulder as they left the barn. "How long is the tour?"

"Five months, but they're doing it in two legs. Three in the spring, two in the fall."

"That's not too bad. You know, you've accomplished a lot in the last few years. Growing your business, mentoring kids like Eli, playing at festivals, and guiding your siblings through a multitude of issues."

"Why do I hear a 'but' coming?"

"I was just thinking that you probably have more you want to do in the future."

"Of course I do."

"Then while you've got your nose in an engine, maybe you should think about how taking five months to do the tour might help or hinder you in accomplishing those things. Right now you're single, but one day you might not be, and taking risks will be harder when you're involved with a partner."

"Do I strike you as the type to settle down and be bossed around?"

"Honey, I don't pretend to know everything about my kids, but I know you're all brass knuckles on the outside and tender heart on the inside."

She rolled her eyes. "What is it with you people and hearts?"

He laughed. "Everybody's got one."

"Well, mine's not tender. That would be Amber or Pepper. Mine's—"

"Guarded?"

"Permanently out to lunch."

# Chapter Five

IT WAS ALMOST twelve thirty when Kane headed outside to the porch of the bed-and-breakfast to check in with his mother before getting tangled up in what he was sure would be another contentious discussion with Sable. He'd spent the morning handling various issues for his businesses and reading through the background checks he'd finally ordered on Sable and her bandmates. He wasn't used to being a step behind, and thankfully, his team of investigators had left no stone unturned. He'd learned a lot about the musically inclined mechanic and her bandmates, but he still wasn't sure why she was adamant about not taking the offer.

He'd figure that out after speaking with his mother, who cheerily answered his call with "Hi, sweetheart. How are you?"

"I'm good, Mom. How are you feeling? Are you resting?"

She'd beaten two forms of cancer within the last year and a half and was currently at home recuperating from her most recent surgery. Thankfully, it had gone well. They'd gotten clear margins, and her blood work had come back showing no signs of cancer. They were all relieved, but since cancer was a sneaky bitch that could return without warning, and it wasn't something Kane could pay off, beat into submission, or slaughter, he doubted he'd ever rest easy again. His parents, on the other hand, had the uncanny ability to find sunshine in the darkest times. Even when his mother had been in the thick of treatments, and Kane had known she'd felt like hell, her sunny outlook had shone through.

"I feel great, honey. You saw me last week. You know I'm up and around and doing well."

This surgery had been much easier than the last. "I also know you push yourself too hard. Are you in any pain?"

"I get a twinge of discomfort every now and then, and I'm a little sore, but no real pain. In fact, I'm currently whipping your father's butt in Scrabble."

Kane smiled. "I bet he's loving that."

"You know how competitive he can be. This is game number two, and Harlow is here cheering him on." Harlow, an actress living in LA, was the older, and feistier, of his two younger sisters.

"Hi, Kane!" Harlow hollered.

"Let me put you on speaker so you can talk to her and Dad," his mother said, and a moment later his father chimed in. "Hi, son."

"Hi, Dad. It's nice of you to let Mom win at Scrabble."

His father laughed. "We all know better than that, but thanks for having my back."

"Hey, Kane, do you miss me?" Harlow asked.

"Like a sore thumb." Harlow was twenty-eight to his thirty-eight, and a bundle of energy. "What're you doing home? I thought your film wasn't wrapping until next month."

"It's not, but the director had a family emergency and gave us the weekend off. So...give me the deets. Have you heard Jilly's friend play yet? Is her band any good? Jilly's on pins and needles waiting to hear how it goes."

"Yeah, I saw them play last night. They're good, and her friend has a voice and stage presence that could put Johnny to shame. Don't tell him I said that."

"Really? I guess that means she's opening for the tour?" his mother asked.

"Jilly will be elated," Harlow exclaimed.

"I haven't gotten confirmation on that yet, so please hold off on saying anything. Sable Montgomery is *not* an easy woman to navigate. She's mouthy and obstinate, and we keep butting heads."

"Of course you do. She sounds just like you," Harlow teased.

"She's worse than me, Har."

"Honey," his mother said carefully. "Don't take this wrong, but are you using your typical hard-nosed businessman approach with her?"

"This is business, Mom. That's the only approach there is."

"Honey, Sable's not a businesswoman—"

"Yes, she is. She owns an auto shop. She's a businesswoman—just a snarky, ornery one."

"But she's also a musician," his mother said. "You know how artists are. Look at your brother and sisters. They might be tough on the outside, but they're sensitive on the inside."

Most people probably wouldn't think Aria, his youngest sister, a tattooist on Cape Cod, was tough, since she had social anxieties and could come across as painfully shy in some situations. But what those people didn't realize was that it took monumental effort for her to be present in those situations, making Aria stronger than most of them.

"Why don't you try showing Sable the guy you are with us?"

his mother suggested. "Relax a little. Show her you're not the big, bad wolf."

"Trust me, Sable is not Little Red. She's more like a she-wolf." A she-wolf with killer legs, a body made for pleasure, and a mouth he'd like to do very dirty things to. He'd promised himself he'd stop crossing those lines with her, even mentally, and silently gave himself hell for it.

"Sounds like you've met your match," his father said.

"Or his rival," Harlow said. "You'd better seal this deal, Kane. I have a hundred bucks riding on it."

"You *bet* on this?" he asked.

"Yup," Harlow said proudly. "So did Aria and Zoey. Aria's in for fifty bucks, and Zoey's in for ten." Aria usually steered clear of drama like bets. Johnny's teenage daughter, Zoey, was another story. She was a savvy little swindler. Kane adored both of them.

"Are you shitting me?"

"*Language*," his mother said.

"Sorry, Mom."

"I'm serious about the bet. Don't let me down," Harlow said. "Jilly said Sable has no interest in making it big and that she didn't think *any* man was capable of changing her mind. But don't worry. Zoey and I have total faith in you."

"Aria bet on *Sable*?" Kane snapped.

"Mm-hm. Sorry," Harlow said. "Jilly said she basically only left Oak Falls under duress, and Aria knows all about standing her ground when she doesn't want to go somewhere."

He didn't know what bothered him more. The fact that his youngest sister didn't have faith in him or that he'd been put in a losing situation from the get-go. "Why did Jilly push to have Sable open for the tour if she knew she didn't want to do it?"

"She said she's too good to be stuck in Oak Falls," Harlow said.

"And it sounds like you agree with her," his mother said.

"It might be time to up your game," his father suggested.

"I'll close this frigging deal, and then Aria and Jilly are going to have some explaining to do." Kane glanced at his watch and gritted his teeth. It was 12:40 and he still hadn't heard from Sable.

Lucy Potter, the woman who owned the bed-and-breakfast, walked out the front door and waved.

Kane waved back, speaking into the phone. "I've got to run. I'll call you when I'm back in the city." He ended the call and put on the charm. "Good afternoon, Lucy. You look lovely."

"Thank you. I have a date with my bridge club."

"I hope you win many tricks. Are you going anywhere near the Oak Falls auto shop?"

"I can be."

KANE CLIMBED OUT of Lucy's car at Oak Falls Automotive feeling like he'd dodged a bullet. The sweet innkeeper spent the whole ride trying to convince him to have dinner with her oldest daughter, which he kindly declined. Unfortunately for his sanity, the only woman he'd like to spend time alone with was the woman who made his blood boil every time she opened her mouth. Since that wasn't something that could happen without impacting the reason he was there, he focused on getting Sable on board for the tour, so he could get the hell out of that town.

He headed for the office. His rental car was parked in the

side lot, which hopefully meant it was repaired and ready to go. As he passed the bays, he saw Tuck working on a car that was on a lift and a teenage boy carrying something to another car that had its hood up two bays over. Sable peered out from beneath the hood. The sea-green eyes that had haunted him all night, turning his dreams into dark fantasies, zeroed in on him like lasers, causing that clench in his chest again, reminding him of their first encounter. How could that have been only yesterday? And why was he so damn attracted to her?

She strutted out of the bay in a snug long-sleeve shirt and jeans that accentuated her curves. "What can I do for you, Mr. Bad?"

"You had a deadline, Miss Montgomery."

She glanced at the clock on the back wall of the shop. "I still have five minutes. How'd you get here, anyway?"

"Lucy Potter was nice enough to drop me off."

"Oh yeah?" She cocked a brow. "Has she tried to set you up with her daughter Arlene yet?"

He couldn't resist toying with her. "How do you know I wasn't with Arlene last night?"

Her eyes narrowed.

"Is that a hint of jealousy I see?"

"More like disgust. You might want to make an appointment at a clinic when you get back to wherever you came from. Let's get this over with." She glanced over her shoulder, calling out, "Eli, you can get started. I'll be back in a few minutes."

"Is he an apprentice?" Kane asked as they walked away from the bays.

"Something like that." She stopped and crossed her arms like they were on opposing sides of a battlefield and she needed the barrier.

"I assume you've thought about the offer?"

"As if I could think about *anything* else? It's not just my life the offer impacts, as you so kindly pointed out, which means I don't really have a choice, do I?"

Here came those claws. "It's your life, Sable. You always have a choice."

"Selfishness belongs in the bedroom. Wasn't that your advice?"

"It's good advice when it comes to business."

"I don't disagree, but I don't have to like it. I'll make this quick. We're going to do the tour, but I have stipulations."

"I assumed you would." He breathed a little easier knowing they were accepting. "But before we get into it, have you considered hiring a band manager?"

"We manage ourselves. Always have, always will."

"You're entering a very different level of business than you're used to in a complicated industry. A good manager can be helpful in navigating contracts, securing record deals, and handling other aspects of the business so you can focus on the music."

Her eyes sparked with a challenge. "Like your brother's manager did?"

"That's one case in a million, Sable. You shouldn't be short-sighted about something this important. I'm sure Axsel can attest to that."

"We're good," she said stubbornly.

He respected her need for control, but she had no clue about what was coming her way. He didn't like the idea of letting her go into this without proper guidance, but he told himself that wasn't his problem. He'd made plenty of business deals with people who should have had better counsel. So why was the idea of Sable flying solo eating away at him? It wasn't like he could manage them. He had enough on his plate, and it would be a conflict of interest. *Jesus Christ. Get the agreement, and get the hell out of town.* "Okay. I'm here if you have questions or if you want me to get you a recommendation for a manager."

"I won't, but thank you."

"That stubbornness is going to bite you in the ass one day."

"Maybe I like to be bitten," she said tauntingly.

*I bet you do.* "Moving on, then. Let's hear those stipulations."

"I want my band taken care of. I know how these things usually work. Marketing and PR focus on the lead singer, and when the lead is female, she's sexualized. I don't want anyone trying to change me, and I want the focus to be on my band, *not* just me."

"I'll make Shea Steele, Johnny's PR rep, who's coordinating marketing efforts for the tour, aware of your request."

"Not just *aware.* I want a guarantee that it will be handled appropriately."

She was sharp. He had to give her that. "Done. What else?"

"We choose the sets and play as much of our original music as we want."

"We wouldn't have it any other way."

"Great." She crossed her arms. "I want Chris and his family to have all the accommodations you promised him at every tour stop."

"My word is as good as gold."

"We'll see if your actions back that up."

"Noted," he said tightly. "What else?"

"Tuck got in trouble as a kid for drinking, vandalizing, and some other things. I don't want that coming back on him in the media."

"Juvenile records are sealed from the public. I know his history, and I don't think he has anything to worry about."

"How can you be sure?"

"I got in trouble for the same kind of things when I was a kid. If word gets out, there might be some initial noise on social media about it, but Shea will spin that to his advantage like my PR rep did for me."

A small smile curved her lips. "Is the city boy a reformed bad boy?"

"Let's just say I redirected my rebellious proclivities to areas that bring richer, more pleasurable rewards."

Their gazes held, the air between them heating up.

"I bet you did," she said just above a whisper. Her eyes widened with surprise, as if she hadn't meant to say it aloud.

*Interesting slip, sweetheart. Did I visit you in your dreams last night, too?*

She cleared her throat and drew her shoulders back, breaking their connection. "I want to be kept off the gossip sites."

"Don't we all? Unfortunately, I have no control over that."

Her jaw twitched.

"But I'll have Shea do her best to quiet the noise where you're concerned. What else?"

She looked at him for a long moment, as if weighing her words. "I'm giving up a lot to do this tour, and I'm not doing it for you or Johnny or Jillian. I'm doing it for my bandmates, and if anything bad happens to them, it's on *you*."

He wasn't going to bicker about blame that didn't need placing, but curiosity about the things she was giving up got the better of him. "I understand this could have an impact on your business, but I think you'll be pleased by the doors it will open for you."

"I told you I don't care about any of that. This tour won't just negatively impact my business. It'll affect my family and every other aspect of my life."

"Isn't that a little dramatic? Unless you get on that stage and do something other than what I saw you do at the pub, the effects should be only positive."

"I'm not talking about what I have to gain from the tour. Do you know how much can happen in five months?" The determination in her eyes morphed into something sadder, more thoughtful, and when she spoke, it wasn't with venom but with deep-seated emotion. "I have a sister undergoing IVF, another who comes over all the time to talk through problems she doesn't share with anyone else. I mentor a kid who could lose focus and go right back to getting into trouble in a *week* without the right guidance, much less several months, and I have a special relationship with someone who could—" She snapped her mouth shut.

He was momentarily struck silent to learn that behind all that toughness was an unexpectedly soft heart. She really was part of a rare breed who wasn't interested in money and fame. He was beginning to understand where her aggression toward him stemmed from. In her eyes, he *was* the big, bad wolf, luring her away from the family and friends she loved, with promises that would benefit other people she cared about—her bandmates. He hadn't realized they had so much in common. He knew how difficult it was to choose between what he wanted to be doing and taking on time-consuming, headache-inducing opportunities simply because it would help the people he cared about. He'd spent a lifetime doing it.

He wrestled with a pang of guilt for pushing her so hard, but at the same time, the last thing she said echoed in his mind, and a streak of jealousy got the better of him. "A special relationship with someone who could *what*? Find another girlfriend?"

Her eyes narrowed. "Do I seem like a woman who gives a damn about losing a man?"

He hated the relief her answer brought *and* the primal need to know what she was dealing with. "Then what is it? Because I'm sure you can hire another mechanic to fill in here. You can be there for your sisters with video calls, and you must have a friend who can help with a rebellious teen while you're gone."

"Like you know anything about helping rebellious teens?"

"Actually, I do. Who do you think kept my sisters safe when they were younger, and still does to this day?"

She held his stare. "*Fine*, so you get that."

Finally, she gave him an inch. But he wanted a hell of a lot more and was surprised by how viscerally he wanted to ease her worries. "Whatever you're concerned about, I'm sure I've already faced it, and I can help."

"I doubt that."

He stepped closer, softening his tone. "Try me."

For a split second, her gaze softened, a fissure in her resolve to shut him out. But in the next breath, it hardened again. "Don't worry about it. I'll figure it out."

Just as he wondered if she fought all her battles alone, Brindle's voice whispered through his mind. *You'll never know what's really going on inside her head...She's always been there for everyone else.*

He knew way too damn much about being the one who was always there on the frontline, fending off adversaries for everyone else. As much as it pissed him off that the idea of any other man getting their hands on her bothered him, if that's what she needed fixed, he'd fucking do it. "I'm not the enemy, Sable. If there's someone special in your life who you need to be there for, I can probably make that happen."

She shook her head. "No, you can't. Just tell me what the next steps are."

He ground his back teeth together, wanting to help her and knowing he needed to take the distance she was offering. Stepping back, he put on his game face and moved on. "Our attorneys will send each of you a contract to review. Once they're ratified, you'll receive a packet detailing schedules and commitments." He extended his hand. "It's been a pleasure doing business with you."

"Your idea of pleasure and mine are very different. Remember, Bad, if things go south, I'm coming after you." A challenge shimmered in her eyes. "Don't disappoint me."

She shook his hand, sending an electric charge straight to his chest, then lower. She must have felt it, too, because she looked down at their joined hands.

He tightened his grip, the caveman in him overriding the businessman. "I never disappoint." He couldn't stop the sly grin tugging at his lips. "My ladies always come first."

# Chapter Six

THE NEXT WEEK and a half flew by as Grace and Reed announced the happy news that they were pregnant and Sable and the band prepared for the tour. Sable made arrangements for coverage at the auto shop as tour contracts were reviewed and ratified, schedules were disseminated, social media pages were created for the band—Sable abhorred the idea and refused to have anything to do with them—and Kane drove her crazy one text and one phone call at a time. She was used to calling the shots, but he always seemed to get the upper hand. She didn't know what it was about them, but every time they communicated, their business-oriented conversations were interlaced with sexual innuendos that left her craving more. If that wasn't enough to put her on edge, word had spread through Oak Falls about Surge opening for Bad Intentions on their worldwide tour. There hadn't even been any press about the decision yet, but the press was no match for the power of Oak Falls gossip. While the band, and just about everyone else, was stoked about the opportunity, Sable was filled with worries and second guesses.

As she sat with Deloris in the recreation room of the assisted living center, those second guesses were hitting hard. She'd planned on telling her about the tour closer to March, but since Deloris's lucidity was precarious at best, and at some point, it would slip away and never return, Pepper had suggested she tell her sooner rather than later. Deloris was having a fairly good day, which should make it easier. Sable had only had to remind her who she was once so far. But as she gazed into the eyes of the woman who had shown her the type of gentle, unconditional love she'd missed out on for so many years with her own grandmother, sharing words of wisdom and lending an ear when Sable didn't want to burden her parents, her chest constricted. Three months was a long time. She hated the idea of losing that time with Deloris. The good moments were so few and far between, she worried Deloris might not remember her at all when she returned.

She couldn't allow herself to get lost in those devastating thoughts. She'd made a commitment, and no matter how much she disliked it, she couldn't renege on the deal. She threw a silent apology up to Lloyd, sure he was watching over his beloved wife, and hoped he wouldn't be too disappointed in her. As she reached for Deloris's hand, Lloyd's slow drawl whispered through her mind. *The best thing about my Dee is the way she makes lemonade out of lemons.* Sable remembered teasing him about that. *She has to, to survive being married to you.* The truth was, Lloyd had doted on his wife right up until the day he died, and Deloris had grieved him for the longest time. Sable knew she still missed him every day, because not a visit passed without conversations about Lloyd.

Gathering all her courage, she said, "Dee, I have some news to share with you."

Deloris tilted her head, giving Sable her full attention. Her silver hair framed her sweet face in short wispy layers. "What is it, dear?"

"You know that I play in a band." She'd learned to remind Deloris of people and certain aspects of their lives, to make things easier for her.

Her brows knitted. "A band."

It didn't come out as a question but more like something she was pondering, giving Sable a pang of hesitation. Sometimes that uncertainty was a precursor to Deloris slipping away. But she didn't want to assume the worst and continued sharing her news. "Yes, and we're going to do a tour for a few months."

"What kind of tour?"

"A musical tour, where we perform in concerts in different towns."

"Well, that'll be something, won't it?" Deloris said excitedly.

"It'll be *something*, all right. But it means I'll be away for several weeks and won't be able to visit you during that time. We can still talk on the phone if that's okay with you." She was worried about how that would work, but she'd talked with one of the aides, and they were willing to try. She'd also asked her mother to keep her updated about Deloris while she was gone, and of course she was happy to do so.

Deloris patted her hand. "That's okay, dear. You can tell me all about it over the phone, and I'll see you when you get back."

"I look forward to it."

Deloris's eyes glazed over with that faraway look that filled Sable with sadness. Her friend looked at their joined hands and withdrew hers. Blinking with confusion.

"Deloris?"

She leaned back, fear rising in her eyes. "Do I know you?"

Sable wanted to say, *Wait! Don't take her away yet.* But

shouting at a disease wouldn't make it stop. "Yes. It's me, Sable—"

"I don't...I don't know you. I don't know *her*," she said louder, looking around, agitated.

Paula, one of the aides, hurried over with an apologetic expression and tried to calm Deloris down.

This was the hardest part, when Sable wanted to be the one to reassure her, tell her that she was safe, and remind her of how much she loved her. But she'd made that mistake when Deloris had first started slipping away, and it had only further upset her. Sable had learned a lot since then. With a heavy heart, she put on her jacket and turned to leave.

"I know how hard this is," Suzie, another aide, said. "Deloris is really lucky to have you in her life, and in her better moments, she's very appreciative of that."

Too choked up to speak, Sable nodded and headed out to her truck.

Her phone rang as she crossed the parking lot, and Pepper's name flashed on the screen. Sable didn't usually need anyone, but her twin often appeared when she did. She tried to pull herself together and put the phone to her ear as she climbed into her truck. "Hey."

"Hi. You don't sound good. Are you okay?"

"Yeah. I just told Deloris about the tour, and a minute later she was gone, like she couldn't handle it."

"Oh, Sable," she said empathetically. "You know that's not how that disease works. I'm so sorry. Maybe I shouldn't have suggested you tell her so soon."

"No, it's better this way. At least I know she heard me. It just sucks."

"I know. Do you want to talk about it?"

"No. I don't even want to think about it. What's going on with you?"

"I got your message about our birthday. It's a bummer that you have a show that night, but we'll toast over video chat. It'll be fine."

She heard the disappointment in Pepper's voice, and her sarcasm came out. "Way to ring in our thirtieth."

"Hey, it's okay. This is going to be a stellar year for both of us. Even though I know you only agreed to do the tour for the guys, I'm really proud of you for stepping out of your comfort zone. You're going to make music lovers very happy, and you might even enjoy it a little."

Sable started the truck. "It's like you don't know me at all."

"Like we never shared a womb," Pepper teased, falling into their old heckling routine.

"Like you never tortured me with scientific facts."

"I think you mean tutored you so you wouldn't flunk high school. Oh yeah, you were busy thinking about getting under cars and arrogant boys' penises."

"I was *not*." She hadn't slept around in high school, but that had never stopped her from making comments about sex just to get Pepper flustered.

"If you say so," she teased.

"Why do I put up with you?" Sable realized she was smiling. Pepper always helped turn her moods around.

"Because I'm the only one you trust with your secrets. Speaking of those tasty little morsels, how's the enticingly sexy arrogant ass doing these days? Still butting heads?"

"Like bulls in a china shop."

"I'm beginning to think that's foreplay for you two. Maybe you should nip it in the bud."

"There's nothing to nip." She didn't know why she bothered lying. If anyone could read her, it was Pepper.

"Really? Is he still sexting you?"

"He doesn't *sext*."

"What would you call thinly veiled innuendos in business texts?"

Just thinking about their conversations made Sable's temperature rise, causing her to feel edgy. She had no idea how she was going to navigate seeing him again when she practically spontaneously combusted from their texts. "Dangerous."

# Chapter Seven

"NOW, THIS IS traveling in style," Lee said from within the luxurious limousine Kane had arranged for them to use while they were in New York City. It was Monday afternoon. They'd already settled in at the hotel, and they were heading to Kane's office to meet Johnny and his band before Surge's promotional photo shoot.

"I could definitely get used to this." JP rolled down the window, taking pictures for Surge's social media pages, which he and Lee were running. He turned the camera on Sable. "How about a smile?"

She held up her middle finger, scowling. She was already sick of having her picture taken.

"Those hotel suites were outrageous. If this is how things will be when we're on tour, Katie won't have a thing to complain about," Chris added.

"Kane owns the hotel we're staying in and lives in the penthouse," Tuck said. "I doubt he owns all the hotels we'll be staying in, but I hope they're all as nice as this one."

As they went on about their accommodations, Sable's phone vibrated with a text. Kane's name appeared on the screen, and she steeled herself against the thrum of desire that had become her constant companion whenever she thought of him. She was determined not to let those feelings get the better of her. She was there for the band, and she wasn't about to allow herself to get sucked into Kane's sexy vortex. From here on out, their communication would be strictly business.

Kane: *Welcome to New York. Have you looked over the schedule changes I sent last night?*

Sable: *Yes.*

Kane: *Any concerns?*

Sable: *Beyond feeling like I'm your marionette?*

Kane: *Lucky for you I have very capable hands.*

She'd experienced several of his very capable body parts in her dreams, but she was *not* going there.

Sable: *I don't like men pulling my strings.*

Her phone vibrated as she hit send, and a message from Axsel popped up.

Axsel: *How's it going so far?*

Sable: *There's too much traffic and the guys have stars in their eyes.*

Volleying texts, she replied to Kane while she waited for Axsel's response.

Kane: *Relinquish control and you might enjoy it.*

Sable: *Do you get off by leading women on?*

Kane: *That isn't a very professional question, but no. Only by getting women off.*

The man was beyond infuriating.

Axsel: *Have you seen delicious Big Daddy Kane yet?*

The car stopped abruptly, and Sable's phone slipped from her hand to the floor. Tuck reached for it, but she snagged it first, quickly replying to Axsel.

Sable: *No, and I bet Big Daddy Kane has a tiny little prick.*

Kane: *I assure you, I do not.*

Sable read the message again, confused about what he was responding to. She scrolled through the messages, and—*Oh no. Nonono.* She'd sent the message intended for Axsel to Kane!

"You okay? You look like you're going to be sick," Tuck said as the driver opened the limousine door for them.

"Fine." Her mind raced as they made their way up to Kane's office. She sent a quick text to Axsel saying she'd catch up with him later and spent the rest of the elevator ride making silent deals with the embarrassment gods in hopes that Kane wouldn't call her out in front of the guys.

A pretty blonde dressed to the nines met them at the reception desk. She offered them coffee and led them to Kane's enormous, elegant office, which was outfitted with mahogany furnishings, leather couches, and an unbeatable view of the city.

Kane stood in front of an impressive desk talking with a stunning brunette holding a thick document. Did everyone who worked for him have to win a beauty pageant? Kane wore another expensive suit that fit him to a tee. Despite Sable's best efforts not to, she reluctantly drank in every inch of the infuriatingly beautiful man as his dark eyes moved over the group, lingering on her. Her body flooded with awareness, and she crossed her arms against the knowing look in Kane's eyes. She narrowed her eyes, willing him not to bring up the text.

He shifted his attention away, speaking coolly. "Make yourselves comfortable. I'll be right with you."

The guys went to sit on the couches, but Sable remained standing as he finished talking with the brunette. He smiled warmly as he thanked her, but that smile turned more business-like when he addressed the band. "I assume your accommodations were acceptable?"

"Dude, they were freaking amazing," JP said, and the guys chimed in with their agreement.

Kane looked at Sable, arching a brow. "Was there a problem with your suite? Hopefully you won't find the bed too *big* or the mattress too *hard*."

*Bastard.* "I don't think there is such a thing, but thanks for your concern."

"Duly noted. Then let's get down to business. We've got a busy schedule. I'm going to introduce you to Johnny and the band before they take off for their interviews, and you'll meet up with them again for dinner this evening. You'll be working with world-renowned photographer and videographer Hawk Pennington for most of the day today. Sable, I believe you know Hawk, since he's Dash's brother."

Sable nodded. She hated to admit it, but Kane was even more impressive than the last time he'd met with them as he went over this week's schedule of photo ops, promotional videos, a PR meeting with Shea Steele to prepare for interviews and podcasts, a meeting with Tom, the tour manager, a recording session, and about a dozen other things, without any notes or the schedule in front of him. He rolled with the ridiculous jokes JP and Lee tossed out and wrangled them back in with minimal effort.

After he was done and had answered all of their questions, he said, "Let's head down to the conference room, and I'll introduce you to Johnny and the rest of the guys."

As her bandmates filed out of the office talking excitedly, Kane sidled up to her, speaking quietly. "Ever heard the saying *curiosity killed the cat?*"

"I'm not concerned. This cat has claws."

A wicked grin crawled into place, and his hand pressed

against her lower back, sending a shiver of heat through her. "Just the way I like it."

Before she could respond, his hand slipped away, and he strode to the front of the group, leading them into a large conference room, where Johnny and his bandmates were waiting. "Gentlemen and Sable, I'd like you to meet the members of Bad Intentions. This is my brother, the one and only Johnny Bad, and his talented bandmates, Adrian, Dion, and Chad. Guys, this is Sable Montgomery, the woman who is going to light the audience on fire with her raspy voice and phenomenal stage presence, and her talented bandmates, guitarist Tuck Wilder, drummer Lee Jenkins, keyboardist Chris Dunn and his brother, bassist JP Dunn."

Sable held back her irritation at that overblown introduction. Had she not made it clear that she wanted more of a spotlight on her band?

Johnny stepped forward with a welcoming smile. He was tall, dark, and gorgeous, but he didn't possess the same striking seductive quality as his domineering brother. "It's a pleasure to meet you all. I'm looking forward to getting to know you."

As their bandmates began greeting one another, Johnny extended his hand to Sable. "I've heard a lot about you. Thank you for agreeing to do the tour."

"We appreciate the opportunity, but please tell your fiancée to leave me out of her future negotiations."

Johnny chuckled. "You'll be able to tell her yourself tonight at dinner. Jilly thinks the world of you, and given the things Kane has said about your performance, I'd say she has an eye for talent."

"Thank you. My band makes me look good."

"Our bands do that for us, but own your talent, Sable."

Johnny's expression turned serious. "It's a part of you nobody else can possess."

"Mind if we interrupt? The other guys would like to meet the man of the hour," Dion said as he and Adrian, an eyeliner-wearing, goatee-sporting Kurt Cobain lookalike, approached. Dion had short dreads, several of which were dyed blond, and a killer smile. His hair and skin were as dark as Adrian's were fair.

"Not at all," Johnny said. "If you'll excuse me, Sable. You're in good hands with Kane today. He'll be overseeing the photo shoot, and we'll catch up over dinner."

As Johnny walked away, Dion said, "How's it going, beautiful? We're really glad you'll be traveling with us."

"Thanks. I've never been on tour, so I'm not sure what to expect," she said, catching Kane watching them.

"Expect a rush like you've never experienced. It's indescribable."

"And exhausting," Adrian added. "The fans are wild, and there's endless booze and just about anything else you could want."

"But don't worry. I'll have your back," Dion said. "And if you want a roommate, I'm your guy."

Adrian scoffed. "You don't want to share a bed with this guy. He never showers."

"You'll have to excuse my buddy," Dion said with a laugh. "He hasn't been the same since his lobotomy."

Sable laughed, enjoying their banter, but there was no escaping the heat of Kane's searing stare as they continued chatting and making jokes.

When Tuck joined them, Dion draped an arm over her shoulder, and Kane barked, "Let's wrap it up. We've all got appointments to get to, and the cars are going to be here any minute."

There was a bustle of commotion as they made their way to the elevator and piled in. Kane stood beside her, but she stared straight ahead. Just as the elevator doors were closing, a hand shot through them, and a group of people piled in, rambling about being late for a meeting. Everyone squished together, and Sable was stuck facing Kane. She avoided looking at him, knowing what his dark eyes were capable of, but it only made her acutely aware of the rest of him, stirring that unrelenting desire. His chest brushed against her with his every inhalation, his potently male scent seeping into her senses. Her body vibrated as she struggled to resist the urge to look up, but his minty breath lured her in, and their eyes connected with the heat of an inferno. For the first time since they'd met, they didn't speak. Sable was suddenly painfully self-conscious. She hated the unfamiliar emotion, but there was no quelling it as they gazed into each other's eyes, something deeper than carnal desire passing between them.

Kane's brows knitted, and his big hand enveloped hers. The world tilted on its axis. He wasn't looking at her like a hungry lion wanting to devour its prey. No, this was a new look. One that said he knew she was rattled and wanted to reassure her, causing her heart to flutter in a way it never had. She didn't know what this was or why it was happening, but as his fingers curled around hers, giving them a gentle squeeze, she felt strangely *safe*. As confused as she was by the unfamiliar emotions, at that moment there was no place else she'd rather be.

The elevator doors opened, and Kane released her hand. She felt a *whoosh* of loss as they followed the others out of the elevator, and she realized everyone else in that elevator was completely unaware of what had just happened. That didn't seem possible when it had felt seismic to her. Kane walked a few steps ahead of her, looking at his hand as he opened and closed it. *You felt it, too.*

She watched the unfairly beautiful, infuriatingly arrogant man who had the power to take her to her knees draw his shoulders back and face Johnny and the other guys, effortlessly shifting into business mode as he directed them toward the waiting cars. Sable couldn't help but wonder what other secret skills he was harboring.

# Chapter Eight

TWO HOURS LATER the photo shoot was in full swing, and Kane was still trying to get his head on straight. He was in negotiations to take over an Australian hotel chain, and he needed to review the most recent round of documents they'd sent over before their meeting later that evening. He'd planned on doing it while the band was busy with the shoot, but his mind kept going back to the vulnerability he'd seen in Sable's eyes and his unstoppable need to help ease her discomfort. He could still feel how right her hand had felt in his, still smell the floral scent of her shampoo, which must've imprinted in his olfactory system, because he smelled her everywhere.

What the hell was *that*?

He never noticed those types of things with other women, much less had ever been utterly captivated by them, and it was fucking with his head.

Sable strutted out of the dressing room wearing some sort of glittery blue bodysuit and matching boots, her eyes finding him like laser beams. He stifled a growl, averting his gaze. He must have been out of his mind when he'd agreed to oversee the photo shoot. Sable was gorgeous in baggy overalls and was hard-on-inducing in jeans and a clingy top. Did the stylist really need to put her in skimpy bralettes, miniskirts, and bejeweled dresses that barely covered her ass? She was a country rocker, not a pop star. But what the hell did he know about wardrobes? He left that to the experts, which rendered him unable to look at her for too long for fear of sporting a hard-on. And forget holding her gaze. Her eyes fucking owned him.

Lee whistled.

"You look smokin' hot," JP called out.

Jealousy burned through Kane. *Hot* was a teenager's word used to describe just about any pretty woman. It didn't begin to fit Sable Montgomery. She was the sexiest, boldest woman alive, and that vulnerability he'd seen had drawn him right fucking in, sparking the possessiveness and protectiveness he usually reserved for family.

He watched her posing. His she-panther didn't have to work to seduce the camera—or *him*—as Hawk guided the five of them through different shots, bringing her and Tuck closer together. Kane didn't miss the way she and Tuck had been passing glances that carried secret messages he couldn't interpret. He was itching to go over there and put space between them. Hell, he wanted to call off the whole fucking gig before every heterosexual male on the planet was jerking off to Sable's image.

She looked in his direction, smiling for the camera, but something was off. He'd noticed it earlier, too. He saw it in her eyes and felt it in his gut.

*Or maybe it's just my head messing with me again.*

He tore his gaze away for the millionth time since they'd left that damn elevator. He must really need to get laid. That was the only explanation he could come up with for how she messed with his head. He owned half of the East Coast, and for the first time in his life he felt out of fucking control.

*The hell with this.*

He strode over to the photographer. "Excuse me, Hawk."

Hawk lowered his camera, brows knitted behind his multi-colored eyeglasses. "Hey, man." He turned his back to the group. "Sable is solid gold through the lens. I knew she would be."

"Excellent." Kane gritted his teeth, unable to shake the feeling that something was wrong. "I've got to make some calls. Is there an office I can use?"

"Sure. Down the hall. Third door on the right."

With a nod, Kane headed down the hall.

In the privacy of the office, he picked apart the nagging feeling about Sable. Was he reading her wrong? Surely Hawk would have picked up on it if something was off. Hawk studied people every damn day through the lens of cameras.

*But he didn't study Sable.*

Neither did Kane, but like it or not, he picked up on her every emotion as if it were his own. He paced a path in the carpet, mulling over that uncomfortable thought. He needed to get his mind off her, and he knew of only one surefire way to do it. He pulled out his phone and scrolled through his personal contacts. What lucky lady would cure him of this nonsense?

Amy was cute. He didn't want cute. Kelly? She was fun and smart. He didn't want fun. Lana? Patricia? Tiffany…

He went through about a dozen women, but he didn't want cute or fun. He didn't want a blonde, or a redhead, or any other brunette. He wanted *Sable*, and no matter how much it bothered him, there was no fucking way he'd read her wrong. He knew exactly what that look was for.

Uttering a curse, he pulled out his phone to fix this mess.

A little while later, he ended that call and was about to call Shea when the office door flew open, and Sable stormed in wearing a purple-and-silver fringed bralette and matching miniskirt, slit up the thigh, and purple ankle boots. She slammed the door and stalked toward him.

"What the hell is this shit you're making me wear?" She didn't wait for an answer and got right in his face. "I told you I didn't want to be sexualized, and you've got me prancing around out there like I'm a fucking Vegas showgirl. You said you'd take care of this, and you won't even look at me."

His pent-up emotions came roaring out. "You want to know why I won't look at you?" He stepped forward and kept going, backing her up against the door. "Because you drive me fucking crazy."

"I drive *you* crazy? *You*, with your stupid chiseled jaw and that handsome fucking face, looking at me like you want to eat me alive?"

"You're fucking right you drive me crazy with those eyes that say fuck me and that mouth that can't stop spewing crap when what you really want to do is suck my cock."

Her eyes narrowed. "Fuck you."

"You'd like that, wouldn't you?"

"Not as much as you would." She grabbed him by the collar, tugging his lips to hers in a smoldering kiss. Their tongues thrust, deep and greedy, battling for dominance. He grabbed a fistful of her hair, taking control as he intensified his efforts. She bowed off the door, rubbing against his cock, moaning hungrily into his mouth. He wanted to fuck that dirty, willing mouth, and then he wanted to fuck *her* against the door, on the desk, and every other place in there. He pushed a hand under her skirt, cupping her sex through her panties, earning another needy moan. A knock at the door had her gasping, but he wasn't done. He kissed her harder, his tongue plunging *deeper*, forcing her mouth open wider as he took his fill. She was right there with him, returning his efforts with fervor.

Another knock sounded, and he reluctantly pulled back just far enough to lock eyes with Sable. Rubbing his thumb over her clit, he barked, "Give us a minute."

"It's Melinda, Hawk's assistant. They're waiting for Sable."

"I *said*, give us a minute," he said sternly.

"Yes, sir."

He heard her heading back down the hall. He must have lost his mind, crossing this line with Sable. But right then he didn't fucking care. Their mouths fused like molten metal in a penetrating kiss that rocketed straight to his dick. She made a needy sound, something between a moan and a whimper, arching and rocking against him. He pushed his hand into her panties, and she inhaled sharply. He drew back, searching her lustful eyes. "Tell me you don't want this, and I'll stop."

Her eyes narrowed. "If you don't make me come, I will."

He plunged his fingers into her tight heat, earning a salacious moan. "Your pussy is so fucking wet for me." He reclaimed her mouth, using his thumb where she needed it most, taking and giving in equal measure. Her thighs flexed, and her breathing shallowed. He quickened his efforts. "Come for me, and next time I'll use my mouth."

She clung to him, eyes blazing. "Who says there'll be a next time?"

He abruptly withdrew his fingers, and a plea fell from her lips. "*Kane*—"

"Be a good girl, and don't fuck with me."

Her skin was flushed, eyes desperate to finish, but her voice was thick with challenge. "How about I be a bad girl, and you *earn* the next round?"

She was wicked, and he fucking got off on it. He crushed his mouth to hers in a punishingly intense kiss, fucking her with his fingers, and zeroed in on the spot that sent her spiraling over the edge. She cried out into their kisses, her sex pulsing tight and hot. His cock ached to be buried deep inside her. He tore his mouth away as she came down from the peak, but he didn't relent in his masterful ministrations, taking her right back up to the edge and holding her there. A stream of sinful noises sailed from her lips. He recaptured her mouth, swallowing the sounds as she rode out her pleasure. *So fucking perfect.*

When she went boneless against him, he lowered her skirt and lifted her chin, making her watch as he licked his fingers clean. "*Mm.* As sweet as honey, but you sting like a bee."

She grinned. "Something tells me you wouldn't have it any other way."

He wiped the smeared lipstick from the edges of her lips with the pad of his thumb, holding her gaze. She was too damn beautiful, and messing around with her was a really bad idea. But he'd never been one to play by anyone else's rules. *Fuck.* This time he was breaking his own rule. "I don't play games, Sable."

"Then tell the stylist to let me dress in my own clothes."

"I already took care of it. That's who I was talking to before you walked in."

Her brows knitted.

"I told you I don't play games. They fucked up. I fixed it."

She didn't move, just looked at him incredulously.

"You'd better get out there and tell everyone you gave me hell, or they're going to know something's up."

"I *did* give you hell." She reached for the doorknob, then hesitated.

"You got more to say? Get it out now."

She glanced over her shoulder, her cat eyes softening. "Thank you."

Hit with a wave of those unfamiliar emotions that had knocked him off-kilter earlier, he leaned into the familiar, trying to force them away. "For the orgasms? My pleasure." He winked.

"You're an ass."

"So you've said. Now get out of here."

She closed the door behind her, leaving him to wonder what the hell he'd just done—and aching to do it again.

# Chapter Nine

SABLE PUT HER key card in her back pocket with her phone and credit card and headed out of the suite. Someone whistled at her, and she turned and saw Tuck coming down the hall, wearing jeans and a gray button-down. She was glad he was wearing jeans, too. She didn't do dressy, and her sisters had put doubts in her head about her wardrobe. But Sable didn't put on airs for anyone and had worn one of her favorite outfits. A clingy off-the-shoulder black top that didn't require a bra, with sheer bell sleeves, a sweetheart neckline, and a scalloped hem that ended just above the waist of her skinny jeans, which were tucked into black suede thigh-high boots, and of course, she'd worn her hat.

"Damn, girl. That's a killer top." He fell into step with her, heading for the elevator.

"Thanks. Morgyn made it. She and Brindle were so excited about the trip, they wanted to *approve* my wardrobe. I nixed that real quick."

He laughed as they stepped into the elevator. "They love you."

"Love can be smothering." She felt a pang of guilt after saying it. Tuck didn't know what being smothered by love felt like. Thea had loved him to the ends of the earth, and Sable and the guys loved him. But Thea had been gone most of his life, and Sable had never been great with touchy-feely emotions. For Tuck, she wished she were, because if anyone deserved extra love, it was him.

"That was some crazy shit today, wasn't it?"

Her mind went straight to making out with Kane. She couldn't have held back from making out with him if someone had put a gun to her head. "You can say that again."

"I have a feeling we're just getting started."

Sable tried not to listen to the *so do I* whispering through her head as the elevator doors opened and they made their way to the restaurant.

They were led to the fanciest private dining room she'd ever seen, complete with an open bar and a waitress serving hors d'oeuvres. The entire room sparkled with gold and white, from the crystal chandeliers to the elaborate place settings. She and Tuck were the last to arrive, and as the others glanced in their direction, her gaze was riveted to Kane, who was talking with Chad, Chris, and Johnny across the room. Her pulse quickened. He possessed something innately mysterious, so powerful and alluring, he penetrated her defenses by simply being there.

He looked over, his piercing dark eyes daring her to enter their fiery depths.

*Damn him.*

She'd been with her fair share of men, and never once had anyone ignited an inferno of lust and longing the way he did. That searing passion had heightened every sensation, sending shock waves through her when she'd come. To say she wanted more was an understatement, but banging a business associate was never a good idea. She was weak earlier, but now she was even more determined not to give in to those desires again.

She wasn't controlled by her libido. She could totally do this.

Resolve firmly in place, she broke their connection and looked around the room. Jillian was chatting with Lee and Adrian by the windows, and Dion and JP were talking by the table. Sable was surrounded by musicians she was excited to get to know, but she couldn't think beyond having Kane's mouth on hers, his hands driving her out of her mind, and the feel of his hard body pressing against her.

Jillian waved, jerking Sable from her thoughts.

She smiled, but she wasn't in the right frame of mind for Jillian's enthusiasm. She needed to tamp down the unwanted desire fueling her anger before facing the friend who'd set her on this torturous path.

"Is it just me, or did the room just get a whole lot hotter?" Dion called out, grinning at Sable.

She wasn't in the mood for *that*, either. Why couldn't she be attracted to Dion instead of Kane? That would make things a lot easier. She felt Kane's eyes burning into her.

"Come on, Bell," Tuck said, heading for Dion and JP.

"I'm going to grab a drink first." She made a beeline for the bar and ordered a whiskey on the rocks. She felt Kane's presence behind her like the electric charge in the air before a storm.

"I can't get you out of my head." His breath coasted over her ear, his body heat warming her back.

"Sounds like a problem. Maybe you should see a doctor."

"I'd rather bend you over that bar," he said huskily.

Heat slithered through her core, but she stared straight ahead, unwilling to give him the satisfaction of a reaction.

The bartender headed their way with her drink, and Kane's

chest brushed her back as he whispered, "I can still taste you."

She feigned a smile as the bartender handed her the drink, as if her body weren't begging for more. When he walked away, she turned to Kane. His black button-down was open at the collar, the ink on his chest and neck taunting her. "Don't flatter yourself, *Big Daddy*." The name dripped with sarcasm. "You could have been anyone. I was just scratching an itch."

"It's good to know we're on the same page," he said arrogantly, and somehow also seductively.

*Bastard.* "Clearly not. I haven't thought of you once today."

"We've already discussed how bad a liar you are. How many times did you think about having Big Daddy between your legs?"

*Too many times to count.* She saw Jillian walking over, and her nerves caught fire. "Is this how you treat all your business associates?"

Jillian's singsong voice cut through the air. "*Hey.*" She was as stylish as ever, despite her burgeoning baby bump, in a long-sleeve black-and-royal-blue cocktail dress.

While Sable struggled to tamp down her emotions, Kane was irritatingly cool. "Hi, Jilly. I was just commending Sable on the excellent performance she put on today. Sable, we'll connect later to discuss the next round of activities. If you'll excuse me."

As he walked away, Jillian lowered her voice. "*Whoa.* You two looked like you were either going to kill each other or fuck each other senseless."

Sable downed her drink and set the glass on the bar.

"For the record, I'm all for option two," Jillian said. "It's way more fun, and there's no prison involved. But if you go for that option, be careful, because sometimes *this* happens." She rubbed her belly with the happiest expression.

Sable might be upset with her for getting her into this mess, but she knew she'd meant well, and she wasn't going to ruin her friend's night. She quickly thwarted any further talk about Kane. "Look at you, all gaga over your babies. It's hard to believe you're the same woman who was freaking out over the idea of being pregnant."

"I know, right? I've missed you." She hugged Sable. "I kind of wish Zoey and I were going on tour with you guys so we could hang out. Did you like the clothes we picked out for the photo shoot?"

"You were responsible for those sparkly outfits?"

"That's what all the hottest musicians are wearing."

"Sorry, but not this one." She didn't want to talk about the tour, and she knew just how to change the subject. Jillian was launching a new clothing line in early March. "Morgyn is excited to walk the runway for your Wanderlust launch. She said your other brothers' wives are walking, too?"

"They are. They were such big inspirations for the line. Are you coming to see it?"

"Sorry, Jilly. I love you, but it's not my scene."

"I *know*, but I'm not giving up. One day I'm not only going to get you to a launch, but I'm going to get you to walk the runway."

Sable laughed. "Fat chance."

"I'm *so* excited about it…"

Sable tried to concentrate on Jillian, but her attention was drawn to Kane talking with her bandmates across the room so many times, she had to turn her back to him until they sat down for dinner. She sat between Jillian and Tuck, which she thought was a safe distance from Kane, who was sitting a few seats down on the other side of the table. But even with the jovial banter and conversations going on around her, there was no escaping the smoldering heat of Kane's furtive glances or the tension humming between them. She was sure everyone could feel it, but if they did, they didn't let on.

Dinner was delicious, and they made small talk as they ate. Johnny and the guys told them what it was like when they were coming up in the ranks. It sounded like pure chaos to Sable, with multiple tours, tons of publicity, and absolutely no privacy, much less downtime with family. But Lee and JP ate it up.

"Remember all the crazy shit we did on our first tour?" Adrian said.

"We had more groupies in our beds than there are people in this state," Dion bragged.

"That was all you guys, not me." Johnny put his arm around Jillian.

Chad barked out a laugh. "You're the only one of us who knocked up a groupie."

Jillian looked lovingly at Johnny. "He's got you there, babe."

"She's the best thing that could have come out of those days," Johnny said.

"*Aw*, she sure is." Jillian kissed him. "I love you."

"I love you, too, babe."

"Damn, man." Dion waved his finger at Johnny and Jillian. "Between you two, Chad reconciling with his wife, and Chris bringing his wife and kids along on the tour, we might as well change the name from the Brutally Bad Tour to the Ball and Chain Tour."

Chuckles rose around the table.

"Sorry, dude, but those days are over." Johnny put his hand on Jillian's belly, smiling lovingly at her. "And I'm not going to miss them."

"They might be over for *you*," Dion said. "But I'm still in the game."

"And we're just getting started. I'd like to get in on a little groupie action," JP said.

"You can have your *little*," Lee teased. "I'll be getting a *lot*, thank you very much."

"Not more than me," JP said.

Lee scoffed. "Dream on, asshole."

"Trust me, there's plenty to go around," Adrian said. "But now that there'll be a woman traveling with us, I'm sure Sable will try to keep us in line, and we'll need to keep an eye out for her, to make sure she's safe."

"Are you kidding? Sable's tougher than half the men in this city. She can take care of herself," Chris said.

"And she gets as much action as we do," Lee added.

Kane's eyes bored into her.

"How about we leave Sable out of this?" Tuck said sternly.

"No, it's all good." Sable met Kane's stare. Lee had exaggerated, but she had no desire to clarify. "I've got nothing to hide."

Kane's jaw clenched.

"Girl power is strong in Oak Falls," Jillian said supportively, bumping shoulders with her.

Dion cocked a grin, arching a brow at Sable. "Sounds like we're going to have a blast."

"And now that Kane's coming with us, he'll be the last Bad standing," Adrian added.

"I doubt he'll be doing much *standing*," Chad said, earning a round of chuckles.

Kane's smug expression got under Sable's skin. She had never been jealous over a man, but the ugly emotion twisted inside her like barbed wire.

"I don't think Kane needs groupies to fill his dance card." Johnny lifted his glass. "Here's to new friends, good times, and a great tour."

"Hear, hear," Adrian said.

As they clinked glasses and drank to the toast, Sable stewed over the idea of Kane tangled up with nameless, faceless women.

"Who wants to hit the hottest club in the city with me and Adrian?" Dion asked.

Everyone talked at once as they got up from the table, and Jillian said, "Sable, you should go. After they make the announcement tomorrow about you guys opening for the tour, you won't be able to go out without being mobbed by people who want a piece of you."

Sable had heard Kane telling Johnny that he had a business meeting to attend after dinner. Time and space away from him were *exactly* what she needed, and a club would be the perfect distraction. "Sounds good to me."

"All right," Dion exclaimed. "Johnny, are you and Jilly coming?"

"No. I think we're going to call it a night," Johnny said.

"I'll call for the car," Kane said, thumbing something out on his phone.

"You're going?" Johnny asked. "I thought you had a meeting about that takeover you're working on."

Kane glanced at Sable. "It can wait."

THE PRIVATE CLUB was the epitome of opulence and

excess. It was a veritable playground for the city's elite, guarded by mountainous, hawk-eyed bouncers. The scent of wealth and overinflated egos hung in the air, and a kaleidoscope of colors swam over the crowded dance floor, illuminating stylishly dressed men and women lost in the bump and grind of foreplay. The beat of the music pounded through Sable as she danced with Tuck, adrenaline coursing through her veins. This was exactly what she needed. Total anonymity.

They'd been there for hours, and she'd escaped to the dance floor because, while she'd been hit on by a handful of rich pretty boys, it turned out there was no distraction big enough to block out the sensual prowess of Kane Fucking Bad. He'd been one lascivious comment away from melting her panties off. As if that wasn't enough to frustrate her, he did it in covert whispers, while those other men were flirting with her and other women were flirting with him. The man didn't have to do anything to gain the attention of beautiful women. They sought him out like cats in heat, offering themselves up on a silver platter.

Sable was totally out of her element in the exclusive club, and those women, dressed in silk and dripping in diamonds, pawing at Kane irritated the hell out of her. But on the dance floor she could pretend she was back in Oak Falls, where nothing intimidated her.

She caught a glimpse of Kane watching her through the crowd, still flanked by women. She fired back against the jealousy clawing at her and turned up the heat, dancing more erotically. Her arms snaked over her head, hips gyrating. Tuck met her move for move. As more people came onto the dance floor, she turned away from where she'd seen Kane and lost herself in the beat.

"I need a drink." Tuck practically shouted to be heard above the music.

She followed him off the dance floor, scanning the crowd for their friends. They were nowhere in sight, but as Tuck headed for the bar, Kane broke through the crowd, a symphony of powerful confidence and raw sensuality, heading straight for her. Her body vibrated with anticipation. A flush heated her skin at the intensity of their connection, the magnetic pull drawing her toward him. He stopped when they were toe-to-toe, the cacophony of music and voices turning to white noise.

The muscles in his jaw bunched. "You looked like you were enjoying yourself out there."

"Yeah. *So?* It wasn't like you were lacking in the entertainment department."

His face was a mask of restraint, her own resolve fraying fast. She grabbed his glass and gulped down his drink, relishing the burn of the alcohol as it coated her throat.

Kane cocked his head, holding up another glass with a colorful drink.

"A fruity drink? What kind of woman do you think I am?" she said loudly.

"I have all kinds of ideas about that, *Panthera.*" He took the empty glass from her and set it on a tray as a waitress walked by, eyes never leaving Sable's.

Her eyes narrowed at the name. Not that it wasn't fitting, but the gall of him, thinking he could coin a nickname for her. "I think you mean, Sable."

He leaned closer, his lips a whisper away. "I know what I meant, and you do, too, *Panthera.*"

Why did she have to like the way it rolled off his tongue, full of seductive intrigue and challenge? She didn't bother wasting her time on the futile effort of arguing a point she wasn't fully committed to. "Is this what you enjoy, City Boy? Getting your ego stroked by women who have as much money as you do?"

The tempest of darkness rising in his eyes sent shivers of heat down her spine. He leaned closer again, his scruff abrading her cheek as he spoke into her ear. "The only thing I want to *do* is get my mouth on the frustratingly stunning woman standing in front of me, and I'd much rather you stroked my *cock* than my ego."

His gruffness bordered on diabolical. She'd never been so greedy for more. The air between them crackled with intoxicating tension. He lifted the glass. Extending his index finger from around it, he trailed that finger just above the neckline of her shirt, along the swell of her breasts. The intimate touch lit sparks beneath her skin. The scent of the alcohol heightened her arousal. He cocked a brow, offering her the drink.

She declined with a shake of her head.

He leaned in again. "Drink, *bad girl.* I want to taste it later."

The scintillating scratch of his scruff and the enticing demand had her drinking the fruity concoction. She was slipping into dangerous territory where need and want overrode everything else. Appropriate business lines be damned. Sable didn't play games when it came to taking what she wanted. She was going to *feed* her greed.

She crooked her finger, beckoning him closer again, and purred, "How disappointing. Sounds like your mouth is going to be in the wrong place."

He rose to his full height, eyes aflame, muscles taut.

*God,* she wanted him. She wanted to make him snap. To feel all that power cut loose as he lost control for *her.*

He put a hand on her back, blazing a path out the front

door of the club. Warning bells went off in her head, reminding her this wasn't a good idea, but they were no match for the desire thrumming through her as he called for the car. A few fevered minutes later, the limo pulled up. The driver got out to open their door, but Kane beat him to it, telling the driver, "We're going back to my hotel." He followed Sable into the back seat, closing the door behind them.

Before the driver had even settled in behind the wheel, Kane's mouth was on hers, his big hands hauling her onto his lap so she was straddling him. Her hat fell to the seat as she rocked along his thick arousal, and they ate at each other's mouths with reckless abandon. He pushed her shirt up, breaking the kiss to seal his mouth over her breast, sucking her nipple to the roof of his mouth. Lightning seared through her core. *"Yes,"* she cried out, thankful for the privacy glass separating them from the driver. She grabbed his head, holding him there, riding him through her jeans. But it wasn't enough. Thoughts of making him lose control took over, and she pushed him back, gritting out, "My turn."

Needing to see the ink that had been taunting her and touch the hard chest that she'd been fantasizing about, she grabbed his shirt with both hands and tore it open, sending the buttons flying. His eyes flamed, a growl rushing out as he grabbed her hair, tugging her into another kiss. Painfully aware of the short drive to the hotel, she pried herself away, unwilling to get out of the car before she got a taste of him.

"I said it was *my* turn." She opened his belt, and as she slithered off his lap, she grazed her teeth over his nipple, earning a sharp inhalation. She drank in the tattoos on his chest and stomach, kneeling between his legs as she freed his formidable erection.

He fisted the base, grinning arrogantly as he aimed it at her.

Even though he was telling the truth when he'd said he earned every inch of his ridiculous nickname, she couldn't resist putting him in his place. "I'd like to get a little pleasure out of this. Try not to come too fast."

He scoffed. "That's not a problem. I have impeccable control."

"We'll see about that." She wasn't like most women, who thought fast and deep was the best way to get a man off, because really, what did that do for *them*? She was all about mutual pleasure and control. She'd done her research, and she knew all the best tricks. Unfortunately, while she'd like to take her time, they had none to spare.

She moved his hand, grabbed either side of his trousers, and yanked them lower, giving her better access to his beautiful cock and perfect balls. She licked him from balls to tip, earning the sexiest hiss she'd ever heard. She did it again and again, until he was growling, his cock glistening, jerking with every slick of her tongue.

"*Suck it,*" he demanded.

Ignoring the command, she wrapped her hand around the thick shaft. His eyes remained trained on her as she stroked him, dragging her tongue lightly around the broad head and over the sensitive glans. "*Fuuck.*" He lowered his chin, moaning deep and guttural. His eyes narrowed as she quickened her strokes, squeezing tighter, and continued lightly teasing the crown. She flicked her tongue around the head of his cock, and his hips shot up, hands diving into her hair. She focused on the crown, teasing until his every muscle corded tight and a glistening bead formed at the tip. She slicked her tongue over it, delving into the slit. "*Fuck*, baby. I need to fuck your mouth."

Loving the desperation in his voice and the fire in his eyes, she continued torturing both of them, until a stream of curses left his lips, and his cock swelled in her hand, ready to blow. "*Shit.*" He grabbed the base again.

"Move it," she demanded.

His brows slanted angrily. "Then take my cock in your mouth *now.*"

"I'll do what I want when I'm good and ready." Watching him struggle was too much fun. Gone was the need to make him come fast, replaced with the craving to drive him out of his mind. "Tell the driver to take the long way."

Jaw clenched, he pushed the intercom button, growling, "Add ten minutes to our drive."

When he released the intercom, she said, "Good boy."

"You're fucking wicked."

"Damn right I am."

He gritted his teeth as she dipped lower, licking and teasing his balls while she stroked him. His thighs flexed, and he groaned, loud and deep, the sinful sound making her wetter. She couldn't take it another minute and lowered her mouth over his shaft, taking him to the back of her throat, and constricted around it. "*Fuuck.*" She drew back, but she didn't bob her head or stroke him. With his heavy cock in her mouth, she ran her tongue along that sensitive ridge, getting off on his pleasure-drenched ramblings. "*Fuck...Holy shit...So fucking good.*" She cupped his balls, teasing and squeezing as her tongue worked its magic. "*Sable,*" he pleaded gruffly. "I need you to suck it, baby." Kane Bad begging was the best aphrodisiac. "I want to fuck your mouth hard and watch you swallow every drop."

She wanted that as much as he did and met his gaze. The

visceral need and untamed emotions staring back at her filled her with pride and something much deeper. She nodded, giving the approval he sought. He moved to the edge of the seat, fisting his hands tighter in her hair, and thrust excruciatingly hard and erotically deep. He was fucking perfect, holding nothing back, pulling her hair, growling with every pump, until his release spilled down her throat, and a slew of curses flew from his lips. On the verge of her own release, she took everything he had to give, soaking in their mutual pleasure.

When he withdrew from her mouth and wrapped his strong arms around her back, his head dipped beside hers. For a few silent beats, her head spun, and her heart wasn't far behind.

"Christ, woman. What the fuck?"

She was asking herself the same thing.

But she knew one thing for sure. She'd been wrong earlier about hearing him beg. Watching this beautiful man *unravel* was the best aphrodisiac of all.

# Chapter Ten

KANE WAS STILL trying to get his brain to function when the limo pulled up in front of his hotel. He'd never come so hard in his life, and he sure as hell had never begged for a damn thing.

Sable wiped the corner of her mouth and settled her hat on her head. "Thanks for the ride." She was out the limo door before the doorman even made it to the car.

*What the...?*

Kane went after her, catching a curious look on the doorman's face. He shoved a hand in his pocket, pulled out a twenty, and handed it to him, remembering too late that his shirt was torn open. *Shit.* He caught up with Sable inside the hotel and put a hand on her lower back as she hurried through the expansive lobby. "Where are you rushing off to?"

"You got what you wanted." She stopped at the elevator, staring straight ahead as she reached for her key card.

He beat her to it, flashing his card instead. "What I want," he said for her ears only, "is your pussy riding my face until you come so many times, you've got nothing left to give."

The elevator doors opened, and they stepped inside. He flashed his card again, pocketing it as the doors shut, and he closed in on her, boxing her in against the wall. "Don't act like your panties aren't drenched from what you just did to me."

Her cheeks flushed despite the tightness of her jaw.

That hint of vulnerability cut him to his core, stirring the urge to gather her in his arms and say something sweet and reassuring. But she was as bullheaded as he was, and sweet wouldn't get either of them what they wanted. Before any other crazy thoughts could take hold, he returned to safer territory and ran his hand up her thigh, rubbing the hot denim between her legs.

Her breathing shallowed, lustful eyes going half-mast.

Damn, that was sexy. "We both know if you go to your room alone, you'll get yourself off wishing your fingers were my mouth."

She lifted her chin defiantly, and he rubbed more intensely. "Imagine how good that would feel if it were my tongue and my teeth driving you out of your fucking mind."

She breathed harder, eyelids fluttering. "Your mouth better be worth it."

"Trust me, Panthera, I'll make you purr like a kitten and scream like a savage, and when you recover from my mouth, you'll beg for my cock." He grabbed her jaw and brushed his thumb along her lower lip. His dick was hard as stone just thinking about the way she'd blown him. "I should punish you for taunting me with this wicked mouth."

"Just fucking *kiss* me already."

He crushed his mouth to hers, rough, greedy, and unrelenting. She clutched his shirt, and he grabbed her wrists, pushing them above her head and holding them there with one hand as he ground his hips against her. He had an animalistic need to dominate her, to touch and taste every inch of her gorgeous body. Pushing his other hand beneath her shirt, he rolled her nipple between his finger and thumb, earning a cock-hardening moan as she bowed off the wall. "I'm going to come on these phenomenal tits tonight." He squeezed her nipple, earning a sharp gasp, and lowered his mouth to her neck, biting and sucking. Eliciting moans and whimpers, *fucks*, and pleas for more.

The elevator opened in his penthouse, and they didn't stop or even slow down. He tore off her shirt, knocking her hat to the floor, and shrugged off his own shirt as they stumbled through the foyer, their mouths coming together again. Feasting, possessing, *claiming*. He opened her jeans and pushed them down.

"My boots," she panted out.

"I look forward to fucking you when you're wearing nothing but your hat and these thigh-high boots," he said, tugging them off and tossing them to the floor.

"Those are awful big fantasies for a guy who has yet to get me naked."

"You're going to pay for that comment." He stripped her bare and tossed her over his shoulder, ignoring her protests and flailing arms and legs as he carried her into the living room.

"Put me *down*," she demanded.

He smacked her ass and dropped her on her back on the double-chaise end of the enormous U-shaped couch. She was a stunning sight, glowering up at him angry as a snake, all gorgeous legs and perfect breasts, hair strewn over her shoulders, pussy practically dripping for him.

"Don't *ever* do that again." The desire in her eyes betrayed her warning.

"I told you not to fuck with me." He sank to his knees between her legs, running his hands up them, feeling her shudder with anticipation. "What didn't you enjoy? Being carried or being spanked?"

She scowled.

"That's what I thought. You're used to having control, and it pisses you off that you can't control me." He spread his hands on her thighs and pushed them apart, brushing his thumbs along her wetness, her cheeks reddening. "This drenched pussy tells me exactly how much you like everything I do. Now, how about you stop bitching and enjoy the ride?" He buried his mouth between her legs, earning a long, surrendering sigh as he devoured her. She tasted so fucking sweet, he couldn't get enough. He used teeth and tongue, fingers and thumbs.

Her heels dug into the cushion as she gasped and moaned, writhing against his mouth. She fisted her hands in his hair as he feasted on her, fucking her with his tongue, using his fingers on her clit and then swapping, sending an orgasm crashing over her. She cried out his name so loud, it vibrated through him. She was a fucking dream come true, cursing and digging her nails into his scalp and shoulders as she rode out her pleasure. When she came down from the high, he sent her soaring again, her sinful noises echoing off the walls.

This time when she sank to her back, he said, "Hold on tight, gorgeous."

He pushed his arms beneath her legs and grabbed her waist. In one swift move, he rolled onto his back, turning her with him so she was straddling him.

She laughed. "You're quite the acrobat."

He smacked her ass with both hands and held on tight, earning the most alluring moan as he pulled her pussy down to his mouth and took his fill. She grabbed the back of the couch, hips undulating. "*Ohgod*," she panted out. "So good. *Don't stop.*" Her voice escalated as she rode his mouth faster, *harder*, allowing him to use teeth and tongue as she panted out sinful sounds that shot through him. He brought one hand to her clit, working her into a needier frenzy. With his other hand, he smacked her ass *hard*. She cried out, her pussy pulsing against his mouth as she surrendered to another intense orgasm. She bucked and cursed, clinging to the back of the couch. He stayed with her, and when she came down from the high, trembling and gasping, he didn't relent. He increased his efforts, wanting *everything* she had to give. Every drop of come, every ounce of energy, every plea, moan, and whimper. "*Ohgodohgodohgod—*" Her voice escalated with every syllable. The third orgasm drew his name like a curse, and the fourth brought begging, music to his ears. "No more. It's too much. Too sensitive. *Please*...Kane. I can't take it." He intensified his efforts, feeling like a fucking king when a loud pleasure-filled sound tore from her lungs, and she spiraled over the edge again.

When she went boneless above him, he eased his grip, pressing a kiss to her inner thigh before shifting her to the chaise, so she was lying on her back beside him. Moonlight spilled in through the wall of windows, bathing her sensual curves and blissed-out smile in a dusky hew. He couldn't resist trailing his fingers up her stomach and between her breasts, earning tiny gasps and bringing rise to goose bumps.

"You're a bastard," she whispered.

He pressed a kiss to her lying lips. "I'll take that as a compliment."

She was so beautifully unguarded, he had the urge to wrap her in his arms, carry her to his bed, and worship every inch of her. The thought hit like a bullet, startling him back to his good senses. Needing to shut that shit down, he pushed to his feet and headed over to the bar.

Sable went up on her elbow, watching him pour himself a drink, looking sweet, satisfied, and intoxicatingly sexy. He downed the whiskey and poured another as he walked back to her. He set the bottle down and stood at the end of the chaise, opening his pants with his free hand.

"Are you going to share that glass of whiskey, or what?"

He took a sip, holding the alcohol in his mouth as he set down the glass and crawled over her. Her eyes sparked with intrigue, and as he lowered his lips closer to hers, she opened her mouth. So fucking sexy. His lips parted, dribbling the liquid into her mouth, and took her in a ravenous kiss, the taste of the alcohol mixing with the taste of her, setting his soul on fire. He grabbed the bottle and tipped it up to his lips, filling his mouth. Their eyes locked as he dribbled it over her nipples, down her stomach, and over her pussy. She sucked in air through gritted teeth.

"Feel that burn, baby." He dragged his tongue around and over her nipple, teasing it to a peak, and sucked it to the roof of his mouth.

"Ah." She arched her back, grabbing his head. "*Yes.*"

He grazed his teeth over the sensitive peak and sucked it again. She writhed and bowed off the cushion as he licked and sucked a path to her other breast, giving it the same titillating attention. She was so fucking perfect, so eager and sexually confident, he was hit with a spear of jealousy knowing she could have gone home with any of the other men who had hit on her tonight. He couldn't resist marking each of her breasts like a Neanderthal marking his territory. He followed the trail of alcohol down her stomach with his mouth, slowing to nip at her ribs and waist, earning more thrilling gasps and sexy noises as he tasted his way lower. He slicked his tongue along the edge of her pussy, and she clutched the cushion. He licked her inner thighs, using his teeth as he neared her sex, sucking and teasing without touching her slick pussy. "Look how wet and ready you are for my cock."

"Kane, *please*—"

Her words were lost to a hungry moan as he licked her swollen sex, her essence spreading over his tongue. He was a greedy bastard for it, but he wanted her even needier, so she'd remember every excruciating moment, so thoughts of *him* obliterated memories of any other man. He pushed his fingers inside her, working her with his hand and mouth, taking her right up to the edge of madness and holding her there. Her eyes slammed shut, and her head whipped from side to side, heels digging into the cushion. "*Kane*. I need more. I need *you*."

"Good girl. Beg for my cock."

He pushed to his feet and pulled his wallet from his pocket, withdrawing a condom. She watched him strip down. He couldn't resist taunting her a little more. He fisted his cock, giving it a few tight strokes and moaning.

"You really are a bastard." She licked her lips as he rolled on the condom, her breasts heaving with anticipation.

"I never claimed to be Prince Charming."

"Hurry up, before I lose interest," she challenged.

He laughed, loving her wit. She reached for him as he came down over her, and he buried himself to the hilt in one hard thrust. She gasped, her eyes blooming wide, her body gripping him like a vise. He gritted out a curse, a surge of desire thundering through him. Their eyes connected, the storm of emotions and confusion in hers mirroring the storm whipping through him. *Holy fuck.* He sealed his mouth over hers, needing to outrun whatever train was barreling toward them. He pounded into her, fucking her like a savage, biting her shoulder, lifting her hips to drive in deeper. She was right there with him, hooking her legs around him, meeting every thrust with a tilt of her hips, her pussy clenching tighter around his cock. This was fucking heaven on earth, tugging at the emotions he was trying to evade. Their connection was overpowering. He needed to temper it.

He pulled out and flipped her onto all fours. Hauling her hips up, he drove into her again. She moaned lasciviously, rocking in time to his efforts, and reached between her legs, teasing her clit. "That's it, baby. Touch yourself while I fuck you." He hammered into her, her gorgeous ass there for the taking. He dripped spit between her ass cheeks, teasing her tightest hole with his finger. She looked over her shoulder, challenging eyes boring into him.

"You are a naughty little vixen, aren't you? Taunting Big Daddy." He pushed his finger past the tight rim of muscles. Her back curled up like a cat, her sex clenching impossibly tighter.

Her eyes met his over her shoulder again. "Finally, a man who knows how to fuck."

The more he took, the more she gave. And the more *he* wanted. He pounded into her, fucking her pussy with his cock and her ass with his finger, driving them both out of their minds. Driving her hips backward, she pleaded, *"Faster."* A symphony of sinful sounds filled the room, taking them both to the edge of a cliff. Her body clenched in an unrelenting grip around his cock. Heat seared down his spine just as she shattered, crying out his name, catapulting him into a hailstorm of erotic sensations that raged through him, arcing and peaking in explosive crescendos carried by the sound of Sable losing herself in the throes of passion.

When the last spasm rolled through him, he collapsed over her, feeling the frantic beat of her heart through her back. "*Jesus.*"

"I know," she panted out. "That wasn't bad."

They both laughed.

He pressed a kiss to her spine and got up to take care of the condom. She remained on all fours, head hanging, trying to catch her breath. That urge to hold her returned, only this time it had fucking talons trying to pull him back to her. He fought against that urge, tearing free from those spiny claws, and forced his legs to carry him into the bathroom before it could take over.

After washing up, he leaned his hands on the counter, taking a minute to try to center himself. He barely recognized the man staring back at him. His eyes were different, softer. What the fuck? He'd gone against all his rules, and it was biting him in his ass. He never brought women to his penthouse. He kept a separate apartment for hookups, but with Sable, he hadn't even hesitated. With any other woman, the only emotion that came into play was lust, and once they'd fucked, he couldn't get rid of them fast enough. He'd immediately get dressed, giving them the push they needed to walk out that door. It was easy and effective.

*So why don't I want to do the same with Sable?*

He told himself it was because having sex with her was more lucrative than his most profitable business deal. More exciting, more pleasurable. Just fucking over-the-top better in every way.

He'd never been good at lying to himself. Having sex with Sable felt intimate, more fulfilling than any fucking business deal ever could. But he'd learned to stand strong behind his walls, and he needed to find that brick and mortar and remember how to do that now. He drew in a deep breath, lowered his chin, shoring up those walls, and strode out of the bathroom.

Sable wasn't on the chaise. He scanned the vast living room and bar area and saw her bending over to pick up her clothes near the foyer. He strode over and smacked her ass. He'd never been much of an ass smacker, but he loved riling her up, and rile her up he did. She spun around, cheeks pink.

"Cut the shit, Kane." It was a half-hearted *almost* plea.

Her eyes still radiated the emotions he was trying to escape, and man, that fucked with his head. He took her hand, drawing her closer. "Where do you think you're going?" So much for shoring up his fucking walls.

"To my suite."

He should let her go, but he wanted more. "Tapping out already?" Marveling at the feel of her soft, naked body against his hard frame, he brushed his lips over hers. "Is Big Daddy too much for you?"

"Tapping out? I'd say half a dozen orgasms make me the winner."

"Is that all you've got, Panthera?" He kissed her jaw, running his hand over her hip and up her waist, and caressed the side of her breast with his thumb. Her eyes narrowed, but the telltale hitch in her breathing gave away her desire. "What do you say we go for ten?"

"Make it an even dozen," she challenged, "and I'm in."

SABLE LAY ON a blanket on the floor of Kane's library, trying to catch her breath, in the wee hours of the morning. What was she thinking, sticking around for more? The man was too damn addicting, from his irritating arrogance and enticing innuendos to his magic penis and talented mouth. And the way he looked at her? She'd never felt so beautiful or so challenged. The last few hours had passed in a blur of dirty talk and mind-blowing debauchery. She'd come so many times, she'd lost track. They'd done it against the bar, on the dining room table, the kitchen counter, and she had no idea where else other than that opulent library. He'd literally fucked her so thoroughly, she hadn't been able to think past the pleasure coursing through her.

"That has to be a record," he said, turning on his side and kissing her shoulder.

Her body warmed with that tender kiss, but she knew better than to stick around. She had no idea how they were going to get past this and work together. She'd never made this mistake before. She'd just gotten roped in by his dirty talk and filthy promises. That's all this was, and it had to end *now* so she didn't mess things up for the guys before the tour even started. No matter how much she hated the idea of walking away from the one man she didn't have to fake a damn thing with.

She forced the words to come. "A record? More like a mistake."

"It's not like you accidentally fell on my dick a dozen times."

She liked the tease in his voice far too much, but she couldn't fall into his hands—or onto his dick—again. "Hindsight and all that." She heard the faint ringing of her cell phone and sat up, glad for the excuse to get out of there before she changed her mind. "I'd better get that." She pushed to her feet.

His piercing gaze traveled down her body. "Who would call you at three in the morning?"

"It's probably Tuck."

He followed her out of the library and down the hall. "At this hour? Booty call?"

"That's none of your business." Her stomach twisted at that. *Ugh. What is wrong with me?*

His jaw tightened. "I think after what we just did, it is my business."

This was why she no longer got involved with guys who had anything to do with her life. They were controlling and complicated everything. "All you need to know is that I'm clean, and this was a onetime thing." She rounded a corner into the living room and went to get her clothes.

He was at her side, eyes icing over. "I'm glad I didn't have to be the one to point that out." He picked up her clothes and handed them to her.

Fury mounted inside her as she dressed. She shouldn't be mad, since he was just agreeing with her, but she was. "Why do you care if I'm hooking up with Tuck, anyway?"

"I *don't*. I care that my reputation doesn't get soiled in the process."

She tugged on her boots, refusing to let him see how much his words stung, and grabbed her hat.

"I assume you'll keep tonight's activities between us." He said it like he was confirming a business deal and pushed the button for the elevator, as if he couldn't get rid of her fast enough.

"I don't waste brainpower on unremarkable events. By the time I reach my suite, I'll have already forgotten what we did." The elevator door opened, and she stepped inside, an angry, cataclysmic crescendo raging between them. As the doors closed, she said, "By the way, that was nowhere near a record."

# Chapter Eleven

KANE STOOD IN Shea's office the next morning, hands fisted by his side, the urge to bash Tuck's face in making him feel like a damn jealous teenager as Shea worked with Sable and her bandmates to prepare for their upcoming public appearances and interviews. Why did he care whether the flannel-shirt-wearing country boy was sleeping with Sable? It wasn't like Kane was looking to be tied down, no matter what kind of connection he'd thought he felt last night. It sure as hell shouldn't bother him that Tuck was sitting next to her or that while she had barely spared Kane a glance, she and Tuck were passing silent messages masked by not-so-secret glances.

But it fucking did.

Everything was pissing him off today. He needed to get a grip.

"As you know, the press release is going out in two hours. From that moment on, everything you do will be documented and scrutinized by paparazzi and the general public. While it will be exciting, public appearances with paparazzi shouting questions at you can also be intimidating, as can interviews and podcasts. I hope to alleviate some of the fear by going over a few things." Shea was the picture of professionalism in a fitted blouse, a pencil skirt, and heels. Her makeup was subtle, her blond hair clipped at her nape with a simple gold clasp that matched her teardrop earrings and gold-and-diamond necklace.

"The image you project in these early appearances holds the power to win fans over or turn them against you. As unfair as it is, every outfit you wear, every word you say, and every facial expression you make will be picked apart on social media," Shea explained. "As soon as fans hear you're opening for Bad Intentions, they're going to be ravenous for information about your lives. We want to start out on the right foot and control public perception as best we can."

Shea gave them a friendly but assessing once-over. The guys wore jeans and boots with T-shirts, Henleys, and flannels. Sable looked like a badass country girl in a faded leather cowgirl hat, a black long-sleeve V-neck under a suede fringed vest, jeans, and Western boots, with a few silver and black charms dangling from black-leather cords around her neck.

Sable shifted uncomfortably in her seat, exchanging another of those annoying glances with Tuck. Kane gritted his teeth, remembering her stipulations for doing the tour and how vehement she was about protecting her bandmates or, more specifically, *Tuck*, and staying off gossip sites. Was she afraid whatever was going on between them would be exposed?

"Boots and jeans are great, but believe it or not, the right jeans can make a difference with fans. We'll take care of that, and we'll swap the flannels for something a little edgier, like leather jackets over your T-shirts," Shea said.

"Awesome," Lee said, and JP nodded in agreement.

Shea glanced at Sable. "Sable, you'll want to lose the hat during indoor interviews and events."

"Why would I want to do that?" Sable asked.

Kane was wondering the same thing. He loved how she looked in that hat. She was never more *Sable*—strong, confident, and sexy—than when she wore it. It was part of her. Her *brand*.

"It's proper etiquette to remove hats indoors, and it'll make you more fan-friendly. Show the public that you respect those social guidelines," Shea said with enthusiasm and directness.

*Fuck that. Her rebellious nature makes her who she is.* It was all he could do to keep from intervening.

"I understand *hat etiquette*," Sable said sharply. "But I'm a country musician, not a people pleaser, and where I come from, plenty of people wear their hats indoors."

"I understand where you're coming from. But you're about to become a public figure. A role model to some," Shea explained. "Millions of men and women and boys and girls will be watching you, learning from you, and making decisions about you based on the glimpses they get."

Sable's eyes narrowed. "So *let* them."

While concern riddled Shea's brow, Kane was once again drawn to Sable's honesty and her strength to stand up for herself and demand to show the world her authentic self. Even if it was that honest side of her that had infuriated him last night. He was also worried that if Shea continued pushing Sable about her hat, the issue would escalate. "Why don't we discuss this later and move on."

Sable looked at him curiously.

Shea forced a smile. "Good idea. Since the band is relatively unknown, people will want to know how the offer to do the tour came about and how you felt when Kane approached you with the offer. Sable, I understand Jillian Braden is a friend of yours, and she set these wheels in motion. So why don't we start there? Did you ask Jillian to hook you up with the gig?"

"Hell no. I was pissed when I found out she was pushing for us to do it."

"We'll talk about that phrasing in a minute," Shea said carefully. "The public will want to know why you weren't interested."

"Not that it's any of their business, but I liked my life the way it was," Sable explained. "I don't care about money or fame or social media likes."

"She hates social media," Tuck added.

"Big-time," JP chimed in.

Shea nodded, her expression serious. "Okay, I see. Sable, let's talk about how we can soften your response to make it more palatable to the audience."

"What does that mean?" she asked.

"It means there are aspiring musicians and experienced bands out there who would give anything to be in your position, and we don't want the public thinking you're ungrateful for the opportunity. There are ways to finesse your answers to make them more relatable," Shea reassured her. "For example, you could say it was such a big opportunity, you were nervous about measuring up or overwhelmed."

Kane didn't like the turn this conversation was taking. Sable didn't scare easily, and she sure as hell hadn't appeared to be overwhelmed when he'd approached her.

Sable crossed her arms. "So you want me to lie?"

"No, we can work with the truth," Shea said. "We just need to find the right way to say it so the audience doesn't dislike you."

"How could anyone dislike her for being honest?" Kane asked.

"That kind of honesty is an acquired taste," Shea said sharply, as if chastising him for interrupting again.

He clenched his teeth. She wasn't wrong, but neither was Sable. "With all due respect, I suggest we move on."

"Yes, that's probably a good idea," Shea said tightly. "Since the band is new on the scene, you're likely to be asked some pretty personal questions about your families and your childhoods and how you got into music. Kane has mentioned some of your concerns, and I'd like to address them."

Shea went on to speak with Chris about his family and to Tuck about his past. After asking Lee and JP if they had any concerns, she returned her attention to Sable. "Since Axsel is a major celebrity, you can expect interviewers to focus on him. They'll probably try to get information about your relationship with him, his relationship with your family, if there's been any strife between any of you. They might even try to goad you into revealing something by asking if you're jealous of his success or any number of other things."

"They can try," Sable said. "But as I told Kane, my family is off-limits."

"Yes, Kane relayed that to me, but you'll be expected to give them *something*," Shea said.

Sable lifted her chin. "Like I said, talking about my family is not an option."

"I'm sorry, Sable, but that's not going to fly," Shea said. "Interviewers will badger you, and if you don't give them some type of palatable response, they'll assume the worst."

*Fuck it.* Kane couldn't take it anymore. "Shea, may I have a word, please?" He headed into the hall, knowing she'd follow.

Shea closed the office door behind her, speaking hushed and urgent. "Sable is out of control. Maybe you can get through to her about the reality of this situation."

"Look, I respect what you're doing. You're excellent at your job, and you clearly know what works, but I've seen Sable command a stage. I've seen her say things that should piss people off, but it's that brashness, that raw honesty, that draws them in. I think you should stop trying to manage her responses and let Sable be Sable."

"You know how critical people are and how they feel entitled to information on celebrities," Shea warned. "Look at what your brother just went through."

"I'm well aware of what Johnny and our family have gone through. Sable is setting up boundaries from the get-go. If Johnny had done that, things might have played out differently."

She shook her head. "Kane, this could come back on Johnny. You know how fast bad press spreads, and that woman in there? *She's* an acquired taste."

It took all his willpower not to snap at her, despite knowing she was right. "Acquired or not, she's got a captivating presence. I was with them last night at a club. I watched men lose track of their thoughts midconversation with other beautiful women to check Sable out and ramble like idiots trying to pick her up while she made no bones about not being interested. People can't help but be drawn to her. When she performs, she is head and shoulders above today's musicians. And that honesty that irks you? That not-giving-a-shit attitude about strangers judging her for protecting her family or for wearing a hat? *That's* more relatable than some song and dance about how she fell to her knees when she got the offer. I respect you—you know that— but stop trying to change her. She's *not* going to bring down Johnny. He's a fucking icon, and trust me. That woman in there? She's going to be one, too, if you let her be herself, because not only does she speak from the heart with no pretense and no bullshit, but she is going to blow the audiences out of the stadiums."

Shea studied him, brows slanted. "Oh my God. *Kane.* I'm sorry. I can't believe I didn't see it sooner."

"See what?" he barked.

"You're involved with her, aren't you?"

He exhaled in frustration, shaking his head. Part of him wished he could say yes, but that was fucked up. He didn't pine for women. And he sure as hell shouldn't be overthinking the one woman who challenged his every breath. "No, Shea. I'm not. Cut the shit. This isn't a game. It's business. Her rough-around-the-edges demeanor and those hard-and-fast boundary lines are big parts of her appeal. Again, please stop trying to put words in her mouth, and trust me that she won't fuck things up."

"It goes against everything I know and believe, but you're Johnny's manager, so I will follow your guidelines. But if shit hits the fan and this comes back on Johnny, that's on *you.*"

"It won't. If anything, it's going to make Sable even more intriguing to the public."

BY LATE AFTERNOON, Kane was regretting that conversation with Shea. He'd had no doubt that any man would have the same visceral reaction to Sable as he did, but after a day of traipsing around the city for the band's interviews, that reality was eating him alive. News of the band opening for the tour had gone viral within twenty minutes of the press release going out. Sable had nailed every interview, even winning over Chuck Winston, one of the most critical podcasters in the industry. But every time they left a building, they were swamped with paparazzi and people trying to get a look at the band. Thankfully, this was the last interview for the day. If Kane had to watch one more man leer at her or hear another asshole make a comment about wanting to fuck her, heads were going to fly.

He was watching the interview from behind the scenes with a handful of other people, their excited chatter floating around him like gnats.

"Look at Tuck's eyes. They're mesmerizing," a young brunette said to the blonde beside her.

"He's too broody for me. I'll take JP. He's got a flirtier vibe," the blonde said.

"Did you see that look Tuck just gave Sable?" another brunette said.

"I think there's something between them," the blonde whispered. "Lucky Sable."

Kane's jaw clenched.

"I'd like to be between those two," a dark-haired guy said.

Kane shot him a dark stare, but the idiot was too busy gaping at Sable to notice.

"That Sable chick is hot," a blond guy said.

"With those legs and those tits, she's the total package," the dark-haired guy said.

"Show some respect," Kane growled, his temperature rising.

"Sorry, man," the dark-haired guy said. "Just stating the obvious."

Kane glowered at him.

The blond guy nudged the dark-haired guy. "Her voice is so

FALLING FOR MR. BAD

damn sexy."

"No shit," the dark-haired guy said. "I could listen to her all day long. Preferably while she's naked."

Kane's hand curled into a fist.

A woman shushed them as Sable explained how she'd gotten the band together when they were teenagers. The interviewer asked the guys what that was like for them, and Lee answered, "When you're a teenage boy and the baddest girl in school asks you to play in a band with her, you don't question it."

"How many of those guys do you think she's slept with?" the blond guy asked.

*Jesus fuck.* Kane ground his back teeth to keep from making a scene.

"I don't know," the dark-haired guy said. "But I'd like to get my hands on her."

*Over my dead body.*

"You and half the male race," the blond guy said.

"No shit," the dark-haired guy said. "I bet she likes to be ridden hard and shared often."

Kane saw red, his restraint snapping like a twig. He grabbed the prick by the collar and slammed his back against the wall, snarling, "Watch your fucking mouth, asshole." The women stumbled backward, and the color drained from the asshole's face. "That woman has more class in her pinkie than you have in your entire fucking body, and if you say one more disrespectful word about her, your head is going through this wall." The prick was shaking, his jaw hanging open, hands up in surrender.

"Sorry," he said shakily. "I...I won't."

"Fucking right you won't." Kane shoved him away from the group, catching appreciative glances from the women as the guy and his buddy hightailed it out of the room.

Kane went back to watching the interview, arms folded, head a fucking mess. He didn't like reverting to violence, but apparently Sable awoke the possessive beast he'd long ago buried and had kept chained down in the dark, dungeonous depths of his soul.

# Chapter Twelve

AFTER A GRUELING day of interviews and insanity, Sable paced her hotel room, feeling trapped. She'd known things would get crazy after the announcements about the tour were made, but they'd been mobbed by paparazzi and fans the entire day. The guys ate it up, but Sable wanted to find a cave to crawl into far away from anyone other than her family and close friends. The life she loved was slipping through her fingers, and she couldn't do a damn thing about it.

Her mind began toying with the things that were bothering her, twisting them into lyrics begging for a melody. *You can run but you can't hide from the people or the lights. You can mask the pain inside, go along for the ride...*

She grabbed the pen and notebook she'd used last night when she'd futilely tried to write her way past the anger and sting of Kane's response when she'd asked him why he cared if she was hooking up with Tuck. *I don't. I care that my reputation doesn't get soiled in the process.*

She didn't want to think about Kane, but he was always there, lurking in the recesses of her mind, trying to push to the forefront, and the hurt came rushing back.

She'd never been the type of woman who'd let anything a

man said get her down, and she was not going to become one. Refusing to let those thoughts take hold, she scribbled down tonight's lyrics, itching to find the right tune to bring them to life. She snagged her guitar and sat on the couch, strumming the familiar strings. But the centering feeling that usually accompanied playing didn't come. She looked around the luxurious living room. The furniture was too perfect, the energy too stale. How was she supposed to be creative in a room that meant nothing to her? If she were home, she'd go outside and let the sounds of nature draw out her inspiration.

She eyed the balcony. At least Mr. Bad did something right.

He did a lot of things right last night.

Until he didn't.

*Stop thinking of him!*

She put on her favorite gray cowl-neck sweater—the one with the frayed hem and rips in the sleeves—and carried the desk chair out to the balcony, bristling against the cold. After retrieving her guitar and notebook, she left the balcony door open, hoping the night air might breathe new life into the stale room. She stood at the railing, taking in the tall buildings towering over busy sidewalks and overpopulated roads, the sounds of traffic and horns infiltrating the night. There was no grass in sight. No space to breathe.

How did people live like this?

Sighing, she sat with the guitar and tried to find the right chords for the lyrics, but the harder she tried, the more off it felt. *Wrong.* It wasn't surprising, given all that was going on in her life, but she had to break through this mental block before she lost her mind. She tried again, and *again*, until she was so frustrated, she wanted to scream. She closed her eyes, trying to conjure her grandmother's image. Sometimes that would help pull her through mental blocks, but Kane's piercing stare was front and center behind her closed lids. *Damn him.*

Maybe she could *play* him off her mind.

She filled her lungs with the brisk air, and without another thought, she began playing "Last Nite" by the Strokes. As she sang about feeling alone and nobody understanding what she was going through, her voice grew louder, angrier. It felt fantastic to lose herself in the music, but it didn't clear her head, so she went right into another Strokes song, playing "I Can't Win." For some reason that made her think of Kane even more, which was why she then played "Bad Decisions," and belted out the lyrics, taking responsibility for her *own* bad decisions.

As she sang the last note, she still felt that soul-deep need to create music out of her frustrations, but how could she when she was trapped there?

There was a hard rap on the door.

*Great.* Someone probably complained about her being too loud. She hated city life.

She set her guitar on the couch and went to answer the door. Peering out the peephole, her breath caught, and her chest fluttered at the sight of Mr. Bad rubbing his jaw, his shirt collar open. She could still taste his hot skin, still feel his muscular pecs beneath her fingers. She shoved those feelings aside and opened the door, planting a hand on her hip. "What do you want?"

"My place is right above you. I was out on my balcony and heard you playing. That was quite an angry concert."

She tilted her head. "I can't think in this place."

"You don't like your suite?"

"It's fine, but it's not conducive to creativity. I thought it would help to be outside, but it's not like I can walk across the street to a park or even go outside at all without getting mobbed, and *you* pushed me to be here."

"Yes, I did, but you made the final decision. I'm holding up my end of the bargain and having your back, am I not?"

Thinking of the photo shoot and the meeting with Shea, she nodded. After Shea had stepped out to speak with Kane, she'd had a change of heart about Sable's responses and wearing her hat indoors.

"Like I said, I'm not the enemy, Sable. Where do you feel most creative?"

"Back home on my balcony, surrounded by nature and not concrete."

"And that usually helps?"

"It always helps. The music and lyrics just come to me. I can't explain it. It just flows."

He nodded. "I get it. It's like you're a radio transmitter picking up a signal."

"*Yes.* That's exactly what it feels like." She wondered how he'd known, but he was a famous rock star's brother. Johnny had probably explained it to him a million times.

"I think I can help with that. Grab your guitar and follow me."

"Where?"

"Up to my place. I want to show you something."

"If you think I'm going to wind up in your bed again, you're wrong."

He cocked a brow, amused. "You've never been in my bed."

"You know what I mean. I'm not sleeping with you again, so whatever it is you're offering, no thank you." She started to close the door.

He put his hand up, stopping it midway, his serious eyes

finding hers. "I'm sorry for my part in the way things ended last night. I had a nice time, and I'm sorry we got derailed."

The sincerity in his eyes was so different from the way he usually looked at her, it caught her off guard, buffering the jagged edges of her attitude. She hadn't exactly been nice last night, and she felt a little guilty for being a jerk. "I'm sorry, too. I'm not very good at having to explain myself."

"Neither am I, so let's move past it. If you'll trust me enough to come with me upstairs, I think what I'm about to show you will make up for my questions last night."

She crossed her arms, a smile tugging at her lips. "What makes you so sure?"

"You really don't trust anyone, do you?"

"Do you blame me?"

"Not really. I don't trust most people, either." A devilish glimmer rose in his eyes. "I'll make you a deal. If you're not pleased with what I show you, I'll find a reason to get you out of the contract and fly you home to Oak Falls."

Her eyes widened. "You can't do that. They just made the announcement."

"There's *nothing* I can't do."

"But I could just pretend to be unhappy with whatever you show me, and it would cause a nightmare for your brother and his band."

"You won't do that. You're not that kind of person."

She swallowed hard. He was right, but still. He'd *just* told her that he didn't trust most people, and after the way they'd been butting heads, why would he trust her? He must really want her to see whatever it was. "Okay. You've piqued my curiosity."

She grabbed her guitar and notebook and followed him up

to his penthouse. He led her through a maze of rooms and up a flight of stairs to an exterior door. As he entered a code into a keypad on the wall, he said, "Please keep this under your hat."

"Speaking of my hat, thanks for convincing Shea to let me wear it."

"I like you in that hat." He wasn't flirting. He said it seriously, as if it were an important fact, and as he pushed the door open and said, "After you, Ms. Montgomery," it felt strangely like it was.

She stepped inside, and couldn't believe her eyes. White-paned glass walls and a matching ceiling formed a massive dome around them. Elaborate marble floors snaked through stunning gardens overflowing with various types of lush greenery and vibrant flowers. Birds flew overhead, chirping out their welcomes, and a gorgeous tree anchored one side of the room.

"Wow. What is this place?"

"It's my escape from the concrete jungle."

"They let you do this?"

"Well, I do own the hotel, so *they* would be me." He cocked a grin.

"Of course you do," she said sarcastically.

As they walked through the gardens, their beauty and the scents of dirt and fresher air snuffed out the piss and vinegar of her sarcasm. She heard trickling water as they rounded a burgeoning plant, and they came upon a waterfall cascading over large rocks, pooling in a pond surrounded by leafy, flowering plants. In the center of the pond was the most beautiful sculpture of a naked woman standing on tiptoes, her arms straining beneath the weight of a sphere she was holding over her head. Her long hair was swept to one side, covering her breast. The detail was so beautifully crafted, her body looked as strong as it did soft and feminine, with rounded hips and a little belly. Sable walked around the pool of water and realized the back of the sculpture was purely male. As if the man's back and the woman's front had fused into one being. The hair on the back of its head was cropped short, his muscular shoulders slightly rounded forward, strong arms and lats also straining beneath the weight of the sphere.

"This sculpture is incredible."

"Thanks. I designed it, and my buddy Justin Wicked made it for me."

"You *designed* it?" She couldn't hide her surprise.

His brows knitted. "Why do you sound so surprised?"

"I guess I don't see you as an art-is-life kind of guy. But then again, I never would have thought you'd have a place like this."

"I'm not an art-is-life guy, but I do enjoy it." They started walking along the path again. "I'd lose my mind in this city without this place."

"Really? You seem so comfortable with your high-class life-style."

"I am. But I'm not one-dimensional. Sometimes I just need to breathe."

*Aren't you full of surprises?* "I guess you're human after all," she teased. "What's the meaning behind the sculpture? It's pretty intense."

He shrugged. "Family. No one carries their burdens alone."

"You seem to."

"So do you," he challenged.

Every time she thought she got a glimpse inside the fortress that was Kane Bad, he turned things around or shut down. Now she knew what it was like for others to deal with *her*. "Do you always picture your family naked?"

"It's not like those are my family members. It's a general concept. Art is supposed to be beautiful. But we're not here to pick apart my sculpture. We're here to get your creative juices flowing." He led her through the maze of gardens to a cozy sitting area, and he motioned to the benches. "Do you think being here will help your creativity?"

She wanted to dig deeper to find out more about him, but she was enjoying getting to see this side of him and decided not to push it. "Definitely. No need to send me home after all." Even if she'd been unimpressed with what he showed her, she wouldn't have taken him up on the offer to go home. She'd never do that to her friends.

As she settled onto a bench, he took out his phone and began tapping and swiping on the screen. The glass panels in the walls darkened, and the lights faded to black as dimly lit flooring lights illuminated the paths. Suddenly the ceiling bloomed to life like a planetarium with hundreds of tiny sparkling stars and stunning hues of blues, purples, and pinks.

Sable was awestruck. She no longer felt like she was in the middle of a noisy, overpopulated city but was sitting in a field back home, where nights were peaceful and serenity was vast. She wanted to say as much and gush about how much she appreciated Kane sharing this amazing place with her. But while sharing those thoughts and feelings would sound perfectly normal coming from any of her siblings, they would probably sound as uncomfortable as they felt coming from her. Instead, she fell back into her comfort zone and said, "Look at you using your money for good and not just evil."

"I have my moments. What were you working on in your suite that got you so frustrated?"

"Just a song I can't get right."

He leaned his elbows on his knees, looking at her thoughtfully. "Let me hear what you've got so far."

"It's just a few lyrics that'll go something like this." She looked up at the stars to keep from meeting that all-seeing gaze and sang softly.

*"You can run but you can't hide*
*From the people or the lights*
*You can mask the pain, go along for the ride*
*But the walls close in, and you scramble up the sides*
*Losing your grip*
*Losing your mind*
*Losing your life, one flash at a time."*

She swallowed hard, feeling the vulnerability of what she'd just shared. She hadn't thought the words would come out sounding so personal, but they felt like they'd been ripped from her heart.

He sat back, eyes serious. "That's how you felt today?"

A lie hung on the tip of her tongue, but when she spoke, the truth came out. "Pretty much."

He was quiet for so long, the muscles in his jaw clenching, she braced herself to be called ungrateful or get an earful about how much the opportunity was doing for her and her friends.

"You need a tense and heartbreaking rhythm for those lyrics." He held out his hand. "May I use your guitar?"

"You play?" She handed it to him, as shocked by that as she was that he wasn't giving her a hard time.

"Like I said, I'm not one-dimensional. I can play an instrument or two."

He settled the guitar on his lap and began playing what sounded like a normal chord progression, until he played a major four followed by a minor four. Her breath caught. The contrast between major and minor chords added complexity, signifying an emotional shift. It was such a simple concept. One that was used all the time. How could she have *blanked* on it? It was the perfect way to take the song from angry strength to melancholy introspection.

"That's *it*," she exclaimed. "That's exactly what it needs. Keep playing." She sang the chorus, and as he played, more lyrics popped into her head. "I don't have the right lyrics, but I've got something." She shared her thoughts as she wrote them in her notebook. "I've spent so many years mapping out my life, and it's slipping away."

"What do you feel? Do you want to scream? Cry?"

"I feel suffocated. I want to shout, *Come back. Fucking stay. I can't breathe this way.*"

"That's good. Keep going," he urged as he played. "What do you do from there? Where do you go?"

She tried to answer that question in her head, but that was the problem. There was no answer, and the question became the lyrics. "*Where do I go? When does it end?*" She scribbled the words on the page.

"How do you leave that land of pretend?" he suggested.

"Yes!" She wrote that down. "But it's not all bad. I feel empowered onstage. Invincible." She continued taking notes about what she was feeling. "The music takes over, and I fade away."

"A voice in the lights," he offered.

"*Only fingers working strings. It's a wonder I'm anything.*" She looked at Kane, excitement bubbling up inside her. "This is really good. Can you play faster?"

He grinned and turned up the beat.

"You don't mind doing this with me? Don't you have anywhere else you need to be?" She couldn't believe how much she hoped he didn't have another commitment. Not just because he'd opened her well of creativity, but because she was enjoying brainstorming with him, hearing him play, seeing him with his guard down, and allowing herself to lower hers as well.

"I'm enjoying it, and I've got all night."

She filled with happiness and rambled on, saying the lyrics that came to her, writing them down and crossing some out. Kane chimed in with suggestions about adding more emotion, playing faster or angrier, and then taking it down to a painfully slow cadence, perfectly matching the emotional waves she felt. She didn't know how long they worked on the song, but by the time they finished, she had pages of notes and a new appreciation for Kane.

"You missed your calling." She set down her notebook. "I haven't been inspired like that in ages."

"That was all you, sweetheart. I just fed off what you were saying."

"I couldn't have gotten there without this place, and you. I was too frustrated. I felt like I was trying to jump out of a burning plane, but I couldn't find a safe place to land." She held his gaze, the energy between them warming and tangling. But it wasn't the urgent, combustible heat that had driven last night's tryst. It was different, more real, more consuming, like a bond rather than a challenge. That made her a little nervous. "I still can't believe I missed something as simple as a major and minor chord transition."

"You were stuck in the muck, watching your life become

public consumption." He continued strumming a slow tune. "It's not unusual for someone going through something painful to miss things they normally wouldn't."

"What do you know about that? You seem like you can buy your way clear of anything."

"I know too much, actually." He set the guitar on his lap. "There are some things money can't fix."

"Such as?"

He paused for a beat, and just as she wondered if he wasn't going to respond, he said, "I don't know if Jillian told you about my mother, but she's had cancer twice."

Aching at the sorrow in his voice, she shifted on the bench, giving him her full attention. "No, she didn't. Kane, I'm so sorry. I shouldn't have been so cavalier. Is your mother going to be okay?"

"Yes." He put the guitar down and turned toward her with so much emotion etched into his face, she could feel it. A fissure in his usual steely facade. "She had surgery a couple of weeks ago, and she's cancer free again. Hopefully she'll stay that way."

She wanted to climb into that fissure and hunker down with that part of him he kept locked away from everyone else. "I don't know what to say. I had no idea you were dealing with that."

"We've been able to keep it out of the media, but I didn't tell you to gain pity. I just wanted you to know that I understand how easy it is to lose sight of the things that are usually second nature when something upends your world. I lost a major business deal during the worst of my mother's illness because of a stupid mistake that I never would have made otherwise."

"I don't know how you concentrated on business at all with

that going on. I would've been a mess if it were my mother."

"I was, but my mess looks different than other people's."

"What does yours look like?" she asked carefully.

"Nothing anyone could see. I have a feeling we're alike in that way."

He couldn't know just how right he was.

His phone chimed. "Excuse me." He pulled it from his pocket, and as he read the text, she saw that fissure seal back up. "About fucking time."

"Booty call?" she teased to lighten the air.

"No, smart-ass." His amused eyes briefly flicked to hers; then he thumbed out a text. "It's from my youngest sister, Aria. She's a tattoo artist on Cape Cod, and she had me check out a client of hers who asked her out."

"Let me guess. He was a douchebag, and you had him taken out."

"No," he said with amusement. "The guy seemed harmless, and I had a buddy ready to keep an eye on them just in case."

"That sounds like something I would do."

"Then you understand why I asked her how the date went instead of telling her that I knew she didn't go on it." His phone chimed again. He read the message, *cursed*, and sent a reply.

"Sure, but then why did her response just piss you off?"

"It didn't piss me off. I'm *concerned*. Aria suffers from anxiety, and accepting a date was a big deal for her. The fact that she didn't go because she was too anxious is the problem. She's twenty-six, and she's an incredible person. She deserves to have a full life. It kills me that her anxieties are still holding her back after all these years."

The concern in his voice tugged at her heartstrings. "I know the feeling."

He cocked his head in question.

"My younger sister, Amber, has epilepsy, and she lived a really careful life before she met her husband, Dash. You met them at a fundraiser a while ago."

"I remember them. Amber is a pretty brunette, right. Sweet? Kind of quiet?"

"That's her. She's the sweetest of all of us."

"Are things different for her now?"

"Much. She'll always be more careful and live a quieter life than most of us. It's who she is. But Dash has definitely expanded her horizons. He gets her out to enjoy life more often, and she's incredibly happy. But getting there came at a price. She had two seizures early on in their relationship. I shouldn't say they were caused by breaking out of her shell. That could be a coincidence, but she *was* having great sex for the first time in her life and getting very little sleep, so who knows. It had been a long time since they'd adjusted her medications, and now that they have, she hasn't had any more seizures."

"That's good. And I bet you'll always worry about her."

"I absolutely will. Do you see Aria often?"

"As often as I can, and we talk every week. Her best friend, Zeke, watches out for her, and he'd let me know if there was trouble. But as with your sister, it's a constant worry."

"I worry about all of my sisters and Axsel."

"I figured as much. We're made from the same fabric. I worry about Harlow and Johnny, too. You know what happened to John, and Harlow is an actress out in LA. You wouldn't believe the cretins she deals with."

"After what I experienced today, I think I have a pretty good idea."

"Yeah, I guess you do." He stretched his arm across the back of the bench and touched a rip on her sleeve. "You know, with all this success, you can probably afford a sweater without holes in it."

"Shut up." She laughed. "My twin sister gave this to me a long time ago. It's my favorite sweater, and I will wear it until it's threadbare."

Amusement danced in his eyes. "I can't imagine two of you."

"You say that like it's a bad thing."

"Scary, not bad," he teased.

"The only thing scary about Pepper is her brilliance. She's a scientist. She develops medical instruments for people with disabilities."

"So you're both smart and creative."

"I'm not *that* smart."

"Sure you are." He brushed his hand along her arm, holding her gaze. "But I admire your loyalty."

"Says the man who dropped everything to take over managing his brother's career. Don't you have like a zillion businesses to run?"

"Yes, but none are more important than family."

He was striking a lot of chords tonight, inching into that panty-melting danger zone. He took her hand, his eyes boring into her, stirring the desires she'd been trying to deny.

"You and I aren't so different after all." He paused, as if he wanted that to sink in, which it did. *Deep.* "Can we circle back to how you're feeling about all the changes that are taking place?"

She didn't want to talk about it, but he'd just shared some pretty private parts of himself, so she agreed. "I guess."

"In my experience, success usually goes one of two ways. People either dive in with both feet and become addicted, or they pull back. I owe you an apology. I thought your views might change once you got a taste of success. I'm sorry you're hurting over this decision."

She swallowed against the emotions stacking up inside her. "Is that what happened to you? You got addicted to the thrill of having money and the ego boost that came with it?"

"Nothing *happened* to me. I set out on a mission to create an empire and made it happen. Was I addicted to that success? Probably." His thumb moved in slow, soothing strokes along the back of her hand. "But the only thing I'm addicted to now is you. You're like a drug I shouldn't want but can't resist."

She liked knowing he was as tortured as she was, and she knew she was playing with fire, but she didn't want to stop. "I know the feeling."

He leaned closer, eyes going impossibly darker. "I nearly pummeled a man today because he was talking about wanting to fuck you."

"Really?" Turned on by his visceral reaction, she said, "That's kind of hot."

A gruff laugh fell from his lips. "It's crazy. I'm almost forty, not a stupid kid who can't control his emotions, and yet there I was, slamming some asshole against the wall, ready to take him out." His large hand slid to the nape of her neck, drawing her closer. "I don't know what you've done to me, but I need to get my mouth on you."

"What are you waiting for?"

He took her in a merciful kiss. Every thrust of his tongue dragged her deeper into his sexual vortex. She leaned forward, wanting more. His arm swept around her, pulling her across the bench, and he lifted her onto his lap. She ground against him, wanting to disappear into him. His cock was hard and insistent against her ass. Her skin prickled with need from the tips of her fingers to the ends of her toes and every place in between. He palmed her breast, his other hand tugging her head back by her hair, eyes blazing.

She was desperate for more but refused to go back on her word. "I'm not ending up in your bed tonight."

"Lucky for you, we don't need a bed for what I have in mind."

He took her in another scorching kiss, burning through her resolve *and* her panties.

# Chapter Thirteen

THURSDAY EVENING KANE sat at the head of the conference table in the boardroom of Bad Enterprises, surrounded by his top legal experts and acquisition executives as they met via video conference with the owners and legal team of the Australian hotel chain he was taking over. The legal teams had been discussing the intricacies of the takeover for an hour, but Kane had barely heard a word. His normally hyper-focused business brain had gone to shit because of the sharp-tongued vixen he'd spent the last three nights with.

Memories of the last few nights taunted him with images of Sable's gorgeous eyes smoldering when he talked dirty and of that sated smile that couldn't help but turn challenging afterward. When he'd heard her playing guitar on the balcony Tuesday night, he'd tried like hell not to go down there because of how poorly they'd left things Monday night. But he'd had a bone-deep ache to see her again. When she'd sung those heartbreaking lyrics, he tried to keep his hands to himself and just be there for her, but the more they'd talked, the stronger the urge to be closer had become. He didn't know all that much about her, but he knew she used physical touch to escape painful emotions, the same way he did, and they'd come together explosively. Just as they had last night, when he'd texted to see how her song was coming along because he'd just fucking needed the connection. One text had led to another, and he'd ended up knocking on her door again with a pocketful of condoms. He'd had a dire urge to stay right there in her bed, wrapped around her soft, sated body all night.

But that wasn't what this was, and he'd forced himself to leave at four in the morning while she'd slept.

He had no idea *what* this was between them, but he never stayed overnight with women. Or at least he hadn't since college, and he had no interest in opening himself up to that kind of heartache ever again. That was why he'd told Sable he couldn't see her tonight. She'd gotten too far under his skin, igniting an obsession he needed to quell.

But he fucking ached to see her.

His leg bounced impatiently under the table. He discreetly checked his watch, gritting his teeth against the mounting need to see her, touch her, *taste* her one last time. She was going back to Oak Falls with her band tomorrow, and he was stuck in that meeting for at least two more hours, when instead he could be worshipping her naked body, hearing her whiskey voice begging him for more. Her voice had become one of his biggest temptations, and don't even get him started on that husky laugh of hers.

He tried again to focus on the meeting, but the importance of the acquisition paled in comparison with the intensity of his desire.

*Fuck it.*

He pushed to his feet, drawing all eyes to him. "My apologies, but I'm afraid I have to cut this meeting short." He didn't bother giving a reason, and nobody questioned him. A testament to the man behind the vast empire that was Bad Enter-prises. "I'll have my assistant reschedule in the morning. I trust you can wrap things up in my absence."

He walked out the door consumed by thoughts of the only woman outside of his family to ever distract him from the business he'd spent his life building.

ON THE RIDE to the hotel, a full-on war raged in his head. By the time he knocked on Sable's door, he was pretty sure he'd lost his mind. But when she answered wrapped in a towel, hair dripping, skin glistening, looking as fresh faced and gorgeous as she had the first time he'd seen her climbing out of that cherry-red truck, he didn't give a damn. If this was insanity, he never wanted to be sane again.

"Kane," she said breathily, cheeks pinking up like a cat caught with a canary in its mouth. "I thought you were going to be tied up all night in a meeting."

Her sexy smile drew him closer. "The only thing I want to be tied up with is you."

Her eyes flamed, and she stepped aside, giving him the invitation he sought. He loosened his tie and unbuttoned his collar as he walked in. She closed the door behind him and met his gaze. What a stunning sight she was.

He trailed his fingers just above the edge of her towel. "Have you been thinking about me, sexy girl?"

"Wouldn't you like to know?" she said sassily.

"You know I would." He ran his hand up her thigh. "How many times have you thought about the way you devoured my cock last night?"

Her eyes narrowed, but there was no hiding the truth in them, even as she said, "*None.*"

"Did you make yourself come in the shower thinking about how I fucked you on that couch?"

She lifted her chin. "No."

"Such a bad liar." He reached beneath the towel, teasing her slick pussy, earning a needy gasp. "Don't you know you can't hide how much you want me?" He backed her up against the wall, rubbing her clit with his thumb, making her pant with desire.

"Maybe I was thinking about someone else."

"And maybe I'm Peter Pan." He bit her lower lip, giving it a tug. "We both know nobody else can make you feel as good as I do." He pushed his fingers inside her, earning a cock-hardening moan. "Tell me the truth, and I'll get on my knees right now and make you come so hard you won't remember your name."

She closed her mouth in a silent challenge.

"You stubborn little minx." That was one of the things he liked most about her. He withdrew his fingers, and her breath left her lungs in a rush. "I don't play games." He turned and reached for the door.

"Wait!"

*That's my girl.* He glanced over his shoulder.

"*Fine.* I thought about you in the shower. Now get over here."

He stepped back, their eyes locking as he took off his shirt and tie, dropping them on the floor. She watched him open his pants and fist his cock and licked her lips as he gave it a few hard tugs. "Tell me, baby girl." He stripped naked and grabbed hold of his cock again. "How many times did you make yourself come thinking about me today?"

"How many times did *you* make yourself come thinking about *me*?" she countered.

"I'm waiting for your answer, Panthera."

"Two can play at this game." She dropped the towel and ran her hands over her gorgeous breasts, moaning sensually.

He gritted his teeth as she lowered one hand to her pussy, those seductive green eyes luring him in. "*Fuuck.*" He stroked himself faster, watching her fingers grow slicker as she quickened her efforts. "That could be my mouth."

"And your hand could be min—"

Her voice was lost to a punishingly hard kiss. They were ravenous, their kisses messy and urgent as he pulled a condom from his wallet. He broke away to tear it open. She kissed his chest and sank her teeth into his flesh as he sheathed his length.

"*Fuck*, that feels good."

He grabbed a handful of her hair and yanked, reclaiming her mouth, devouring her as he lifted her into his arms. Her legs wound around him, and she sank onto his dick, sending bolts of electricity through him. They both went a little wild, kissing, biting, and clawing as she rode his cock. "So fucking tight. So damn perfect." Using the wall against her back for leverage, he thrust so hard she cried out. Heat pooled at the base of his spine, making him even greedier for more of her. He grabbed her ass and slid his fingers along her pussy, using her arousal to tease her tightest hole. She tore her mouth away with fire in her eyes. "You like that, baby girl? Want me to fuck that hole while you ride me?"

"God, *yes.*" She crushed her mouth to his as he pushed his finger into her ass. Her pussy clamped so tight, he cursed, thrusting his hips and pumping his finger, until "*Kane—*" flew from her lungs, and a string of curses flew from his. He gritted his teeth to keep from coming as they rode out her pleasure, her sinful sounds heightening his arousal. Desire boiled and swelled inside him like lava ready to blow. When she went soft in his arms, he sealed his mouth over hers, rougher and more possessively, taking them right back to the edge of ecstasy and holding them there, pumping slower, intensifying every sensation as she slid along his cock.

"*Kane. Ohgod. Faster.*"

That voice was the sound he craved, expressing the desire he hungered for. Memories of her pleasure-drenched pleas had carried him through the day, and he was in no hurry for them to end. "Fuck no," he gritted out. "This is our last night, and I'm not rushing a damn thing."

He kissed her again, deep and slow, trying to last, soaking in every second he could. But she felt too good; the needy noises she made were too enticing. Need burned beneath his skin, pulsing through his veins like a serpent seeking release. "*Please,*" she begged. Her fingernails cut into his flesh. He quickened his thrusts, and her thighs locked around him, her body trembling. She gulped sharp inhalations, riding him like she was born to do it. "*I'm gonna...Ohgodohgod...Kane—*" she cried, loud and untethered, severing his control. The world spun away, their bodies thrusting and rocking to their own chaotic beat.

This time when she collapsed in his arms, panting against his neck, he was right there with her, their bodies jerking with aftershocks. "Damn, woman." He kissed her cheek and buried his nose in her hair, breathing her in. "What the hell are you doing to me?"

She lifted her face, eyes at half-mast, a sated smile on her lips. "Using you for sex—what else?"

"So bold and so fucking beautiful." *You're a dangerous woman.* "Glad we're still on the same page." He carried her into the bedroom, trying to convince himself it was still true as he laid her down. "Don't move."

"As if I'd go anywhere when you're naked? I know what Big Daddy's capable of, and I'm a needy girl."

How could someone so tough be so adorable? He kissed her hard, trying to silence the words blaring through his head—*Tonight, you're my needy girl*—and headed into the bathroom to dispose of the condom.

When he returned, she was lying with one arm over her head, eyes closed, like she didn't have a care in the world. But he knew she had big worries. Worries he'd pushed on her. The urge to wrap her in his arms and tell her everything would be okay was stronger than his need to breathe. A knock sounded at the door, jarring him from his thoughts.

His muscles tightened. He didn't comfort or soothe. He *fucked*, and he was nowhere near done fucking the worry out of her. Sable's eyes met his, stirring that now-familiar clench in his chest. Struggling to ignore it, he said, "You expecting someone?"

"Dessert. I figured since you were footing the bill, I'd enjoy my last night of luxury."

"Stay put." He wrapped a towel around his waist and went to answer the door.

He grabbed his wallet and tipped the guy who'd brought the dessert. On his way back into the bedroom, he lifted the silver dome off the dish to see what she'd ordered. Chocolate silk pie with extra whipped cream. *Perfect.* He found Sable standing beside the bed, looking good enough to eat. Funny. That was exactly what he had in mind.

"I thought I told you to stay put." He set the tray and his wallet on the nightstand.

"I had to wash up." She dipped her finger into the whipped cream. As she brought it to her mouth, he grabbed her wrist.

"I'm going to enjoy getting you messy again." He guided her finger into his mouth, swirling his tongue around it, and sucked it clean. "*Mm.*" He swiped his fingers through the whipped cream, holding her gaze as he dragged it down the center of her chest. Going back for more, he painted whipped cream and chocolate over the swell of one breast and around her nipple. He followed the same path with his mouth, earning appreciative moans as he teased her with his tongue and teeth, sucking her flesh, taking sinful pleasure in the marks he was leaving.

He scooped more pie onto his fingers and sucked her nipple to the roof of his mouth as he cupped her pussy, covering it with the sweet treat.

"*Kane,*" she panted out.

He lowered her to the edge of the bed and dropped to his knees, burying his mouth between her legs and devoured her. "*Oh...Yes...Don't stop.*" She dug her nails into his scalp as he brought his fingers into play. It didn't take long to turn her moans into cries of pleasure. She rocked and moaned as he feasted, soaking in every sound, savoring every drop of her arousal. He was a greedy bastard, making her come time and time again, until she clung to his shoulders, breathless and panting. But he wasn't nearly done. He crushed his mouth to hers, fucking her with his tongue as he was about to fuck her with his cock. She kissed him hungrily, as eager as he was for more. He broke the kiss and pushed to his feet. She watched him scoop more pie into his hand and fist his cock, coating it in the dessert. "On your knees, beautiful. Time to choke on Big Daddy's cock."

"I thought you'd never ask."

As she sank to her knees, he tangled his clean hand in her hair. "Eyes on me. I want to see the pleasure in them as you take me deep."

Her eyes flicked to his. "You're a greedy bastard."

*For that mouth? For this woman?* "Fucking right I am. Now get busy."

She lapped up the pie, licking and sucking, taking her time and driving him out of his fucking mind. When she finally wrapped her fingers around his cock, stroking tighter as she increased her pace, he growled and hissed, gritting his teeth to stave off his release. Pleasure shimmered in her eyes as she took him to the back of her throat and then swallowed him deeper. "That's it," he gritted out. "Take it all." She moaned, and it vibrated along his shaft, sending spikes of pleasure down his spine. He had the overwhelming need to possess *all* of her. He buried his hands in her hair, reclaiming control, pumping harder. It wasn't enough. *Nothing* was enough with Sable. He withdrew from her mouth and tugged her to her feet by her hair. "I want to finish inside you. Get on your hands and knees."

He grabbed a condom and tore it open. Sable took it from him, rolling it on with a look of pure seduction before climbing onto the bed. The image of her on all fours, eagerly watching him over her shoulder, seared into his brain as he buried himself to the hilt with one hard thrust. Too fevered for each other to slow down, they rushed to find their rough, agonizingly perfect rhythm. Her hands fisted in the sheets as she met every thrust with a rock of her hips. He reached around her, using his fingers on her clit, sending her crashing into ecstasy, her pussy pulsing around his cock. He was utterly consumed with her, with their connection, the way they fed off each other. He clutched her hips, pounding into her, trying to outrun the emotions clawing at him, but there was no escape. She fucking *owned* him.

If he couldn't outrun the excruciating emotions, then he'd take everything she had to give and ruin them *both* for anyone else. He pulled out and flipped her onto her back, coming down over her. Their eyes connected with the powerful impact that never failed to blow him away. She closed her eyes as their bodies came together, and he wondered if she felt it too. But he knew even if she did, she'd never admit it.

He pinned her hands to the mattress beside her head and brushed his nose along her cheek, growling in her ear, "You can close your eyes, but you can't hide. We both know it'll be my face you see late at night when you're all alone and you need to come." He thrust his hips, gradually increasing the intensity as he spoke. "It'll be my cock you imagine fucking your mouth and your pussy. My voice coaxing you over the edge."

Her eyes opened, a mix of anger and lust staring back at him. "As if you won't feel my mouth on you every time you fist your cock?"

"I look forward to it, and I'll enjoy every second knowing that I've ruined you for all other men." He crushed his mouth to hers, both of them grinding and thrusting, groping and biting. Fucking like the greedy, untamable beasts they were. They took and claimed, giving only enough to make the other even wilder, until they lay tangled in each other's arms, sweaty and breathless, unable to think, much less speak.

# Chapter Fourteen

SABLE LAY IN a fog as Kane climbed back into bed after taking care of the condom. She couldn't help but marvel at the exquisite exhaustion coursing through her. At the same time, she wished she'd never gotten together with him, because now she knew what she'd been missing for all these years. The arrogant billionaire who represented everything she hated was her sexual and emotional equal. He challenged her, pushed all her buttons, and fucked her like his sole purpose in life was to bring her pleasure.

He leaned over her and kissed her lips. "You're awfully cute with that look on your face."

She couldn't remember the last time anyone had used *cute* to describe anything about her. He sounded like he really meant it, and that made her feel less inclined to overthink and more playful. "What look?"

"The one that says half a dozen orgasms should be enough to relieve your stress, but your brain refuses to cooperate."

"You have an annoying ability to read my mind." As uncomfortable as that made her, it also felt kind of nice knowing he saw the real her.

"What's going on? Thinking about how much you'll miss

me?"

"*Hardly.* My life has turned into one big complication. The last thing I have time for is thoughts of an arrogant, egotistical pain in my ass."

He laughed. "You like the pain, Panthera."

"Don't call me that." *I like it too much, which is also irritating as hell.*

"Sorry. When the claws fit..." He kissed her again and brushed his fingers over her cheek, his expression turning serious. "All kidding aside, are you worried about the fans and paparazzi and what it'll be like when you go back home?"

She shook her head. "It's Oak Falls, not the Big Apple or LA. Nobody bothers Dash, and it's been years since anyone has hounded Axsel when he's in town. I can't imagine fans or photographers showing up there for us."

"You might be surprised. You're new on the scene, and people want to know more about each of you. I've got a team watching your families—"

"You *what?*" She sat up, but he gently pushed her back down.

"Before you bite my head off, you said you didn't want your family affected by the tour, and you were pretty determined to protect your bandmates, too. I figured that extended to their families, and I always keep my word. I sent a very discreet team to Oak Falls and another guy to Charlottesville to keep an eye on Pepper."

"*God.* What is it with you?" She was equally touched by what he'd done as she was irritated by it. "Everything you do makes me want to smack you *and* kiss you."

He laughed. "I'll take the kisses and give you the smacks on your ass."

She shoved him playfully. "My family hasn't said anything about security."

"And they won't. I told you the team is discreet. Oak Falls has been quiet, but my guy in Charlottesville caught an amateur photog trying to get pictures of Pepper."

"What? Does she know? If anything happens to her—"

"She's fine, Sable. She's safe, and she doesn't need to know. You didn't need to know, either, but I don't want you worrying when you go back home. My cousins own Elite Security, and their guys are top-notch. They'll stay under the radar."

"Elite? Isn't that owned by Brett and Carson...*Bad.*" She rolled her eyes. "The whole tall-dark-and-way-too-handsome thing should have clued me in to the cousin thing. I forgot Brett was in security. His wife, Sophie, is my sister Grace's best friend, but they only live in Oak Falls half the time, so I don't see them very often."

"I know. Brett filled me in about Grace and Sophie, and it was in the background report they ran for me."

"Is there anything you *don't* know about me?"

"Yes, many things, but you're not naive, Sable. You had to know we'd check out the band."

"I did, but hearing it from you while we're naked is a different story. I feel even more exposed."

"Want me to run a background check on myself and give you the reports?"

She smiled. "Yes."

"Consider it done. Fair is fair."

"You're not worried that I'll find out all your secrets?"

"The important ones won't show up on a background report."

She guessed that meant that hers wouldn't, either, and she

was glad about that. "Thank you for watching out for my family and the guys' families, but I don't need security at home. I don't like the idea of strangers lurking around watching my every move. I can take care of myself. Besides, the Jericho brothers will watch out for creeps."

"Jericho brothers? I met Jeb and JJ Jericho at that pub where you played. Is that who you mean?"

"Yes. My sister Brindle is married to their brother Trace, and they have another brother named Shane. They'll keep an eye out for us."

"Jeb seemed awfully interested in keeping you in town. Is there something between you guys?"

She appreciated the lack of jealousy in his tone. "Once upon a time there was, but he wanted more and I didn't, so now we're just friends."

"Mind if I ask why you didn't want more?"

She shrugged. "I don't like complications. Never have."

"I know how small towns are. The gossip can kill you."

"It wasn't that. Nobody knew about us."

He cocked a curious grin. "Have the men in your life always been your dirty little secrets?"

"Not the way you make them sound, but I guess they are. I'm a private person. I don't even go out with guys from my hometown anymore. I haven't in years."

"Then where do you meet men?"

"Music festivals usually, or at gigs we play in other towns. It's too weird to be with someone you see all the time if it's not going to be a long-term relationship. Like with Jeb. His family has community jam sessions in their barn, and they have since we were kids. It would've been weird if anyone had known we'd hooked up, and my sisters would've been all up in my business."

"I get it. Is that how you got into music? Jam sessions with your old fling?"

"No. Jeb and I didn't get together until six or seven years ago. I've always loved music. There was always music on in the barn and garage when we'd do chores or fix things, and my grandmother was a musician before she got married. She used to sing *all* the time. She taught me to play the guitar. My parents say I sound just like her when I sing."

"She must have really been something, because I've never heard a voice as sexy as yours."

Sable went up on her elbow, mirroring his position. "In case you haven't noticed, I'm already naked. You don't have to blow smoke up my ass to get a little action."

"I believe we've already clarified that I never blow smoke up anyone's ass." He pulled her closer, squeezing her butt. "But I am obsessed with yours."

"Shut up." She'd never been one for pillow talk, but she liked it with him. She was enjoying their playfulness, and seeing him smile made her feel happier.

"Okay. I won't tell you about how I've been fantasizing about your ass all day. Tell me about your grandmother."

"She was amazing. She played at festivals and local events and never wanted to make it bigger."

"Sounds familiar."

"Yes, but that's where our similarities end. She was all about settling down. She met my grandfather at the summer music festival in Romance, Virginia, and once they were married, she stopped performing to focus on family. She used to take us to music festivals, but she passed away when I was eight." A wave of longing moved through her as memories rolled in. "After that my parents took us to the festival in Romance, Virginia, and

FAROUK®

CHI® | BIOSILK®

## 2-YEAR WARRANTY CARD IF HAIR TOOL IS LESS THAN 2 YEARS OLD

For a hair tool replacement with a 2-year warranty, please send the following:

• Completed Warranty Card
• Your hair tool
• Original receipt indicating the place and date of purchase.
• $15.00 USD check or money order payable to Farouk Systems, Inc. to cover the shipping
  and handling if your tool is less than two years old. **If you return a tool that is older th**
  **2 years old, we will promptly return your tool and $15.00 USD check or money orde**
  **to the address below.**

**Mail to:**     Attention: Returns Department
                 Farouk Systems, Inc.
                 880 E.Richey Rd.
                 Houston, Texas 77073

Name: _____

Address: _____

City: _____ State/Prov.: _____

Zip Code: _____ Country: _____

E-mail: _____Phone#: _____

Model (ex. GF1001): _____

**Store Purchased From**: _____

City: _____ State/Prov.: _____

Zip Code: _____ Country: _____

Date of Purchase: _____

Describe Problem: _____

_____

✂ – – – – – – – – – – – – – – – – – – – – – –

KEEP FOR YOUR RECORDS

Shipping Tracking Number: _____

Date Tool Was Sent: _____

then Grace got her license, and eventually I was able to drive myself."

"It's nice that your family kept up the tradition, but it's a shame your grandmother never got to see you play professionally. You must miss her."

"I do. A lot, actually. She was my person. She understood me. I could talk to her about anything."

"That's rare for people like you and me, who aren't open books."

The truth in his words hung between them, binding them together in a way she'd never felt before. It felt more intimate than the bond she had with Pepper or Tuck, and she was surprised she didn't want to push him away because of it. She knew she'd do enough of that tomorrow and allowed herself a brief respite from holding up her walls.

"I feel like she's smiling down on me when I play. Especially when I play the summer festival in Romance, since it was so special to her."

"I'm sure she is. You're incredible."

He kissed her again, then lay back, pulling her against his side. Her cheek rested on his chest. He felt familiar and safe, and she had a niggle of a need to push away, but a bigger part of her wanted to stay right there.

"You know, I DJed at that summer music festival when I was in college."

"No way." She looked at his face to see if he was kidding. "You *DJed*? Were you DJ Big Daddy Kane?"

"No," he said coyly. "I was DJ *BDK*, thank you very much."

"Ohmygod. *Seriously?* You called yourself that at *what?* Twenty?"

A boyish grin softened his features. "Actually, I grew up

listening to Dr. Dre, Tupac, and Biggie Smalls. I became BDK when I was about ten."

Laughter burst from her lips, and she fell onto his chest. "Did you wear baggy pants and gel your hair, too?"

"*Yes*, and I was cool."

"I'm sure you were." She cracked up, making him laugh, too. "What did your parents think of Baby BDK?"

"They were proud of me. They supported my love of music. It wasn't until I hit puberty and discovered girls that BDK took on a different meaning."

That only made her laugh harder. "I can just see you strutting down the halls of your high school in your baggy pants, with a chain attached to your wallet, going, *Hey, baby. Let Big Daddy Kane teach you a thing or two. Meet me under the bleachers after school.*" She cracked up and buried her face in his neck.

He smacked her ass, and she squealed with laughter.

"Are you telling me you never went through an awkward stage?" he asked through his own laughter.

"Nope. Never." She wasn't about to share those details. "But now I have to know how you went from rockin' DJ Baby BDK to billionaire extraordinaire Big Daddy Kane."

He clasped his hands behind his head with a smirk. "After the way you're making fun of my *early* career, I'm not sure I can trust you with such a personal story."

She leaned on his chest, schooling her expression. "Are you serious?"

"It's not something I typically share. Especially with someone who lies about their awkward years."

"*Fine.* I was gangly when I was younger, all knees and elbows, and I didn't get boobs until I was in tenth grade. But I was tough, so nobody messed with me."

He cocked a grin. "Woman, even without boobs, you were probably the hottest girl in Oak Falls, and I'm sure that fiery attitude made you even more alluring. All young guys love a challenge."

"Apparently so do *old* guys," she teased, then kissed his chest. The second her lips left his skin, she was struck by the tender intimacy of what she'd done.

She moved to lie beside him, but their eyes connected, the moment pounding like thunder between them. Kane's lips twitched into an *almost* smile. He pulled her against his side again, kissing her temple, and held her there, as if he were refusing to give her space to pick apart this strange new thing building between them.

"You want to know how I got to be a ruthless business-man?"

Still caught up in *him* not pushing *her* away, "Uh-huh" was all she could manage.

"I'm like all those country songs, where a guy gets his heart broken, goes on a bender, bangs women, gets more tattoos, and when he finally gets his head out of his ass, he comes back with a vengeance."

She couldn't imagine him getting his heart broken any more than she could see herself in that light. "You were in love in college?"

"Yeah, or so I thought, until she dumped me for a pretty-boy prick whose parents had money. He was a real asshole who had a reputation for treating women like shit. She married him a year later."

"*Ouch.* When you say vengeance, do you mean Carrie Un-derwood style? Did you slash their tires and ruin their fancy cars?"

"No. That's never been my style. I made it my mission to be wealthier than that guy's parents. I convinced my father to invest in real estate with me, and after a few lucky breaks, I decided to go bigger. I secured more capital from him and other sources, quadrupled it in the first two years, and kept learning, growing, and investing. I took my revenge a few years later in the form of a hostile takeover when that pretty boy was given a piece of the family business, and then I drove it into the ground."

"Holy crap." She pushed up to see his face again. Tension lines mapped his forehead. She imagined a younger, heartbroken version of him and knew he had to have been cut to his core to have taken it so far. "But that means you lost your own money."

"I didn't give a fuck, and in the end I didn't lose much. Just prior to the takeover, I'd acquired a floundering family-owned syrup company in Pennsylvania that was being run by the ill-equipped grandson and granddaughter of the original founder. I offered the best execs and support staff of the other company generous compensation packages to relocate and be part of the renewal of the syrup company and gave equally generous severance packages to the people I let go. I revamped and rebranded the syrup company, created hundreds of new jobs, and breathed new life into the town's economy. Then I renamed and rebranded the company I'd torn apart, revived it, and sold it off."

"Ruthless, clever, *and* bighearted. Don't worry, I won't tell anyone about that big heart of yours. But I wonder what it says about me that I find your viciousness as much of a turn-on as your kindness."

He hugged her against his side. "It says you and I really are made from the same cloth."

"I don't know about that. You did it all for love."

"No. I did it for revenge."

"Because you loved her and you were heartbroken. There's no shame in that."

He leaned up on his elbow again, piercing eyes drilling into her. "I *thought* I loved her, but it didn't take long to realize that while I cared for her, I wasn't in love with her. When you love someone, you fight for them. I didn't fight for her. I just hated having something taken away from me." His tone softened. "What about you? What's your first-love story? What poor sap did you leave crying in his hat?"

"My first love and I are still going strong. I ride him every chance I get."

His brows slanted. "So you *are* involved with someone back home? Your *special friend*, of course," he said with distaste. "Is that who DA is?"

"*DA?* Did you go through my planner?"

"It was open on the desk, and I might have glanced at it…and turned a few pages."

"You nosy little shit," she teased.

"Give me a break. I hadn't done the background check yet, so I was trying to figure out who you were."

"You could have asked."

"You wouldn't have answered."

"True." But for some reason, she wanted to answer now. "DA is Deloris Aiken, and yes, she's the person I was referring to when I mentioned having a special friend. She's like a grandmother to me, and her husband, Lloyd, was like a grandfather. He taught me everything I know about mechanics." She told him about how she and her father used to tinker in the barn together and how, at fourteen, her father had suggested she talk to Lloyd about learning from him at the auto shop. "I followed him around the shop, learning everything I could, and since he and Deloris had no kids, they treated me like part of their family. I spent a lot of time at their house, helping them with things."

"What kinds of things?"

"Whatever they needed. I'd wash the car, mow the grass, chop wood. I helped make flower beds and bring planters in for the winter and out to the porch in the summer. Deloris loved gardening, and their house was filled with flowers. Lloyd loved her so much. He used to say he loved her more than flowers loved the sun."

"That's beautiful."

"Yeah. He passed away six years ago and left the shop to me in his will." She told him about how she'd been taking care of Deloris and why she'd had to move into the assisted living facility.

"That must be hard."

"It is. I have to remind her who I am a lot, and sometimes she gets upset and scared when she doesn't remember, which they told me is normal. In her more lucid moments, I can't help but hope she won't get worse, even though I know it's not realistic. So I try to spend as much time with her as I can."

"No wonder you didn't want to leave."

"That's one of the many reasons."

"I'm sorry you're going through that. It's a lot to deal with, but at least you've had a surrogate grandmother for all these years. That's something to be thankful for."

"I am thankful." She traced one of his tattoos with her finger, thinking about how she was thankful for this moment, too.

It was usually more difficult for her to share her feelings, but tonight it felt nice. "How did we get on that subject anyway?"

"We were talking about your first love. If it wasn't DA, who's the special someone who stole your heart?"

"It's not exactly *someone*. My truck was my first love, and I take very good care of him."

"Oh, I see how you are." He bit her neck, both of them laughing, and then he was on top of her, his delicious body rubbing against all her best places as he pinned her hands to the mattress, his eyes glittering devilishly. "You need to be punished for trying to trick me."

"If my punishment involves your mouth on me, I'm all for it."

"That's *not* a punishment."

"It is if you make me wait for what I really need."

A sinful growl rumbled up his chest, eyes flaming. "Your punishment is *my* pleasure."

He kissed his way down her body, slowing to tease and titillate, making her want to be very, *very* bad.

# Chapter Fifteen

THE SOUND OF knocking dragged Sable from a deep sleep. Freaking hotels. She reached for the extra pillow to put it over her head and touched a scruff-covered jaw, flooding her with warmth as memories of their sexy night tiptoed in. She opened her eyes, drinking in the man who had surprised her in so many ways last night sleeping beside her, gloriously naked. One arm was tucked under her pillow. His other hand rested on his ink-covered chest. She wanted to know the meaning behind those tattoos. Her gaze followed the treasure trail down his body to his erection poking out from beneath the sheet. Her mouth watered to tease him awake. She inched down the bed, trying not to wake him. Another knock rang out, and she froze, realizing it was on the door to her hotel suite.

"Sable?"

*Tuck. Shit.* She slipped carefully off the bed and threw on a T-shirt. She was pulling on underwear when another knock sounded. She hurried out of the bedroom, stepping over the towel and Kane's clothes they'd left strewn across the foyer, and opened the door just a few inches. "Hey, what time is it?"

"Almost nine. We missed you at breakfast." Tuck's brows slanted. "Are you just getting up?"

"Yeah. Late night."

He arched a brow. "You got someone in there with you?"

"*No.* I was up late trying to hash out a song." The lie tasted bitter. Tuck probably wouldn't care about her and Kane, but why bother telling him about something that wasn't going anywhere? A pang of sadness moved through her with that realization, and she had to work hard not to let that disappointment, or the discomfort of it, show.

"Hope it's a good one. Our car leaves in forty minutes. Want me to grab you some breakfast while you pack?"

"No. I'm good. I'll meet you downstairs in half an hour."

"A'right."

She closed the door, and when she turned around, Kane was leaning against the doorframe, his legs crossed at the ankle. Guilt slayed her as he pushed from the doorframe and started dressing. "Hey, I didn't say anything to Tuck because this isn't..." *Real?* That stung, because, for the first time in her life, something had felt real. "Because you and I aren't..." She searched for the right words and came up empty, save for the memory of how angry he'd been when he'd asked about Tuck the other night. "Not that Tuck and I have anything going on, but I didn't think you wanted—"

"Sable, it's *fine*," he said calmly, buttoning his shirt.

She was too frustrated to think straight. "I just didn't want to make it weird. But it's not because—"

"I *didn't* ask," he said firmly.

As he finished dressing, she wondered why he wasn't asking. After everything they'd shared, didn't she owe him the truth about Tuck? "Kane—"

He held up his hand. "You don't owe me an explanation. We both know what this was, and there's no reason for anyone else to hear about it." He stepped closer. "This week has been great. I'm glad I've gotten to know you." He kissed her cheek. "I'll see you in seven weeks, when the tour starts."

"Yeah, okay," she said absently, as if a spear wasn't puncturing her heart as he walked out the door. A wave of sadness consumed her, and she squeezed her hands into fists, steeling herself against the unwanted emotion.

With a deep breath and a fast exhalation, she headed into the bedroom to shower and pack. The sight of soupy pie remnants, condom wrappers, and other evidence of their pleasure-filled night stopped her in her tracks.

*I'm stronger than this.*

She lifted her chin, refusing to get caught up in man drama the way her sisters and friends always had, and forced herself to walk past those reminders, into the bathroom. She locked the door behind her—as if those inanimate objects could follow her in—and turned on the shower, averting her eyes from the mirror.

If there was one thing she couldn't stand to look at, it was a liar.

# Chapter Sixteen

KANE ANSWERED THE phone as he walked into his penthouse after a long day at the office. "Hey, Johnny. What's going on?"

"I just hung up with Dad. I hear congratulations are in order."

After months of negotiations, Kane finally signed the last of the legal documents transferring ownership of the Australian hotel chain to Bad Enterprises. He should be riding the highest high, thrilled with his latest accomplishment and excited about the challenges he faced to turn the hotel into something extraordinary. But while he was glad to have expanded into international territory, he'd been so knotted up since Sable left, it was as if he couldn't find the same high as he'd experienced with her. Like his world wasn't quite as bright as his snarky bedmate had made it. It had only been a week since she'd left, but it felt like a fucking month. It didn't help that Surge desperately needed a manager, and Sable was too bullheaded to work with one. Kane had stepped in to ensure they had all the appropriate insurance and legal documentation in place to protect them during the tour, which meant he had to stay in contact with her. He'd forwarded the information to her via email to keep things professional. Professional was safe. Silence was safer, but he wasn't going to let her or the band fall through the cracks.

"You must be stoked," Johnny said.

"Yeah. I am. It's going to be a great project."

"Should we start looking for a new manager for the band?"

"Hell no. Why would you do that?"

"You've already got a lot on your plate running your companies, managing us, and making sure Surge is protected. You're burning the candle at both ends. How can you possibly do more?"

*The more distractions, the better.* "Lucky for you, my candle never burns out."

"I don't know, bro. You're not Superman."

"You're right. I'm more like Iron Man."

Johnny laughed. "That's definitely more fitting. Listen, I can't thank you enough for all you're doing for the band, and for Surge. It means a lot to me and Jilly that you stepped up to help Sable and the guys."

"No problem. We're all on the same team, trying to knock this tour out of the park. From what Shea has said, we're well on our way."

"Yeah, it's pretty incredible. Be forewarned, Jilly swears you and Sable were hooking up in the city, but don't worry, I told her Sable wasn't your type."

Kane looked out the window at the lights of the city. He was right. Sable wasn't anything like the women he usually went out with. Those women were a dime a dozen. She was one in a million. And those were the thoughts that were fucking with his head, which was why he chose to bury them down deep. "Jilly's barking up the wrong tree."

"No shit. You like women you can wine and dine and impress with your success."

"You make me sound like an asshole."

"I don't *make* you sound like anything." Johnny chuckled. "You know who you are, and Sable strikes me as someone who's more impressed by a big engine or a kick-ass guitar than Armani suits and thousand-dollar bottles of wine."

There was more to Sable than mechanics and music, but Kane buried that, too, and redirected the conversation. "How's Jilly feeling? Is she excited about the launch of Wanderlust?"

"Yeah. We all are. The prelaunch buzz is off the charts. She's gained international attention, and they're touting the line as affordable designs that represent female empowerment and femininity, which is exactly what she'd hoped for. You're still coming to the launch, aren't you?"

"I wouldn't miss it for the world. I talked to Harlow yesterday, and she said she's walking the runway in it."

"Yeah, Jilly's thrilled about it, and guess who else is walking the runway? Hold on. Jilly and Zoey just walked in."

"Is that Kane?" Zoey shouted.

Kane smiled at his niece's exuberance. She'd come a long way from the sullen, rebellious teen she'd been last fall. After missing out on so much of her life, he tried to keep in touch every week and see her as often as he could to be the uncle she deserved.

"Yes," Johnny answered.

"Did you tell him?" Zoey asked. "What did he say?"

"Tell me what?" Kane asked.

"I'll let her tell you."

He heard him handing the phone to Zoey.

"Kane, guess what? Jilly's showing some of the Rocker Girlz

outfits at the Wanderlust launch, and she's letting me and Ginny and Cara model them! Can you believe it?" Ginny and Cara were two of Zoey's closest friends, and Rocker Girlz was the name of the clothing line for young teens that Jillian and Zoey were designing together.

"That's awesome. I can't wait to see you rock the runway."

She went on to tell him about the clothes she and her friends were going to model and to describe, in detail, the outfits she and Jillian were in the process of making, barely slowing down to take a breath. "I've got to go. Jilly and I want to finish a shirt tonight. Love you!"

"Love you, too, kid. Put your father back on the line."

"Sorry about that," Johnny said. "I didn't know she was going to talk for ten minutes."

"You know I love hearing from her. Every time we talk, it makes me realize how great a father you've been. Her happiness is a reflection of you and Jilly."

"Thanks, man. But it's a reflection of you, too. There was so much going on at the time, I couldn't have managed without the peace of mind of knowing you were handling the business. You allowed me to focus on building a relationship with my daughter."

"And your soon-to-be wife," he reminded him.

"Yeah. I'm a lucky bastard for a lot of reasons, and having you as a brother is at the top of that list. I hope one day you'll have this, too. I know it's not what you think you want, but there's nothing like being in love or being a parent."

Kane's lingering feelings after his fling with Sable were further proof that caring about people outside his family only led to pain. But he hadn't burdened his family with that bullshit back then, and he wasn't about to start.

"That's not my thing, but I'm happy for you. Listen, I've got to run. Give my love to Jilly."

After ending the call, he texted his assistant, Anne.

Kane: *What can I send Zoey to celebrate a big event?*

Anne: *A cupcake tower. Kids love those.*

Kane: *Great. Send her the biggest one they've got, with a card that says "Watch out fashion world, Zoey Bad is on the scene. Congrats, kid. Looking forward to seeing you on the runway. Love, Uncle Kane."*

Anne: *You've got it.*

His thoughts circled back to Sable.

Kane: *I need one more favor…*

Five minutes later, he rolled up his sleeves and headed into his music room to blow off some steam. He cranked the music, sat at the drums, and tried to play his frustrations away. But twenty minutes later, he realized he was no longer playing the songs he was listening to. He was playing the damn song Sable had sent him in an audio file earlier in the week. The song they'd worked on together in his rooftop escape. The one she'd aptly named "In Too Deep."

He'd listened to her belting out the heartbreaking lyrics so many times he knew every word and every note by heart. He'd wanted to call her when he'd received it, but he had no control around her. He knew she'd lure out the animal in him without even trying, and they'd end up falling into the lustful abyss that consumed them every time they spoke. He was already hanging on to his sanity by a thread.

*Time to end this shit.*

He pushed to his feet, heading out of the music room as he scrolled through the contacts on his phone. Finally settling on one, he made the call.

"Kane," Angie purred. "It's been a while."

Her voice wasn't doing it for him, but that was okay. He wasn't in the mood for chitchat. "What are you up to? Want to grab a drink or dinner?"

"What do you think?"

"I'll pick you up in twenty."

"I look forward to it. But I'd much rather enjoy *dessert*."

Fuck if his mind didn't go straight to chocolate pie—and Sable.

# Chapter Seventeen

SABLE PARKED BESIDE Reed's truck and gazed up at the farmhouse that had felt like a second home for nearly her whole life. She could still picture Lloyd and Deloris sitting in rockers on the wide front porch on warm summer evenings, two glasses of iced tea on a table between them as Deloris knitted and Lloyd read. Her throat thickened. She'd give anything to see them like that one more time.

Tucking those feelings away, she grabbed the paint out of the back of the truck and headed up the porch steps. Reed had already replaced the railing and fixed the crooked middle step. It was strange how life kept moving no matter what changed—a death, a move, an unexpected opportunity. *An unexpected man.*

Sable hadn't known what to expect when she got back to Oak Falls, but her quiet hometown hadn't let her down. There were a lot of congratulations and just as many *You're not going to run off and leave us now, are you*s, and a few kids had asked for her autograph when she was picking up lunch at the Stardust Café. She'd been home for a little more than two weeks, and thankfully all of that had tapered off, and life had pretty much gone back to normal.

Or at least as normal as it could after a dirty-talking, sex-machine billionaire had awakened parts of her that she *still* wasn't able to quiet. Like the inescapable ache to see him, the irritating urge to verbally spar with him, and that late-night desperate desire to lose herself in his capable hands. That wasn't even the worst of it. The worst part was the yearning to talk about what she was feeling. Sharing bits and pieces of herself with Kane must have opened some sort of door inside her, and she was having trouble kicking it closed.

She never talked about her personal life, and she hadn't intended to talk about Kane. But when she'd visited Deloris this morning, Deloris had been having a relatively good day, although she'd believed herself to be a young woman in love again, and she'd called Sable *Lara*. Sable didn't mind. They'd reminisced about Lloyd, and Deloris had asked if Sable had a special man in her life. Sable had given Deloris her standard response. *I don't need a man telling me what to do.* But some-how, during their conversation, she'd digressed and had ended up with verbal diarrhea. She'd told Deloris about *a* man she'd met in New York and had vacillated between bitching about butting heads with him and raving about how incredible it had been to be with someone so bright and virile. Deloris had called him a *hot-sauce guy* and had said that was what Lloyd had been to her at first. *My Lloyd used to be the kind of man that burned my britches, but I couldn't resist him. I kept going back for more. One day I realized the burn had eased, but the spiciness had remained. It turns out he is exactly what I need...*

It pissed Sable off that she'd even mentioned Kane to her.

She shouldn't *want* to talk about him. The bastard had been able to flick a switch and revert to business mode without missing a beat, which meant she was the only one tortured by this nonsense. He'd sent her professional emails as if he were the band's manager, and though she appreciated his expertise, it was beyond frustrating. Especially since she'd sent him a copy of the song they'd written together, and he'd merely replied with *It's phenomenal. Fans will love it.*

That was almost as irritating as the background check she'd received by FedEx from his personal assistant two days ago with a note that simply read, *As promised, from Mr. Bad.*

The fucker.

He was like the worst type of hangover, and there was no cure in sight.

When she went inside, she could hear Reed working upstairs. It was just as well. She wasn't exactly good company lately, and he and Grace were so happy about Grace's pregnancy. She didn't want to bring him down. She headed into the dining room to try to paint her frustration away.

Grace breezed through the front door a few hours later carrying a large pizza and a pink bakery box. They said pregnant women glowed, and she looked like sunshine on a rainy day. Her thick dark hair billowed around her face as she set the food on the tarp covering the dining room table. "Hi. I hope you're hungry. I had a craving for pepperoni pizza and chocolate éclairs."

The mention of chocolate sent Sable's thoughts right back to Kane. "Thanks." She set down the paint roller. "I'm surprised you're getting cravings already."

"Oh, these aren't pregnancy cravings. They're just regular pig-out cravings."

Grace had always been curvier than Sable and their other sisters, and Sable loved that she'd never been one of those girls who was afraid to eat what she wanted. Grace's confidence was just one of the many things she admired about her oldest sister, along with her good sense to follow her heart and not give up on her dreams because of a man. She and Reed had gone through so much heartbreak when they were kids, but you'd never know it looking at them now.

Her sisters made love look like it was worth the heartaches, headaches, and compromises that had led to their happiness. They'd married strong, capable, loving men who talked out problems and never seemed to fly off the handle. Sable would lose her mind with a man like theirs. There was a reason she was drawn to rebellious, challenging men who weren't emotionally available. They were always on the same page as she was.

So why was she having such a hard time getting past Kane?

*And why am I thinking about him again?*

Trying for the umpteenth time to push him out of her head, she said, "How are your auditions going? Have you found your leads yet?"

"We found the female lead. I'm really excited. She sent in a video audition that blew me away, and she drove down yesterday to audition in person. She's twenty-two, and she's got this Elle Fanning vibe going on. She looks super sweet and innocent, but she's got the ability to rein that in, and when she read her lines, every single one of them carried an emotional punch. If she ends up being as good in the play as I think she will be, I'll hook her up with my friends on Broadway."

"She's that good?"

"Yeah. She's been working in a dinner theater for three years. She's like you—a hidden gem."

"*Please.* I'd like to stay hidden. Have you seen all the crap they're writing about me on social media? Women are saying I'm not that pretty, my voice is too rough, and they're speculating about who I slept with to get the gig. Half the comments from guys are about fucking me or saying I'm banging the guys in my band."

"Don't pay any attention to that garbage."

*Easier said than done.* "Did you see the article about me and Axsel?"

"The one that emphasized you're his *older* sister?"

"Yes. Someone commented that I shouldn't wear shorts because of cellulite. I don't have cellulite, and who cares if I do? What I look like has no bearing on my talent."

"They're just jealous. You're lucky. At least you have thick skin. Don't you remember how I nearly quit and moved back home when critics first started reviewing my plays in New York?"

"Yeah, but they didn't attack you on a personal level. It was all about the plays. I don't know, Grace. My skin isn't *that* thick."

"Oh, Sable. I'm sorry." Grace hugged her.

"It's fine. I'm just bitching. But I have to do the tour, so let's not talk about it. It just pisses me off. Reed is upstairs. Do you want to let him know you're here?"

"I texted him before I came in. I'm sure he'll be down in a minute. I'm sorry about the comments. Just don't look at social media anymore. It's not like you have to."

"Trust me, I never will again. Now can we let it go?"

"Yes. Sorry." Her eyes brightened. "Have you driven through town today? It's all decorated for the Valentine's Day Festival. I can't remember the last time Valentine's Day fell on a weekend."

Tomorrow was the Oak Falls annual Valentine's Day Festival, a fun-filled day of community and chaos. Surge was playing at the festival, as they had for nearly a decade. It had always been one of Sable's favorite events because while *she* wasn't looking for love, every other person around her seemed to be, and love was always in the air at the festival. This year she'd tried to ignore the banner hanging over the road and the vibrant red hearts and love-in-the-air decorations adorning the storefronts along Main Street. Her band planned to play the new song she'd brainstormed with Kane, and she was dreading it. She loved the song, but it was hard to get through when every word reminded her of their time together.

"Yeah, I saw it when I was picking up paint."

Grace opened the pizza box and plucked a pepperoni off a slice. "Is it just me, or do the decorations get better every year?"

"They're definitely striking a different chord this year."

"Is that paint on your shirt?"

"Yeah. Who cares?"

Grace's brows knitted, and she motioned to Sable's leg. "You got paint on your jeans, too. Why didn't you wear your overalls?"

*Because they reminded me of the first time I saw Kane standing on the side of the road looking like my wildest fantasy come to life.* "I forgot to change."

"Bummer. Those jeans are so cute on you. You can get the stains out. It'll be hard with the splatter, but it's doable. When you get home, scrape off the dried paint with a butter knife and then flush the stain with warm water and saturate it with detergent. Keep flushing it out until the stain is gone, or try stain remover, but not until after you've tried the detergent."

"Listen to you. You get pregnant and suddenly you're Helpful Heloise."

Grace's grin widened, and she whispered, "I still can't believe I'm pregnant. Since we decided to embrace the excitement instead of letting our worries steal our joy, part of me wants to shout it from the rooftops. I know we're doing the right thing by not telling anyone outside the family yet, but it's hard to keep it in. Brindle doesn't know how good she had it."

Brindle hadn't been trying to get pregnant, and she'd been a mess when she'd found out. "That was really stressful for her. I understand why you think it might have been easier, but I don't think either of you had it easy. I wish it were easier for you and Reed, but at least IVF worked, and I know you're going to be an amazing mom."

"I totally am," she whispered excitedly.

"Just one thing. Please tell me you're not going to follow that kid around with a stain stick."

"My husband comes home with new stains every week, and I don't follow him around...except to get him naked."

They both laughed.

"What are you guys laughing at?" Reed asked as he came downstairs. He flashed a lopsided grin, drawing a swoony sigh from Grace.

"The thought of you naked," Sable teased.

Reed drew Grace into his arms and kissed her. "Hi, beautiful. You're not laughing at me naked, are you?"

"Not a chance."

Reed looked at the freshly painted walls. "The room looks great."

"It would look better if the real estate agent would let me add some color," Sable said. "The house feels flat with white walls. It was so full of life when Lloyd and Deloris lived here."

"That was because of them, not the color of the walls," Reed said.

"This is really hard for you, isn't it?" Grace asked.

"No," Sable lied, not wanting to burden them with her hard time. "I just think a little color would help."

"You're probably right, but some people don't like color," Grace said.

"It'll sell quicker this way," Reed said. "You're doing the right thing listening to the agent."

*Am I, though?* The little girl in her wanted to paint the walls black so nobody would buy the house and erase the memories of the people she loved. Her emotions were all over the place today. "You probably shouldn't be near paint fumes. Why don't we take this stuff into the kitchen. We can open the patio door"—*to clear my head before band practice tonight*—"and eat at the table." Sable picked up the pizza and bakery box.

"Good idea. I didn't even think about the fumes." Grace and Reed followed her into the kitchen. "Thanks for looking after me."

*It's a lot easier than looking after myself.*

LATER THAT NIGHT, Sable's fingers danced across the fretboard of her guitar with restless urgency as she and the band played "In Too Deep" for a fourth time. Memories of the night she and Kane had worked on the song competed with the music blaring through amplifiers. The sounds reverberated through her as if she were a tuning fork that'd been hit. The guys were jamming like they were feeling every beat, but it all sounded off to Sable. As she belted out the lyrics, the keyboard and bass were harsh and jarring, the notes disjointed, the tempo too fast. Even her own voice sounded off, tearing from her lungs in a strained crescendo, culminating in a frustrated *"Shit."* She stopped playing. *"Sorry.* I can't…"

It took a minute for the guys to realize it wasn't just a momentary slip and for them to stop playing. "What's wrong?" Tuck asked.

"Everything sounds off."

"Off?" JP snapped. "What are you talking about?"

"Yeah. We fucking nailed it," Lee said.

"It sounded great to me," Chris agreed. "What didn't you like?"

"I don't *know*. All of it." She looked around, avoiding their incredulous stares and searching for answers. Moonlight streamed through cracks in the old barn walls, spilling over the equipment, tattered couches, and mismatched chairs they'd collected over the years. It looked the same as it always had. There were no new holes in the walls or other elements that would change the sound of their music. Kane's image flashed before her, sitting on the bench in that rooftop escape, playing her guitar. She tried to push it away, but it only morphed into his cold goodbye, and she realized it wasn't their playing that was off. It was *her*. She couldn't play that damn song without thinking of Kane. Hell, she couldn't breathe without thinking of him.

*"Sorry,"* she said, annoyed with herself. "I'm just not feeling it tonight. I can't get out of my own head."

"A'right, then let's grab a drink and come back to it later," Tuck suggested.

"I'm starved," Lee said. "Let's hit that new sushi joint in Meadowside."

"That sounds great," JP said.

"Sorry, guys." Sable put her guitar in its case. "I'm spent. I just want to go home and chill."

"What about the new song? We're stoked to get new material out there. Are you going to be able to play it tomorrow?" Lee asked.

They'd been practicing every day since they got back from New York. She knew the material. She just needed to get Kane out of her head. "Have I ever let you down at a gig?"

Lee shook his head. "But you've been on edge since we signed on for the tour. I just had to ask."

"Come on, man, let it go," Tuck said. "We all have off days. Shit, you've had years when your head was up your ass for several weeks, and we didn't give you shit about it."

"You're right." Lee held up his hand. "Sorry, Sable. It's cool."

"No worries." She was more disappointed in herself than any of them could ever be.

They put away their equipment, and as they left the barn, Tuck sidled up to her. "You want me to swing by and hang out for a while?"

"No, thanks. I'm fine. I just need to be alone."

He studied her for a beat. "A'right. You know how to reach me."

She climbed into her truck, cranked the music to drown out thoughts of Kane, and headed home. As she turned into the auto shop parking lot, she saw a sleek black Aston Martin parked by the bays and—her breath caught in her throat—Kane Freaking Bad leaning against the wall beside the office door, legs crossed at the ankles, arms folded over his broad chest, dress shirt straining against his biceps, and those piercing dark eyes tracking her as she parked.

# Chapter Eighteen

SABLE CUT THE engine, trying to make sense of the irritatingly beautiful man suddenly appearing in her life again. But she couldn't think beyond how much she'd missed him. How could someone who frustrated her to no end also stir so much longing?

How could she let him?

It had been a mistake. A fiery, unexpected, intensely emotional mistake. She hadn't even realized how emotional until now, when it took all her strength to straighten her spine and throw the door open.

As she climbed out of the truck, he pushed from the wall, watching her like a lion studying his prey. Hot sauce had nothing on this man. His burn scorched hotter with every step. She stopped a few feet away, needing the barrier to keep from giving in to the ignorant organ in her chest, which was trying to break free to get to him. "Hello, Kane. What are you doing here?"

He stepped closer, his eyes never leaving hers. "I was in the area and thought I'd swing by to see how you were."

"You expect me to believe you just *happened* to be in Oak Falls?"

"It would be nice." His lips quirked as he closed the gap between them, making her heart race even faster. "Then I wouldn't have to admit that I can't stop thinking about you."

Her stomach dipped, but this was Kane Bad, not Joe Schmoe. "You can have any woman you want without traveling hundreds of miles. Why are you really here?"

"Because that's the fucking problem. I can have any woman except the only one I want. I can't get you out of my head, and trust me, I've tried." His tone turned dark, impassioned. "I met a woman for drinks the other night, and I had every intention of fucking you out of my system."

Her heart sank.

"But I sent her home from the bar *alone* because she didn't have seductive green eyes that challenged me and a whiskey voice that set my body on fire. She didn't make me smile or laugh or *want* until I was crazed with desire by merely existing. She wasn't the one infiltrating my thoughts twenty-four-seven. There's only one person who does that for me, and that's you, Panthera."

She'd known he had the power to take her to her knees with his dominance, but what he'd just said and the way he was looking at her like he meant every word had her at a loss for words. He slid an arm around her, drawing her tight against him, and Lord, he felt *good*.

His eyes bored into her. "You can't tell me you haven't been thinking about me, too."

*Lie. Just fucking lie.* "You've already messed with my head so badly, I couldn't even concentrate at practice tonight." She didn't know why the truth came out, but there was no stopping it now. "I don't need more complications when we go on tour, and you're the other band's manager. That makes you one giant complication."

He held her tighter and brushed his scruff along her cheek, speaking sternly into her ear. "I understand. I don't have time for complications, either. I know you're not looking for anything serious, and neither am I."

She closed her eyes against that truth for just a second, her fingers curling into his shirt.

He lifted his face, eyes serious. "The tour doesn't start for another month, and it sounds like we've both already wasted too much time trying *not* to think about each other. I'm here now, and no one has to know what goes on between us. How about we stop torturing ourselves and take advantage of this time together?"

Her mind spun, but her body was egging her on. She didn't know if being with him tonight would make things worse or if it would get him out of her system, but at that moment she wanted him too much to care. "I do like taking advantage of you."

A wicked grin spread across his handsome face. "There's the feisty woman I came to see."

He lowered his mouth to hers in a slow, passionate kiss, easing the frustrations that had rattled her to her core in his absence. As if *he* was the cure for the Kane hangover.

"*God,*" he growled against her lips. "I've missed your mouth."

He kissed her again, harder, more possessively, devouring her in the dimly lit parking lot where anyone could see them.

"*Inside.*" She grabbed his hand, pulling him around the building to the outside entrance to her apartment. Their kisses were fierce and urgent as they stumbled through the door and up the stairs. She must've been moving too slowly, because he belted one arm around her waist, lifting her off her feet, and ascended the stairs two at a time, both of them laughing into their kisses. Laughing with this man who made her want and crave like an animal felt *amazing*. He set her down on the landing, and she fumbled with the keys.

"If you make fun of my place, you're out of here," she warned.

He looked at her like she was speaking a foreign language. "What's wrong with your place?"

"My entire apartment could fit in your foyer."

He hulked over her, pressing her back to the door, grinding his erection against her. "Does it feel like I'm interested in your apartment? Open the door, Sable, or I'll fuck you right here."

Her temperature spiked at that tempting thought, but she pushed the door open, and then he was on her, hands and mouth everywhere. She was just as eager as he pushed off her jacket. She tore at his shirt as he tugged hers off. Her skin was on fire, her panties wet, and as his shirt fell to the floor, revealing his sculpted chest and all that beautiful ink, a hungry moan fell from her lips. He yanked open her jeans, dark eyes scanning the room. "Get these fucking jeans off and bend over that couch."

Desire burned through her at his unwavering demand.

She tugged off her boots and socks as he toed off his shoes and opened his slacks. He watched her strip. The hunger in his eyes took her breath away. Her insides vibrated with need as she bent over the back of the couch, and he moved behind her.

He rubbed his palm over her ass. "So fucking perfect." He pushed his cock between her legs, sliding the length of it through her wetness. She moaned, and he did it again. "I've missed your pussy."

"Don't fuck with me, Kane."

In the next breath, the broad head of his cock rammed into her, burying him to the hilt. She cried out with the immense pleasure *and* relief of his thick shaft stretching her, pressing against the secret spot inside her as he found a hard-and-fast rhythm. Everything, from the air filling her lungs to his hands on her hips and his cock driving into her, felt different, *better,* more intense. Tingles started in her core, radiating outward, taking her higher and higher, until she was holding on to her sanity by a thread.

"Christ, you're so tight, so hot and wet...*Fuck.*" He stilled.

"Don't stop!"

"I forgot the fucking condom," he said through gritted teeth. "I lose my mind when I'm with you."

He started to pull out, and she reached behind her, grabbing his thigh and holding him there, locking eyes with him over her shoulder. "I'm on birth control. Just fuck me."

A sinister grin curved his lips. "You want me to fuck you bare, baby girl?" He began moving excruciatingly slowly. "You want Big Daddy to make you come on my cock?"

"*Kane,*" she warned, but he continued taunting her. He gyrated his hips, sliding one hand to her clit, teasing her so exquisitely, he took her right back up to the edge of madness. "*Faster,*" she pleaded, but he continued the torturous pace.

"I love the feel of your tight pussy wrapped around me."

The tingles returned, desire mounting inside her, pounding through her veins. She felt a thousand pins prickling her skin, an orgasm hovering just out of reach. She rocked with him, trying to get him to go faster, her legs shaking. "*Harder,*" she begged.

"That's it, baby. Beg for my cock." He thrust a little faster, a little harder.

*"Oh God...Kane...please."*

He grabbed a fistful of her hair, clutching her hip with his other hand, holding her at a ninety-degree angle as he pounded into her. "Drench my cock, baby. Come for me." *This* was what she craved. Kane's power, his dire need to *take*, and the guttural sounds of restraint he made with every thrust as he sent electricity arcing through her. She couldn't think, couldn't see past the pleasure exploding inside her as she cried out "*Kane*—"

"That's it, baby girl. *Fuck*, that feels good." He continued driving into her, magnifying her pleasure, until she collapsed over the couch, panting for air.

The man was a master of control. She had no idea how he hadn't come, but she loved that he could go all night. He tugged her upright, turned her roughly around, and grabbed her hair again, crushing his mouth to hers in a mind-numbing kiss that brought her right up to the edge of release again. But he tore his mouth away and pushed her down to her knees. "Suck my cock."

She reached for him, taking him deep, sucking and stroking, teasing his balls. He gritted out, "Touch yourself." She reached between her legs, wanting to make him as crazy as he made her. He tugged her head forward, fucking her throat. She greedily soaked in every growl, every thrust, and when he buried both hands in her hair, fucking her mouth instead of her throat, making it easier for her to breathe, and said, "That's it, tease that pussy as you take my cock," she reached up with her other hand, cupping his balls, and tugged. "*Fuuck*" tore from his lungs, and he pulled out of her mouth, hot jets of come streaking her breasts.

His eyes bored into her as he pulled her up to her feet on

shaky legs. "Look at you. So fucking beautiful with my come on your tits." He ran his fingers through the sticky mess, using it to tease her nipples.

"Marking your temporary territory?"

His eyes narrowed, jaw clenching. "I'm going to fuck you on every surface and make you scream my name so many times, it echoes off the walls after I leave." He dragged his come-covered fingers down her stomach and teased her clit with deathly precision. She went up on her toes, chasing the high. His mouth covered hers, tongue thrusting, teeth gnashing, as he sent her soaring again. He broke the kiss as his name tore from her lungs. The greedy bastard. She barely registered his gratified smile as he captured her mouth again, swallowing her moans and whimpers.

She was trembling all over as she came down from the peak. He said, "Shower," and she panted out, "Bedroom, but my legs need a minute."

"It'll cost you." He lifted her into his arms, lowering her onto his hard shaft with a groan.

"Best fee *ever*."

She covered his mouth with hers, riding his cock as he carried her into the bathroom. He turned on the shower a few seconds before stepping in. Warm water rained down on them, slipping between their lips as they feasted on each other's mouths and between their bodies as she rode his cock, making every thrust and grind feel even more erotic. Her back hit the cold tile, and he thrust harder, sending jolts of pleasure through her. He slowed their kisses to a tantalizing pace, making her entire body tingle and burn, and teased her bottom with his fingers, making her insides clench and crave. She tried to keep up with the sensations, but it was like being in a thunderstorm with no shelter in sight, so she stopped trying and gave herself over to all of them. "I can't get enough of you," he said gruffly. She was about to say, *I can't get enough of you, either*, but he reclaimed her mouth in a luxuriously deep, passionate kiss that sent her careening. Her head fell back, and "*Kane—*" shot from her lungs as "Sable—" flew from his.

They rode out their high, and he held her as their breathing calmed, a whirlwind of emotions coursing through her. When he set her on her feet, he did it gently, drawing her into his arms and turning, so she was beneath the warm shower. He didn't say a word, and she couldn't have if she tried. He kissed her forehead, the tenderness and his lazy smile getting her even more twisted up inside. They didn't speak as he poured body wash into his hand and began bathing her. His touch was sensual and calming as he washed her breasts, dipping his head to kiss each one. Seeing this powerful man care for her in a way she'd never allowed another to, a way that seemed to bring him pleasure, too, intensified her emotions. He continued moving down her body, caressing and bathing, kissing and nipping, until she was panting for more.

He spread his hands on her thighs, heat flaring in his eyes as he slicked his tongue along her sex. "*OhgodKane*," she said in one long breath, and pushed her hands into his thick hair as he used teeth and tongue to send her spiraling into oblivion again, his name echoing off the walls.

She collapsed over him, and he rose to his full height, lifting her chin with his fingers and kissing her again. The taste of her mixed with the addicting taste of him, leaving her in some kind of drunken sex fog as he washed himself off and turned off the water. He grabbed a towel, drying her before tending to himself, his eyes never leaving hers.

What was he thinking? Or was his mind as hazy as hers?

She turned to go into the bedroom, but he snagged her hand, eyes full of mischief.

"What?" she asked with a soft laugh.

"You said a dozen orgasms wasn't a record. I heard a challenge." He eyed the sink. "This surface cannot go unclaimed."

Her body ignited. How could she want him again so soon? "Sure you can handle it?"

"Bads always rise to the occasion." He drew her closer, their naked bodies brushing as he kissed her neck and nipped at her earlobe, causing goose bumps to chase over her skin and his cock to press temptingly against her belly.

# Chapter Nineteen

KANE'S ARM WAS numb, but he didn't dare move as Sable was using it for a pillow as she lay sleeping beside him on her bedroom floor, entangled in rumpled sheets. They'd left no surface untouched. He couldn't remember exactly how they'd tumbled off the bed to the floor, but he'd never forget their fits of laughter and kisses or how good it had felt when she'd rested her cheek on his chest, saying she needed to power up for the next round, and had promptly fallen asleep.

His gaze rolled over her beautiful face. She looked peaceful with the morning light misting through the curtains, as if she might open her eyes, smile warmly, and snuggle into his side. But that wasn't his Panthera. She was more likely to kick his ass out the second she realized he was still there. He grinned at the thought. He adored her fierceness. Seeing the woman who drove him mad climb out of that cherry-red truck that meant so much to her and force a scowl—*so damn cute*—had loosened all the knots in his chest. That was the first time in almost two weeks he could breathe without feeling like his lungs were clogged. For all his second-guessing and worries about showing up to see her, the reward was definitely worth the risk.

But it came at a price.

She'd left a lasting impression on him when she'd returned home from New York, and after last night he knew he was in for an even worse time after he left this morning. He was still trying to process how moments when they fell silent and time seemed to stand still had coalesced with the vulnerabilities that had gone unsaid—but were felt as deeply as a spear to the heart—and how their raw, animalistic passion had given way to lighthearted banter and laughter as naturally as breathing when they'd needed sustenance at one o'clock in the morning and had raided her pantry.

All those pieces of themselves had intertwined and imprinted on him in a way he wasn't fully prepared to face. He'd lain awake most of the night struggling with those emotions, wishing they'd remained undiscovered, and at the same time marveling at the fact that he was capable of feeling more than lust or greed. He'd thought he'd all but killed that part of himself years ago.

Sable sighed, and her eyes fluttered open. Her smile didn't falter, and she didn't scowl as she said, "I guess last night wasn't a dream," and rolled onto her back, wincing. "*Nope.* Definitely didn't dream it."

He chuckled and went up on his elbow. "A little sore?"

"Get that smug look off your face. You try having a two-hundred-pound man between your legs all night."

"I'd rather not." He massaged her hip. "But a beautiful brunette with challenging eyes?" He kissed one of the marks he'd left on the swell of her breast. "All night long, baby, and don't even try to tell me we didn't set a record."

"No comment." She threw off the covers, revealing the other marks he'd left on her stomach and thighs. She got up and sauntered into the bathroom, gloriously naked, giving him a great view of her heart-shaped ass, which he'd also marked like a Neanderthal.

He got up from the floor and tossed the sheet and comforter on the bed, taking in the simplicity of her bedroom. Several plants decorated a tiered stand spanning the length of the double windows. Pale green walls with white trim contrasted nicely with the simple oak bed and dresser. Two notebooks were on the nightstand, reminding him of when they'd knocked other notebooks off quite a few surfaces in the other room. She must like plants and color, because there wasn't a white wall in the place, and there were a number of plants and flowers by the patio doors in the living room. But while the other rooms had family photos decorating the walls, there was an enormous white tapestry on the wall behind the bed, with yellow flowers and green leaves painted along the top and draped down the sides unevenly, partially framing a line drawing of a naked woman. She was drawn from her mouth down, lips slightly pinched, knees pulled up to her chest, arms draped around them. A few muted orange and peach butterflies danced around flowers and ivy snaking up her side. It was the perfect imagery of simple elegance and fierce femininity with an undertone of guardedness. The tapestry was signed by Morgyn in the lower-right corner. Did her sister see her as guarded and feminine as he did? Or was it just a tapestry she thought Sable would like?

Sable came out of the bathroom, still naked, hair still messy, face freshly washed, stirring all those emotions he was trying to ignore. She reached into a drawer and grabbed a T-shirt. "Don't you have to catch a flight or something?" she asked as she put on the shirt.

He needed to shake off the feelings gnawing at him and walk out that door. But no part of him was ready to do that. He didn't know if or when he'd get another chance to be with her, and that had him closing the distance between them. "Since it's Sunday and your shop is closed, I was thinking I'd stick around."

"*Here?*" She didn't even try to mask her shock.

"Yes, here." He pulled her into his arms and kissed her. She tasted minty, and she was trying to suppress a smile. "We can have breakfast, a little *dessert*, hang out."

She pressed her lips together, her eyes giving away how much she liked the idea. "As fun as that sounds, I can't. Today's the Valentine's Day Festival, and we're playing at it."

"Valentine's Day?" *Shit.* How could he have forgotten? He'd had his assistant send theater tickets to his parents and baskets of candy to his sisters and Zoey, but he'd arranged it a few weeks ago and hadn't given it another thought.

"Yes. I guess you didn't drive down Main Street on the way here?"

"Why would I?" He grabbed her ass, trailing kisses down her neck. "That would have delayed me from getting here and seeing you. But a festival sounds fun." He had no idea where *that* came from. He hadn't gone to a festival since he was a kid, but what the hell. If that was the only way he could get more time with her, he'd take it. "I drove all this way. Might as well enjoy the day."

"*Kane.*" It was more of a plea than a complaint. "How would I explain that to people?" She bent her head to the side, giving him better access. "My mother and sister have booths at the festival."

"Just say I'm here going over a few things for the tour." He slicked his tongue along her collarbone. "I'll drive separately. Nobody will think we've been together." He sealed his teeth over her neck, earning a needy moan that had him aching to be inside her again.

"You can't park an Aston Martin at the fairgrounds." She breathed harder as he pushed his hand between her legs, teasing her wetness. "*Door dings.*"

"Then I'll go with you," he said in her ear as he teased her clit. "When does the festival start?"

"Eleven," she said breathily as she greedily fisted his cock. "How do you always make me want you so badly?"

"Just lucky, I guess." He tore off her shirt and teased her nipple with his tongue and teeth.

She moaned, grabbing him by the hair, holding him there as he worked her with his fingers and mouth. "*Kane—*" She went up on her toes, panting out, "Fuck me, you bastard."

He lifted her onto the dresser, crushing his mouth to hers as he drove into her, and their bodies took over.

KANE WAS FEELING pretty fucking fantastic as they climbed into Sable's truck to go to the festival. Sable, however, was another story. She'd gone from a state of blissed-out sass to spending twenty minutes engrossed in taking care of her plants and flowers, to being as edgy as the last person hired in a failing company.

She was pure country-girl beauty, in her cowgirl hat, long-sleeve black shirt, sexy leather fringed jacket, curve-hugging jeans, and her ever-present boots. "I need to make a quick stop to pick something up and drop off this gift for Deloris." She set a gift bag on the seat between them and started the truck.

"No problem. Why didn't you mention your plant and flower fetish when I showed you my rooftop sanctuary?"

"I don't have a fetish. I told you I liked nature." She drove out of the lot.

"That's a lot of nature."

"Morgyn filled my place with plants over the last few years. She said it's good for my soul to nurture something."

"And the flowers?"

"They were Deloris's. She knew she'd forget to water them, and even though I thought she should have them in her room and let the staff help care for them, she said she would rather they were with me. I'm just trying to keep them all alive."

She didn't seem that cavalier when she was studying each one, whispering as she picked off dead leaves and watered them. "If you don't like caring for them, why not give them to someone who does?"

"Because they're important to Morgyn and Deloris, so..." She shrugged.

"They're important to you."

"I guess."

"Is that why you talk to them?"

"I don't talk to them," she snapped.

"So you were whispering to yourself when you were watering them?"

"You're such a pain. I talk to them sometimes, okay?" She said it sharply, but she was smiling. "It helps them grow."

"I think it's great. Do you name them?"

She gave him a deadpan look, but laughter burst from her lips. "I wouldn't tell you if I did."

"Hey, no judgment here. But who's taking care of your brood while you're on tour?"

"My *brood?*" she asked as they drove into a neighboring town. "Morgyn, while she's in town, and then my mom will take over."

"Family is the best. I happen to agree with Morgyn, by the way. It's good for us to nurture things."

"Says the guy who probably has an entire staff to water his plants."

"Yes, I do, but I nurture my businesses."

She shook her head.

"I noticed the tapestry behind your bed. Did your sister make it?"

"Yes."

"Is it supposed to be you?"

She shrugged, but the pink staining her cheeks told him it was. She pulled over in front of a diner, and he spotted a florist at the end of the block.

"I need to run in and pick up a pie for Deloris. Do you want anything?"

"You? Pie?" He arched a brow. "Need I say more?"

"Now, there's a thought." A sexy smile lit up her face. "But keep it in your pants, BDK. This pie is for Deloris. Lloyd used to bring her cherry pie and candy on Valentine's Day." She reached into the gift bag, showing him a box of chocolates.

"And you've been keeping up the tradition for her?"

She nodded, putting the candy back in the bag.

*You sweet thing, taking care of everyone else.* He wanted to lean across the seat and kiss her more than he wanted his next breath, but he refrained and took out his wallet instead, handing her a fifty. "Get her two." She opened her mouth, and he was sure she'd complain, so he climbed out of the truck before she could. "I'm going to the drugstore. I'll meet you back here."

Sable was already in the truck when he climbed inside carrying two bouquets—an assortment of flowers in a glass vase and a mix of roses in a colored ceramic vase. She arched a brow. "Drugstore, huh?"

"Pie is nice, but I thought Deloris could use some flowers on Valentine's Day."

Sable looked at him with disbelief. "You just had me get her an extra pie."

"She lost her husband. We can't bring her enough on a day like today. They didn't have many roses left, but I bought all they had." He handed her the ceramic vase with a mix of orange, pink, yellow, white, red, and lavender roses. "Happy Valentine's Day."

Her lips parted, but her brows knitted, her gaze moving between the roses and him. She blinked several times, emotions swimming in her eyes. "Kane...?"

"What? Can't a guy give you flowers?"

"No one ever has."

Now it was his turn to be momentarily stunned. He wished he'd bought out the entire flower shop. Were all of the men in Oak Falls blind, deaf, and dumb? He couldn't be near her without wanting to be closer. "Well, I'm honored to be your first."

"Thank you, but what is this? Why are you really staying today?"

He could make a joke and probably get away with it, but he couldn't look in her eyes and not give her the truth. "I don't fucking know."

SHE SHOULD LET it go, laugh it off, and change the subject. But she wanted to know what was in his head, because her own thoughts and emotions were all over the place. "What does that mean?"

"It means I had a great time last night and I like being around you. But I'm not trying to make something of us. I'm just not ready to leave, and it's Valentine's Day, so I bought you roses because I'm not a complete dick, and they're mismatched, like us. It seemed like they were meant for you."

She was at a loss for words.

"Don't overthink it. It's not like I have hearts in my eyes and I'm asking you to be my Valentine. It's rare for me to want to spend time like this with anyone outside my family, so I decided to go with it. I know you're concerned about people finding out we slept together, and I hope you know I'd never jeopardize your reputation. I'm not going to touch you or do anything stupid at the festival. But if this freaks you out and you want me to take off, just drop me back at your place."

*If* it freaked her out? Her heart was racing and playing tricks on her, filling with feelings she wasn't used to. She looked down at the roses, at the pies on the seat between them, and at the flowers at his feet. When she finally met his gaze, vulnerability—his and hers—lingered in the space between them. He'd told her the truth. Didn't he deserve the same? "I'm kind of glad you're staying, but it also sort of freaks me out."

"Do you want me to leave?"

She shook her head. "Not really." She swallowed hard, unable to believe she'd said it, and sprinted back to her comfort zone as she started the truck. "Just try not to be so billionairish at the festival."

He laughed. "What does that mean? I'm wearing jeans."

"You stand out like a sore thumb with your thousand-dollar dress shirt and shiny black dress shoes."

"Stop at that farm supply store we passed. I'll run in and get a flannel shirt and boots."

She pulled away from the curb. "You don't have to."

"Jesus, woman. Stop at the damn store. I don't want all the women gawking at me like fresh meat. I'd rather fit in."

"You couldn't fit in if you took lessons." *You're too beautiful and powerful. Like a Martin guitar among a world of Yamahas.*

"Do I hear a challenge? Watch me nail it."

AFTER A QUICK trip to the farm store, Kane sported a gray T-shirt beneath a green plaid flannel, and brown leather work boots. He looked even more delicious than he did in dress clothes, and he turned every head in the assisted living facility. When he asked to be introduced to the staff, Sable was pretty sure the women were silently swooning as he explained about the tour and handed out his business cards with a promise to make sure all urgent messages were relayed to Sable in a timely fashion. Sable had never wanted to be taken care of, but with Kane watching out for Deloris's well-being, and in turn, for her own, her heart was tripping up big-time.

Sable was a little nervous as they made their way to the recreation room to see Deloris. She didn't want to overwhelm her.

Kane must have sensed her unease, because he shifted the flowers he'd bought for Deloris to one hand and put the other on her back. "Are you okay?"

"Yeah. Fine." She clung a little tighter to the pies and the gift bag. They stopped in the doorway, and Sable pointed out Deloris, sitting on a couch staring absently at the television. "I don't know if she'll get upset when she sees us. I never know until I'm with her."

"I did some research after you told me what she was going through. I know what to expect."

She was hit with another onslaught of emotions. "You did?"

"You're going on tour with us. I needed to know what you were dealing with."

The matter-of-fact way he said it brought her back to reality. It was a good reminder that he was a businessman first, and she shouldn't allow herself to get carried away with the things he did or said. "Of course."

As they made their way across the room, Sable hoped for the best. Deloris looked up, her eyes brightening. "Aren't those beautiful flowers?"

"They're for you," Sable said.

"For me?" As Kane set them on the coffee table in front of her, she said, "Are they from Lloyd?"

Before Sable could respond, Kane said, "Yes. He said to tell you he loves you more than flowers love the sun."

Deloris beamed. "My Lloyd knows just how to make me smile *and* how to ruffle my feathers."

Sable could say the same thing about Kane.

"Where is Lloyd?" Deloris asked. "At work? He loves his cars…"

As they chatted about Lloyd, Kane lowered himself to the couch beside Deloris, giving this woman he barely knew his undivided attention. Even the melodies in Sable's most emotional songs had nothing on the highs and lows Kane put her through without even trying.

# Chapter Twenty

THE FESTIVAL GROUNDS were hopping when they arrived. Throngs of people filed in, taking pictures of one another standing beneath red-and-white balloon arches and by enormous wooden letters that spelled LOVE. Couples strolled hand in hand, parents chased after giggling children, sticky with cotton candy and anxious for more, and groups of friends chatted animatedly as they meandered through dozens of colorful tents decorated in crimson and pink displaying arts and crafts, clothing, jewelry, and other wares. Attention-grabbing bells and whistles of carnival games and festival rides competed with the alluring scents of barbecue, fresh-baked goods, and popcorn.

"Oak Falls sure knows how to throw a festival," Kane said, steeling himself against the urge to put his hand on Sable's back, just as he'd had to refrain from putting his arm around her when they'd left Deloris. She'd put up a strong front when they were there, but he'd felt the emotional toll seeing her friend staring absently at the television had taken on her. They had time before meeting up with her bandmates, and he was hoping she'd be able to relax and enjoy the festival until then.

"We sure do," Sable said. Her gaze had been darting around

them since they arrived.

"Breathe, Sable. You look like you have something to hide."

"That's *your* fault," she said in a hushed voice. "I'm not used to caring what people think."

"Then don't."

"I have to. People on social media are jerks, and you never know where the jerky ones are hiding."

The security he'd hired was still in place, and they hadn't picked up on any trouble. "What I meant was stop trying to *act like* you have nothing to hide, and just be yourself."

"I *am*."

He arched a brow.

"*Ugh.* You're right. It's not like anyone can tell we've been together. Just keep your hands to yourself."

He cocked a grin. "What about my mouth?"

She shoved him.

He laughed. "Good to see you're back to normal." As they followed the crowd around a line of tents, he spotted her mother's booth for her service dog training business, Canine Companions. "Come on. I want to talk to your mother about a service dog for Aria."

"How do you know...? The background check. *Right.*" She drew in a breath. "I guess you're meeting my parents."

He assumed by the way the couple behind the table's eyes lit up when they saw Sable that they were her parents, and he recognized her sister Amber from when he'd met her at the fundraiser with Dash. She had a service dog by her side, and she was talking with a young couple.

"Hi, honey," her mother, an attractive brunette with a warm smile, said as her parents came out from behind the table. "I was hoping to see you before you went onstage." She hugged Sable, eyeing Kane curiously.

"Mom, Dad, this is Kane Bad. He manages the main band we're opening for, Bad Intentions."

"Kane, it's so nice to finally meet you. I'm Marilynn, and this is my husband, Cade."

"It's a pleasure to meet you both. You have a very talented daughter."

"She's pretty remarkable," Cade said. He was fair haired with sharp blue eyes.

"Kane's here to go over a few things with the band about the tour," Sable explained as her sister joined them, her dutiful service dog by her side. "Amber, you remember Kane."

"I do. It's nice to see you again." The sweet brunette had a kind smile and gave off a girl-next-door vibe.

"It's nice to see you, as well. How is Dash?"

Amber's smile widened. "He's great. He's running a booth for kids on the other side of the festival, fundraising for the kids' football program."

"Wonderful. I'll have to find him and say hello. I was hoping to get some information about service dogs. My sister suffers from anxiety, and I'm wondering if it might help her to have one."

"Well, you came to the right place," Cade said.

"Amber has had Reno for several years," her mother added. "Amber, honey, why don't you tell Kane about how Reno became your service dog and how he's helped you."

Amber told him about how she hadn't wanted a service dog at first because she was afraid it would be just one more thing that made her different from the other kids and how that changed as she got older and wanted companionship. She reached down and petted Reno. "Reno senses when there's a seizure coming on and alerts me with behavioral changes, like barking, whining, circling, or pawing at me. When he does it early enough, it allows me to move to a safe place and sit down so I don't hurt myself by falling. Knowing he's watching out for me gives me an enormous sense of peace."

Marilynn and Sable filled in the gaps, telling him what Reno did when Amber had a seizure. Sable was as passionate about the benefits of her sister's service dog as Amber and her mother were. Marilynn explained how she trained the dogs and gave him a business card. "You'll find personal stories, information on available dogs, and articles about the benefits of service dogs and care and ongoing training on my website."

"Thank you," he said as Sable stepped away to chat with a couple. "I'll pass all this along to Aria. I hadn't thought about a dog bringing unwanted attention. Amber, would you be willing to speak with Aria if she has questions?"

"Of course," Amber said.

"Bring her for a visit," Cade suggested. "She can spend time with the dogs to see how she feels around them."

He welcomed the idea of having another reason to visit. "That sounds like a fine idea. I'll speak with Aria about it."

"Wonderful," Marilynn said. "Our dogs go through extensive training, and we want to make sure they're a good match on all levels, including commitment. You should know that applicants have to go through a pretty lengthy process before being approved for one of our dogs."

"I understand. I'm sure all that training costs a pretty penny. How are you funded?"

"Donations, mainly," Marilynn said.

"You can donate by buying some of these heart-shaped dog treats." Amber held up a bag of treats.

"I'd be happy to." He took out a fifty-dollar bill and handed it to her. "Keep the treats for Reno."

"Really? Thank you." She put the fifty in the donation basket. "Excuse me." She went to answer someone else's questions.

"Kane," Cade said. "I want to thank you for getting Sable out of her comfort zone."

"I think her band is responsible for that more than I am."

"Well, as happy as I am that she's spreading her wings," Marilynn said, "she hasn't spent any extended time outside Oak Falls. She's tough, but she's a small-town girl at heart. I'm a little nervous about the tour."

*The apple did not fall far from the tree.* She reminded him of the way Sable had tried to protect her family with her stipulations before accepting the contract. "She's a small-town girl with big-city talent, and she's going to soar. But don't worry, she'll have ample security at all times, and I'll personally keep an eye on her and make sure she's safe."

"Her safety is important, but I'm more worried about her emotions," Marilynn said. "I remember how trying Axsel's first tour was. I know Sable will have Tuck and the guys with her, but that's different than family."

He glanced at Sable, chatting with Amber and an attractive couple who were holding hands. His challenging vixen stole a glimpse at him. He winked, and her eyes narrowed. *Put your claws away, Panthera. I'm not outing you.* He met her parents' gazes. "I'll make sure she's well taken care of, emotionally and physically."

"Thank you. That makes me feel better," Marilynn said.

"I hope you enjoy the rest of the festival," Cade said. "One word of advice. If Sable challenges you to the Cupid's Bow and Arrow game, you might want to pass on it."

"Why is that?"

"She's been the reigning family champ since she was a kid."

He was an expert marksman. He'd been on the archery team in high school and had kept it up for sport. "I'll keep that in mind. Thank you." He headed over to Sable and started to put his hand on her back, catching himself before it connected.

"*Kane*," Sable said a little sternly. "This is my sister Grace and her husband, Reed."

"It's nice to meet you." He shook Reed's hand and nodded to Grace. "My cousin Brett told me about what you've done with the Majestic Theater. I haven't seen it in person, but I've seen the pictures online. It looks spectacular, and Grace, Brett, and Sophie have raved to me about your plays. I hope to catch one myself one of these days."

Sable's brows knitted. "You want to see a play? *Here?*"

"Yes, I would." Another trip to town to see Sable was sounding better by the second. "We've talked about my affinity for the arts. My sister Harlow is an actress, after all. She started in local plays."

"I met Harlow," Grace said. "It was only briefly, when I visited the set during filming. She probably doesn't even remember, but I wrote the screenplay for the film adaptation for Charlotte Sterling-Braden's novel *Anything for Love*, which Harlow starred in."

"That was a great story," Kane said. "Harlow was very proud to be cast as the lead."

"She did a great job, and Char is an incredible writer," Grace agreed. "I have a new play coming out at the end of August. Maybe you can catch that one."

"I'll try to fit it in." He glanced at Sable. Her mouth was pinched, but he couldn't tell if she was irritated or suppressing a grin.

"I'd be happy to show you the Majestic later this afternoon if you're going to be around," Reed offered.

"I would love that. Thank you."

Sable's eyes narrowed, but she looked more like she was trying to figure him out than wanting to slap him. "We should get go—"

"Say Say! Gwace." The cutest dark-haired little girl carrying a stuffed teddy bear that was almost as big as she was toddled toward them. Brindle was behind her, holding hands with a dark-haired man who must be her husband.

Sable knelt to tap the little girl on the nose. "Wow, that's a huge teddy bear, Emma Lou."

"You're a lucky girl," Grace said.

"It only cost her daddy seventy-five bucks in the baseball toss," Brindle said. She turned a mischievous grin on Kane. "I didn't know you were going to be here." She gave Sable a curious look.

"I needed to review a few things for the tour with Sable and the guys," he explained, and went for a subject change. "I take it this little princess is yours?"

"Yes. This is Emma Lou, and this is my husband, Trace."

"How's it going?" Kane said.

Trace ruffled Emma Lou's hair. "It's a pretty great day, right, Emma Lou?"

She beamed at her daddy.

Kane knelt in front of Emma Lou. "Hi. I'm Kane. I like your bear."

She hugged her bear and twisted side to side. "*Dat?*" She touched the tattoos on the back of his hand.

"They're tattoos. Like drawings." He held his hand out. "Would you like to touch them?"

SABLE HAD NEVER felt anything even remotely swoony when she'd seen men with little kids the way her sisters sometimes did. But watching Kane talk to Emma Lou about his tattoos with a tenderness that he must reserve only for children gave her a fluttery feeling in her chest.

"Looks like Emma Lou has a new friend." Brindle smirked. "Sable, since you and Kane have *business* to take care of, Trace and I can stay in tonight so you don't have to babysit. I'll still take pictures for Surge's social pages while you perform."

"There's no need to stay home," Sable said. "I'll be there."

Emma Lou bounced on her toes. "Cookies?"

As Kane rose to his feet, Sable said, "That's right, peanut." She hiked a thumb over her shoulder. "We'd better get going." *Before Brindle makes things more uncomfortable.* "See you guys later."

As they walked away, Brindle said, "Let me know if you change your mind!"

Sable was going to kill her. "I won't!"

"Looks like we're babysitting tonight," Kane said.

*We?* "I am. You're leaving." A little voice inside her hoped he'd stay, and another hoped he'd leave. "What do you know about babysitting, anyway?"

"*Little sisters*, remember? I have mad skills with females of all ages."

She rolled her eyes. "We're just making cookies. You'll be bored."

"Impossible. I'll be with you."

*God, the things you say.*

He lowered his voice. "You know you'd like to spend another night with me worshipping every inch of you."

"I would, but…" *Why is this so hard?* She liked being with him too much. Another night would make it even more difficult to walk away.

He leaned closer. "Nobody will know."

"Did you hear the innuendo in Brindle's voice?" It was a halfhearted attempt at convincing herself to make him leave.

"She's guessing, but she's not going to gossip about it. She loves you too much to hurt you like that."

She met his gaze. "How would you know?"

"Because of how she was at the bar that first night. Tell me you don't want me to stay, and I'll drop it."

She couldn't lie to him.

He stepped closer, holding her gaze, his voice low and caring. "Why is it so hard to admit you want one more night with me?"

"I don't know. Because you're *you*, and I might want it, but I don't know if I'll survive it."

He laughed. "Now, that's a five-star recommendation if I've ever heard one. I'll go easy on you."

"Shut up. I meant survive it in a different way, because you mess with my head. Never mind."

He checked his watch. "Since you're not telling me to leave, let me make this easy for you. We have thirty minutes until we have to meet your bandmates. I'll play you in one of those games over there." He pointed to the row of carnival games. "If I win, I stay. If you win, you decide what happens."

"You're on. Cupid's Bow and Arrow. Let's go."

A few minutes later, they stood across from their respective heart-shaped bull's-eyes, bows in hand, three arrows lined up in front of them. Sable picked up an arrow. "You're going down, Bad."

"I look forward to it, Montgomery."

A thrill skated through her as she lined up her shot and let it fly. It hit the outside edge of the bull's-eye. "Beat that."

"If I must." He lined up his shot.

She held her breath as his arrow flew to the center of the bull's-eye. What the...? She turned on him. "Have you done this before?"

He shook his head. "I can't recall ever encountering a cupid game in Manhattan. But I've always been pretty lucky."

"Skill wins over luck every time." She lifted her chin, snagged another arrow, and nailed the center of the bull's-eye.

"Now, *that* was impressive. You've obviously done this before."

"A few times. Let's see what you've got, BDK."

He chuckled. "Talk about pressure." He drew in a deep breath and blew it out slowly before lining up his shot. He let it fly, and it landed on the outer edge of his bull's-eye, just like her first arrow. "Holy shit. Look at that! What are the chances?"

"Are you playing me, Kane?"

"I swear I've never played this game before. I'm as shocked as you are. I might actually win. *You* might be going down, Montgomery, and I'll enjoy every second of it."

Memories of last night trickled in, warming her from the inside out. She drew her shoulders back, forcing herself to focus on the game instead of how much she wanted him to stay. "Don't go fluffing your feathers just yet." She grabbed an arrow and took the shot. The arrow burned through the air, nailing the bull's-eye right beside her last arrow.

"Damn, woman. Where'd you learn to do that?"

"Lloyd was a hunter. He said it would be good for me to know how to use a bow and arrow in case there was ever an apocalypse."

"He sounds like quite a character. Do you hunt?"

"No. I could never kill an animal."

He arched a brow. "Only a man's hopes?"

"Are you going to take your shot or procrastinate?"

"It's not my fault. I've got a lot riding on this, and you keep distracting me."

She held her hands up. "I won't say another word."

"It's not the words that distract me." He shot her a sexy look as he lined up the bow and arrow. "It's where they come out of." He released the arrow, and it hit the outermost ring. "*Damn.*"

"Yes!" She flashed a victorious grin. "Aw, what's wrong, Big Daddy? Can't perform under pressure?"

He scowled as she picked her prize and waved the little red stuffed devil in Kane's face.

"That's fitting," he teased. "So, what'll it be? Are we co-babysitting, or am I leaving after I watch your band take the stage?"

She'd gotten so into the competition—and *him*—she'd forgotten the stakes.

"Sable!" Tuck was running toward them, his gaze moving curiously between her and Kane.

Kane's jaw tightened.

Sable had texted Tuck and the other guys to let them know Kane was in town to go over a few things and would be watching them perform, but the way Tuck was scrutinizing them made her nerves flare.

"Kane," Tuck said with a nod.

"Good to see you again, Tuck."

"Sable, we've got a problem. Lee's sick as shit. Food poisoning. He brought home extra sushi and left it on his counter. The fool ate it this morning."

"And he *just now* told you?" Panic flared in her chest. "We're on in half an hour."

"He thought he'd feel better," Tuck explained.

"We can't play without a drummer." She pulled out her phone. "Have you seen Shane? Is he around this weekend?"

"Shane?" Kane asked.

"Jericho. He plays the drums," Tuck responded. "But he's not here. He left town this morning with his old man to look at cattle or some shit."

"I can play," Kane said.

She looked at him like he'd lost his mind. "You play the drums?"

"Yes, and I've got a great ear. If you've got the equipment, I can keep up."

"Lee's equipment is already here," Tuck said. "Kane's better than nothing. We just won't play your new song."

"If you're talking about 'In Too Deep,' I can play it."

"Kane—"

"I can play it," he said sternly. "Do you want to argue, or do you want to put on a show?"

*Is both an option?* "Fine."

"I'm going to hit the head," Kane said. "I'll meet you by the stage."

As he strode off, Tuck and Sable headed for the stage. "What's up with you two?" Tuck asked.

"Nothing. Why?" She hated lying to him again, but she wasn't in the mood to be given any crap, and if she told him the truth, he'd have every right to give her hell.

"You're out here playing games with him instead of hanging with us. Are you sure there isn't something going on between you two?"

"A city boy like him? Don't be ridiculous. He came all this way to help us. I just figured I shouldn't ignore him."

Twenty minutes later they were onstage. The excitement of the gathering crowd had Sable's adrenaline pumping. For the first time in years, she was nervous about playing. She'd shed her jacket, and Kane had rid himself of his flannel shirt. He looked more than comfortable behind the drums—and too damn sexy twirling the sticks like they were an extension of his fingers. The man had more secrets than Homeland Security.

She stepped away from the mic, and with her back to the crowd, spoke to Kane. "You really think you can keep up?"

"I wouldn't have offered if I didn't."

"Then let's do this." She headed back to the microphone. "Happy Valentine's Day, Oak Falls! We're Surge, and we're here to set your hearts on fire." Cheers and applause rang out. "Unfortunately, Lee is under the weather. In his place, please welcome all the way from New York City, our friend BDK!" She motioned to Kane, sending him a smirk as more excitement filled the air.

Kane waved to the crowd, shooting her a devastating smile, but those piercing eyes told her she'd pay for that comment later.

*Bring. It. On.*

She began playing "Bloody Valentine," and the crowd went wild. Kane blew her away, keeping up like a pro, as they played "Love Is a Battlefield," "Love Story," and "Heartbreaker." He didn't miss a beat as they rolled into songs for anti–Valentine's

Day fans, like "Before He Cheats," "Hide the Wine," and "I Knew You Were Trouble." She saw Brindle taking pictures of them playing and felt Kane's eyes on her when she sang a duet of "Don't You Wanna Stay" with Tuck.

She stepped up to the mic before the last song and waited for the crowd to quiet. "For our last song, we've got a new one for you called 'In Too Deep.' We hope you like it as much as we do." She glanced at Kane, remembering the night they'd worked on the song. He winked, nodding reassuringly. As she started playing, the discomfort she'd felt at practice was nowhere in sight. She grabbed hold of that brass ring and sang her heart out.

When they played the last note, the audience erupted with appreciation.

"We love you, Oak Falls," she said into the mic. "Happy Valentine's Day!"

As they prepared to leave the stage, the guys gathered around Kane. "Man," Tuck said. "You didn't tell us you could play like Travis Barker."

"I wouldn't go that far," Kane said. "You guys are a lot to keep up with, but that was a blast. Thanks for letting me join in."

"Dude, you were great," JP said.

"You can play with us anytime," Chris added. "Sable mentioned you had a few things to go over with us."

"I do. I need to make sure you're prepared for what it's like when we're on the road. We'll go over pre- and post-stage timelines and discuss what you can expect at meet and greets, the press, fans, security. I don't want there to be any surprises," Kane said.

It sounded like he really did have things to discuss with

them. Sable wondered when he'd have gotten around to it if he hadn't stayed for the day.

"Mind if I grab a drink first?" JP asked. "I've got to get my head out of the show."

Kane shook his head. "Not at all. I need a few minutes to cool off anyway."

She followed them off the stage, trying to make sense of the man who seemed capable of doing anything. When the others headed for a refreshment stand, Kane waited for her to put her guitar away. "Did you just make up all that stuff to go over?"

"No. It was on my agenda to discuss with you next week. Concerts are utter chaos, but don't worry. I'll make sure you're all prepared."

"Thank you. I guess we kind of did need a manager."

"You can still hire one."

"I didn't say I wanted one."

He shook his head. "You're pretty quiet about the show we just did. I hope I didn't slow you down too much."

"You weren't bad." She tried to keep a straight face as she closed her guitar case and put the stuffed devil on top of it. "I can't wait to see if you're as good at babysitting as you are at playing the drums."

# Chapter Twenty-One

THE REST OF the day passed without a dull moment. After Kane spoke with Sable and the guys about the tour, they grabbed a late lunch. Then Kane insisted on catching up with Dash. On their way, they stopped by Morgyn's booth, where he bought gifts for his sisters and mother and spent an hour talking with Graham about one of his upcoming eco-friendly development projects. After finally chatting with Dash—and cheering on kids who were throwing footballs for prizes—they went with Reed and Grace to the Majestic, where Reed gave Kane a tour, while Grace grilled Sable about her relationship with him.

Now it was early evening, and she and Kane were making cookies with Emma Lou, but something Grace had said kept rolling through Sable's mind. *I hear what you're saying, but I think if a guy drives all the way from New York to go over something he could easily discuss over the phone, there's more to it. At least on his end.* Kane had told her as much when he'd shown up, but Grace was all about love, and she and Kane *weren't.*

As she got the rolling pin and baking pans from the cabinets, she glanced at Kane and Emma Lou. Emma Lou was standing on a chair by the counter in front of him, her little hands cocooned by his as they cracked eggs into a bowl. Emma

Lou's clothes were covered in flour, and like Sable, Kane was sporting tiny flour hand prints on his jeans and T-shirt.

"Good job, princess." He lifted his gaze, catching Sable staring, and his lips tipped up. "Let's wash our hands, and then you and Auntie Say can finish mixing the ingredients." He wrapped his arm around her and set her on the counter beside the sink.

He wasn't kidding about having mad babysitting skills. He looked as comfortable washing Emma Lou's hands as he had behind the drums and discussing the tour with her band.

"You *are* good with kids."

"Thanks. I've been around them my whole life. My parents had trouble getting pregnant. I was four when Johnny was born, and twelve when we adopted Harlow. She was only a year old, and the happiest little girl. She could get me to do anything with a single smile. Four years later, they adopted Aria."

"How old was she?"

"Four, and she'd been through hell with foster families. She had nightmares for months. Sometimes I'd get into her room before my parents did, and I'd hold her, telling her she was safe and that I wouldn't let anyone hurt her. She was so little and so scared." He dried Emma Lou's hands, emotions brimming in his eyes.

"I can hear how much you love them."

"They wrapped their tiny fingers around my heart, and to this day, if they call, I go." He set Emma Lou back on the chair, waiting until Sable was behind her before stepping aside.

She was touched by how deeply he loved his family. "Did you bake with your sisters?"

"Yes, but Harlow is a chocolate fiend. If I didn't watch her close enough, she'd eat half a bag of chocolate chips and get a wicked stomachache." He watched them stirring the ingredients. "How about you? Did you bake with your mom and sisters?"

"No. I was more interested in tinkering with my dad in the barn and playing music. Deloris tried to teach me to knit once. That was a disaster. I have no patience for things like that."

"What did you want to do instead?" Kane asked as he cut a piece of wax paper off the roll.

"Anything. But I think that day I helped him clean out the barn and hang Christmas lights."

"I bet he appreciated that."

"Uh-oh, Emma. Some of the dough is trying to sneak out of the bowl," Sable said, earning giggles from her as they ran the fork around the sides of the bowl. She glanced at Kane. "Lloyd appreciated everything, until the year I hung their holiday lights by myself while he was out with Deloris. He was in his seventies, and I didn't want him on the ladder, but when he got home, he read me the riot act and told me never to do it again."

Kane's expression warmed. "He was worried about you getting hurt."

"He *knew* I could handle ladders and lights, but he was always trying to dote on me like he did with Deloris."

"I bet that went over well," he teased.

"Cookie ball?" Emma Lou asked.

"Yes. I think we're ready to make a cookie-dough ball." She kissed the top of Emma Lou's head, and together they scooped up the cookie dough and began forming it into a ball.

"So, did you let Lloyd dote on you at all?" Kane asked.

"Dote? No. But he did spoil me. When I put the band together, we needed a place to practice, and he let us use his old barn. We still practice there."

His brows knitted. "Do you have another place lined up for after the house sells?"

"Not yet. I've been a little busy getting my life in order for a tour." She bent so she could see Emma Lou's face. "What do you think, Em? Is it perfect?"

She nodded excitedly and exclaimed, "Look, *Kay*."

"That's the best cookie ball I've ever seen," Kane said. "I think you're ready to roll."

He swapped the bowl for wax paper, and Sable moved a bowl of flour closer so they could reach it as they rolled the dough. Emma Lou plunged her hand into the bowl and threw a fistful of flour onto the wax paper, sending particles flying all over them.

Sable gasped. Kane tried to stifle a laugh as Emma Lou giggled uncontrollably and did it again. "*Emma*." Sable grabbed her little hands. "The flour is for the wax paper, not for throwing, okay?"

Emma Lou nodded, but as soon as Sable let go of her hands, she reached for the bowl again. Sable caught her hand, and Kane turned around, his shoulders shaking with his silent laughter as Sable said, "You are just like your mama, Emma Lou." She pushed the bowl of flour out of reach. "Are you ready to roll the cookie dough, or do we need to stop?"

"Weady," she said.

Kane turned around, and Sable's entire being tingled at the joy lighting up his eyes.

She tried to ignore the feelings as they rolled out the dough and used heart-shaped cookie cutters to make the cookies. When they'd filled the baking pans, Sable said, "Would you mind sticking them in the oven while I give her a quick bath?"

"No problem."

"I hungy," Emma Lou said.

"We'll eat right after we wash up." Sable tried to get her head on straight as she took Emma Lou upstairs and got her cleaned up and into her pajamas.

When they came back down, the dishes were washed, the table and counters were sparkling, and Kane was plating grilled cheese sandwiches by the stove. "I hope she's not allergic to cheese. I found some broccoli in the freezer and cooked it, too. I hope that's okay."

"You didn't have to do all this. I could've helped."

"I heard her say she was hungry, and you were a little busy." He grabbed the heart-shaped cookie cutter and used it on a grilled cheese sandwich. As he set the plate in front of Emma, he said, "Do you like trees, princess?"

Emma Lou nodded, wide-eyed, as she climbed into her booster seat.

Sable melted inside and wondered how a heart-shaped sandwich, calling broccoli *trees*, and calling her niece *princess* could make her swoon.

"Say Say! *Hawt*," Emma Lou exclaimed.

"Don't worry, princess. I've got one for Auntie Say, too." He used the cookie cutter on another sandwich and handed Sable the plate with a wink.

Her stomach flip-flopped. *What are you doing to me, dastardly Bad?*

AFTER DINNER THEY played zoo with Emma Lou and her stuffed animals. Kane didn't hesitate to sit on the floor with them. When her yawns took over, he carried her to the couch and held her on his lap as Sable read her a story. Emma Lou was so tuckered out, she fell right to sleep.

Kane carried her upstairs and laid her in bed. He brushed her fine dark hair away from her face and whispered, "Sweet dreams, princess."

Sable tucked Emma Lou's blanket around her and kissed her forehead. "Good night, baby. I love you."

As they left the room, Kane put a hand on Sable's back and pulled the door partially closed behind them. "Now I see who you save all your sweetness for."

"I could say the same about you. You're pretty good at this babysitting stuff."

"*Pretty good. Not bad.* What's a guy got to do to earn higher praise?"

"Oh, a little of this and a lot of that," she teased. "Honestly, you kind of blew me away today. How long have you played the drums?"

"Since I was a kid. Music has always been a passion of mine, and when Johnny got discovered, I got more serious about it."

"Did you want to play in a band?" she said as they went downstairs.

"No. That was Johnny's dream. He was fifteen when he was discovered, and he was playing solo. I figured I'd get good enough that if he ever put a band together and needed a drummer, I could step in. But by the time he was ready to do that, I was in college, working as a DJ and loving it, and he had his own guys in mind."

As she came off the last step, she turned to face him. "I don't get it. You said music was your passion, but you just let BDK go for revenge on your ex and her new boyfriend."

He drew her into his arms. "Let's just say my love of music was tabled for the sweet taste of success."

"But you must still play to have kept up with my band and played my new song so well."

"I still play to let off steam." He brushed his lips over hers. "And as for your song, I told you, you got under my skin. I listened to that damn song so many times, I could play it in my sleep."

She loved knowing that, and she was aching to kiss him, but something was still nagging at her.

"You've got that look in your eyes again. What is it?"

"It's just…It sounds like you've created your path in life for everyone else. You learned to play better in case Johnny needed you, and you gave up doing what you loved to take revenge. Then you took over as Johnny's manager because *his* life imploded. I'm sure you love being a billionaire, but what do you do just for you? Not because you have to or because someone needs you, but for the sole purpose of bringing yourself pleasure?"

"That brain of yours is really something." He kissed her softly. "Don't waste your time trying to figure me out. It's an impossible task."

"You can say that again." She wound her arms around him. "You're the most complex man I've ever met."

"All you need to know is that I take great pleasure in everything I do. Especially *you*." His lips touched hers, soft as a feather, and he whispered, "Stop thinking, and just be with me."

As his lips claimed hers, there was no place else she'd rather be.

# Chapter Twenty-Two

THE AIR HUMMED with excitement at the launch of Jillian's Wanderlust line. True to Jillian's eccentric brand, she'd rented out a warehouse in Brooklyn and had transformed it into an elaborate showroom with lights strung over metal rafters, sparkling strings of crystal lining the walls, and an enormous screen behind the runway announcing WANDERLUST BY JILLIAN BRADEN against a backdrop of a beautiful meadow blowing in the breeze. The fashion show was in full swing, and the place was packed. Jillian's extended family, and Kane's, had turned out to support her, along with everyone who was anyone in the fashion industry, including Jillian's cousin and his wife, famed fashion designers Josh and Riley Braden, and all the major media outlets. Everyone was eager to view the cutting-edge designs that represented freedom from everything that held women back. Despite having been advised against it, Jillian had brilliantly forgone using professional models. In addition to her sisters-in-law and mother, women with varying abilities of all ages, shapes, sizes, and skin color were making their way down the runway. The audience and media were eating it up. Johnny beamed with pride beside Kane.

Kane admired Jillian even more for sticking with her passion and her principles, but his mind was elsewhere. He'd been thinking a lot about passion lately, thanks to Sable. They'd been texting daily, which often led to sexting, and he'd nearly gone out of his mind missing her. In the three weeks since Valentine's Day, he'd spent six days in Australia and had gone to see Sable twice. He would have taken her to Australia if it wouldn't have caused a shitstorm for her and the band. He pulled out his phone for the tenth time in as many minutes. He hadn't heard from her since last night, and it was driving him insane.

"Who are you waiting to hear from?" Aria asked from beside him.

He looked at his younger sister, her simple gold nostril ring gleaming under the lights. Like a certain brunette, Aria was most comfortable in jeans, but tonight her dirty-blond hair fell in gentle waves over the shoulders of her black turtleneck, which she'd paired with a black-and-white checked miniskirt, black tights, and black ankle boots. Like Kane, Aria had a body full of tattoos, none of which were currently visible. His gaze dropped to her hand, which was gripping her thigh like a lifeline, and his heart took a hit. It had taken a lot to get her to the event. She hated crowds, but she loved Jillian, and in the end her love for her future sister-in-law won out. Kane had sent a car to pick her up on the Cape and had met her at his hotel, where he'd arranged for each of his sisters and his parents to have their own suite.

"Work," he said as he put his phone in his suit coat pocket.

"I would hate to be you." Aria bumped him with her shoulder, smiling sweetly.

He wouldn't wish this feeling on anyone. Sable hadn't just gotten under his skin. She'd fucking burrowed into his soul. It was hell trying to keep his emotions from boiling over. They didn't talk on the phone or video chat, and that was purposeful on his end. He'd thought if he didn't hear her voice or see her face, it would help to keep his emotions in check, but all it did was make him want her more.

"Mom looks pretty tonight," Johnny said, bringing Kane's mind back to the moment as he motioned to their mother getting up from her seat on Aria's other side.

"She always looks pretty," Aria said.

Kane agreed, even when she'd lost her hair during her chemo treatments. Now she had a soft sheen of blondish-gray waves, not much longer than his hair. He watched his father getting up, probably to escort her to the ladies' room, but she wasn't having it. With a kiss on his cheek, she headed out alone in her pretty floral dress. His father watched her with the adoring smile Kane had seen his whole life.

Kane turned his attention back to the event as Harlow led a line of women down the runway, one of whom was in a wheelchair. He nudged Aria. "That could be you up there."

She shook her head, eyes wide.

Harlow was gorgeous in a flowing silver-and-black gown with side cutouts and mile-high heels, her blond hair twisted into a fancy updo. A few minutes later, Morgyn followed two other women down the runway, wearing a colorful layered minidress with a black scarf around her neck, a flower wreath in her long blond hair, and fringed suede boots. She flashed a special smile at Graham, and hell if Kane wasn't envious of what they had. He'd do anything to have Sable by his side, and he knew how messed up that was. He wasn't looking for a wife, and she didn't need the media catching wind of their tryst. He wasn't a man who dicked around. He usually took what he wanted and didn't give a damn what anyone else thought about it. But he'd protect Sable with everything he had.

As Jillian's other sisters-in-law made their way down the runway, each as beautiful as the last, Kane tried to talk himself out of checking his phone again. But the urge was too strong. He looked down as he reached for his phone, but Aria nudged him, motioning to the runway with tears in her eyes. Instinct had him taking her hand as he looked up, and his heart stuttered at the radiant, strong woman walking down the runway. His mother looked stunning and ethereal draped in layers of taupe tulle with a deep V neckline and a sheer, ruffled floor-length skirt. Her eyes sparkled, but it was her effervescent, confident smile—the smile that had carried him through his toughest days as a kid, and many rough times as an adult—that clogged his throat with the emotions that had been building since her first diagnosis.

She tossed a wink their way, her head held high as she walked to the end of the runway, pivoted like she'd been practicing her whole life for that moment, and made her way past them again. Aria squeezed his hand.

Johnny wiped his eyes, uttering, "Shit," as Kane blinked away tears and put his arm around Aria, pulling her against his side. He glanced at his father, the rock of their family. The man who never cracked through the worst of times, at least not in front of them. He, too, was wiping his eyes. Kane's chest constricted. Love was a powerful, terrifying thing, but his parents made it look like the pinnacle of their existence.

For the first time since college, that thought didn't scrape like nails on a chalkboard.

After their mother cleared the runway, the lights dimmed and the music faded. Whispers rose around them as the screen changed from WANDERLUST and a meadow to ROCKER GIRLZ and a Bad Intentions video. Colorful lights bloomed to life as Johnny's music blared through the room, and Zoey strutted onto the runway in a newspaper-print top with black sleeves and a black faux leather skort tied at the hip. Kane knew it was a skort because Zoey had told him about it in painful detail three days before the event. She looked adorable. Her dark hair was shiny and parted to the side, just as it was every other day. Her tough-girl attitude gleamed through her bright eyes and serious expression. Kane knew how nervous she was. She'd called him last night, afraid she'd look stupid smiling on the runway. He'd told her to just act like she was playing poker with him, and she was *nailing* it.

"She's got her daddy's confidence," he said to Johnny.

Johnny nodded, eyes glassy again.

"Softie," Kane teased, though his own heart was thudding with pride for Zoey, too.

Zoey's friends walked the runway with a handful of other young girls. As they left the runway, the screen changed to show both brands side by side, and the music tamed as all the models for both fashion lines strutted out and lined the runway, clapping as Jillian appeared at the far end.

Johnny beamed proudly, rising to his feet along with Kane and the rest of the audience, applauding as Jillian moved gracefully and confidently down the runway. She was gorgeous in a sparkling gold minidress with sheer sleeves and her signature sky-high heels, her baby bump leading the way. She took a bow at the end of the runway, her mahogany hair tumbling over her shoulders as she straightened and blew a kiss to Johnny before heading back the way she'd come.

"Congratulations, man. That was a hell of a show," Kane said as the applause went on and on.

"I can't believe that amazing woman is going to be my wife."

"You deserve her, and she's a lucky woman to have you as a future husband." He kept Aria close as they made their way away from the aisle with their father and Johnny. "You okay, Ar?"

She nodded. "I can't get over Mom. She looked so beautiful. She and Zoey are *so* brave."

"Hey, listen to me." Kane held her gaze. "You're *here*. That makes you brave, too."

She blushed. "Thanks."

"I mean it, Aria. It takes courage to face your fears. Have you thought any more about getting a service dog?" He'd called her the day he'd left Oak Falls, and they'd talked for an hour about the idea. But she'd had a list of reasons why she didn't want one. Most had made sense, but he couldn't shake the feeling that having a constant companion would help her.

"I'm thinking about it. Zeke thinks it's a good idea, but it's a big commitment."

Zeke was Justin Wicked's brother and one of Aria's closest friends. He was a member of the Dark Knights motorcycle club, and Kane could always count on him to keep Aria safe. He was glad she was talking to Zeke about the idea. "As I said, I'd be happy to take a ride down there with you to check it out."

"You leave for the tour in two weeks."

"I know, but if you want to go, I'll make it happen."

Their father put a hand on Johnny's shoulder. "You should be very proud, son. Jillian and Zoey are both incredibly talented. But you could have given me a heads-up about your mother walking the runway. My old heart could hardly take seeing her up there."

"I didn't know." Johnny looked at Kane and Aria. "Did you guys know?"

"No," they said in unison.

More applause rose around them, and they joined in as the models filed into the room. Kane spotted his mother, Harlow, and Zoey and her friends just as Jillian appeared behind them, and the applause grew louder. Jillian was swept into the crowd as his mother and the others made their way toward them. They stopped to chat with some of Jillian's family members, and Aria ran over to them. She hugged Zoey and Harlow, and then she plastered herself against their mother in a hug so tight, Kane felt that tightening in his throat again.

"You okay, son?" his father asked.

He cleared his throat. "Yeah. It was really good to see Mom up there. She was so…" He searched for the right words.

"Full of life?" his father asked.

Kane nodded. "I didn't realize how much I needed to see her doing something for herself."

"For herself? This is your mother we're talking about. I think she had a few other people in mind when she made that decision," his father said as she and the girls joined them, and a flurry of commotion ensued.

Kane gave his father and Johnny the first shot at congratulating the girls and his mother. He didn't have to wait long, as Harlow made her way over to him.

"Get over here, hot stuff." He pulled her into a hug. "You were great up there."

"Thanks. Mom outshone us all. Could you see the tears in my eyes when we lined up?"

"No. But you weren't alone in that."

"Hey, BDK!" Zoey said as she and her friends hurried over.

Harlow laughed. "You'll never live that down."

Kane shook his head. Pictures of him playing with Surge had appeared on social media the next day. Someone had tracked BDK back to Kane's DJ days, and social media had been abuzz with ridiculous speculation about him being jealous of Johnny and trying to get into the music business. Kane had been quick to have Shea shut that shit down. She'd made a statement on his behalf about how honored he'd been to step in and play with Surge and that it was a onetime thing. He'd just been glad no one had turned the tides to him and Sable.

"I'll give you BDK." He hauled Zoey into a tight hug, making her laugh as the others joined them. "I'm proud of you, kid. You nailed it up there." He smiled at her friends. "You all did."

"Thank you," Ginny and Cara said, beaming with pride in the outfits Jillian and Zoey had designed.

Zoey chimed in with "Of course we did. We rock."

"We're going to have to lock you girls up so boys don't knock down your parents' doors," his father said.

"Jilly and I are installing bars on the windows," Johnny said.

Aria nudged Zoey and said, "You can live with me or Harlow."

"Thanks, but I'm not going to need to live with anyone," Zoey declared. "I'm going to be a designer, not a model. Then I'll be rich enough to build my own house."

"Attagirl," Kane said. "Go for the gold."

"Soon you'll be managing her career," Harlow said.

"Unless I start a band. Then he can be my drummer," Zoey teased, earning laughs from everyone.

As they joked around, Kane sidled up to his mother, and she stepped away from the others. "Way to steal the show, Mom. You looked gorgeous up there." He embraced her, feeling a lot like Aria must have felt when she'd hugged her, because he didn't want to let go.

"Thank you, honey. I still can't believe I did it. I was so nervous, but once I got up there and saw you kids and your father, all that nervousness slipped away."

"I'm proud of you. What made you decide to do it?"

"Jilly asked me to. I said no at first. I wasn't feeling very pretty or like I wanted all those eyes on me."

"Mom, you've always been beautiful, and you always will be."

"I appreciate that, sweetheart, but it's a *me* thing. This old body has been through a lot, and I didn't want to disappoint Jilly on her big day. But then she said, 'How great would it be for your family to see you up there in the spotlight?' and I started thinking about it differently. I thought about how much joy you've all brought to my life, and I thought maybe she was right, and you'd all like seeing me up there."

"It was quite a gift."

"I'm glad, but don't get me wrong." She lowered her voice as if sharing a secret. "I did it for myself, too. I mean, really, Kane. When would I ever have this opportunity again? Not that I ever dreamed of being a model, but doesn't everyone want a few minutes in the spotlight?"

His mind went directly to Sable. "Not everyone."

She was looking at him the same way she had when he was a boy and her mom radar picked up on something only she could see. "Thinking of Sable?"

"What makes you say that?"

"You mentioned she wasn't chomping at the bit to do the tour, *and* you've brought her up quite a few times over the last two months."

He hadn't realized he'd done that, but even if he hadn't, he had a feeling she would have known Sable had become important to him. Just as she'd been the only one who had known about the breakup that had turned him from a rebellious DJ into a cutthroat businessman. "It's her band's first tour. There's a lot to coordinate."

"I'm sure there is, and I know how much Johnny and Jilly appreciate all you're doing so they can focus on Zoey before the tour. Actually, from what Jilly has told me about Sable, it sounds like she's a lot like you."

"Stubborn?"

"Oh yes, without a doubt. But I have to wonder if her spotlight has been on her family for so long, she's afraid if she shifts it to herself, her world will come crumbling down around her."

"How is that even remotely like me? I'm focused on Bad Enterprises and have been forever. I'm not afraid of my world falling apart."

She touched his arm, her voice soft and thoughtful. "Aren't you, though?"

"What do you mean? My businesses are solid."

"Yes, you're a brilliant businessman and a master at protecting everyone. But I worry that you've worked so hard for so long to protect that generous heart of yours, you've forgotten that not all failed *enterprises* are precursors for what's to come."

She smiled at Johnny heading their way, and as they fell into easy conversation, Kane went to get a drink, chewing on what his mother had said.

As the night wore on, Jillian made her rounds of the room and finally made her way over to them. She was glowing as everyone congratulated her, and they chatted about her designs and the event. Eventually Zoey and her friends went to get

sodas with Harlow and Aria, and their parents went to mingle
with some of Jillian's family members, leaving Kane with Jillian
and Johnny.

"What a night." Jillian rubbed her belly.

"This is what happens when you're a superstar designer. It
looks like everyone you know came out to celebrate your big
day," Kane said.

"Almost everyone. We're missing some of the Montgomery
sisters." She eyed him curiously.

When the Valentine's Day buzz had hit the internet, Jillian
had held nothing back, pushing him for information about
what he was *really* doing in Oak Falls. He'd divulged nothing,
despite wanting to tell someone how fucking insane he was over
Sable.

"You sure missed that boat with Sable. I thought you two
had crazy chemistry when her band was in the city. I can't
believe my hookup radar was off."

"Jilly," he warned.

"I could put in a good word for you," she offered.

"Stop matchmaking, babe. He already told you there's nothing there." Johnny kissed her temple.

"I think you two have mixed business and pleasure enough
for all of us. If you'll excuse me, I need another drink." *Or six.*

BY THE TIME Kane got home, it was after eleven, and he still
hadn't heard from Sable. When they'd texted last night, she
hadn't mentioned having a gig tonight. When she hadn't
responded to the text he'd sent this morning, he didn't worry.

He knew she wasn't attached to her phone. He'd waited hours to hear from her on other occasions. But he was beginning to wonder if something had happened to her. Although if ever there was a woman who could take care of herself, it was Sable, and surely if she'd been in an accident, someone would have reached out to him because of the tour. She was probably just busy.

Or maybe she was rethinking this thing between them.

He fucking hated that thought, but he wouldn't blame her. She had a lot more at risk if anyone found out about them than he did. He took off his jacket, tossed it over the back of the couch, and went to pour himself a drink. The solitude of his penthouse, which had once brought him so much satisfaction, grated on his nerves. He couldn't look around his place without remembering Sable being there. But it made no sense. She'd spent so little time there. How could it eclipse everything else?

How could it not?

She was on his mind every minute of the day. When he'd seen Jillian's brother Nick, an elite freestyle horse trainer and showman, and his wife, Trixie, who owned a miniature horse therapy business, at the event tonight, their frigging Western boots had sent his mind sprinting right back to Sable. It hadn't helped that Trixie brought up the tour and told him she'd grown up with Sable in Oak Falls. Trixie's maiden name was Jericho, and she was all too happy to share stories about how close Sable was with her brothers.

Fucking small towns.

He downed his drink, then poured another, carrying it over to the windows. He looked out at the lights of the city, trying to ignore the truth he'd been denying. But there was no escaping it. It ate away at him like a rabid animal trying to gnaw its way out.

He was in too deep, which was ironic.

He knew they didn't make sense.

Their lives were too far apart in distance and lifestyle, and she was embarking on a life-changing opportunity. She had been nothing but honest about not wanting complications, which meant he was heading for a world of hurt.

His phone vibrated. He told himself not to check it, but he was already pulling it out of his back pocket.

# Chapter Twenty-Three

SABLE SAT ON her balcony bundled up in a sweater and blanket, staring at her phone. She needed to put a little distance between her and Kane, and she'd told herself to go twenty-four hours without communicating with him. But it was like trying not to breathe, and she'd caved. Now her heart was racing as she waited for his reply, which was silly, considering she'd *just* sent the text. Her phone rang, startling her as Kane's name appeared on the screen. She held her breath, her nerves pinging like pinballs. They didn't *call* each other. Why would he call her?

Her mind spun. Why was she nervous about a phone call?

*I'm definitely losing it.* She put the phone to her ear. "Hey."

"Hi, beautiful."

His deep voice brought a shiver of heat. "This is *different*."

He was quiet for a beat. "I wanted to hear your voice."

*Ohgod.* It felt really good to hear that, but her nerves caught on fire. "That's different, too."

He was quiet for so long, she looked at the phone to see if the call had dropped.

"Kane?"

"Yeah, I'm here. I know it's different. I've been missing you, and figured I'd call."

Now she fell silent, soaking in his confession and weighing one of her own. They didn't say things like that, but that didn't mean she didn't feel it.

"I'm not asking you to say it back, Sable. I just wanted you to know."

She closed her eyes, feeling like an idiot. She wasn't afraid to take on anyone or tell people off, but when it came to opening up like this, she wanted to climb into a guitar case and zip it closed. But that wasn't fair to either of them. She opened her eyes and her heart. "I've been missing you, too. That's why I haven't texted all day."

"I'm not following your logic."

"Self-preservation. It turns out that you're more than an arrogant ass who gives great orgasms."

"Ah, *denial*."

She heard the smile in his voice.

"I've been practicing that tactic myself. How do you feel now that you've shown your hand?"

"Like I want to run away," she said softly. "You?"

"Like I want to chase you." He paused, and she held her breath. "But I have a feeling it would be like running through a minefield."

"It would probably be something like that. I don't know if I can keep this up. You're all I think about, and it's messing with my work and my music."

"Need me to back off?" he asked gruffly.

"No," she said quickly. "Not yet."

"Good, because I *won't*."

She smiled. "Then why did you ask?"

"Because I was trying to be a gentleman, but it turns out I'm not one."

She laughed softly.

"We agreed to stop when the tour starts. That gives me two weeks to get back there and pleasure you until you beg me to fuck you."

She squeezed her thighs together. She had no idea how she'd resist him when they were on tour, but she'd have to find a way. She couldn't take a chance of being distracted and screwing up their first tour.

A truck drove by and honked, drawing her from her thoughts.

"Are you outside?"

"Yeah. I'm on my balcony. Some city boy did dirty things with me all over my apartment, and I can't be in there without thinking of him."

"Who do I need to kill?"

"Look in the mirror, but I'm pretty sure he's unkillable."

He chuckled. "At least you have good taste. How was your day other than thinking about getting naked with me?"

That idea hadn't been far from her mind for weeks, but it wasn't just sex she'd been thinking about. It was how good it felt to be near him, talking, joking around, just lying in his arms, and how much she wanted more. How much she wanted *this*. Friendship, conversation, companionship that went beyond fantastic sex.

"Busy. Everyone and their brother had car trouble today, but I let Eli help replace pads and rotors, so he was happy, and band practice wasn't a nightmare, so that's a plus. How was Jilly's launch?"

"She had a great turnout, and everyone loved her designs."

"How did Zoey do when she walked the runway? Did she smile?" When he'd texted last night, he'd told her about his call from Zoey, and he'd been worried about her.

"She was incredible, and there were no goofy smiles." He paused, and when he spoke again, his voice was thick with emotion. "My mother surprised us all and walked the runway, too."

"Wow. Good for her. How was she?"

"Stunning and graceful and..." His voice trailed off, and he cleared his throat. "Anyway, she did great."

"What am I hearing in your voice? Was it hard for you to see her up there? Were you worried she might fold under the pressure?"

"No, it's not that."

She waited for him to say more. When he didn't, she knew it was too much, too intimate for whatever this was between them. That hurt, but she understood. "I wasn't trying to pry. Sorry."

"It's okay. I'm just trying to figure out what I felt. She always acts like everything is fine. She's the kind of person who finds light in darkness and hope at the hardest of times, so it's hard to know when she's having trouble and when she's not."

"She sounds resilient."

"She's one of the strongest women I know, and it's been such a roller coaster with treatments and a second bout of cancer and surgery. But when she was up there in front of all of those people, she was so vibrant and confident, I saw the woman I'd grown up with. It was like she'd kicked a rock and an avalanche of realizations came tumbling down at me. I realized how quickly life can change and how much I want to keep her around."

The pain in his voice made her ache.

"I know death is inevitable for everyone—"

"It's your *mom*, Kane. That isn't something you need to just accept without feeling like it'll rip your heart out. I'm like a kid when it comes to my parents." A nervous laugh escaped at the confession. "I still have breakfast with them every week. I can't even *think* about losing them without physically hurting inside."

"*Christ*. That's exactly what it's been like while she was sick. Like a piece of me was being tortured."

"That's what I feel like when I'm with Deloris and she's having a rough day. It's scary, knowing you can't control things like diseases…or protect your family from jerks." She'd never admitted that to anyone, but Kane had become anything *but* anyone.

"Especially for control freaks like us."

"I don't recall calling myself a control freak."

"Okay, Miss You Have to Be Out by Six A.M."

"That's for your own good." She was thankful for the levity. "If you were still here when the guys showed up for work, I'd have to kill you. Then there'd be the issue of getting rid of the body, and your car, and quite frankly, that's a lot of work for a few orgasms."

"A *few* orgasms? What kind of math did they teach you in that Podunk town?"

"Says the man who thinks eight inches is nine."

"Hey now," he said with a laugh. "That's been verified with a ruler."

She cracked up. "A ruler?"

"I was fifteen—give me a break. It's probably bigger now."

"Guys are so weird," she said.

"Are you trying to tell me that teenage girls don't worry about the size of their breasts? Because I was a teenager once, and I have it on good authority…"

Two hours later, Sable was lying on her bed and they were *still* on the phone, sharing secrets and making each other laugh. They talked about growing up in small towns, the pressures of high school, and what it was like watching their younger siblings navigate them. He told her he'd grown up on Cape Cod, near where his sister Aria lives. She told him about what her father considered the first time she'd sung onstage. They shared their favorite musical artists and how they've changed through the years and commiserated about bands breaking up and artists passing away. They talked about how lucky they were to have careers they loved, and he told her he'd just acquired an Australian hotel chain, his first international venture.

Sable rolled onto her back, staring up at the ceiling, feeling like she'd finally gotten to know the real Kane Bad. "Why did you wait so long to go international?"

"It takes a lot of time to manage the businesses I already own, and I like knowing that if my family needs me, I'm fairly close."

"So why did you decide to do it now?"

"I felt like I was missing something and figured it was time. This hotel deal came up right before my mother was diagnosed the first time. I put it on hold, and once she was given a clean bill of health, I lit the fire again. When she was diagnosed the second time, I was going to put it off, but my mother told me not to. She said it would hurt her knowing I was putting my life on hold because of her. I fought with her about it, but my father pulled me aside and said being a parent is different from anything I could imagine, and that my mother needed me to move forward. He said it would give her strength, so I did it."

She drew in a deep breath, thinking about how hard that must have been for him. "That's heavy."

"It was, but I think he was right. She'd ask about it when negotiations first started, and she'd get excited about certain aspects. Now she's anxious to see what I do with the project."

"The pictures you sent me when you were there last week were beautiful. Out of all of the places you've been, is there one place you go where you feel like you can let down your guard and breathe?"

"Anywhere my family is."

She closed her eyes, warming with his words. He couldn't know he was singing her heart song.

"I miss your face," he said huskily.

She reveled in how special that made her feel. "My face is not very attractive right now. It's been a long day."

"How about you let me be the judge of that?"

A video call rang through, and her pulse quickened. She answered it, and Kane's face appeared. His hair was tousled, and he was lying on the couch with one hand tucked behind his head. He looked so relaxed and happy, she wanted to climb through the phone and lie beside him. She hadn't realized how much she'd missed his face until seeing it brought a sense of excitement *and* contentment. "You're a pain, BDK."

"And you're beyond beautiful, Panthera."

She smiled and shook her head. "I hate video calls."

"I've never been a fan of them myself except with family. Until right now."

"Liar."

"I swear it's true. Do you video chat with Pepper or Axsel?"

"No. We usually text."

"You and Pepper probably don't even have to text, do you?"

"What do you mean?"

"Don't you have some kind of twin telepathy?"

"*No.* Well, I don't, but sometimes I think she does."

"Because she can read your mind, and texts you a million times a day to say stop thinking about Kane naked?"

"*No.*" She laughed. "She just knows when I'm feeling off." She'd texted Sable so many times over the last few weeks, it had to be a record. "But it's not like that for me."

"What's it like for you?"

She'd never told anyone the truth about what it was like for her, but she wanted to share it with him. "It's like we're two parts of one person that are at odds with each other most of the time."

"That doesn't sound comfortable. What do you mean?"

"It's not bad. It's just what it is. I feel more connected to Pepper than to my other sisters or Axsel. But at the same time, I feel disconnected because we're so different."

"Do you wish you were more alike?"

"Sometimes, but I wouldn't change either of us."

"I'm glad to hear that, because I wouldn't change you, either."

# Chapter Twenty-Four

THE LAST TWO weeks before the tour flew by. Sable had seen Deloris as often as she could. She'd spent loads of time with her family and made sure Carter, Buddy, and Eli knew how to handle any emergency. She'd written down instructions on every little thing from answering the phones to where to order supplies, more for Eli's benefit than the men's. Kane came to see her five times, and they talked on the phone every night. She'd thought they were building something real, something special. So much so, she finally understood why her sisters often rattled on about the men in their lives. She'd wanted to, desperately. But she was glad she hadn't. The last time Kane visited, he hadn't spent the night like he had the other times. She'd felt him flip that switch between businessman and lover before he'd even said he was going to miss their time together and had wished her luck on the tour as if they were friends who had enjoyed a coffee date. And he'd done it just as easily as he had in New York. She'd thought he might fight for her—for *them*—but he hadn't even hesitated. The worst part was knowing he was doing the right thing. She had too many people counting on her to risk being sidetracked by their relationship or risk the public finding out and ripping her to shreds. But that didn't mean it didn't hurt worse than she ever imagined it would.

She was envious of his ability to escape the feelings she was drowning in, which made their encounters even more uncomfortable now that the tour had started. They were in the second week of it, and minutes from playing their fifth concert. Sable swore the excitement from the crowds, and her desire for Kane, multiplied with every show. The thunder of excited fans crackled in the air backstage, feeding the adrenaline pumping through her veins as Kane filled shot glasses for what had become Surge's pre-show ritual.

His eyes locked with hers as he filled her glass. He always seemed to be watching, keeping her safe, batting away handsy fans at the after-parties and signings, and finding reasons to pull her away from the press when she reached her breaking point. She had no idea how he could tell, but the man had some kind of shitstorm radar or something. He must not realize that he was the source of her mental shitstorm.

"You good?" he asked.

She lifted her chin. "Always."

With a curt nod, Kane stepped aside.

Self-preservation was the name of the game. She wouldn't give him the satisfaction of knowing what she felt, and she sure as hell wouldn't let the media catch wind of her frustrations. The press and cell-phone-toting fans were everywhere. Like mosquitoes. You never knew they had you in their sights until they'd already drawn blood. She avoided social media like the plague, but her bandmates devoured the praise from fans and press and talked shit about the nasty comments.

She lifted her glass, focusing on the four men who had stuck with her through thick and thin and would fight to the death to defend her and not the one who had stolen a piece of her heart like a thief in the night.

"Let's rile 'em up!" She clinked glasses with the guys, downed the whiskey, and headed onto the stage.

The rush of spine-tingling trepidation and the thrill of feverish anticipation pounded through her as colored lights swept across the stage and she picked up her guitar. The crowd erupted into an exhilarating roar of cheers and shouts, applause and waving arms, as the chant that had begun at their third concert rose around them. "*Surge! Surge! Surge!*"

Sable stepped up to the microphone, looking out at thousands of fans cheering for them, and filled with awe. "How's it going, Miami?" More whoops and cheers rang out. "We're Surge, and we're here to get you wet for Bad Intentions!"

The crowd went wild as they started playing their first song, the bass hammered in Sable's chest, the melody vibrating through her limbs. All her fear and worry fell away, just as they had during each of the previous concerts. She felt electrified, overtaken by the highest high, carried by the excitement of the fans, the emotion of the music, and the power of performing, to a state of complete and utter euphoria.

It *almost* drowned out her silent screams for Kane.

# Chapter Twenty-Five

KANE ENDED HIS phone call, muscles cording tight as he turned back to the sea of people clamoring for the musicians' attention. He'd spent time with Johnny while he was touring in the past but never as his manager. He'd always been able to avoid the circus of the deluge of press and fans backstage. But meet and greets were important, even if overwhelming.

They'd just played their eighth concert in as many cities. The media was hailing Bad Intentions as the band of the century and Surge as the hottest up-and-comer of the decade. They'd only been on the road for three weeks, and the musicians were already riding a roller coaster of adrenaline rushes and sleep deprivation, and Johnny had twins on the way. Tension was running high and patience dangerously low. The schedule had been too grueling for Chris's family, and Katie had taken their kids back to Oak Falls after only a week. Their leaving was definitely putting a strain on Chris. Hell, Kane was wound so tight, he'd been one twist away from snapping ever since the first damn concert, when he realized how hard it was going to be keeping his distance from Sable. In the time since, his body had become a painful cauldron of want and need and a host of deeper emotions that were seriously threatening his sanity.

He scanned the crowd, quickly finding his beautiful mark. He never let her get far, but some phone calls couldn't be avoided. He cut through the mass of people, eyes trained on Sable in her long-sleeve black minidress, fringed leather vest, and cowgirl hat and boots. She was answering questions from the press with Tuck and Dion and signing autographs for eager fans. Kane didn't give two shits about the thousands of male fans vying for her attention at each venue, but fucking Dion was always with her, flirting and making her laugh, and the other morning Kane had seen her coming out of Tuck's hotel room. He'd felt like a volcano ready to blow and had forced himself to go for a run. He fucking hated running. Give him a pool and a weight room, and he was good. Those hadn't done shit to ease his tension lately any more than the run had.

Sable managed a strained smile for the fans, but even from a dozen feet away Kane could see her claws coming out at the press. They were always pecking at her like vultures, trying to get information about her personal life and future plans for albums. He wanted to step in and shut them down long enough for her to breathe, but he'd done that at the beginning of the tour, and it had made keeping his hands to himself even harder.

Johnny finished with an interview and sidled up to Kane. "I'm grateful to be on top of my game, but *fuck*. All I want to do is kick back with Jilly and Zoey."

"I bet." Kane had never been a kick-back-with-a-woman kind of guy, but he'd give anything to have a night with Sable to do just that. He watched her smile as a fan took a selfie with her. When she turned to sign another autograph, her eyes locked on Kane like homing devices, the air between them as volatile as a brewing storm.

"I had a long talk with Sable last night," Johnny said. "Given how much she hates this part of the gig, she's doing a hell of a job. It sounds like Victory started wooing her to sign with Blank Space this past week, but Sable's pretty much made up her mind that this isn't what she wants in the long run. I can't blame her. This is nothing like what she's used to. But she's so talented, it would be a shame if she didn't make the most of it for a while. Don't you think?"

"Yeah." Jealousy seared through him. Sable should be talking with *him* about those things, not his fucking brother, but the tension between them was so thick, he couldn't get more than a clipped response from her about anything.

"Maybe Tuck can talk some sense into her."

Kane gritted his teeth.

The tour manager waved Johnny over to a line of fans. "Duty calls. I heard there's a mob of fans waiting outside by the bus. Looks like it's going to be a while before we get on the road."

Kane stewed as Johnny walked away, frustration building inside him as another hour passed. When it was finally time to head out, Johnny and his bandmates led the way past the equipment crews loading the trucks, heading for the screaming fans lining the gate just past the bus. Kane fell into step beside Sable. Tension rolled off her in waves. "Why didn't you tell me Victory was trying to get you to sign on?"

"Why would I?" she said sharply, not looking at him.

"What the hell does that mean?"

She stopped walking, breathing hard, and turned on him. "It means why do you care what I do?"

"What are you talking about?" He lowered his voice. "You *know* I care."

253

"You mean about the business. Well, don't worry your pretty little head about it, *sweetheart*. I put her off."

He saw red, speaking through gritted teeth as the rest of her band followed the others to the gate. "After everything we've done, you think I'm only interested in the fucking business? Let me make this perfectly clear. My interest is in *you*. Helping Surge is just an extension of that."

"I can't do this with you right now," she whisper-barked.

Her gaze darted to the screaming fans and back to him with a mix of longing, frustration, and so much fucking resilience, his restraint snapped. "The hell you can't." He took her by the arm, dragged her onto the bus, and locked the door.

"What are you doing? What if someone saw us?"

"Then I'll say you weren't feeling well. I've had enough of this bullshit." He tightened his grip on her arm, backing her up against the wall. "You think I don't care about you? You think because I'm doing what you asked that it's not killing me? That I don't want to kiss you and tear off your clothes every damn time I see you?"

"I don't *know*. You went back to being all business like it was—"

Unwilling to waste another second arguing, he crushed his mouth to hers, making his emotions clear in the best way he knew how, pouring them into their kiss. "I did it for *you*," he said against her lips. "I'd do anything for y—"

She pulled his mouth back to hers, grinding against his cock. God, he'd missed her. Her smell, her taste, her feverish kisses. They devoured each other, and he ate up her moans and whimpers, the feel of her clutching his shoulders. He pushed his hand beneath her dress, thrusting his fingers inside her. They both moaned. "*Fuck.* I miss how wet you get for me." He grabbed her hair, angling her mouth beneath his, taking her in a brutal kiss, and used his thumb where she needed it most. She went up on her toes, fingernails digging into his biceps, her hungry noises filling his lungs. Her thighs flexed and her pussy tightened around his fingers as her orgasm took hold, and she cried out into his mouth, riding his fingers like she couldn't get enough. He devoured her mouth, soaking in every sensual sound as waves of pleasure consumed her. As she came down from the peak, he tore open his pants, shoved them down, and lifted her into his arms. Her legs circled his as he drove into her balls deep. Exquisite pleasure radiated through him. *"Fuuck"* sailed from his lungs as a moan flew from hers.

Their eyes connected, and there were so many things he wanted to say, but he was painfully aware of their limited time, and he wasn't about to waste a second of it. He reclaimed her mouth, and they pounded out a frantic rhythm, fucking like they'd never get another chance. She clung to his shoulders, fingernails digging through his shirt. He quickened his thrusts, need coiling hot and tight inside him as she rode his cock. Her legs squeezed around him, her pussy tightening like a vice, and *"Kane—"* flew from her lips, pulling him over the edge with her. They thrust and moaned, riding the highs of their passion until they had nothing left to give and she went soft in his arms, her head lolling back, eyes closed.

"Look at me," he demanded. Beautiful sated green eyes met his. "You're *mine*, Sable."

She shook her head. "We can't. You know what they'll say about me."

"We'll be careful. Nobody will know until well after the tour is over, but we're *done* fighting this. I need you in my arms, and I know you don't think you need a man, but you fucking need me."

Her eyes narrowed, but there was no anger in her voice. "Such an arrogant asshole."

"Tell me I'm wrong. Tell me the second I was inside you, it didn't obliterate the chaos of the tour and all the other bullshit."

She touched her forehead to his. "I can't," she whispered. "It would be a lie."

"Damn right it would. Now tell me you're mine."

With a sexy smirk, she said, "Don't push it, Bad."

"Fucking say it, or you'll never get my cock again."

She glared at him. "I'm yours, you ass. Don't make me regret it."

# Chapter Twenty-Six

SABLE LAY AWAKE in her bunk as the tour bus sped along the highway. Six weeks on the road felt like a lifetime. She longed for fresh air and a little space to breathe without always having someone five feet away. She listened to the sound of Lee snoring. Would she ever get used to it? At least Tuck wasn't talking in his sleep tonight, like he often did. Sometimes he woke with a start, sweating and anxious, and had to get up and walk around. She wondered if he was still having nightmares, as he had after Thea had been killed. If he was, he wasn't sharing them with her. When she'd tried talking to him about it, he'd said he was just stressed.

Weren't they all?

She felt things changing between all of them and wondered how Johnny and his bandmates made touring work without killing each other. She'd asked Dion about it after one of the concerts. He'd said they'd argued like cats and dogs on and off, but after a while they'd gotten used to it. She wasn't sure if he meant the arguing or touring.

They were all short-tempered. JP was fucking groupies left and right, and Lee was perpetually pissed off about God only knew what. Katie was driving Chris crazy with jealousy, and then there was Sable. She missed her family despite texting and calling often, and she missed seeing Deloris. She'd gotten to speak with her a few times, which had helped, but it wasn't the same as being there. She also missed working at the shop, the smell of it, getting her hands dirty, and that sense of accomplishment that only working on vehicles could bring. She even missed Buddy shuffling at a snail's pace and Eli rattling on as he shadowed her. But what she missed most was living on her own timeline. Doing what she wanted when she wanted.

Ever since the night Kane had dragged her onto the bus three weeks ago, what she *wanted* was him. Knowing he'd been as desperate for her as she'd been for him was *everything*. While she and her bandmates seemed to be drifting farther apart, she and Kane were becoming closer. The only time they fought their feelings was in public, and it was torture, but they were finding their way through it. On breaks and in their downtime, they gravitated toward each other. When she'd see him working on his computer, she'd sit nearby working on songs, and vice versa. Not that Kane had any real downtime. He always seemed to be *on*. If he wasn't doing something for the bands, then he was focused on his own businesses or checking in with his parents or sisters. She'd heard him on the phone negotiating a business deal like he knew he couldn't lose, and she was as attracted to that arrogance as she'd been turned off by it at first. Five minutes after that business call, she'd heard him talking gently to Aria, and she'd been even more drawn to him.

They were always ravenous for each other, and while they'd been able to steal away without anyone noticing for a few minutes here and there when they weren't on the road, they were careful not to cross any lines in front of anyone. They tossed barbs as they always had, only now those teases were accompanied by furtive glances and interspersed with longing whispers and dirty promises. When they'd hang out with the guys, she got to see a lighter side of Kane, joking with his brother and the other guys he'd known for years. One evening he'd ridden on their bus for part of the trip, going over changes to the schedule with them. Afterward, he'd brainstormed a song with her and Tuck, which had reminded her of that night in New York in his rooftop sanctuary. They couldn't touch openly, but their legs had brushed under the table, and she'd gotten butterflies like a schoolgirl with a crush.

She liked those silly moments she'd missed out on as a teenager, as much as she liked their sexy nights when they stayed in hotels. On those nights she'd sneak into his room, which was always farther away from the band than hers. After satiating their desires, they'd lay tangled together, talking until they fell asleep. They set alarms so she could leave by four in the morning, but she treasured those stolen hours. But she also liked when he'd notice that she was overwhelmed before or after a show or ready to lose her shit with the guys, and he'd walk by, put a hand on her back, and whisper, *You doing okay?* or, *Breathe, baby. Just breathe.*

Kane had become her chorus between chaotic verses.

*My safe place to fall into.*

It was strange thinking about herself in a relationship, even if a secret one, but with Kane she didn't feel trapped the way even the thought of a relationship had felt in the past. But those warm, fuzzy feelings made their nights apart, like this one, when they were riding on separate buses, painfully difficult. She wanted to see him, talk to him, *touch* him.

If only the vibration of the bus would lull her to sleep. Or at least drown out the ache of missing him. She wondered if he was still awake, working on his computer or doing business over the phone with his team in Australia. She couldn't imagine keeping track of all of the business entities he owned, even with a staff to oversee them.

She picked up her phone, ignoring the voicemail messages from Victoria, who was reaching out to her again about signing with Blank Space. Sable didn't have the bandwidth to think about that. She wasn't even sure she'd make it through this tour without losing her mind.

Pushing those thoughts aside, she thumbed out a text to Kane. *Miss you.* She stared at it, her thumb hovering over the send icon. They might not be holding back their feelings, but it still felt weird to put it out there unsolicited. She deleted that and typed, *Hey,* and added a smiley emoji. *Still up?* That felt too cheery, so she went with, *Hi. You up?*

Kane: *Depends on what sense you're asking about.* A devil emoji popped up.

Sable: *If you're that kind of UP on a bus full of men, I have questions.*

Kane: *I have answers. I can't stop thinking about the hot chick I saw onstage tonight.*

She grinned.

Sable: *I doubt she'd be impressed by your billions.*

Kane: *No, but she does have a thing for tattooed drummers who are good with their hands.*

Sable: *Among other body parts.*

She sent a flame emoji, loving their banter. But she wanted him to know he was more than sexy banter and good times to her.

Sable: *I miss you.*

The second she sent it, she worried she sounded clingy.

Sable: *I know that sounds ridiculous since I just saw you a couple of hours ago. I'm shutting up now.*

She closed her eyes, cursing herself.

Kane: *Why do you think I'm still awake at 2am? I miss you, too. The only time I can sleep anymore is with you in my arms.*

Filled with relief and warmth, she sent a smiley-face emoji with hearts around it.

Kane: *Tomorrow night you're all mine.*

They were staying at a hotel tomorrow night. In her heart, she was his no matter where they stayed.

Sable: *I look forward to it. I hate 4am.*

Kane: *You could always meet me at the hotel pool at 5am.*

Sable: *Not if you want to get any swimming in.* She sent a smirking emoji and realized she had no idea why he swam when they were at hotels. *What's with all the swimming?*

Kane: *It's good for stamina.*

Sable: She sent an eye roll emoji. *So it started in high school when you discovered Big Daddy wasn't just your rapper name?*

Kane: A laughing emoji popped up. *My parents put me in team sports when I was a kid, and I hated running, but I'm competitive and had to work off my energy, so I joined the swim team.*

Sable: *Funny, I had you pegged as a football guy or maybe baseball.*

Kane: *Think again. What has the higher payoff? Being surrounded by guys in shoulder pads or girls in swimsuits?*

She sent a smirking emoji.

Kane: *I wish I had known you in high school.*

Sable: *No you don't. Jocks have never been my thing.* But she wished she'd known him then, too.

Kane: *Until now.*

Sable: *You're hardly a jock, Mr. I Don't Run.*

Kane: *You would have liked me. I can see you sitting in the stands, cheering me on with my fan club.*

She sent another eye roll emoji.

Kane: *My mother and sisters never missed a swim meet.*

She smiled as she typed, *I love that.*

Kane: *If we won the meet, we'd go out for ice cream.*

Sable: *No celebrating with friends?*

Kane: *Family first. Friends and parties later.*

Sable: *Your sisters must have been crazy about you.*

Kane: *Not as crazy as I was about them. They changed my life for the better.*

She wanted to hear his voice and thought about going to another part of the bus to call him. But she was worried someone might wake up, so she continued texting.

Sable: *In what way?*

Kane: *When a little girl comes to your family with nothing more than a bag of clothes and eyes full of hope and fear, it changes your perspective on everything. Johnny and I never went without anything. Most importantly, we had endless love and support. From the moment I met them, I wanted that for them. I was twelve when Harlow came to us and sixteen when Aria joined our family, and I wanted to protect them and give them the world.*

She imagined him as a serious-eyed boy, guarding his baby sisters with everything he had, and she fell a little harder for him.

Sable: *They're lucky to have you.*

Kane: *Like I said, not as lucky as I am to have them. Was it like that for you and your younger siblings?*

She started to weigh her answer, but she knew she could be honest with him.

Sable: *Not really. I didn't want to give them the world. I wanted to protect them from it.*

Kane: *Did something happen that made you worry for their safety?*

Sable: *Not really. I just knew I had to be strong for them.*

Kane: *How did you know?*

Sable: *Because I saw them get their feelings hurt. They're strong in their own ways, but they didn't always stand up for themselves.*

Kane: *What were they like back then?*

Sable: *Grace got along with everyone, but she was sensitive, and Pepper was all about school, which made her a little nerdy and a target for some jerks. Amber was quiet and too nice. I think she would have liked to be invisible, and while Morgyn lived in a state of happy hippieness she and Brindle were all about being sneaky. Someone had to make sure they didn't get into trouble. Then there was Axsel. As the youngest and the only boy, he was spoiled by everyone. He didn't know people could be rotten, and it was hard on him when they were.*

Kane: *And what were you like?*

Sable: *Rebellious as the day was long. My grandmother once told me that the greatest thing a person could be was loyal, and I guess I took that to heart.*

Kane: *She sounds like she was a smart woman. I can't imagine growing up with all those personalities. I bet your parents have some great stories.*

Sable: *There was never a dull moment.*

She laughed softly, remembering an epic food fight.

Sable: *This sums up what it was like. One night my parents took us to the Stardust Café for dinner. It was a big deal because we didn't go out that often. Brindle didn't want to eat her peas, and she pushed her plate away, knocking over Morgyn's glass and spilling juice all over her. Morgyn thought Brindle did it on purpose, and she threw mashed potatoes at her. But she was never good at sports, and they landed in Grace's hair. Grace shrieked and threw potatoes at Morgyn, but they hit Pepper and Morgyn. I went after Grace for nailing Pepper, and then all hell broke loose. We were all throwing food and laughing. Axsel was probably four or five at the time, and he'd climbed onto the table in the middle of it all and began stuffing everyone's rolls into his mouth.*

Three laughing emojis popped up from Kane.

Kane: *What did your parents do?*

Sable: *Shit a brick. My father whistled really loudly, like he does when he's calling the dogs, and we all froze. That's when we realized the other customers had scattered, and Amber was hiding under the table, which just made us laugh harder. There was food everywhere. My parents made us wash every dish, every table, every inch of the floor.*

She hadn't thought about that night in forever.

Sable: *That's actually one of my favorite memories.*

Kane: *That's hilarious, but your poor parents.*

Sable: *I don't think they took us out for months after that. What about you? Do you have a favorite memory?*

Kane: *I have many. When I was ten or eleven, Johnny and I were playing with friends down the street, and we got into a brawl with them and came home with black eyes. We thought we were super cool, but our parents weren't very happy about it.*

Sable: *I hope you won the brawl.*

Kane: *We did, but our school pictures were taken the next day.*

Sable sent a laughing emoji and thumbed out, *I guess that wasn't your mom's favorite memory.*

Kane: *Nope. Her favorite story is from the Fourth of July the year Aria came to us. Johnny and I were kicking a ball around the yard and tackling each other. My dad was grilling burgers, and my mom put platters of corn on the cob and watermelon on the table on the patio, where Aria and Harlow were playing with dolls. She told me and Johnny to wash up and went inside to get something. We got to the table a minute before our parents. Every ear of corn had tiny bites out of it, and Aria had corn all over her face and clothes. Harlow had scarfed down several pieces of watermelon and had juice dripping down her face and the front of her shirt. When our parents got to the table, I said I was too hungry to wait and told them I'd eaten the corn and the watermelon.*

Sable's heart filled up, and she thumbed out, *You're the best big brother.* She sent three red hearts. *What did your parents do?*

Kane: *Nothing! They said I must have been hungry and to try to save some for everyone else next time. You can imagine how funny it is when they tell the story.*

Sable sent a laughing emoji, but inside she wasn't laughing. She loved hearing about his life. His story made her want to know his family, too.

Sable: *I wish we were on the same bus.*

Kane: *The tour won't last forever.*

The tour wouldn't, but Sable wondered if maybe *they* could. Their worlds were so far apart, she didn't know how they could possibly make it work. But maybe Kane wasn't supposed to just be her chorus between chaotic verses. Maybe he was supposed to be her love song.

# Chapter Twenty-Seven

AS SABLE CAME off the stage, a roadie handed her a towel and a bottle of water. "Thank you." She wiped her face with the towel, heading for the green room as the crowd erupted for Bad Intentions. They'd been touring for nine weeks, and she was ready to throttle everyone. Victoria was hounding her, and Sable was doing her best to ignore her. Lee and JP were at each other's throats, Chris was fighting with his wife nearly every time they spoke, which made him a bear to deal with, and Tuck was barely speaking to her. He'd caught her coming back to her hotel room at four in the morning last week and had given her an inquisition. She'd said she couldn't sleep and had been pacing the halls. On top of everything else, every time Sable tried to call Deloris, she was told she wasn't having a good day. Her mother kept her up to date on their visits and reassured her that Deloris still had plenty of good days, which was great, but Sable was missing them. Her only reprieves from the stress were a few stolen minutes with Kane here and there, the occasional hotel room tryst, and their midnight texts from bus to bus. As far as she was concerned, the tour couldn't end soon enough.

"What the fuck happened out there, JP?" Chris barked as they entered the green room.

JP glowered at him, pouring himself a shot of whiskey. "What're you talking about?"

"You screwed up that last song," Lee snapped.

"The hell I did." JP drank the shot. "You missed a beat in the bridge."

"Fuck off. I did not." Lee grabbed the bottle from him. "You've got to cut back on this shit."

"Fuck you." JP grabbed the bottle, and they started fighting over it.

"Damn it, you idiots. Cut the shit." Sable tried to get between them and caught a fist in the jaw, sending her reeling backward. She caught herself on the coffee table before she went down, watching her worst fears play out before her as Tuck slammed JP against the wall.

"You don't fucking hit a woman, you asshole." Tuck had his forearm against JP's neck.

"What the hell, JP?" Chris snapped.

"It was an accident. It was meant for Lee." JP looked at Sable, wild-eyed. "Sorry."

She tasted metal and wiped her lip. Her finger came away bloody just as the door flew open and Kane strode in. "What the hell is going—" His eyes landed on her. His nostrils flared. He reached past Tuck, grabbed JP's collar, and lifted him off his feet, seething through clenched teeth, "You fucking *hit* her?"

*Shitshitshit.* "Kane, *stop!*" She ran over to them. "Let him go."

"He's *not* getting away with this." He shoved JP harder into the wall.

"He didn't mean to do it. I tried to stop him and Lee from fighting and got in the way. But this is between *me* and *them*. *Please* just go, and let us work it out." She looked at him imploringly, all too aware of Tuck watching them.

Kane set a dark stare on JP as he lowered him to his feet. "Touch her again, and it'll be the last thing you do." He shifted his attention to the others. "That goes for all of you. Accident or not." He walked out of the room without a backward glance.

"Fuck." JP rubbed his chest where Kane's fist had been.

"This shit *has* to stop," Sable said.

"I told you it was an accident," JP said.

"It's not just that," Chris snapped. "Drinking all night and fucking any woman who'll get in your bed? You're out of control."

JP scoffed. "Now you're the pussy police?"

"Jesus, JP. I don't even know who you are anymore." Chris stalked away.

"You're no better," Lee pointed out. "Bitching at everyone because you can't stop fighting with Katie."

"Watch it," Chris warned, glaring at him. "She's my *wife*, and this time apart sucks for her and the kids."

"It's a few months," JP said. "Get over it."

"Like you've *ever* had someone important in your life?" Chris seethed.

"Can you all just shut up?" Sable hollered. "This is why I didn't want to do the tour. We're all exhausted, and all you can do is take it out on each other. Get your shit together." She reached for the door.

"Where are you going?" Tuck asked.

"I need air." She stalked out of the room, and Tuck followed. A bodyguard stood outside the door, and she saw Kane down the hall, watching them. She turned her back to him, and Tuck was *right there*. "I need a fucking break, okay? Give me some space."

"Why are you lying to me?"

"What are you talking about?"

"You know *exactly* what I'm talking about." Tuck lowered his voice. "You think we've changed? Look in the fucking mirror, Bell." He looked down the hall at Kane, and she chanced a glance, catching Kane returning Tuck's stare.

*Damn it.* "Tuck—"

"Don't bother." He stormed back into the room.

Kane took a step toward her, but she held up her hand, shaking her head, and turned to the bodyguard. "Can you get me to the bus?"

SABLE PACED HER hotel room later that night feeling like a caged tiger. Tensions were still running high when they finally left the venue. The silence had been deafening on the bus on the way to the hotel. She didn't know how to make anything right. She felt bad about lying to Tuck and about sending Kane out of the room, but what else was she supposed to do? Kane had texted her, and Pepper had called for their weekly chat, but Sable had been too upset to text or talk with either of them. She'd texted Axsel, hoping he had some advice about how to deal with the band, but he'd basically told her that what they were going through was par for the course.

Her life was unraveling around her, and she needed to find something to hold on to. She wished it could be Kane, but he was probably furious with her for sending him away, so she pulled out her phone and called the one person she could always turn to. Her father answered on the second ring.

"Hi, sweetie. How's my girl?"

His familiar voice was as comforting as a hug. "Hi, Dad. I'm okay. How is everyone there?" She texted with her siblings often, but it made her feel closer to home to hear about them.

"Everyone's good. Morgyn and Graham are on the road again, and Grace and Reed were here for dinner."

"I'm glad for Morgyn and Graham. They love traveling. How are Grace and Reed?"

"I've never seen them so happy. It's funny how a baby can make everything look brighter. Reed said Deloris's house is almost done."

"Yeah, I know. He needs to know what to do about fixing up the barn, but I haven't had time to figure that out yet." The truth was, she didn't want him to touch the barn. It felt like the last piece of her relationship with Lloyd. The place where she and the band had come together, where they had battled and made up and created music that came from their souls. With everything that had gone down tonight, she wanted to crawl into that barn and never come out.

"Reed knows you have a lot on your plate," her father said. "He didn't seem in a rush to finish. But if you're worried about where you'll practice, we can clean out the garage and you guys can practice here."

"Thanks, Dad, but you didn't like the racket when we were kids. I don't think you and Mom need it now." At this rate, she may not even have a band to practice with. Her stomach sank with that thought.

"You and the guys are a little more talented than you were back then. Just know the option is there. I stopped by your shop the other day. Carter and Buddy are holding down the fort, and Eli seemed darn proud of himself for knowing as much as he does. Carter said he's a real help. You've done well by Eli."

"Thanks. He's a good kid."

"They're all proud of you and the boys, honey. The whole town is."

They wouldn't be if they knew what was going on, but she kept that to herself.

"Is something on your mind?" her father asked.

"Not really. It was just a stressful night, and I wanted to hear your voice."

"I'm always here for you, sweetheart. I can't imagine how stressful it is to travel all the time and perform three or four nights a week. I bet you wish you had an engine to disappear into."

Music and mechanics had been her go-to stress relievers forever. Now she added Kane to that list. "Wouldn't that be nice? Maybe I can go take apart the bus."

Her dad chuckled. "I'm sorry today was stressful. Do you want to talk about it? Is there anything I can do? Want me to get your mom on the line?"

A knock at the door startled her. "I don't have time. Someone's at my door, but thanks, Dad. Just talking to you helped. Love you."

"Anytime, sweetie. I love you, too."

She ended the call and went to look out the peephole. Her heart stumbled at the sight of Kane's dark eyes staring back at her. She opened the door, looking down the empty hall at her bandmates' rooms. "What are you doing here? Someone might see you."

He pushed past her, walking into the room. "Get your bag. We're getting out of here."

She closed the door. "We can't just leave together. People

will see us."

"We can and we *are*. It's already taken care of." He put his fingers under her chin, lifting it, visually inspecting her jaw. "I could have killed that fucker. Did you ice it?"

"Yes." She'd iced it when Bad Intentions was onstage and had covered the redness with makeup before the meet and greet. "Kane, what do you mean it's taken care of? I can't just disappear with you. What am I supposed to tell the guys? We're leaving for Seattle in the morning."

"*You're* not telling them anything. You all need time to defuse. I told Johnny and Tom what happened, and they agreed that you guys need space, which is totally common on tours. As soon as we leave, Tom will tell them that you'll meet them in Seattle the day after tomorrow for the next concert."

"What? *No*. I need to be here to fix things."

"*Damn it*, Sable. Stop being so fucking stubborn. You got *punched* in the jaw. You all need a break from each other, and since you'll never ask for one, much less admit to needing one, I'm making sure you get it. Now get your shit and let's go. Our car is waiting."

She grabbed her bag from the closet and began stuffing her things into it. "This will make things worse. They'll think I'm turning into a diva."

"First of all, that could never happen, and they know it. You'd tear their heads off before you'd turn into that type of person. Second of all, give me some credit. I know how to handle people. Tom's going to tell them that he forced you to travel separately."

"With *you*? How's that going to look?"

"They know you hate having bodyguards around. It'll look like Johnny, who I *work for*, tasked me to go with you to make sure you don't run into any trouble."

"And if I say no?"

"I'll carry your ass out of here kicking and screaming if I have to. You need downtime, and I'm not taking any chances of things escalating and you getting hurt again." He pulled her into his arms. "Why are you fighting this so hard? We'll get twenty-four hours together. No roadies, no bandmates, no cameras. Just *us*."

She wanted that more than he could know, and she appreciated how hard he was fighting to take care of her, but she wasn't used to it, and she didn't want to let the guys down. "Because I can handle my own problems."

"Nobody is doubting that, and you *will* handle them after everyone's had some time to cool down." He kissed her softly. "We've got a couple of masseuses traveling with the guys tomorrow. Hopefully that'll help them work off steam so they can chill, too."

"JP will try to sleep with them."

"I don't give a damn if they all do if it means you're getting the time and space you need."

How could she not appreciate that? "Where are we going?"

"To my plane, and in a few hours we'll be at my private villa in Punta Mita, where I can pamper you properly, so please finish getting your stuff together and we'll grab whatever else you need from the bus, like those cutoffs you wore onstage last week."

*Pamper me?* "I don't even know where Punta Mita is."

"Mexico. It'll be warm, and I've got a security detail there to make sure we're not disturbed." He kissed her again. "Now, please stop asking questions and trust me."

A little while later, as they boarded Kane's private plane, her phone vibrated with texts from JP and Lee apologizing and one from Chris asking if she was okay. She replied to JP and Lee, telling them not to worry about it, and to Chris, reassuring him she was fine and just needed a little space.

The fact that Tuck hadn't reached out hurt like hell.

After they were safely in the air, Kane moved the armrest and pulled her against his side, kissing her temple. As the tension drained from her shoulders and neck, she realized Kane hadn't been upset with her about kicking him out of the green room. He'd seen past it and had somehow known exactly what she needed.

He'd given her something—*someone*—to hold on to.

KANE HAD A mountain of worries beyond the band fighting. He'd seen how hurt Sable was when everyone but Tuck had texted her, and he knew how hard it was for her to let him take her away tonight when she'd rather barrel into the lion's den and fight her way out. But he'd be damned if he'd let her traipse into an already volatile situation or deal with all this shit on her own. He pressed a kiss to the top of her head. "Are you okay?"

"Mm-hm."

"Do you want to talk about what's going on with the band?"

"No."

He held her a little tighter, concerned about how much she was holding in and how explosive things must have gotten for her to get hurt the way she did. "If you change your mind, I'm all ears."

"I won't." She was quiet for a solid two or three minutes, before sitting up and looking at him, the bruise on her jaw showing through her makeup, cutting him to his core. "This is what I was worried about. Everything is a mess. This life changes people. It puts you under so much stress, you forget how to cut each other slack. And it's not just them. I'm guilty of it, too. Sneaking around with you makes it even harder. I'm not used to keeping secrets from Tuck. I feel like I'm losing my best friend on top of everything else, and I don't know how to fix any of it."

His jaw tightened, his feelings for her burning him up inside. She'd never answered him about whether she'd been hooking up with Tuck. He had no doubt that if she had been, it had stopped weeks ago. He and Sable might not talk about their feelings, but he could feel how much she cared for him in her touch, saw it in her eyes. Just like he saw the hurt in them now. "Do you and Tuck usually share everything?"

"Pretty much. We have since we were kids."

"You've been close that long? Before you started the band?"

"Forever. He used to have a twin sister, Thea, and I was close to her, too."

"I read that in his background check. She died in an accident when they were young, right?"

She nodded. "His parents are rough, and they treated him and Thea like crap."

"Were they physically abusive?"

"No. They were always fighting, and they'd holler at Tuck and Thea all the time and tell them they weren't worth a shit. When things got really bad, Tuck and Thea would sneak out at night and throw pebbles at my window. We'd go out to the barn and talk for hours so the hatred didn't eat away at them.

After we started using Lloyd's barn, that's where we'd go. We stashed extra blankets there for them, but they always made it back home before daylight."

"Couldn't your parents do something to help them?"

"Tuck thought they'd have to tell the authorities. He was afraid they'd split up him and Thea, and he didn't want his parents to get into trouble. No matter how they treated them, they were still his parents, you know? I wanted to tell my dad, but he begged me not to. The thing is, it's a small town, so people knew things weren't good. One night when we went to the barn, we found an old couch in it. Lloyd must have known what we were up to, and as time went on, there was food, clean blankets, pillows. I heard Lloyd talking at the shop with Buddy one afternoon about how he and my father had gone to speak with Tuck's parents, but I couldn't ask about it without making things even more complicated for Tuck. But at least there were people trying to make things better for them."

"Did it help?"

"Things were never great, but they got better for a while. Until Thea died, at the end of their sophomore year." The pain in her eyes had Kane reaching for her hand. "Their parents were fighting late one night, and Tuck and Thea were sneaking out. Their bedrooms were on the second floor, and they'd climb out the window onto the roof and then climb down a tree. But that night Thea slipped and fell. Tuck tried to grab her, and he fell too. She landed headfirst on the concrete beneath him and was killed instantly." Tears spilled from her eyes.

"Jesus." Kane pulled her into his arms, holding her against his chest, his heart breaking for all of them. "Those poor kids. I'm so sorry." He pressed a kiss to her head, trying to get his arms around the guilt and pain Tuck must have suffered. "That had to be devastating for all of you."

She nodded against his chest, sniffling, and stayed there for a minute or two before pulling away and wiping her eyes. "They blamed Tuck, and things got bad again. You asked if Tuck and I were hooking up. We weren't when you asked, and we haven't since we were teenagers, but we did after he lost Thea. Nobody knew, but we'd meet in the barn, and..." She shrugged. "She was part of us, and then she was gone. It was impossible to comprehend. We were trying to hold on to her and escape our pain." Her eyes teared up again, and she blinked them dry.

"Jesus, Sable. I can't imagine what you went through. It's no wonder you two are so close. How long were you together?"

"I don't know. A few weeks. It wasn't like we were a couple. We were friends, and we'd meet at night and cry and talk and have sex. Eventually he wanted more, and I didn't, and we ended it."

He was surprised, given all they'd been through together. "Why not?"

"I didn't have a good answer back then, and I still don't. I've just never been one of those girls who needed a boyfriend. I was a junior, working with Lloyd after school, and we'd started the band that year. I loved Tuck. I still do, and I'm sure I'll always will. But I wasn't in love with him." She shook her head. "I don't know why I wasn't or why I didn't want to be his girlfriend. I guess I'm just wired differently. I never wanted more with anyone until I met you."

"Nobody else was arrogant enough for you." He leaned in and kissed her. "You are wired differently, and that's what makes you so special. You gave him the love and comfort he needed."

"I needed it just as badly. I don't know what that says about me, but it doesn't matter. I did it, and I don't regret it."

"You shouldn't regret it. You followed your heart, and this might sound strange coming from a guy who hasn't given that particular organ much thought in almost two decades, but that's a beautiful thing. It sounds like you two helped each other through the worst of it, and you were able to remain friends afterward. That says a lot about both of you."

"Things were tough between us for a while, but we missed each other, and we found our way back to being friends. I'm pretty sure the band and our friendship are the reason he's still here."

"Was he suicidal?"

"No, but I think if he hadn't had us, things could have gone that way. Anyway, we've always told each other everything, so not telling him about us feels like a betrayal. And he's pretty much figured it out anyway. When you saw us in the hall at the venue, he basically said he knew without spelling it out."

Fuck. He hated that their relationship was causing her this much anguish. "We're playing by your rules, babe. If you want to tell Tuck and you trust he isn't going to out you to the media, then tell him. Unless you think he's in love with you and it'll cause more problems?"

"It's not like that. At least I don't think it is. We've both been with other people, and he's never had an issue with it."

"He could still be harboring feelings for you."

"I don't think so, although I've never been this serious about anyone. Maybe he senses that."

That was the first time she'd admitted to being serious about Kane, and he was glad she didn't immediately try to qualify it or take it back. "If it feels like a betrayal to you, I'm sure it feels like one to him, too, and that's enough to trigger lots of feelings for a friendship like yours. He was your friend long before I came into the picture. I don't want to be the guy who upends your life, so do whatever feels right for your friendship and know I support it. No matter what the fallout."

"I appreciate that. I need to think about it."

He'd tell the world tomorrow and annihilate anyone who disparaged her if she'd let him, but he'd also wait a lifetime for her if that was what she needed. "Of course. What about the rest of the band? When you hit rough patches, how did you get past them?"

"They've never gotten this bad. We'd usually just take a break and blow off some steam. Once we all calmed down, we'd figure it out."

"Good, then it seems like we're on the right path with them."

Troubled eyes met his. "I don't know, Kane. This feels different. Like it has sharp edges that could break our friendships apart."

He pulled her closer again. "It feels that way because you're all in a pressure-cooker situation. But these are your lifelong friends. It might take some time, but they love you. I'm sure it's going to be fine."

"I hope you're right."

"Do you regret doing the tour?"

"Honestly? In some ways I do. There's no bigger high than being onstage and knowing people are loving our music, but I hate the rest of it. There's so much pressure with fans and the press, and sleeping on the bus sucks. We're exhausted all the time and at each other's throats. I haven't been able to connect with Deloris the last few times I tried, and that makes me even edgier. It's a lot to deal with."

"Do you want to talk about replacing your band with another for the last three weeks of the tour and for the international tour in the fall?"

She looked at him incredulously. "Would you really do that?"

"It wouldn't be my first choice, but if it's too much for you, then we can figure something out."

Her brows knitted. "It means a lot to me that you would even consider doing that. It's overwhelming, and I hate what it's doing to the band, but I made a commitment, and I'll stick to it."

"That's admirable given that bruise you're sporting." That earned him a smile. "I'm not sure how I can help with the guys, but I know how worried you've been about Deloris. You've mentioned her quite a few times lately, so I called the administrator of the facility and explained what was going on. She has my direct number, and I told her to call whenever Deloris is lucid enough, day or night. As long as you're not onstage, I'll make sure you get to speak to her."

"You did that for me?"

He took her face between his hands, gazing deeply into her eyes, needing her to see the truth in his words. "I'd do anything for you. Even when you fight me tooth and nail."

She smiled and it finally reached her eyes, loosening some of the knots in his chest. "Then kiss me, because when you do, nothing else matters, and I could really use a little disappearing into you right now."

He lowered his lips to hers in a tender kiss so as not to hurt her jaw. He continued kissing her, softly and sensually, hoping to silence the pain and sadness and breathe hope into her lungs, passion into her body, and with any luck, his love into her heart.

# Chapter Twenty-Eight

SABLE AWOKE TO a warm breeze coming in through open glass doors that spanned the length of the wall, and an empty bed. She sat up, soaking in the breathtaking views just outside the bedroom of Kane's private villa in Punta Mita. The infinity pool looked like it spilled over a cliff and into the ocean. Kane swam into view, and she watched his sleek naked body move across the pool, flip at the wall, and head back the other way. She warmed all over. When they'd arrived last night, she'd been mentally and emotionally exhausted. They'd climbed into bed naked, and she must have fallen right to sleep, because the last thing she remembered was his arm around her, drawing her back against his chest as he kissed her cheek and said, *Sleep, baby. I've got you.*

She watched him doing laps, her heart swelling for the man who made her feel safer than anyone ever had. She could let her guard down with him in a way she'd never been able to with anyone else. She never would have thought she'd want a man like Kane in her life, much less be unable to imagine her life without him in it. She climbed out of bed and went to use the bathroom and brush her teeth. The bathroom was very *Kane*. It was big and luxurious, with marble floors and walls and a glass shower that was larger than her entire bathroom back home.

When she was done, she padded through the spacious bedroom, stepping onto the sun-drenched terrace. The two-story cliffside villa had views of the ocean on three sides and was surrounded by lush trees, with no other houses in sight. She could almost taste the peacefulness as she took in the fancy lounge chairs and covered outdoor dining area complete with a bar and built-in barbecue, rectangular firepit, and hot tub. She made her way over to the pool and sat on the edge. The stone was cool on her bare skin. Her legs dangled in the water as Kane swam toward her.

His arms cut through the water, his handsome face turning slightly to breathe, then going face down again. He looked like he was going to swim right into her, but he broke the surface, put a hand on either side of her legs, and pushed himself up so they were eye to eye. "Morning, beautiful. Give me that mouth."

A thrill chased through her as she leaned forward to kiss him. He tasted deliciously familiar.

"*Mm.* You taste much better than coffee." He kissed her again and swept one arm around her, crushing her breasts to his slick, hard chest as he kicked off the wall, shooting them into deeper water with him on his back and her lying on his front.

They laughed as he shifted upright, and she wound her arms around his neck, his strong legs keeping them afloat. She felt like she was laughing for the first time in years, and she couldn't stop grinning. He looked like he couldn't either. She hadn't realized how much she'd needed this freedom to just *be* with him. How much *they* needed this. She felt like a whole different person, and with him she was different than she'd ever been with any man, so it kind of made sense. She should probably feel guilty, being there with Kane while her bandmates were traveling in a bus. But she was doing the tour *for* them. Didn't she deserve this for herself?

"I didn't know the house came with a pool boy," she said playfully.

"Only for you."

"Do you always swim naked?"

"I had a hell of a time keeping my hands to myself this morning. There's no way my swim trunks would fit over my greedy cock."

She laughed, loving the way he held nothing back, and wiggled her hips, taunting him. "Feels like he's getting greedy again."

"What'd you expect, you fiery temptress?" He bit her neck, emitting a low growl that sent lust slithering through her.

She reveled in happiness and gazed up at the house and out at the ocean, feeling like she'd woken up in someone else's dream. "God, Kane. You sure know how to pamper yourself. This place is outrageous. It belongs in a travel magazine."

"This place is an investment. I've got a dozen more like it in other locations. Having you with me? *That's* pampering myself. No matter where we are." He kissed her again, as if he hadn't just bowled her over with his words. "I'm sorry I couldn't take you home so you could see your family and Deloris." He brushed his scruff along her cheek, sending prickles of arousal down her core. "I was afraid the press would catch wind of us, and it would make things worse."

Her heart filled up anew with his thoughtfulness. "I would give anything to see them, but you did the right thing."

"My phone is on the table over there in case they call about Deloris."

"You thought of everything."

"I thought of *you*." He kissed her again, slowly and sensually, moving through the water until his feet reached the bottom. "I'm always thinking of you."

He looked so serious, and she knew he was. She felt it in her bones, because she was always thinking of him, too. "How did we get here?"

"I don't know. But I'm sure glad we did."

He kissed her again, slowly at first, but with their naked bodies sliding against one another, and her heart—*both of our hearts*—open for the first time in years, there was no holding back. Their kisses grew hungrier, their hands roving over each other's bodies, as she rocked against his hard length. He smiled against her lips and moved his hand between her legs, teasing her as his mouth came down over her neck, sucking and biting. Her entire body ignited. "*Kane*—" came out as desperate as she felt.

"Feel good, baby?" He nipped at her jaw.

She closed her eyes. "So good."

"Look at me when I make you come," he said gruffly. His fingers quickened, and her heart rate followed. She held his stare, feeling the pull of an orgasm low in her belly. "There it is. Come on, baby. Show me how much you love coming for me."

Her fingernails dug into his skin, her breaths coming in fast, hard gusts. "Show me how much you love touching me," she challenged. He flashed a wolfish grin and grabbed her hair with his other hand, tugging just hard enough to sever her control. "*Ohgod*—" He reclaimed her neck, intensifying her pleasure. "That's my girl. So fucking sexy." The huskiness of his voice and the taunt of his thick fingers had her wanting so much more. He sealed his mouth over hers, kissing her slow and deep as she came down from the high.

As their lips parted, he kept her close. "See, baby? I'm always thinking of you."

With the sun warming her back and the man she adored holding her like he never wanted to let go, she was overcome with emotion and barely managed, "Me too, you," before covering his mouth with hers. He tightened his fist in her hair, taking her in a ruthless kiss. She ground against him, anticipation stacked up inside her, but he held her ass with one hand, keeping her from sinking down on his cock. He tore his mouth away with a curse and clutched her waist with both hands, lifting her until he could reach her breast with his mouth, and proceeded to tease her to the brink of madness. She dug her fingernails into his shoulders as he gave her other breast the same exquisite attention, making her want and need and *ache* for him. "Kane, *please*—"

That was all it took for him to lower her onto his cock and feast on her mouth. Her jaw stung, but the pain intertwined with the pleasure radiating through her as he thrust hard and deep. She clung to his shoulders, cool water swishing around them as she met every thrust with one of her own. Tingles climbed up her limbs, consuming her core and spreading like wildfire. He bit down on her shoulder, sending pleasure crashing over her like a tidal wave, dragging *him* under, too, in a frenzy of thrusts and moans and curses as they rocked and pumped and, finally, *blissfully*, collapsed in each other's arms.

"Jesus, Sable," he panted out. "How can it be *more* intense every time we're together?"

"You're too arrogant to have it any other way."

He laughed and kissed her again.

"Sorry I interrupted your workout."

"Are you really?" He nipped at her lower lip.

"Not even a little, but it seemed like the polite thing to say." Feeling playful, she pushed out of his arms and swam away.

"Since when are you polite?" He caught up to her, hauling her back into his arms, both of them laughing again. "Now you're at my mercy."

"There's no place else I'd rather be."

SABLE SHADED HER eyes from the sun, looking at Kane lying beside her on a lounger, bare-ass naked and beautiful as could be. She couldn't remember the last time she'd let herself relax, and she'd sure never relaxed like this. They'd been lying on thick, fluffy towels for what felt like an hour. She must have needed it, because she usually couldn't sit still doing nothing, but she hadn't felt fidgety until just now.

Kane reached for her hand and opened his eyes, a lazy smile giving him a boyish charm. "Getting hungry?"

"A little."

"Come on. Let's get dressed, and I'll make you breakfast." He pushed to his feet and pulled her up beside him, drawing her into a kiss. He snagged his phone on their way into the bedroom.

"Do we need to get groceries?"

"No. I had the kitchen stocked before we came."

She put on a T-shirt as he pulled on shorts. "It must be nice to have staff at your beck and call."

"It's convenient."

"I'm surprised you don't have a chef." She put on her underwear and shorts.

"I do, but I wanted to take care of you."

"I don't need taking care of. I can cook for myself."

"I'm sure you can, but today is your day to relax and rejuvenate and my day to pamper you, so you don't burn out."

"Kane, I'm not—"

He drew her into his arms, cutting her off with a kiss. "Stop with the knee-jerk reactions, and hear what I'm saying to you. I know how capable you are, and I know you're not used to anyone doing things for you, much less some pushy guy who's not going to take no for an answer. I'm not used to *wanting* to do things for anyone outside my family. So how about we humor each other and just go with it?"

She loved that he understood the way she was wired, but what she liked even more was that he was wired the same way. "How about we cook together?"

"How about I swat your ass?"

He lifted his hand, and she scooted out of reach, laughing. "It's called a compromise."

"I don't compromise. I win." He flashed that devastating smile and hauled her in for another kiss.

"I got kissed. I'd say I'm the winner."

He laughed and said, "You're a brat," tugging her in for another kiss.

They headed out of the bedroom, through the main living area, which was tastefully decorated with a calming mix of cream, brown, and taupe, lavish furniture, and what were probably hand-carved wood tables. Gallery-worthy art decorated the few walls that weren't glass. Two sets of sliders spanned the length of the back wall, leading to the terrace.

The room opened into a dining area with a massive table

that seated twelve and a kitchen the size of Sable's apartment, with black marble countertops, dark wood cabinets, and stainless-steel appliances. A vase of fresh flowers sat on the island beside a large oblong dish of fresh fruit.

"I can't believe you live like this. It's beautiful, but I'm afraid to touch anything."

"Just don't be afraid to touch me." He leaned in and kissed her.

She pulled him back for another. "I like being with you without people looking over our shoulders." So much so, she wished the tour were over and enough time had passed that nobody would care if she was sleeping with Johnny's brother or the manager of Bad Intentions.

"Me too." He pulled out a stool by the island. "Set your pretty ass here while I cut up some fruit."

"I know how to use a knife," she said as she sat down.

"Yes, but you don't know how to let me do things for you, so sit down and chill while I pamper you." He grabbed a knife, cutting board, and bowl and placed them on the island. "Do you have an aversion to any type of fruit?"

"Nope. I like it all, but honeydew is my favorite."

"Honeydew it is." He turned on the coffee maker, then picked up a melon and set it on the cutting board.

He was shirtless, his hair still damp. She watched him cutting the melon into bite-size chunks. He looked so relaxed, so different from the man who walked around wrangling band members and roadies and making sure nothing fell through the cracks. She'd gotten glimpses of this side of him during their stolen evenings together, but even then he was never quite this unguarded. She tried not to think about him being in the villa with other women, but she couldn't help it.

She plucked a piece of melon from the bowl, and he smiled as she ate it. "So, Big Daddy, how often do you bring your lady friends here to *relax?*"

His brows slanted. "I don't."

"Ever?" she asked with surprise.

"Ever." He emphasized his response with a hard cut with the knife.

"Why not?"

"I don't form attachments to the women I hook up with. I don't bring them to my penthouse, and I sure as hell wouldn't lavish them with trips to my investment properties."

"But I'm here." She snagged another piece of melon.

He stopped cutting, giving her his full attention. "Have I not done a good job of showing you how special you are?"

"No. You have."

"Are you worried about me sneaking off to be with other women behind your back?"

"No. I don't think you'd do that. I just don't know much about your personal life. I guess I'm curious."

"Then let me fill you in. Other than you, I haven't formed a romantic attachment with any woman since college, and I respect you too much to ever do anything behind your back." He put a handful of strawberries on the cutting board and began slicing them. "So you can leave your worries behind, and as far as my daily life goes, which you didn't ask about, but I'd imagine you wonder about, there's not much to tell. I work a lot. Any other questions?"

She shook her head. "I've never been the jealous type, but I guess I am with you." She ate a strawberry.

"You're not alone in that. If JP had hit you on purpose, I would have murdered him, and you'd be visiting me in prison."

"Not until after the tour," she teased. "Do you come here often?"

He set down the knife and poured them each a cup of coffee. "You don't need a cheesy pickup line. I'm a sure thing." He added cream and sugar to hers and set the mug in front of her.

She rolled her eyes and sipped her coffee, which was perfect. She'd been surprised the first time he'd made her coffee at her apartment and had wondered how he'd known the way she liked it. But he was like that, always figuring her out.

"Come on. How often do you come here?"

"Not very," he said, and went back to cutting the fruit.

"Why not?"

"I'm usually working, and when I get time off, I tend to visit my family. With Harlow in LA, my parents in Boston, and Aria on the Cape, it takes time to see them. And now that Johnny's living in Maryland, I'll be going there to see Zoey and their new babies."

"I don't know how you can stand living that far from everyone." She ate a piece of melon and picked up another piece, holding it out for him. He ate it from her fingers. "I don't think I could do it. I hate that Pepper is so far away and that Axsel and Morgyn travel so much."

"If I had my way, we'd all live within twenty minutes of each other." He threw a handful of blueberries into the fruit mix and began taking eggs and other things out of the fridge. "Do omelets sound okay?"

"Sounds delicious."

"Is there anything you don't eat? Cheese? Spinach? Tomatoes?"

"Healthy omelets," she teased. "Actually, I eat all those things. I just haven't had one in forever."

He began making the omelets. "You mentioned having breakfast with your parents, but how often do you see your sisters and Axsel?"

"I only see Axsel two or three times a year because of his schedule. I see Pepper more. Maybe eight or ten times a year. But breakfast is a family affair at my parents' house. I go once or twice a week, and everyone who can be there usually is, husbands included. I need that, and I know that's weird for someone my age, but it is what it is."

"I don't think it's weird. I think it's nice. Family is everything, and Oak Falls is where your heart is. I can't see you ever moving away from there."

*I always thought it was where my heart was, but now you own a piece of my heart, too.*

She sat with that thought for a minute, letting the truth of it settle in before responding to him. "Me either. I love being around the people who know me and love me for *me*. Even when they drive me batty. The same way you like being close to your family. It's comforting knowing I'm there if they need me. I love seeing the mountains and horses in one pasture, cows in another."

"And small-town life?"

"I like it, despite the gossip. I like that at any time of year there's a barn bash right around the corner. I love knowing everyone will be there, dancing and teasing one another. I love that Grace's and Brindle's kids will grow up together, and they'll be close to their grandparents and their favorite aunt." She flashed a cheesy grin.

"That sounds like a lot to love. What about you? Do you want a family one day?"

She thought about that for a minute. "Know what's funny?

A full-time guy in my life was never on my to-do list, but a family of my own has always been there. What about you? Is New York your place now? Do you think you'll ever want to live anywhere else or have a family?"

He plated the omelets and put them on the island. "That's a big question." He grabbed forks and napkins and sat on the stool beside her.

"Too personal?"

"No, just big." He took a drink. "New York isn't where my heart is. It's where my business is. I can see myself moving away at some point, and there was a time when I wanted a family."

"Pre-vengeance?" she guessed.

"Exactly. I haven't thought about it in a long time."

She found herself hanging on in his silence, wanting to know if children were in his future, but when he didn't say more, she let them both off the hook. "No pressure. I was just curious." She took a bite of her omelet. The cheese melted in her mouth, bringing the other flavors to life. "This is delicious. You make an excellent houseboy."

He turned on his stool, swiveling hers and bringing her knees between his. "And you make an excellent bedmate."

"Is that what I am?"

He kissed her softly and stayed close, speaking just above a whisper. "I think you know you're a hell of a lot more than that to me."

# Chapter Twenty-Nine

THE DAY WAS moving too fast for Kane. Deloris called while they were eating breakfast, and Sable had spoken to her for a long time. He'd seen a weight lift from her shoulders, but he knew she was worried about how to handle things with her bandmates. He figured she'd talk about it when she was ready and tried to help her relax. The trouble was, neither of them was very good at doing nothing. They tried lying in the sun again, but both got antsy after a few minutes. They ended up jumping in the pool, playing around *and* fooling around. No complaints there. He couldn't get enough of her. They showered and went downstairs to play a game of pool. Sable was a lot better at it than he'd anticipated, which made it even more fun.

It was midafternoon, and they were walking hand in hand on the private beach below his house. There was a gentle breeze as the waves kissed the shore, and their bare feet left tracks in the cool, wet sand. He wanted more of this. More time with Sable when they weren't under a fucking microscope. Not having to hide their relationship showed him just how right they were together. It uncapped a well of emotion, and he wondered how either of them were going to rein them in when they went back to reality tomorrow.

Sable touched a shell with her toe and gazed out at the water. "I've always been a creek and mountain girl. I never saw the appeal of beaches, but I'm starting to understand why people are so enamored with them."

"It's the ocean. My mother says it soothes the soul. She says it washes away bad mojo and confusion, bringing clarity and making room for better things."

"It sure has for me." She bumped him with her shoulder. "I realized I like you a little."

"Is that right?" He squeezed her hand, loving the way she took baby steps in sharing her heart.

"You must have spent a lot of time at the beach when you were growing up."

"I did, with my family and friends. I surfed with my buddies, and we went to bonfires a lot."

"That sounds like fun, but you said you don't love small towns. Did you not like living there?"

"I liked my friends, but I couldn't stand the gossip."

"I get that. I hated gossip until this tour."

"Why until the tour? Isn't that the primary reason we're hiding our relationship? To keep you out of that realm?"

"Yes, but I meant Oak Falls gossip. When my sisters text me about what's going on back home, I feel closer to everyone."

"You really miss being there, don't you?"

"More than I thought I would. I never thought I'd say anything positive about the grapevine, either."

"Were you ever the focus of town gossip?"

"No. I think people have always been afraid to talk shit about me."

He laughed. "That's not a bad thing."

"What about you?"

"I guess I wasn't scary enough. I made the mistake of bringing that girl I dated in college home for a weekend right before we broke up. After that, it seemed like every time I went home, some well-intentioned friend would ask about her. But you know how people are. They didn't just ask. They *pushed*, wanting to know every little detail. I stopped going home so often for a while after that."

"That would be tough. Did you miss your family?"

"Yes, and some of my friends. But not as much as I hated answering those questions. My ego took a pretty big hit with that breakup."

"I'm sorry. I've never been in that position, but I've been there to pick up the pieces for my sisters when they have. At least you've recovered nicely, and if you ask me, you dodged a bullet. I hate materialistic users."

"Really?" he teased. "You hide it so well."

She bumped him with her shoulder, smiling. "What you see is what you get with me."

"I like that about you. That level of honesty is rare these days."

"I like it about you, too. If you took away the gossip, do you ever miss the Cape?"

He thought about the town where he'd grown up and those well-intentioned friends. "I guess I miss being surrounded by people who like me for me and not what I have. The people there did. They still do. I see them when I visit Aria, but it's not the same as it was."

"It's not the same or you're not the same?"

That gave him pause. "Good point, Montgomery. It's more likely me." His phone rang. He pulled it out of his pocket and saw a video call from his mother. "It's my mother. I should take it."

"Of course."

He gave her a quick kiss, reluctantly released her hand, and stepped away as his mother's face appeared on the screen. "Hi, Mom. How are you?"

"I'm good, honey. I just hung up with Johnny. He said he sent you to look after Sable. Is she okay?"

He glanced at Sable in her sexy cutoffs and T-shirt, dipping her toes in the water. "Yeah, she's good. The band just needed a break from each other. You know how touring is."

"It's no wonder. I never understood how Johnny and the boys could maintain such a crazy schedule."

"It's all part of the business," he said. "How are you and Dad?"

"We're great. Where are you, sweetheart?"

"At my place in Punta Mita."

"With Sable?" Her eyes brightened. "How *interesting*."

*Shit.* He tried to cover his tracks. "She needed privacy."

"Of course she did, and bodyguards would never take as good care of her as you can."

"Exactly." Catching himself, he said, "I mean, things were stressful. We didn't think she should be alone. But I have security watching the grounds."

"I'd expect nothing less." Her eyes narrowed. "Is that Sable behind you?"

He looked at the image of himself on the screen and saw Sable shielding her eyes from the sun, gazing out at the water. "Yes, that's her."

"Can I say hello? Or would that be uncomfortable?"

It would be wildly uncomfortable, but it would only make her more curious if he told her that. "No, it's fine." He headed for Sable, and she turned with a question in her eyes. He lowered the phone. "My mother wants to say hello. Do you mind?"

She whispered, "Does she know about us?"

"No. She thinks I'm just here in case you need anything." She looked a little nervous but agreed to say hello. He lifted the phone so they could both see his mother's face. "Mom, this is Sable Montgomery. Sable, this is my mother, Jan."

"Hi, honey," his mother said excitedly. "Johnny and Kane have told me so much about you."

"And you still wanted to meet me?" Sable joked.

His mother laughed. "You are a spitfire. I like that. Is Kane taking good care of you?"

"Yes. He's quite the host." Sable eyed him. "Very *generous*."

He squeezed her ass, and she made a surprised *squeak* sound.

"Are you okay?" his mother asked. "What happened?"

"Sorry. I seem to have attracted a pest." Sable gave him a cursory *thanks a lot* glance.

His mother looked between them, eyes alit with curiosity. "A good swat usually goes a long way."

"I'll try that next time," she said.

"Are you getting any rest, Sable?" his mother asked.

"Yes. It's beautiful here, and it's nice to be away from the stress of the tour," Sable said. "I even got in two good pool workouts."

*Christ.* She was playing with fire, and he was having a hard time keeping a straight face.

"Oh, you're a swimmer, like Kane?" his mother said. "How wonderful."

"She has a good, hard stroke." *Paybacks are hell, Panthera.* "Much better than mine."

Sable stifled a laugh. "I don't know about that. You had all the right moves, although I did beat you to the finish line. *Twice.*"

Laughter bubbled out, and Kane coughed to mask it.

"That's surprising," his mother said. "Did Kane tell you he was the breaststroke champ in high school?"

Kane and Sable burst into hysterics.

"*What* is so funny?" his mother asked.

"Sorry, Mom." Kane tried to quell his laughter. He looked at Sable with a question in his eyes—*Can we tell her?* That sobered her up, and she gave a small nod. He was so grateful, he slid his arm around her, drawing her closer. "Mom, I've got something to tell you. Sable and I are seeing each other, but no one knows, so please keep it quiet."

"*Finally,*" his mother exclaimed. "I didn't know how much longer I could keep up that act. Especially with you two flirting the whole time."

"You knew?" Sable asked.

"A mother always knows when her children are hiding things. I knew weeks ago, at Jillian's launch."

"Why didn't you say something?" Kane asked.

"I did, honey. Does *failed enterprises* ring a bell?"

Her voice trampled through his mind. *I worry that you've worked so hard for so long to protect that generous heart of yours, you've forgotten that not all failed enterprises are precursors for what's to come.* That statement had given him the courage to take that final leap with Sable and call her even if it meant he might get hurt. "I remember." He met Sable's gaze off-screen and could tell she was thinking about that night, too. "That was a special night."

"*Good gracious.* You two have more chemistry than a lab,"

his mother said, making them all laugh. "I'm so happy for you both. Kane, I'm glad you finally cleared your mind enough to let your heart lead the way, and, Sable, I look forward to getting to know you and meeting you in person."

"Me too." Sable glanced at him. "You raised a pretty incredible son."

"Thank you. I was so happy when we found out we were pregnant and scared to death about doing things wrong. But Kane was an easy baby, which allowed me to learn without all the chaos of colic and other typical baby troubles. Given the man he is, I think he was taking care of me as much as I was taking care of him back then."

Kane warmed at her praise.

"That sounds like him. The great protector," Sable said.

"He's always been that way. Kane, I have to tell your father about you two. He's going to be home any minute, and he's going to know something is up the second he sees me. You know I can't lie worth beans."

"I know, and that's fine. I'll tell Harlow and Aria, but please don't tell anyone outside our family. It'll put Sable in a bad position."

"I promise I won't," she said. "Now, give me all the details. Not the dirty ones, but how long have you been smitten with each other? When did this start?"

Kane laughed and shook his head.

"What?" his mother said. "I've been waiting a lifetime to see that look in your eyes."

"I'm happy to share the details," Sable said. "I don't know about Kane, but for me it started the second I saw him standing on the side of the road looking pissed off. He was quite a sight. It was purely physical, of course." She smirked. "But then he opened his mouth, and I wanted to smack him."

They all laughed.

"Oh, *Kane*. What did you do?" his mother asked.

"*Me?* She practically took my head off."

"*Please*. You were quite the Casanova." Sable looked at his mother. "Can we talk about his use of *sweetheart?* I mean, really."

His mother laughed and looked over her shoulder. "Oh good, your father's home. Hi, honey, come here. Kane's on the line, and he's with Sable."

The happiness in his mother's voice was contagious. Kane pulled Sable closer and kissed her.

"Whoa. What's going on here? Kane's *smooching* Sable," his father said with a laugh.

"Hey, Dad," Kane couldn't stop smiling.

"Hi. When did this happen? I mean, I'm thrilled, but...*wow*," his father rambled, and they all laughed.

They talked for a long time and had each other in stitches. Before they ended the call, he caught an approving nod from his father. He didn't need it, and if he hadn't gotten it, it wouldn't have changed his feelings for Sable. But hell if it didn't feel better than any pat on the back ever had.

SABLE COULDN'T HAVE asked for a more perfect day. She'd loved meeting Kane's parents. They were warm and funny and had taken the time to get to know her. They'd asked about her family and the auto shop and had commiserated about how hard it was to be away from them. Kane seemed freer after talking with them, and Sable felt that way, too. It was hard keeping their relationship to themselves. But it was worth it.

They'd had a great afternoon. Kane had taken a number of business calls, but he'd handled them in stride. He tried to wait on her hand and foot despite her protests, bringing her drinks and fruit and making them lunch. They had been running on little sleep and had caught a nap in the late-afternoon sun. She'd fallen asleep on his chest and had woken up two hours later to Kane, relaxed and happy, working on his laptop beside her.

They cooked a shrimp and pasta dish for dinner and ate it on the terrace while watching the sunset, talking about everything and nothing at all. They'd taken a moonlit walk on the beach, during which Kane kept her tight against his side. Now they were on the patio with music playing, and she was sitting between his legs on the double lounger with her back against his chest, flames from the firepit dancing in the darkness. Kane had kept her close all day, and she was thankful. She wanted to savor every second they had together. She wasn't looking forward to pretending they weren't crazy about each other and sleeping separately again. Nestled in the safety of his arms, she could almost forget she had a world of trouble waiting for her in Seattle.

"Thanks again for meeting my parents. I think we made their day."

"It kind of made mine, too. I really like them. Your mother is really funny, and your father is such a charmer."

Kane held her tighter. "He can turn it on when he wants to."

"The way they teased each other reminds me of my parents. Your dad looks at your mom like he's crazy in love with her."

"He is."

"I love that. I know it was scary for all of you when you found out she had cancer, but I can't imagine how terrifying it was for him, thinking he might lose the love of his life."

"He looks at her differently now than he did before her diagnosis."

The emotion in his voice had her wrapping her arms over his and turning so she could see his face. "Like he doesn't want to live a single day without her?"

"He's always looked at her like that," he said softly. "I can't explain it. It's like he fell in love with her all over again when he realized he might lose her."

"He probably did. How long have they been together?"

"Since their first day of college. My mom was trying to find a class, and he walked her to it. The way they tell the story, they fell in love on that ten-minute walk across campus."

"I'm always amazed when I hear stories of couples who have been together that long. It must be a generational thing. I can't imagine falling in love at eighteen and staying together. I've changed so much since then. Although Brindle and Trace have been together since they were teenagers, and Grace and Reed were secret teenage sweethearts. So what do I know?"

Kane pressed his cheek to hers, his scruff tickling her skin. "Does that mean the dirty-little-secret thing runs in your family?"

"*No*. Grace and Reed went to rival high schools. He was a football player, and she was a cheerleader."

"Yeah, yeah. A likely excuse."

She felt his heart beating sure and steady against her back. "Can we just stay right here for the rest of the tour?"

His arms tightened around her. "Worried about seeing the guys tomorrow?"

"A little. I thought Tuck would reach out by now."

"He obviously needed the space. It's not too late for you to reach out to him."

"I think this is a conversation that should take place in person."

"Maybe that's what he's thinking, too. Hopefully everyone will be less uptight tomorrow. When I spoke to Johnny earlier, he seemed to think things were calming down."

"Good." She exhaled with relief. "Then let's not talk about it. I don't want to spend our last night together stressed."

"Sure. But you know partners are supposed to lean on each other. You might feel better if you talk about it."

She looked up at him again. "Is that what we are? Partners?"

His lips quirked, and he kissed her. "As long as you're mine, you can call us whatever you'd like. I just want you to know you don't have to deal with this on your own. I'm here and happy to talk about it."

"I appreciate that, but I'd rather not talk about it."

"Okay. In that case, I know the perfect way to help you relax." He patted her hip. "Stand up."

"Usually *I know the perfect way to help you relax* is followed by, *lie down* or *take your clothes off.*" She pushed to her feet and followed with a devilish grin.

"I was getting there." He leaned in and kissed her. "Take your clothes off. I'll be right back."

"You want me to strip while you ...*what?* Make a phone call? Strike a business deal? Take over a hotel chain?"

He pulled her into his arms. "I'm going to get some massage oil so I can help you relax."

"Massage oil?"

"Yes. Why do you sound so surprised? I had my staff pick

some up for us. You do like massages, don't you?"

"I don't know. I've never had one."

"You're kidding. *Never?*"

She shook her head. "I don't like strangers touching me."

He arched a brow, amusement shining in his eyes.

She shoved him playfully. "You know what I mean."

"If I'd known that, I would've been giving you massages this whole time."

"You've been depleting me of tension in *other* ways."

"I'm not done doing that yet. We've got to stock up for the weeks to come." He adjusted the lounger so it was lying flat. "Get naked and lie down, baby. Let these hands work their magic."

She undressed as he headed inside and was lying on her stomach, warmed by the fire, when he returned a few minutes later. She watched him slow his gait, admiring her as he approached, those dark eyes growing hungrier by the second. She couldn't resist teasing him and wiggled her butt. "Is this what you had in mind?"

"Yes, but I don't know what I was thinking."

"I *do.*"

"Believe it or not, I wasn't thinking about sex. I just wanted to pamper you."

He'd been using that word a lot, and he was really good at pampering. She'd never felt so spoiled. But what she loved most about this time together were things that surprised her, like sleeping in his arms, holding his hand, making him laugh, and just being with him without the stress of hiding. "Sex with you *is* pampering me. You're all about bringing me pleasure."

"That's because pleasuring you is *immensely* pleasurable for me."

He moved her hair away from her shoulders and poured oil into his hands, rubbing them together as he straddled her, and began massaging her shoulders. His strong hands slid over her skin, warming it with the oil. She closed her eyes, reveling in the luxuriousness of his touch. She sighed as he kneaded the tension out of her shoulders and neck.

"That feels so good."

"You're all knotted up. I'm going to work it a little harder. Let me know if it hurts."

She moaned as he worked the knots from her shoulders, lingering on certain areas that caused a little pinch, but then she'd feel the knot loosen, the stress she didn't realize she carried, fading away. "Feels so good."

He rubbed and caressed his way down her back, massaging away from her spine. He was so thorough, working muscles she hadn't realized were tight, drawing moans and other sounds of relief and pleasure she couldn't hold back. "You're killing me, baby," he gritted out as he took off his shirt and tossed it aside. His hot hands moved over one hip, his fingers pressing into her flesh, loosening knots there. He rubbed her ass with the same strong, sensual touch, turning her on, coaxing more sighs and moans. As he massaged and caressed her ass and upper thighs, his fingers trailed between her cheeks and thighs in a mind-numbing rhythm. She spread her legs wider, lifting her hips, giving him better access, and hoping for more.

"*Christ*, baby. I'm trying to behave."

"So am I," she said breathily. "But you make it impossible. It feels too good when you touch me."

He slid one hand around her waist, and she lifted her hips again. He teased her where she needed it most. His mouth found her pussy, and she sucked in a breath, desire building with every slick of his tongue, sending titillating sensations up her core. She lifted her hips higher, wanting more, earning a sexy growl.

"You taste so fucking sweet." He spread her ass cheeks, licking from one entrance to the other. "*Kane.*" She clutched the chair as he licked her harder, his fingers moving faster. "*Feels so good. Don't stop.*" He quickened his efforts, every flick of his fingers and slick of his tongue taking her closer to the edge. She closed her eyes, lost in a world of sensations, soaking in his hungry sounds. She was panting, dizzy with desire. When he pushed a finger into her ass, she shattered and cried out, rocking her hips with the excruciating pleasure coursing through her. He gripped her hips, relentlessly devouring her as shuddering moans tore from her lungs.

Just as she started coming down from the peak, he got up and took off his shorts, then came down behind her on his knees, driving into her pussy in one hard thrust. She cried out, and he grabbed her by the waist, pounding into her, sending pleasure rocketing through her. The pleasure was so exquisite, she wanted to live in it. She begged him not to stop, willing herself not to come again, trembling with her efforts to resist her release. But her demanding man slowed his pace, dragging his cock out until only the head was inside her, then pushing in slowly, heightening the sensations every time he hit that magical spot inside her. "Kane, *please.*" Her toes curled under, and she clung to the edges of the chair. He continued his slow, sensual invasion until she couldn't think, couldn't beg, could only *feel* the want and need swelling inside her, like she was one big bundle of nerves. "It's time for you to come for me, baby. Come on my cock. Show me how much you like it." He reached around her, zeroing in on her clit, catapulting her into a world of dark and light, hot and cold. Ecstasy so all-consuming, she was lost in it. He stayed with her, pumping and grinding as she soared on clouds of pleasure, and held her there.

She was floating, her body tingling as he kissed her spine, murmuring against her skin. "You're so fucking beautiful." He withdrew from between her legs, and she whimpered with the loss, stuck in a post-orgasmic haze. "Straddle me, baby. I want to watch you ride me."

He lay down, holding her gaze as he helped her straddle him. She sank down on his hard length, pleasure radiating outward through her core. He reached up and stroked her cheek. "I'm so damn lucky. Fuck me, baby. Fuck me like I'm yours." Spurred on by his greed, she started moving slowly, using his chest for balance. "That's it, baby. God, you feel good. Ride me harder. Faster." He was so thick, at that angle the sensations were almost too much to take. He palmed her breasts and teased her nipples, squeezing hard enough to make her pussy clench. "*Fuuck.*" He used his fingers on her clit, taking her higher, as she rode him. Every move, every stroke and touch, intensified the need building inside her, until it was all she could do to remember how to breathe. He worked her clit faster, sending lightning searing through her. Her fingernails dug into his chest as she surrendered to another whirlwind of pleasure.

This time when she came down from the high, he lifted her off his cock. "Lie down, baby. I need to be closer to you." She lay on her back in a blissful state, reaching for him, *needing* him. He laced his fingers with hers, holding them beside her head as their mouths and bodies came together. He kissed her deep and sensually, gyrating his hips in slow circles, then thrusting and gyrating again. His moves were intense, measured, *purposeful.*

She tried to keep up with the sensations engulfing her. He broke their kiss, gazing so deeply into her eyes, emotions thickened between them. He gradually increased their pace, magnifying every sensation. They were both barely breathing, their bodies moving without thought or direction. Just when she was on the verge of coming, he slowed them down again, putting her through the same exquisite torture. Needy sounds fell from her lips as pressure mounted inside her. His jaw tightened as he took them higher again. She rocked her hips, begging for more. His eyes turned feral, and he released her hands. They both went wild. Their hands were everywhere at once. She clawed at his shoulders, hooking her heels around the backs of his legs. He pushed his hands beneath her ass, angling her so he could take her impossibly deeper.

"*I'm gonna...Ohgod*—" The edges of her vision went dark as her orgasm hit like a freight train. He was right there with her, gritting out her name through clenched teeth, hips pounding, fingers digging into her flesh as their bodies thrashed and bucked, until they'd given all they had and collapsed in each other's arms.

Sable felt high. Her skin tingled. Her mind was hazy and happy. Her heart felt full as Kane cradled her beneath him, dusting kisses over her lips and cheeks, his handsome face coming back into focus. His dark eyes mirrored the emotions that felt like they'd bored into her bones.

"Welcome back, beautiful."

She managed a smile, wishing they could stop time and stay in that moment forever. "I like the way you pamper me."

A gravelly laugh tumbled from his lips. "That's good, because I love pampering you." He rolled them onto their sides, keeping their bodies flush, and rasped against her neck, "How am I supposed to go back to acting like you don't mean *everything* to me?"

He kissed her then, slow and sweet and delicious, as if he hadn't just sent her heart tumbling down a dangerous hill.

# Chapter Thirty

AS THE PLANE descended toward Seattle, Kane felt Sable tense up beside him. He'd been tense the whole flight. He could walk into any company and figure out how to take it over, take it apart, and make it better, but he had no fucking idea how he was going to pull off acting like there was nothing between him and Sable. He'd damn well find a way to make it happen. He'd do anything to protect her. He wanted a future with her. He may not know how or where, but if they could make their relationship work on this fucking tour, nothing could come between them.

He took her hand, drawing her worried eyes to his. That familiar clench gripped his chest. "Breathe, baby. It'll be fine." He laced their fingers together and pressed a kiss to the back of her hand as the plane touched down.

She nodded but didn't say another word as they taxied along the tarmac. She drew her shoulders back, inhaling deeply. *Righting her armor.* "Thank you for yesterday."

*It was the best day of my life.* He leaned in and kissed her, their phones chiming as service returned and messages rolled in.

"Back to reality," she said as they pulled out their phones.

He had about a dozen messages from Shea, Johnny, and the

rest of his family. He opened Johnny's first in case there was trouble with the band. A number of screenshots popped up from *TMZ*, *Page Six*, and other gossip sites, showing a succession of pictures of him and Sable on the tarmac in Mexico—Kane helping her out of the car, another of his hand on her back as they went to board the plane, and a picture of her looking over her shoulder at the top of the landing and him leaning in, kissing her just before they'd boarded. He was vaguely aware of Sable saying, "*Ohmygod. No. Nonono,*" but blood was rushing through his ears as he scanned the headlines.

THE GIG IS UP: BAD INTENTIONS MANAGER KISSES
SURGE LEAD SINGER ON PRIVATE JET
BEDDING MR. BAD: DID SABLE MONTGOMERY
SLEEP HER WAY TO STARDOM?
HOW SURGE REALLY GOT THE GIG

Rage burned through Kane, growing hotter and sharper with every word.

He'd fucked up. He was supposed to protect her, and he'd been so caught up in the moment when Sable had turned to him and said, *Maybe you can stow away on my bus,* he hadn't thought twice before kissing her.

"Fuck. Sable." He looked up and saw tears in her eyes. His gut seized, and he said, "Baby, I'm sorry about the pictures in the press. I wasn't thinking." At the same time, she said, "Grace had a miscarriage," and tears spilled from her eyes.

"What?" they said in unison.

"*Grace miscarried.*"

"Shit. Baby, I'm sorry." He pulled her into his arms, his heart breaking for her and for Grace and Reed. How the hell was he going to tell her about the press with this on her shoulders? "Let's get you home."

"I can't *leave*. We have a concert tonight. What did you say about the press?"

His heart hammered against his ribs. "Someone got a picture of us kissing as we boarded the plane."

A pained sound fell from her lips. "I only read my mom's message about Grace." She frantically scrolled through her messages, her face crumpling and hands trembling. "*Ohmygod—*"

"I'll shut it down and take care of it. I'll sue their asses if I have to."

"That's not going to change what people think," she snapped, pushing to her feet. "I *knew* I shouldn't have gone. This whole thing is one big mistake."

He stood as she paced the aisle, the anger and sadness brimming in her eyes slaying him almost as much as her words did. They weren't a fucking mistake, but he couldn't deal with that right now. He had to take care of her and get her home. "It's my fault and I'll take care of it, but don't get lost in the bullshit. Focus on what matters. Do you want to be with Grace?"

"*Yes*, of course. But the band is already pissed at me, and with *this*." She waved her phone. "Tuck will *never* forgive me." She swiped at her tears.

"What's more important, placating them or being with Grace?"

"*Grace.*"

"Exactly. We're going to Oak Falls. Tuck can take the lead at tonight's concert. I'll call Johnny and Tom and work it out."

"You can't go," she snapped. "It'll make everything worse."

"If you think I'm letting you deal with this on your own,

you're wrong."

She lifted her chin, and he could tell it was taking a herculean effort to try to keep it from trembling. "I can take care of it myself."

"Don't you fucking get it? I *know* you can take care of it yourself. You can fight with Tuck and take a punch and deal with whatever else this damn tour or life hands you. But I'm in *love* with you, Sable, and damn it, I *know* you're in love with me. And when you love someone, you don't let them walk across a battlefield alone even if they're armed with shields and AK-47s. You *become* their shield, you *become* their guns, and you battle and win the fucking war *together*."

"Don't…" She continued pacing the aisle, shaking her head. "You can't say that."

"I absolutely can, and I meant every word of it."

"*Kane*, my life is blowing up." Her voice escalated. "My sister is hurting, and I'm a million miles away from her. My band is pissed at me, and the whole world thinks I fucked my way onto that stage." She was shouting, wearing a path in the aisle. "Now my family has to watch as my reputation is dragged through the mud. I can't handle *this*"—she motioned between them—"on top of everything else."

He stepped in front of her, and she crossed her arms, pressing her mouth into a firm line. Her eyes narrowed angrily, but they were so full of love and pain, they practically bathed him in it. As he stepped closer, he swore her gaze softened for an instant before hardening with a warning. He wanted to shake her out of the place she retreated into, pull her into his arms, and tell her they'd figure it all out. But he wouldn't do any of those things because he recognized her reaction. It was like looking in a mirror before he'd met her, when he'd lived within the confines of his own protective armor and had shored up his walls when things got hairy.

"*Fine*," he said evenly. "I'll table it for now, but this isn't me giving up. It doesn't change a damn thing."

She swallowed hard, lifting her chin again.

The move was so very fucking *Sable*, his chest constricted. "I'm going to arrange for Tuck to take the lead tonight and make a call to Shea about the other mess, and then you and I are going to Oak Falls."

She opened her mouth to speak, but he cut her off. "Don't bother trying to change my mind. My plane. My rules."

# Chapter Thirty-One

THE DRIVE INTO Oak Falls was tense and silent as Sable
fielded texts from her family and friends. Chris and Lee had sent
well-wishes for Grace and Reed, but she felt their resentment
toward her in their curt messages. JP and Tuck hadn't even
tried to mask their resentment. JP had said, *You and Kane? Hope
you enjoyed your Mexican vacation. Who the fuck are you?* and
Tuck's message only made her feel worse. *Now you're just like
every other lying asshole?* Kane wasn't pushing her to talk, and she
was grateful. She'd forced herself to read more of the headlines,
but they infuriated her so much, she wanted to rage at everyone
who was speculating and spreading lies about her. She had to
diffuse her anger before seeing Grace, and she didn't want to
take it out on Kane.

She glanced at him behind the wheel as they pulled down
Grace and Reed's tree-lined driveway, and her heart hurt. Kane
had been beyond good to her during the flight, and she had no
idea why after the way she'd shut him down. He'd sneakily
taken care of her, despite her telling him she didn't need
anything. She hadn't caught on at first, when he'd gotten up to
get a drink and had said he could pour her one if she'd like, or
later, when he'd gotten a sandwich for lunch and had simply

placed half of it in front of her and said he wasn't hungry enough to eat the whole thing. He'd gotten himself a pillow and had said it bothered his neck, and she'd taken it. She still hadn't caught on at that point. But when she'd woken up with a blanket draped over her and the window shade pulled down, with Kane wide-awake beside her, his hand on hers, she'd realized he'd been giving her the space she demanded, while making sure she was getting what she needed, despite her bullheadedness.

She hated herself for the way she'd handled things with him, but she didn't have the bandwidth to deal with those emotions then, and she sure as hell didn't now. She was barely holding it together.

He parked by her parents' and Pepper's cars, and gazed up at the old Victorian, his dark eyes roaming over the gingerbread trim, wide front porch, and octagonal tower anchoring one side. "That's a beautiful Painted Lady."

"Reed remodeled it for them. According to Grace, they used to dream about living here when they were teenagers."

"I guess some dreams do come true." He gazed into her eyes, and she was sure he could see her clashing thoughts and inner turmoil. "Are you ready to go in?"

*No* was on the tip of her tongue, but tonight wasn't about her. Shoving her pain and anger down deep, she nodded.

"You still can't lie worth shit." He kissed her and reached into the back, grabbing the flowers he'd bought for Grace and Reed.

Sable ached anew for their loss.

He must have seen it in her eyes, because he handed her the flowers and caressed her cheek the way he'd done so many times, his expression solemn. "She'll be glad you're here."

"I know," she said softly.

"I'm sorry they're going through this. Hopefully it'll happen for them at some point, and if it doesn't, there are other ways to build a family."

She nodded, her throat thickening. She remembered how long he'd said it had taken his parents to get pregnant with Johnny and how many years they'd tried before adopting Harlow and Aria. As he climbed out of the car, she hoped it wouldn't take Grace and Reed that long. She opened the door and stepped out as he came around to do it for her.

He arched a brow. "Are we starting at square one again?"

"No. I'm just anxious." Why was she fighting letting him take care of her?

He drew her into his arms, his eyes searching hers. What was he looking for? Answers? How could he find any when she didn't even know the questions?

"Give them my best, and stay all night if you'd like," he said. "I'll be out here if you need me."

"You came all this way. You don't have to wait outside."

"I'm here for *you*. Grace and Reed don't need extra people hanging around, and I need to do some damage control for both of us."

As he walked her up to the door, she realized how selfish she'd been, and her stomach sank. "Are *you* okay? I've been so worried about Grace and the band and the bullshit, I didn't think about how the bad press affects you."

"Don't give that another thought. I don't give a fuck what anyone says about me."

"But you have a reputation to worry about with your business associates."

"It's none of their business what I do with my personal life, and if they have an issue with it, they can fuck off. I don't want you worrying about me or the press. I'll get my arms around the situation, and together we'll figure out how we want to handle it. But tonight is about being with your family. So, as my mother would say, *clear your mind, and let your heart lead the way.* Grace needs you, and you need to be with her." He kissed her forehead and descended the porch steps.

Sable dragged air into her lungs, trying to suppress the emotions he stirred and push aside all the other chaos in her mind. She drew her shoulders back, and as she'd done a million times before, gathered all her strength for Grace. She knocked once and pushed open the door. "Grace?" she said, stepping inside.

"In here," Pepper called out.

She headed through the archway into the living room and found Grace sitting on the couch in a T-shirt and sweats, her thick dark hair tied back in a low ponytail, her feet propped up on Pepper's lap on the other side of the couch. Grace smiled, but when her green eyes met Sable's, the pain in them nearly brought her to tears, reminding her of all those years ago when Grace and Reed had broken up just before they'd graduated from high school. Grace had confided in Sable about their relationship, and she'd been so devastated, Sable had had serious concerns about how her sister could possibly survive such heartbreak.

She found herself wondering the same thing now.

Pepper moved Grace's feet, concern written all over her face as she hurried over to Sable in stylish white capris and a red top. Her golden-brown hair fell over her shoulders as she threw her arms around Sable, holding her tight.

"Hey, Pep." Sable embraced her, struggling to hold herself together.

"I missed you," Pepper said against her cheek.

"I missed you, too."

Sable set the flowers on the coffee table beside an enormous gift basket overflowing with teas, honey, a leather journal, cookies, a candle, a fuzzy blanket, and who knew what else and went to sit on the edge of the couch beside Grace. "I'm so sorry, Gracie." She wrapped her in her arms, embracing her as tightly as Pepper had held her. They didn't speak, didn't rush to pry apart, or move at all beyond the embrace. Just as Sable had done years ago, she took her cues from her older sister, letting Grace have whatever time or energy she needed.

"I can't believe you're missing a concert to be here," Grace said.

"*Please.* Entertain a hundred thousand people or support my big sister? That's a no-brainer."

Grace sat back, smiling, but it was a sad smile. "Thank you for the gift basket. That was really thoughtful, and these socks are super comfy." She lifted a fuzzy-socked foot and wiggled her toes.

Confused, Sable looked at the basket and plucked the card from it. *Grace and Reed, I'm so sorry. I know how much this pregnancy meant to you. I love you. See you soon. Sable.* Her heart swelled. The gift had Kane's thoughtfulness written all over it. Why didn't he tell her? *Because he handed me his heart and I stepped all over it.* She felt like she was going to cry again. Biting back those feelings, she set the card down. "I'm glad they got the card right."

"I'm really happy you're here," Grace said.

"I'm sorry I couldn't get here sooner. I was on the other side of the country."

"We heard," Pepper said, sharing a knowing glance with

Grace as she sat down and put Grace's feet on her lap again.

"We *also* heard about you and Kane," Grace said.

"You and the rest of the world." Sable was having a hard enough time trying *not* to think about the man who'd turned her heart inside out and the accusations surrounding them and hold her shit together for Grace. She didn't need to test her limits, so she went for a subject change. "Where's Reed? And Mom and Dad?"

"They went for a walk," Grace answered. "I know they worry and they mean well, but I was feeling smothered."

"I get it. Did you hear from Axsel?" He'd texted Sable and had tried to talk her off the ledge, but she hadn't been in the mood for it. "I know he wants to be here, but he had a gig he couldn't get out of."

Grace nodded. "He called, and we talked for a while. He's worried about you."

Sable sighed. "I'm fine."

"It's true, then?" Pepper asked. "You and Kane are together?"

"I think we need to focus on Grace right now. What do you need, Gracie? Do you want to talk? Do you want anything to drink? A snack?"

"Thanks, but I don't need anything," Grace said. "People have been doting on me all day. I'm sad and I'm angry, and I'm probably going to feel that way for a while. One day I might want to talk about it, but right now I could really use a distraction."

"And I could use some answers," Pepper urged.

"I get the whole distraction thing, but can't we talk about your play or something else?" Sable asked.

"Nothing else is as important as you," Pepper said.

"How can you think my personal life is at *all* important with what Grace is going through?"

"I think a better question is how can you think it's not important?" Grace asked. "You've never had any kind of love life. At least not that I've known about, and now it seems like you do have one and it's been publicly exploited in the worst way."

"We're worried about you. People are saying horrible things," Pepper said.

"Thanks for the reminder." Sable pushed to her feet and paced.

"Brindle and Morgyn are up the butts of all those internet trolls, commenting on everything they can and setting the record straight," Grace said.

"This is a lot to handle, even for you," Pepper said. "Don't you want to talk about it?"

"*No. I'm fine.*"

"That's just like you," Pepper said.

Sable stopped pacing and crossed her arms. "What's that supposed to mean?"

"It means you'll go to the ends of the earth for any of us, but you won't give yourself the same support." Pepper started rubbing Grace's feet. She always fidgeted when she was nervous.

"I'm not like you guys. I don't need to hash out my crap."

"It's not *crap*," Pepper said. "This is your life, and you're important to us."

"You've always been. Just because we don't normally push you to talk doesn't mean we don't care." Grace's brows knitted. "Brindle said she thought you and Kane were together on Valentine's Day when he came to town. Were you?"

"Yes. So what?" There was no sense in denying it, no matter how much she hated anyone knowing her personal business.

"We've been together since the end of January, when I went to New York."

Pepper's eyes widened. Grace's brows knitted, and her jaw dropped.

"*What?*" Sable snapped.

"It's *May*," Grace said. "You've been with him for all these months and you didn't tell anyone?"

That stopped Sable cold. *May?* Everything had been such a chaotic blur since she'd first met Kane, she hadn't even realized it had been so long.

Pepper's brows knitted. "Are you okay?"

"*Fine.* It's just…Time doesn't really exist on the tour. It's like one long span of performing, being mobbed by fans and the media, and endless traveling. I didn't realize we'd been together for so long."

"You must really like him," Grace said.

Sable looked at the sisters who had trusted her with their deepest secrets for as long as she could remember, and for the first time in her life, she wanted—*needed?*—to share her own. They'd trusted her with so many things over the years, and she didn't want them to think she didn't trust them. Mustering a kind of courage she'd never tapped into before, she said, "I do. I like him a lot." *Way more than a lot.*

"That's great," Pepper said. "Does he feel the same about you?"

"Yes." She got choked up saying it, and she had no idea why. But it felt so good to finally tell someone the truth, she proceeded to tell them about how he'd come to see her before the tour started and how they'd been sneaking around while on tour. She told them about their all-night texts, how awful she felt about lying to Tuck, and about fighting with the rest of the band, and how Kane had stolen her away to Mexico and had taken care of her there. Then she told them how he'd sneakily taken care of her on the plane and had fought to come with her tonight.

"No wonder you like him so much. He sounds amazing and like he's as bullheaded as you are," Pepper said.

"He is," she said with a soft laugh. "But he's always looking out for me, so he probably has to be since I'm not exactly good at backing down. And, Grace, I wish I was the one who sent you that basket, but it was Kane. He didn't even tell me he sent it. Not that I blame him. Between the press and wanting to get home, I was a mess. He probably feels like he's walking on eggshells around me right now."

"I'm sure he understands," Grace said.

"Most guys wouldn't think about sending anything, especially if you were already headed home," Pepper added.

"Reed and I really liked Kane," Grace said.

"From what I heard, so did everyone else," Pepper added. "Not that we were talking about you before the news broke."

"*Actually*, we kind of were," Grace admitted.

Sable blew out a breath. "Why were you talking about *us*?"

"It wasn't bad. Reed said when he was giving Kane a tour of the theater, Kane asked about the band and Deloris and our family. Not in a stalkerish way or anything. Reed said he seemed genuinely interested in learning more about you and your life here."

"Why didn't you tell me?"

"Because every time I've *ever* tried to talk to you about your personal life, you'd bite my head off. I'm shocked you're talking about it now."

Sable opened her mouth to deny it but couldn't. "Sorry I'm

not more of a talker."

"It's fine," Grace reassured her.

"I would be more worried if he *hadn't* asked about you," Pepper said thoughtfully. "I'm sure there are tons of women trying to bed the billionaire. I think he's smart to try to find out as much about you as he can."

"*Bed* the billionaire?" Grace laughed. "Nobody says bed *anything* anymore, Pep."

"Yes, they do," Pepper insisted.

"Bang the billionaire, bag him, snag him, fuck him," Sable suggested. "Anything but *bed* him."

Pepper looked between them a little sheepishly. "Didn't you guys see the headlines? BEDDING MR. BAD: DID SABLE MONTGOMERY SLEEP HER WAY TO STARDOM?"

Sable's stomach roiled. "I read so many headlines, they all blurred together. I've *never* used sex as currency, and as far as that visit in February goes, *he* showed up on my doorstep that weekend. It wasn't like I chased him down. He knows I don't give a crap about his money."

"We know you didn't sleep your way into the job, Sable," Grace said.

"And anyone who knows you knows you don't care about money," Pepper added.

"I know. But I haven't made things easy for him. When we first met, I gave him all sorts of crap about everything."

"It's good to hear you treat him the same as everyone else," Grace teased.

"It's hard to believe he's stuck around, isn't it?"

"No," Grace said. "You're every man's wet dream. A gorgeous musician who loves sex and fixes cars."

"It's harder to believe that you let him stick around," Pepper said.

"Yeah, that baffles me, too." Sable was only half teasing. She was still trying to wrap her head around what he'd said on the plane, and she hoped her sisters could help her do that. "He said he loves me."

"Oh, *Sable*." Grace beamed.

"I'm so happy for you." Pepper ran over and hugged her.

"Let's not make a big deal out of it." Sable shrugged her off.

"Why not?" Pepper asked carefully. "You don't feel the same or think you could fall in love with him?"

"It's not that. I'm just not wired like you guys. I'm not good at relationships. I don't like relying on other people. I like my independence and the freedom to be here for all of you without someone else telling me if I can or not or making me feel bad." Even as she said it, it felt wrong in a way it never had. She started pacing again.

"You can be independent and still let someone in without giving them control of your life," Grace said. "Look at me and Reed."

"I thought I could," Sable admitted. "When it's just the two of us, I want *more* time with him, and I can see us together in the future. I have no idea how or where, but that doesn't matter, because when the plane touched down and we found out about what happened to you, and about the press, all I wanted was to shut him, and everything else, out and get here."

"When you texted earlier, I thought you said he was driving you here from the airport," Pepper said.

"He was. I wanted to be here, but I wasn't sure I could miss the concert. He refused to let me stay for it. He called Johnny and the tour manager and made arrangements for Tuck to sing, and he wouldn't let me come here on my own. He's outside right now, trying to figure out what to do about the press. He said he'd stay out there all night to be here for me."

Grace and Pepper exchanged confused glances.

"Sable, it doesn't sound like he's trying to take away your independence," Grace said softly. "It sounds like he's watching out for your best interests by taking you to Mexico to make sure you didn't burn out and taking care of your heart by getting you home."

"I know he is. But I can't just let someone else handle things for me or take care of me. I'm not wired like that."

"That has nothing to do with your wiring," Pepper said.

Sable gave her a deadpan look. "How can you say that? You know I've always been different."

"No, you haven't. You let..." Pepper looked at Grace, then back at Sable with a secret message in her eyes. "*Someone* in a long time ago. You're just afraid to do it again."

"I've never been afraid of anything." Sable crossed her arms.

"You're not afraid of much," Pepper said. "But you're afraid if you're in a relationship, you'll be so focused on yourself, you won't be there for us."

Sable rolled her eyes. "That's not true. I've just never wanted a relationship."

"Yes, it *is*," Pepper whispered insistently. "Remember the night of the accident?"

"What accident?" Grace asked.

Sable glowered at Pepper. She'd never forget that night. "This has *nothing* to do with that."

"It has everything to do with that," Pepper insisted.

"Would someone please clue me in?" Grace snapped. "Are you talking about Sable's car accident? When you guys were in high school?"

"Yes," Sable said, eyes locked on Pepper. "I made a stupid mistake that night, and it has nothing to do with this."

"No, you *didn't*," Pepper said firmly. "I made the mistake, and I never realized how it affected you until last week, when a friend of mine told me about something similar she'd gone through and how it had affected her. Think about it, Sable. You stopped sneaking out to meet Tuck the next night."

Sable tried to swallow past that jagged truth.

"You used to sneak out to meet Tuck?" Grace asked.

Sable narrowed her eyes at Pepper.

"You guys are driving me nuts," Grace snapped. "What does the accident have to do with any of this?"

"That's when she changed," Pepper said softly.

"No, it's *not*." As she said it, that night came rushing back. She remembered the excitement of getting Pepper to agree to go to a party at the creek and the desperation she'd felt when convincing her to drive home alone so she could meet Tuck in the barn. Pepper hated parties almost as much as she hated driving at night, but Sable had *needed* to be with Tuck so badly, she'd have sold her soul to the devil to make it happen. Chills ran down her back as memories of Pepper's frantic phone call slammed into her. Sable could still feel her lungs burning as she'd sprinted two miles to the site of the accident and the gut-wrenching devastation she'd felt at the sight of their car crumpled against a tree, blood splattered on the broken windshield, and Pepper, shaking and terrified, huddled by a dead deer in the long grass. She'd almost lost Pepper, and for what? Because she was selfish. She'd ended things with Tuck the next day and had vowed never to make that same mistake again.

*Holy shit.* Maybe Pepper was right.

"Yes, it is," Pepper insisted. "And it's my fault."

"No. It was my fault. I should've been there."

"Been *where*? You were driving the car when you crashed," Grace said.

Sable looked at her, her stomach twisting into knots, but she'd kept Pepper's secret this long. She wasn't going to give it up now. "Nowhere. Let it go. It doesn't matter."

"Yes, it does." Pepper sat beside Grace and said, "I was driving. I made a mistake, and Sable covered for me by saying she was driving, and she's been paying the price for it ever since."

As Pepper told Grace what had happened all those years ago, Sable relived every moment, wishing she could go back in time and change what she'd done.

"It was an accident, Pepper," Sable said. "And it wouldn't have happened if I hadn't been so selfish."

"That's *not* true." Pepper lifted sorrowful eyes to her. "I lied about the deer. It didn't run into the road, like I said it did. I got a text, and my phone was on the passenger seat. I only took my eyes off the road for a few seconds to reach over and grab it, and when I looked up, the deer was *right there*, just standing in the road. I couldn't go around it because I was driving too fast. I was reckless."

Sable wanted to fight against it. She wanted to protect Pepper, erase the memory, and make the lie the truth. That would be a lot easier than believing she'd gone her whole life keeping her heart under lock and key because of a selfish teenage decision, misplaced guilt, and a fucking text.

# Chapter Thirty-Two

KANE CALLED SHEA again to see what had transpired over the last few hours. Then he called his parents, Aria, and Harlow to try to settle his family's worries. He ended the last call and pocketed his phone, cursing himself for the hundredth time for taking that kiss when they were boarding the plane. He turned at the sound of voices and saw Sable's parents and Reed walking across the grass toward him. Marilynn and Cade were holding hands. He'd assumed they were inside with the girls. He waved and went to meet them on the front walk.

"Kane, how nice to see you again." Marilynn leaned in for a hug.

"I wish it were under different circumstances."

"We all do," Cade said, and surprised Kane by leaning in for a hug, too. "Thanks for bringing Sable home."

"Of course. She needed to be here." He turned to Reed, knowing nothing would take away the pain or sadness he must be feeling. "I'm really sorry about what you and Grace are going through." He offered his hand, and when Reed took it, he pulled him closer and clapped him on the back. "I'm here if you need another ear."

"Thanks. I appreciate that. Did Grace kick you out, too?"

"No. I thought I'd give Sable some alone time with her, and I needed to make a few phone calls. How is Grace doing?"

"About as well as can be expected," Reed said. "We tried to manage our expectations, but that's hard when you've got all this love for each other, and suddenly your dreams of sharing it with a baby look like they're coming true."

"I can't imagine how difficult this is for you. I know you've got the support of family, but if I can do anything, please let me know."

"Thanks. I think I'll check on Grace. Excuse me."

As Reed headed up to the house, Kane turned his attention to Cade and Marilynn. "I want to apologize for how my relationship with Sable came to light. I'm in the process of trying to manage that nightmare, and I assure you, I'll do everything I can to protect Sable and your family and make sure the truth gets out."

"Thank you, but we're worried about you and Johnny, too. Will this affect your relationship or your business?" Cade asked.

"No. I was up-front with John before Sable and I went to Mexico. He supports us, and I won't let it affect the business. What can I do to help your family get through this?"

"Oh, honey, this isn't our first rodeo," Marilynn said. "Axsel suffered keyboard warriors, too."

"That must have been rough," Kane said.

"It wasn't easy, and I think Sable was even angrier than Axsel. He was upset, but he doesn't have the same visceral instincts Sable does. She wanted to hunt down everyone who had hurt him and take them out," Cade said with a laugh.

"I swear she feels her siblings' pain deeper than her own. Why don't we sit on the porch." Marilynn motioned to the chairs on the porch. After they sat down, she said, "When she and Pepper were infants, Sable would scream and cry at night, and we'd try everything to calm her down: feeding, changing, pacing the floor with her. Cade even took her out in the car, thinking the vibration would help her sleep like it had with Grace, but nothing worked. I was at my wit's end, and one night I put her in the crib with Pepper so I could grab a fresh diaper, and within seconds, she stopped crying. She wiggled closer to her sister and put her arm around her, happy as a clam."

"*We* didn't get any sleep," Cade added. "We stayed up all night making sure they didn't block each other's airways. But eventually we figured it out, and they slept in the same crib until they got twin beds."

"And then every morning we'd find Sable in Pepper's bed with her arm around her."

Kane laughed. "I can see her doing that. One of the biggest reasons she didn't want to do the tour at first was because she wanted to be here in case anyone needed her."

"That's our Sable," Marilynn said. "She's a handful, but she loves fiercely."

"I can sum up our girl with one Christmas story if you have a minute." Cade and Marilynn exchanged humorous glances.

"I've got all night. I'd love to hear it."

"It was the year their grandmother passed away, and the kids had all been rather prickly, as you can imagine. They'd gotten into some trouble and thought they were on Santa's naughty list. They got the idea that they'd wait up for Santa and bake him cookies to sweeten the pot. They laid out sleeping bags and thought they had it all figured out."

"That meant Cade had to buy a Santa outfit on the sly," Marilynn pointed out.

"We had a good plan," Cade said. "I was going to traipse by the window in my Santa suit so the kids would see me. I'd jingle a few bells, get up on the roof and stomp around a bit, and then Marilynn would tell them Santa wouldn't deliver presents until everyone's asleep."

"But you know what they say about the best-laid plans," Marilynn said. "While the kids were safely tucked into their sleeping bags watching a movie, I went upstairs to wrap Cade's presents and take a bath, and Cade went to the barn to change into his Santa suit. But it took me a little longer than I anticipated because my sister called."

"I came up the hill with a big red sack full of hay over my shoulder and dutifully traipsed by the window jingling my bells. I was feeling pretty darn good as I climbed up the ladder and tossed the sack onto the roof. But as I stepped off the ladder, a flashlight beam blinded me."

"Oh man. Sable?" Kane laughed.

"Who else?" Cade said. "I couldn't see her face at first. She was crouched real low beside a big cookie tin, and she was blinding me with the light, so I stayed in character and said, *Ho, ho, ho!* I thought she'd say something like *Caught ya! I knew there was no Santa Claus.* But my little spitfire had other plans. She said, *I've got thirty cookies, a handful of Hershey's kisses, and twelve lollipops. That's five cookies, some kisses, and two lollipops for each kid. That should make up for the bad things they did. You can keep me on the naughty list, but my sisters and brother need presents. They didn't mean to be bad, and I won't let you ruin their Christmas. Do we have a deal, or do I need to show you who's boss?*"

Kane laughed.

"She wasn't kidding," Cade said. "She sounded pissed, and

she meant business. There I was, hoping she doesn't fall off the roof, and at the same time, in awe of my little girl for taking care of her sisters and brother and throwing herself under the bus."

"What did you do?" Kane asked.

"For a second I just stood there, trying to figure out how Santa would respond, and *that's* when she stood up, and I reacted. I said something like, *Don't move,* and went to grab her so she wouldn't fall. But she saw my face and said, *You're not Santa.* I tried to play it off, disguising my voice, but she didn't buy it. Then she really *was* pissed because she didn't know how she was going to convince Santa if she couldn't meet him. So I did the only thing I could. I came clean about Santa Claus and told her that all kids do bad things and not to worry. Everyone was getting presents."

"And she told him *they damn well better,*" Marilynn said with amusement.

"Now, *that* sounds like Sable," Kane said. "Did she spill the beans about Santa to the other kids?"

Cade shook his head. "She'd never burst their bubbles. She kept the secret and let each one discover it for themselves." He reached for Marilynn's hand. "We did something right with her."

"Or she turned out great despite us," Marilynn teased. "Sable is resilient. She'll find her way through this media mess, and she'll probably hurt for a while for Grace and Reed, but she'll work through it."

"She won't have to battle any of it alone," Kane reassured them. He didn't know where Sable's head was right now, but even if she claimed she couldn't handle their relationship on top of everything else, there was no way in hell he'd walk away. "I know she's strong, but the type of accusations that are going around aren't easily deflected, even by the thickest-skinned celebrities. Part of me wishes she'd never accepted the offer to go on tour. But the world would have missed out on a spectacular entertainer, and I would have missed out on"—*the love of my life*—"a very special woman."

The front door opened, and his beautiful, troubled girl walked out, eyes downcast, looking emotionally drained. He wanted to gather her in his arms, buffer her from the grief billowing off her like the wind, and anchor her from her own storm of anger at the press when it finally rose to the surface, which it would at some point. But he held back, not wanting to add more pressure to her already overloaded heart.

She looked up, spotting her parents first, and it was as if her next step carried her into a suit of armor. Her shoulders squared, and inner fortitude rose in her eyes. He recognized that determination to be strong at the worst of times all too well and knew the weight it carried. He wanted to take that away, too, and show her she didn't need to be strong all the time. The irony in feeling like Iron Man and wanting to show a woman who was just as strong and stubborn as he was that she didn't need to be Wonder Woman was not lost on him. She looked at him, and that shored-up resilience gave way to a glimmer of relief that had him pushing to his feet, the knots in his chest loosening ever so slightly.

"Sable, sweetheart," Marilynn said as she and Cade stood, and she drew her daughter into her arms.

"Hi, Mom." Sable closed her eyes.

She so rarely allowed herself to step away from being the strong one, Kane was captivated by the sight of her soaking in the comfort only a mother could give. She was passed from her mother's loving arms to her father's, and she did the same thing, closing her eyes and allowing herself to soak in his strength. What a sight that was. Kane hoped she'd allow him to be that strength for her, too.

"How're you holding up, honey?" Cade asked.

"I'm good," she said too strongly, and then softened a little. "Just sad for Grace and Reed."

"We all are, and we're worried about you, too," Marilynn said.

"Don't be. I'm *fine*." Sable crossed her arms, eyes briefly flicking to Kane. "You know I don't care what people say about me."

*Oh, baby, how I wish that were true.* But he realized he didn't really wish it were true. He liked her sensitive side, and he wouldn't change a damn thing about her. He just wanted to protect her.

"The people who love you know the truth, and we're all very proud of you." Marilynn hugged her again.

"Why don't we see how Grace is doing and give these two some privacy?" Cade suggested.

As they headed inside, Kane went to Sable and opened his arms, but he didn't reach for her, allowing her a choice. A flash of hesitation shone in her eyes before she stepped into them. He gathered her close, holding her as she pressed her cheek into his chest and breathed deeply. He kissed the top of her head, holding her tighter, and felt her clutching the back of his shirt.

"Are you okay, baby?"

She nodded against his chest. "It's just so unfair. Grace and Reed would be incredible parents. I wish I could make it happen for them."

"I know you do. Listen, I know we have a lot to talk about with what's going on with the media and the band and the things I said, but all that can wait. If you want to stay with

Grace, or you need some space and want me to get a room at the bed-and-breakfast, just say the word."

"And hand you over to Lucy so she can pimp you out to her daughter?" She tipped her face up, eyes narrowing. "Sorry, Mr. Bad, but you're not getting away that easily."

"I never said I wanted to get away. I want to make sure you have what you need, and if that means giving you space, I can deal with it. But don't think for a minute I wouldn't be on your doorstep at dawn."

"At *dawn?*" She grinned.

"I figure you'll be texting me all night, trying to coax me back into your bed because you know, you've been a little spoiled, and you'll probably go through withdrawals. But I know how you are. You don't like things that are too easy, so I'd hold out until dawn. Then all bets are off."

"You think you've got me all figured out?"

"Not even close, but I'm learning."

Her expression turned serious. "I thought I had myself figured out, but I learned some things tonight, and now I'm not so sure."

"Isn't that what life is about? Learning and growing and *becoming?* I didn't think I wanted a woman in my life, but then you came along and made me realize I just hadn't wanted the *wrong* woman in my life."

She pressed a kiss to his chest. "I'm sorry for how I acted earlier and for what I said. I was overwhelmed and worried about Grace."

"It's okay. I understand." He took her hand, and they sat on the steps. He put his arm around her, holding her close. "I'm not easy to deal with, either."

"I never said I wasn't easy."

He arched a brow.

She smiled, and then her expression turned thoughtful, and she was quiet for a moment. "You were right about what you said on the plane."

*Thank God.* "That's a pretty broad stroke. I'm afraid you're going to have to be a little more specific."

"You know what I'm talking about."

"That you can take a punch?" he asked teasingly.

"*No.*"

"That you can deal with whatever life hands you?"

She leaned into him. "Do you really need to hear me say it?"

"I think I might," he whispered.

"*God*, you're a pain." She met his gaze, and he could practically hear her giving herself a pep talk.

"It's okay, babe. Don't force it." He leaned in to kiss her.

"I don't have to *force* it. I feel it. I'm just…"

"Afraid to say it?"

"You had it easy. You were frustrated, so it came out in the heat of the moment."

"You think that was easy?" He scoffed. "It was torturous."

"That's not very romantic."

He laughed. "Do you want romance, or do you want the truth? Because I know if this were easy, we'd both have walked away a long time ago. You and I are a different breed. We need mountains to climb."

"So you're hoping things never get easier?" she asked carefully.

"I'm hoping after the tour things will get easier logistically. A long-distance relationship isn't ideal, but we made it work before the tour, and we're both too stubborn to let a few hundred miles ruin a good thing. But I also know that as one aspect of our relationship gets easier, one of us will be stubborn about something else. There's nothing easy about us. That's just who we are." He slid his hand to the nape of her neck. "I fell in love with a stubborn, rebellious, wild child." He threaded his fingers into her hair. "And you fell in love with an arrogant, competitive asshole. We feed off each other, and that will never change." He tightened his grip on her hair, tugging her closer. "Are you hoping things will get easier?"

She shook her head. "I love who we are."

He feigned a wince. "So close and yet so far."

"I can't make it too easy for you," she teased.

"Such a temptress." He lowered his mouth to hers, kissing her like he'd been dying to do all afternoon, and then he kissed her longer, to settle the worries in her mind and heal the hurt in his heart.

"Why didn't you tell me you sent Grace that beautiful basket?"

"I'd already stepped in a bear trap. I wasn't about to pull it tighter."

Worry rose in her eyes. "Was I that bad to you?"

"No, babe. You were that bad to yourself. Withholding all this"—he motioned to his body—"from the woman I love?" He shook his head. "That was a dick move."

She laughed. "I can't believe I'm going to say this to a man who just called me a dick, but *God* I love you."

His heart filled to near bursting. "Enough to bribe Santa when I'm naughty?" He pulled her onto his lap.

"I can't believe they told you that story."

"Why? There's nothing better than my fierce girl taking on Santa. So, what do you say? Will you have my back and bribe Santa for me?"

She wound her arms around him. "I'll have your front, your back, and every other part of you. Now give me that mouth."

He laughed as he lowered his smiling lips to hers.

# Chapter Thirty-Three

SABLE TOOK KANE'S hand as she stepped from the car in front of her parents' house for breakfast. Everyone would be there except Grace and Reed. Grace told them last night she wasn't up to a family gathering. As they walked past the other cars in the driveway, Sable thought about how different things were with Kane now than they'd been in February, when he'd shown up on her doorstep. They'd been like ravenous animals then, devouring each other in every room of her apartment like they'd never get another chance. Last night hadn't been all that different, because that's who they were, and she loved that about them. But afterward, as they lay tangled together, talking about everything from what they were going through to how they wanted to try to make their relationship work after the tour, she felt the difference.

There was an ease about them despite the media issues they had yet to handle, and she knew it was not only because they'd shared their true feelings but also because they no longer had to hide their feelings. Somehow, now that people knew about them, she felt like they were a team, buffered from the rest of the world in their own little bubble of debauchery, challenges, and love. Maybe *partners* was the right word after all, because after years of flying solo and loving it, she couldn't imagine being any happier than she was with her smart, sexy, irresistibly arrogant copilot.

"Are you sure you're ready for this?" she asked.

"What do you mean? I've already met everyone."

She'd introduced him to Pepper last night, and they'd stuck around for a while. Pepper had asked him a dozen questions, and he'd had a chance to talk with Grace and extend his sympathies. He'd told her and Reed what his parents had gone through when they were trying to have their family, and they seemed to appreciate hearing it. When Sable had hugged Pepper good night, she'd whispered, *He's so special. Please let yourself be happy.* Sable hadn't been able to stop thinking about those words. She'd always been protective of her family. Even before the accident that had snapped her out of her selfish teenage phase and had led to her ending things with Tuck and becoming even more vigilant about protecting them. But she hadn't realized she'd built such solid walls around her heart. Those walls had been reinforced for so many years, she knew it wouldn't be easy to change, and she wasn't sure how much she wanted to. She liked who she was, and apparently so did Kane, but she'd felt both of them changing for a while now, and she had a feeling that's what people meant when they said to let nature take its course.

"Yes, but not as my scorching-hot boyfriend."

He laughed. "Is that what I am now?"

"I'm afraid so."

He pulled her closer and kissed her. "Bring it on."

They headed inside, and the noisy chatter and familiarity of her family gathered around the breakfast table brought a smile.

"Sable!" Amber exclaimed, sparking a flurry of activity as

everyone got up to greet them.

"Kay!" Emma Lou popped up from the floor where she was playing with the dogs and toddled over to Kane with the dogs on her heels.

"Hey, princess." He scooped her up, and she threw her arms around his neck, pressing her tiny lips to his cheek.

"She's definitely your daughter, Brin," Sable said, making everyone laugh as hugs were shared, and handshakes and claps on the back were exchanged. While her family headed back to their seats, Sable glanced at Kane, talking with Emma Lou as she petted his scruff and chirped, "*Doggy?*"

"Did my daughter just call you a dog?" Brindle asked.

"Like Sable said, she's your daughter," Pepper teased.

Emma Lou wriggled in Kane's arms. "Down!"

He set her down, and Sable picked her up and hugged her before she could toddle back toward the dogs, earning the sweet little-girl giggles she'd missed. "Love you, Em." She set her down, and she scampered off to play.

"Sable, Kane, come sit down and eat. I'll get you coffee." Her mother pushed to her feet.

"I've got it, Mom," Sable said.

Kane reached for Sable's hand. "Want help?"

"No. It'll only take a second."

He tugged her into a kiss, and Brindle cheered, which made the girls laugh, and the guys start catcalling.

Sable rolled her eyes. "Idiots."

"Might as well give them an encore." He pulled her in for another kiss, making her laugh as more cheers rang out. "I like this not hiding stuff," he said for her ears only.

"Me too." She had a niggle of worry about how they were going to deal with the press. They'd talked about it, but she was still on the fence about whether or not they should address it. She went to get them coffee as Kane headed over to the table.

Dash pushed to his feet, blocking Kane's way. "So, Bad. You're pretty good with kids. Have you got any of your own?"

"No," Kane answered.

"You mean none that you *know* of," Dash said.

"*Dash*, what are you doing?" Sable asked as she carried their coffee cups to the table.

"Oh boy. Here we go," her father said.

Dash flashed his too-big grin. "Someone's got to look out for you."

"Put that toddler grin away. I can take care of myself, thank you very much." Sable shook her head.

"Sable's got a lot on her plate right now," Trace said as he and Graham pushed to their feet, staring down Kane as they flanked Dash. "She doesn't need whatever brand of BS you're bringing to the table."

"But my brand of BS is so good," Kane said. "It'd be a shame for her to miss out on it."

Her family stifled laughter. Sable loved that he played right into their banter.

"Have you got any crazy exes we need to worry about storming in here?" Graham asked.

"Just a couple, but I think Sable can take 'em." Kane winked at her.

Brindle stalked over to him, all proud-of-herself attitude in her cute floral dress and cowgirl boots, and planted her hands on her hips. "Sable has a heart bigger than the moon." She poked him in the chest. "Break it, and I'll break your pretty-boy face."

Kane held his hands up in surrender. "Now I'm shaking in

my boots."

Everyone burst into hysterics.

"All right, you've had your fun." Sable gave the guys playful shoves toward their seats, and as she pulled Kane down to the chair beside her, she said, "Sorry about that."

"Don't be," Kane said. "That was almost as impressive as this feast." He motioned to the platters of eggs, bacon, pancakes, toast, fruit, and biscuits on the table.

"Thank you, Kane," her mother said.

Her father lifted his coffee cup as if he were toasting. "Good job holding your own with these guys."

"I've been the interrogator a few times," Kane said, passing a platter of eggs to Sable.

"Does that mean your family is nutty, too?" Amber asked. "Sable interrogated all three of these guys."

"Which is why I'll never bring a date home," Pepper said.

"That would require having a date," Morgyn teased.

"Just because you don't hear about my dates doesn't mean they don't happen." Pepper sipped her coffee.

Sable nudged Kane. "We might need to make a pit stop in Charlottesville on the way back."

Her family chuckled, and Pepper gave her a deadpan look.

"Kane, how long are you in town?" Trace asked.

"We're going to see Deloris after breakfast, and then we have to leave," Kane answered. "We're meeting the band in Portland for tonight's concert."

Sable was not looking forward to facing *that* firing squad.

"Did they know about you two?" Graham asked.

"No, and they're pissed, but that's my fault. It was my choice to keep it a secret," Sable said.

Kane reached for her hand, giving it a squeeze. "We thought

it was best, given that we were working together and that Surge was not very well known when they got the offer."

The kitchen door opened, and they all looked over as Axsel walked in, shaggy dark hair curling at the ends, hazel eyes dancing with mischief. "Axsel!" their mother exclaimed.

"Hey, y'all. Look who I found along the way." Axsel beamed as Grace and Reed walked through the door, looking tired but happy to be there.

There was more commotion as everyone got up to greet them. Sable was aching to get her arms around her little brother, but she let everyone else hug him first, and she went to Grace. "Did *chill boy* drag you here against your will?"

"No!" Axsel said loudly. "I gave her a choice."

Reed scoffed, but he was grinning. "He told her she could come to breakfast, or he was going to camp out in the living room and invite everyone over."

"That *is* a choice," Axsel pointed out as he petted the dogs and gave Emma Lou a squeeze.

"I wanted to hide in my bed for the next month," Grace said as Reed slid his arm around her. "But Axsel reminded me that I don't need to pretend that I'm not sad when I'm here, because you guys love me anyway."

"Always, baby doll," their mother said, her love-drenched gaze moving over each of her children. "Our love is unconditional, and we're so glad you decided to come."

There were murmurs of agreement and support as Kane made his way back to Sable, and lowered his voice, speaking into her ear. "Your family is pretty damn special."

"I know how lucky I am." She saw Axsel heading their way. It was hard to believe he was almost twenty-five. He'd changed so much in the last few years. He no longer looked like a lanky kid sliding into manhood. His gray T-shirt was stretched tight over his broad chest. His jaw was sharper, eyes still as kind as ever, but wiser.

A sly grin curved Axsel's lips, those hazel eyes moving between her and Kane. "You done good, sis. Are you going to introduce me to *Big Daddy?*"

Kane grinned and offered his hand. "Kane Bad, it's a pleasure."

"The pleasure is *all* mine." Axsel pulled him into a hug. "Hurt her, and *she'll* castrate you."

Kane winced.

"Don't worry. I'll be there to console you." Axsel winked.

"Get over here, twerp." Sable hauled him into a hug as her father and the guys put an extra leaf in the kitchen table and brought in more chairs from the dining room. "I missed you, but I'll still kick your ass."

"I have no doubt," Axsel said. "How are you holding up with all that shitty press?"

"I'm fine." She didn't want to get worked up, so she changed the subject. "Good job getting Grace here."

"She needed to be here," Axsel said. "But she paraphrased what I said. She was worried about being sad around us, and I told her that we love *you*, and you're not exactly Little Miss Sunshine, so she needed to get her ass out of bed and come see everyone."

"Of course you did," Sable said as they took their seats.

Axsel sat across from her and Kane. "All kidding aside, Kane, you must be a hell of a man to have hooked this one's heart. Please be careful with it." He looked lovingly at Sable. "I wouldn't be where I am professionally, or who I am personally, without her."

"*Aw,*" Morgyn and Amber said in unison.

"You'd be great with or without me in your life," Sable said.

"Yes, but not as great," Axsel said thoughtfully. "You showed me how to be strong in so many ways. You're the one who gave me the courage to tell everyone I was gay."

"It's not like we didn't know," Pepper said.

"Yeah, you were always checking out guys," Morgyn agreed.

"That doesn't mean it didn't take courage to come out," Axsel said. "You guys have always been supportive, but Sable knew my secrets from the time I was really young and confused. I had some really hard times, and she was always there to help. She showed me that I was just as awesome as everyone else, and when I got hurtful press that made me want to climb into a hole, she checked in with me every day, sometimes talking with me for hours."

Kane squeezed her hand again, and she realized how much she loved all his support and affection, from the knowing glances to the warm embraces.

"I didn't know you guys talked daily," her mother said.

"Neither did I," Pepper said, and everyone else chimed in with the same.

"That's because Sable doesn't do things for pats on the back," Axsel said. "She does them out of love. So, Sable, while you're dealing with the media storm, I hope you're asking yourself the same thing you told me to ask myself."

Sable's throat thickened.

"What was it?" Grace asked.

Axsel held Sable's gaze. "She said, *Who are you living your life for? Those smug, attention-seeking a-holes, or yourself?* When I said I was living for myself, but I couldn't take knowing people were saying horrible things about me, she reminded me that the opinions of the people in this room right now are the only ones that matter."

"It's true," Sable said, reminding herself as much as him.

"It sure is." Axsel looked around the table. "She followed that up by saying if y'all didn't like me, then you could go to hell, but she made her point."

Soft laughter rose around them.

As her family discussed the ups and downs of social media and the importance of family, Sable looked around the table at the people she loved most. She knew how much she'd missed them, but she hadn't realized how much she'd needed to not only get her arms around Grace and the rest of her family but also to simply be in their presence, soaking up their teasing banter and unconditional love. They didn't give her hell for keeping her secret, and the way they welcomed Kane into the fold of their family filled her with strength, giving her the answers she was searching for.

She took out her phone and leaned closer to Kane. When he turned those love-drenched eyes on her, she kissed his smiling lips and took a picture of them.

A collective "Aww" rang out from her sisters. "Send me a copy of that," Pepper said, and the rest of the family asked for the same.

Sable looked at the picture, floored by the joy and love in their eyes. It was no wonder Tuck had called her on it. She showed it to Kane and said, "Mind if I post this on social media?"

His grin told her his answer before he even said, "Go get 'em, Panthera."

Excitement bubbled up inside her. "Brin, I need your help." She handed Brindle her phone. "JP put the band's social accounts on all our phones, but I've never used it. Can you post this picture for me?"

Brindle's eyes lit up, and she snagged the phone. "Yes!"

"Now, *that's* the Sable I know," Reed said.

"What's your hashtag?" Trace asked.

"I know!" Brindle exclaimed. "What do you like better, *Sane* or *Kable?*"

Sable made a face. "Neither."

"Come on. Every cool couple has one," Brindle pleaded. "Trace and I were Team Trindle. Remember?"

"No. I'm not going to be reduced to a hashtag. Forget it." Sable held out her hand, motioning for Brindle to give her back the phone.

"Fine, no hashtag," Brindle relented. "What do you want it to say?"

"It's my life. Fu—" She looked at Emma Lou and said, "Eff off."

"*Sable,*" Amber chided. "You'll infuriate fans."

"They're not fans if they're not supportive," Kane pointed out, and winked at Sable.

"Tell 'em, Big Daddy," Axsel chimed in, making everyone laugh.

"Wait, I have a better idea for a caption," Sable said. "Just write *Loving life and this man.*"

"Perfect!" her mother said.

Sable looked across the table at Grace and Reed and thought about what was going on with her band and about Deloris's declining health and having to sell her house and realized she couldn't post that, either. "*Wait.* That's not right with what Grace and Reed are going through and everything else that's going on right now. I'm not loving certain parts of life."

"You're always putting everyone else first," Grace said sweetly. "You could do this just for yourself, and it would be fine."

"No, I can't. It would be a lie."

"How about just posting the picture with a middle finger emoji?" Axsel suggested. "That'll get your point across."

"Now, *that's* perfect," Sable said.

As Brindle posted the picture and everyone chatted excitedly, Kane pulled Sable closer and said, "I think I just fell even more in love with you."

"Maybe I'll have to start giving people the finger more often."

# Chapter Thirty-Four

SABLE'S VISIT WITH Deloris had been bittersweet. She'd had to reintroduce herself several times, and Deloris had spoken about Lloyd as if he were still alive, but at least she hadn't gotten scared when she'd forgotten who Sable was. Things were changing so fast, Sable wanted to put on the brakes. But at the same time, she couldn't wait for the tour to be over. The trouble was, she wanted it to be over so life could go back to normal, and the normal she knew no longer existed.

She and Kane had just arrived at the hotel in Portland where they were meeting the guys, and she was a nervous wreck. The long plane ride had given her too much time to think about lying to Tuck and keeping her relationship with Kane from all of them.

"Are you sure you don't want me to go with you to tackle the conversation about us?" Kane asked.

"I'm positive. It would come across as us against them, and that's the last thing any of us needs."

He nodded, his jaw tightening as he pulled her into his arms. "I hate that you're in this position."

"I'm not loving it, either, but I put myself here. I can handle it." She stepped out of his arms despite wanting to stay right there, where she felt stronger and safer. "I'd better get going."

"Where do you want your luggage? My room or yours?"

"It's so weird that we have that option now. Can you have them put it in mine, please?"

He cocked a brow. "You sure about that?"

"Yes." She paused long enough for him to nod curtly, before adding, "Feel free to put yours there, too, but just remember, my room, my rules."

Those devastatingly dark eyes narrowed, and his grin turned wicked. "Feeling controlling, are we?"

"Not at this moment, but I don't know what I'm walking into. My claws may come out later, and you might need an escape route."

"Fat chance. I look forward to it." He pressed his lips to hers in a hard kiss. "Go get 'em, babe."

She made her way to Tuck's room and took a deep breath, telling herself not to get riled up. They were all at fault, and she needed to take responsibility for her part. She knocked on the door, and several nerve-racking seconds later, Tuck opened it. She'd hoped there might be a modicum of ease between them, but his normally soulful eyes were cold, and he didn't say a word as he stepped back, allowing her to walk past.

Her muscles corded tight as he closed the door behind her and followed her in. Her nerves prickled as she took in Chris's solemn expression as he leaned against the dresser, JP standing by the window with his back to them, and Lee sitting by the table, long legs outstretched, arms folded over his chest. Lee lifted his chin in acknowledgment, but there was no warm welcome there.

Chris pushed from the dresser. "How's Grace?"

"She's not great, but she'll be okay." *Kind of like me.* "Sorry

I had to take off so quickly."

JP turned around, eyes shooting daggers. "Are you?"

"*Yes*, of course I am. My sister had a miscarriage. It wasn't like I was on vacation."

He scoffed. "You expect us to believe you didn't enjoy extending your little fuckfest with Kane?"

"Don't you *dare* dismiss what Grace is going through." It took everything she had not to raise her voice. "And since when is it any of your business who I sleep with?"

"Since the guy you're fucking has been acting like our manager." Lee pushed to his feet. "And now everyone thinks *we* didn't earn this gig."

"Why do you think I didn't say anything?" she snapped. "I was trying to avoid this nightmare."

"It makes sense not to tell anyone outside of this room," Chris said gruffly. "But why did you keep it from us?"

Tuck stared her down, jaw tight, eyes boring into her.

"I don't *know*." She started pacing. "Because it started before the tour, and I was worried about how you'd react."

"Because you knew it was wrong," JP barked.

"Is that why you didn't tell us about the offer from Victory?" Tuck's tone was as rough as sandpaper.

Sable spun around, meeting his cold, hard stare. Shit. With everything else that was going on, she'd forgotten about the offer. "How do you know about that?"

"Who cares *how* we found out?" Lee fumed.

"She showed up at the concert last night," Tuck said evenly. "What the fuck, Bell? How long were you going to wait to tell us about it?"

"She probably wasn't going to tell us at all," JP sneered.

Guilt swamped her, and she snapped. "You want to know

why I didn't say anything? Because the offer was only valid if I stayed on as the lead singer, and I couldn't even think about making a decision like that with everything else that was going on."

"You mean going on with you and Kane," JP accused.

"No, you idiot. I mean the chaos of the tour. There was so much tension between all of us, I couldn't think straight. This tour has turned us into people I don't recognize."

"So what? We're a little tense," Lee snapped. "That's normal. Just ask Johnny and the other guys."

"A *little* tense?" Sable asked incredulously. "You and JP were ready to kill each other the other night, and I got clocked in the jaw. Honestly, after everything that's happened, I'm *glad* I didn't tell you about the offer, because now I know that I don't want it. I don't *want* to live like this, riddled with tension, arguing with my friends, and not seeing my family. I didn't want to do this fucking tour in the first place. I only did it for all of you."

"Yeah, *right*," Lee said sarcastically. "If you were doing the tour for us, you'd have told us about the offer and we'd be signed with a major label, planning our own worldwide tour, and cutting albums that would be bringing in big bucks."

"You said you started hooking up with Kane before the tour," Tuck added coldly. "I guess you got the guy, and that's all that matters."

His words cut like knives, and she held his gaze, her heart shattering. "If that's what you believe after all these years, then you don't know me at all."

"I guess not," Tuck said, driving those knives deeper. "But don't worry. I'll be out of your hair after the fall tour. Victory heard me sing last night, and she said if Surge passes on the offer she gave you, then she's got a deal on the table for me to go out on my own."

Anger and sadness whipped through Sable like angry vipers battling with happiness that Tuck would finally get out of Oak Falls and live the life he deserved. She tried to get her arms around her emotions and finally managed, "That's great."

"Yeah, except *we're* all fucked, thanks to you," JP seethed. "I'm out of here." He stormed out the door with Lee and Chris on his heels.

"Chris," Sable said as he stalked past. "You wanted it, too? Even with what the tour has done to your family?"

"No, but I thought we could trust each other."

She could do little more than stare after him as the door closed. She heard Tuck sit down behind her and closed her eyes, steeling herself against the emotions threatening to drown her. When she turned around, he was sitting on a chair, elbows on his knees, his hair hanging in front of his eyes.

"Tuck, I'm really sorry."

He looked up through his hair, his expression solemn.

She went to him, remembering the day after the accident all those years ago, when she'd met him at the barn after school. He'd reached for her, and she'd stepped back, knowing if he touched her, she'd never do what she had to. That had been the start of learning to lock down her emotions, and she'd said she didn't want to be with him anymore. He'd pleaded and argued, then had finally sunk down onto a crate, looking at her the same way he was now.

What she hadn't allowed herself to see way back then was more than clear now.

Tuck wasn't solemn. He was *heartbroken*.

Guilt swamped her, making it hard to breathe. She opened

her mouth to speak, but her words wouldn't come. But she mustered all her strength and all her courage, because this was Tuck. Her friend, her confidant, her first love, and he deserved the truth. "Tuck." His name came out strangled. "I owe you an apology."

"You owe us all apologies," he said stoically.

"Yes, about the band and the offer, but I owe you a different one. When we were kids and Pepper got into that accident, I blamed myself, and I completely shut down. I stopped letting myself feel anything that would take my attention away from my brother and sisters. That includes shutting down my feelings for you and not acknowledging your feelings for me. I didn't realize I did it, and I feel horrible about it."

He was quiet for a beat. "You haven't changed."

Tears burned her eyes. "I know it seems that way, but I *have*, or at least I've started to. I never put two and two together until last night when I was talking with Pepper about the accident. I must have blocked that part out, and I was so good at shutting down my feelings, it became part of who I was. Like a habit I didn't realize needed to change." She pulled out a chair and sat in front of him, bringing them eye to eye, willing her tears to remain at bay. "If I could go back and change how I hurt you, I would."

"We're not kids anymore, Bell." He sat back and pressed his hands into his thighs. "So, is being with Kane worth it?"

"Worth changing and fighting with the band?" She didn't have to think twice, but it came with another heap of guilt. She realized she'd begun changing—allowing herself to have feelings for Kane—before the tour had even started, when she hadn't allowed herself to change for Tuck when he'd needed her most. "Yes, it is. I love him, and I didn't think I was capable of feeling that. But I don't want to lose you because of how I handled everything."

He held her gaze. "Did you ever love me?"

She nodded, tears sliding down her cheeks. "I don't know if I realized it back then and just shut it down, but I do now." *Now that I know what love feels like.* Her love for Tuck had been different. It had been confusing kid love, while her love for Kane couldn't be locked down if her life depended on it. "I know I loved you, and in my confused teenage mind, I couldn't love you and be there for my sisters and Axsel. That's why I ended things. But you *know* I love you, and I always will."

He didn't respond or even indicate he'd heard her, driving her anguish deeper.

She grasped for something to fill the silence. "Are you going to take the solo deal?"

"Are you really walking away from everything we've built?"

Was she? Was she ready to say goodbye to it all? To lose the friends she loved, the band she put together, and the man who had been her best friend forever?

# Chapter Thirty-Five

KANE CLOSED HIS laptop and pushed to his feet, looking at his watch for the umpteenth time. Sable had been gone for quite some time, and his mind kept circling back to the last time she'd seen her bandmates, when she'd gotten clocked in the jaw. He'd give her fifteen more minutes, and then he—

The door swung open, and Sable traipsed in like a storm cloud threatening to burst. Her brow was furrowed, lips tightly pursed. Kane went to her. "What happened?"

"Nothing good," she snapped, and crossed her arms. "They're furious with me for not telling them about us or about the offer from Victory."

"I thought you put that on hold."

"I *did*. Did you know Victory was coming to last night's show?"

"No. What the hell was she doing there?"

Her eyes narrowed. "Did you know she offered Tuck a solo deal?"

"*No*. If I had, I would have told you, but I'm not your band's manager. Victory and I don't discuss offers for Surge. What happened with the guys?"

"They're pissed. Everything is messed up." She started pacing. "I don't know how things got so out of control. I told Victory I'd give her a decision at the end of the tour. I didn't think she'd run to the band since the offer is contingent upon *me* staying on as the lead singer. Now they all think I've fucked them over, and I have to make a decision about signing with the label. I'm screwed if I sign, and they're screwed if I don't."

He stepped into her path. "Slow down for a second."

She crossed her arms again, looking at him expectantly and too damn tortured.

"You're not back to square one. Surge has gone from an unknown band to a worldwide sensation."

"I know, and I'm grateful for that. But this is just the US tour. We still have two months of touring overseas in the fall, and look at what it's already done to my band. The guys think I screwed them over. Everyone except Chris *wants* this life. They want to tour and make albums and become bigger and better, and I don't blame them. We've been doing this forever. Why wouldn't they want that?"

"And what do *you* want?"

"I want you, and I want my old life back. I want to work at my shop and play at JJ's and festivals, and *not* lose my friends because of it." Her eyes glassed over. "But that's not realistic. If I don't sign with the label, I lose my band and my friends. I'm not sure I haven't already lost them."

"They're hurt and angry, in some ways rightly so. They were blindsided about us, and you probably should have told them about the offer from Victory even if you were putting it on hold."

"I was *protecting* them. If I had told Victory I wasn't interested, they never would have known about the offer, and they wouldn't be hurt because she didn't say she wanted them no matter what."

"I know that, and I love the way you think of everyone else first, but this time it bit you in the ass. You couldn't have factored in Grace's miscarriage and Tuck taking the lead, or Victory showing up at that concert. I know you're used to handling everything yourself, but I'm here for you to lean on. I wish you had talked to me about the offer instead of stewing over it for all this time."

"*Why?* What difference would that make?"

"We could have figured it out when you weren't so upset and saved you and the guys a lot of stress. Things in this industry aren't black or white. That's why I suggested you get a manager for the band, to walk you through this type of thing." He stepped closer, knowing she'd hate what he had to say next, but he'd never forgive himself if he didn't. "You know I support whatever makes you happy, but you should know all your options so you don't spin around in a few years wishing you would have done things differently."

She crossed her arms again, lifting her chin defiantly. "I know what I want, but go ahead and say whatever it is you have to say."

"Maybe there's a way you can meet the guys halfway. You love performing with them, and you have a lot of history together. With the right manager, you can do everything yourselves. You can develop music, distribute it, and market it at whatever pace you'd like. You can play festivals or you can tour, but you and your band would be in control. The downside is that it can be more stressful and expensive to go that route. Signing with a label makes all of that easier, and it can be very lucrative and make or break a career. You can sign with a label and write your own ticket—negotiate tours and albums and anything else you want. Are you sure you don't want to reconsider either negotiating an offer you're happy with and doing those things with your band or hiring a manager and meeting the guys halfway?"

"*Yes*, I'm sure. They want it all, and I don't. I don't want to be committed to creating music on a schedule. I want to make music because I *feel* it, and once we're done with the fall tour, I never want to tour again. I want to be there if my family needs me. I hate living my life in the spotlight and hiding all the time. It's going to be hard enough for us to make things work long distance. I want to be able to go out with you whether we're in New York or Oak Falls or anywhere else and not have to worry about who's taking our pictures or saying shit about us online. I know it'll take time once the tour is over for all of that to die down, but eventually it will, and I can't imagine that you like all of this fanfare, either."

"I don't, but I'd deal with it if there were any part of you that wanted it."

"I never wanted it in the first place, and I sure as hell don't now. I just wish there were a way JP and Lee didn't get screwed because of me."

"Why don't we talk to Tuck about taking the guys along as part of his contract."

"They offered him a solo deal. There is no band."

"Solo artists have supporting bands, and Lee and JP would probably jump at the chance to back him up."

"Do you really think you could get Victory to agree? Wouldn't she have offered that out of the gate if it was a possibility? I don't want to get the guys excited if it's not an option."

"I wouldn't mention it to JP and Lee until Tuck says it's

what he wants, but Victory is an excellent businesswoman. Tuck is a great singer and guitarist, but he's not as strong a performer or singer as you. My guess is that Victory wants to capitalize on Surge's success, and taking Tuck solo would be an easier deal with more options. I bet she'll take all three if that's what was on the table. But you have a concert tonight, so if we're going to speak with Tuck, we should do it soon."

"Okay, but I think I should talk to him by myself first." She lowered her eyes briefly, and when she lifted them, they were more troubled. "I laid some heavy stuff on him earlier, and I don't want to make things worse. Remember when I said I had learned some things about myself while I was with Pepper and Grace?"

"Yeah."

"I think I did love Tuck when we were kids, and I told him as much. But it wasn't like I love you, and I'm not in love with him—"

"Babe, it's okay." He gathered her in his arms. "You don't have to explain. I know you well enough to realize you couldn't have gone through what you and Tuck went through without falling for your best friend. That's another reason this is so hard for both of you, and I respect that."

She exhaled with relief. "Thank you for understanding. I want to tell you everything eventually."

"I'd love to hear it when the time is right, but there's no rush."

She looked at him for a long moment, her brows drawn tight. "I'm sorry that being with me is so complicated."

"Being with you is the best part of my life." He pressed his lips to hers, earning a smile. "Go talk to him before you run out of time. I'll be right here if you need me."

TEN MINUTES LATER, Sable followed Tuck into his room. He turned around and slid a hand into the front pocket of his jeans. "What's up?"

He didn't ask it with an edge to his voice, as he had earlier. He sounded worn out, which was how she felt. She hoped they could pull it together for their concert tonight. "I wanted you to be the first to know that I'm turning down the offer from Victory."

"I assumed as much. You never wanted to do this in the first place."

"So you don't think I'm turning it down because of Kane?"

He shook his head. "I only said that because I was pissed."

Relief swept through her. "I hate how things have gone south between all of us, but you have to know that I want everything for you and the guys. That's the whole reason I agreed to do this tour."

"I know, and so do they, but they are screwed, and that's not going to be easy for you to overcome."

"That's kind of why I'm here. Kane thinks he can negotiate with Victory if you want to take JP and Lee with you."

His brow furrowed. "Really?"

She nodded. "He thinks so. He's a good businessman. You should let him help you. None of this is his fault. It was my choice to hide everything from everyone. He didn't even know the particulars about the offer. I told him I put it off weeks ago, and we never talked about it again until tonight."

"I knew this was all you."

"How?"

"Because that's who you are, Bell. You protect the things you love, and sometimes that means keeping secrets."

She wasn't sure if he meant she'd protected him all those years ago by keeping their relationship secret, or if she'd kept her relationship with Kane from him to protect one of them from being hurt, or if he meant something else altogether, but she got choked up all the same. When she opened her mouth to speak, he cut her off.

"I'd love to keep playing with JP and Lee, but only if JP can pull his shit together."

It was just like Tuck to cut her off *and* shut that conversation down. "You'll have to talk to him about that, and you might want to wait until he cools off."

"Ya think?" Tuck *almost* smiled. "Are you going to be okay at the shop if I take this gig?"

She was touched that he thought of her with everything that was going on. "I'll be fine."

"What's your plan with the other guys?"

"I don't have one. I'll take my cues from them and hope for the best. I appreciate you talking to me. I'll get out of your hair." She turned to leave, but a pang in her chest stopped her, and she turned back. "I know I screwed up, but do you think we'll ever be okay again?"

"It's going to take some time," he said solemnly. "But we always find our way back to each other."

Relief *whooshed* through her. "Yeah, we do." She fought the urge to hug him, knowing it was too soon, and headed for the door.

"So you and Kane are the real deal, huh?"

She nodded. "I think so."

"In that case, you should talk to Chris about taking over the back bedroom on the bus." He opened the door for her.

"We only have three weeks of touring left. I don't want to ruffle more feathers."

"Bullshit. You love ruffling feathers, and if I have to listen to you text all night any longer, I might pull my hair out."

"You heard me texting?"

"Well, not so much texting, but you talk to yourself when you text, and you sound different. Happier. Like he's texting special shit, and you laugh sometimes, real soft, like those giddy girls who annoy you so much."

"*Ugh.* Seriously?"

He nodded.

"Sorry…for everything."

"Me too. I hate how all this went down, but I'm happy for you, Bell."

Too choked up to speak, she nodded and headed down the hall.

"Talk to Chris," he called after her. "And tell Kane to get us all soundproof earbuds."

She waved without turning around so he wouldn't see her happy tears.

# Chapter Thirty-Six

SABLE SAT ON the bed in the back of the bus, gazing out at the dusky predawn sky, as they cruised along the highway en route to Pittsburgh for their last concert of this leg of the tour. It was a bittersweet feeling. It had been a trying three weeks, but they'd all survived.

The media had had a field day with the picture she'd posted of her and Kane kissing, but Brindle and Morgyn continued to fiercely defend her online. Sable was once again learning to ignore the keyboard warriors, and to her surprise, that picture had also spurred many fans into rallying in support of her and Kane's relationship. Tuck called it their cult following.

Things were looking better on that front, too. Her relationship with the guys would never be the same as it was before the tour, but at least they were all friendly again. JP had reined himself in after Kane had renegotiated Tuck's deal and secured deals for him and Lee. She and Chris were planning on putting another band together so they could play at JJ's and festivals, with one hard-and-fast ground rule: No more tours. *Ever.* She and Tuck were back to brainstorming songs and hanging out, but there had definitely been a shift in their relationship. They weren't quite as close anymore. Conversely, she and Kane were closer than ever. Pepper called that transition *the changing of the guards*, because while Tuck had once been Sable's secret keeper, now that her heart belonged to Kane, he'd taken over that role.

She had gotten spoiled with all the time she and Kane had been spending together, and she was nervous about what tomorrow would bring. It wasn't like she didn't have a full life to go back to. They both did. Kane had already scheduled another trip to Australia, and although it was only late June, she still had two more months of touring this fall. They'd talked about taking a trip to see his family next weekend, since Harlow was visiting his parents for a couple of weeks while she wasn't filming. She was looking forward to getting to know his sisters better. They'd spoken over video chat several times, and Aria was planning to come out to Oak Falls over the summer to meet Sable's mother and Amber so she could see what it was like to have a service dog. Kane was thrilled that she was taking that step. He'd confided in Sable that he worried about Aria being lonely, but the more she learned about Aria and her friend Zeke, the more she wondered if they might have secrets of their own.

She looked at him sleeping beside her. Her in-control man could be the poster child for animal magnetism the way he stirred lust, love, and those flutters in her chest and belly that had only gotten stronger as their relationship deepened. He was always handsome, but he was even more beautiful when he slept, free from the tension that riddled him when he was awake. They were alike in that way. She was always on guard, too, except when it was just the two of them. She was still floored by the power of their love and that she'd allowed herself to love and be loved. But it wasn't like she'd had a choice. Their connection was bigger than both of them. Morgyn said they were fated to be together.

Sable had never believed in fate for herself, though she did for others.

Was it fate that Deloris's sister had gotten an offer on the house? While Sable hated the idea of their beloved barn changing hands, Deloris needed the money, and with the band breaking up, it felt like the end of an era.

Kane shifted in his sleep, and she felt herself smiling.

It might be the end of an era, but it was the beginning of something even more special. So much had changed in every aspect of her life since meeting Kane, she had to wonder if Morgyn was right, and everything in life was fated to be.

Needing to feel closer, she took off her T-shirt and lay beside him. His skin was warm, his scent familiar as she drank in his tousled dark hair and all his glorious ink. The other night she'd finally gotten around to asking about the meaning behind each of his tattoos. There were so many, each representing something significant in his life. But three stood out among all the rest: The one over his heart that mirrored the sculpture he'd designed, because it showed the very heart of him. The tally marks on his neck, which he'd started when he was young and vengeful, representing the number of businesses he owned, and had stopped as the number grew too high. She loved those because they were so very Kane, and lastly, the little musical notes that were hidden in all the other tattoos, because her man was so passionate, he could never leave his love of music behind.

Those little notes also made her wonder about that little thing called fate.

The sheet was bunched around his hip, exposing the outline of the trouser snake that never failed to bring her pleasure tucked beneath his black boxer briefs. He knew how to use that particular organ well, but it was another organ—*the one no one can see but I feel every time you look at me. The one that guides you to stay close to your family and to support my need for the same. The one that made you fly Pepper in for our birthday last week*—that had drawn Sable in so deep, she never wanted to leave.

She pressed a kiss over his heart, whispering, "How did you make me love you so much?" She trailed kisses down his chest and stomach. He moaned as she kissed the warm skin just above the waist of his boxer briefs, his cock hardening. His fingers threaded into her hair, sending prickles of arousal skittering through her. *God*, that touch in and of itself never failed to turn her on, because it was always the start of something more, and she knew whatever followed—kissing, touching, loving, *fucking*—would leave them both swimming in a sea of pleasure. She pulled down that cotton barrier, needing to taste him, and slicked her tongue along his length as she drew them down his legs.

He moaned again, kicking off the briefs. His dark eyes found hers as she palmed his length. "There's my sexy girl."

*Oh*, how she was going to miss his gravelly morning voice. She'd become an expert at making him want and need and *beg* for more, and this morning she wanted to hear it all, even if in hushed whispers. She held his gaze as she swirled her tongue around the head of his cock, earning a deep, guttural growl that made her neediest parts clench with desire. She licked and stroked, taunting him without lowering her mouth over his shaft. The muscles in his thighs flexed, and she watched the tension crawl up his torso, cording his abs, chest, neck, and shoulders. She loved seeing him so needy for her. The trouble was, it made her needy, too.

"I need to fuck your mouth," he gritted out through

clenched teeth, fire blazing in his eyes as his other hand pushed into her hair.

"This mouth?" she teased, taunting him with flicks of her tongue along the edge of the head of his cock, his shaft twitching in her hand.

"*Sable.*" His eyes narrowed, fists tightening in her hair, sending scintillating sensations through her core. His warning was clear, but she couldn't help smiling as she stopped stroking and kissed his thighs. He groaned. "Jesus, you're killing me."

"I wouldn't want you to die unhappy."

She lowered her mouth over his cock, taking him deep, earning a gruff "*Fuck yeah.*" She worked him with her hand and mouth. His hips thrust in time to her efforts, rough and greedy. Loving that he didn't hold back, she took him deeper, chasing his release as much as he was. "*That's it...So fucking good...Shit...baby...*" A string of curses fell from his lips as warm jets hit the back of her throat, and she didn't slow down, taking everything he had to give.

His body shuddered with the last of his release. "I fucking love your mouth." His eyes bored into her as she licked her lips. "Get up here and kiss me."

She crawled up his body, and he tugged her into a kiss. He pushed one hand into her hair, crushing their mouths tighter together. His other hand traveled down her back, groping her ass, then sliding up her side and palming her breast, as if he couldn't get enough of her.

He broke the kiss on a curse, grabbed her hips, and said, "Straddle my face."

Thrills darted through her as he helped her into position and slammed her down on his mouth so hard, he sent shocks of pleasure darting through her. She clenched her teeth to keep from making a sound, even though Kane had bought the guys noise-canceling earplugs. He feasted on her, fucking her with his tongue, then using his teeth on her clit, and going back for more. His fingers dug into her skin, controlling her movements, taking her right up to the edge of ecstasy and holding her there. Prickling sensations riddled every inch of her as he tangled one hand in her hair, groping her breast with his other, sending more overwhelming sensations raining down on her. The pleasure was so intense, she panted for air, her muscles tightening and back arching as an orgasm closed in on her like a raging tide. He tugged her hair, sending lightning streaking through her. She cried out, clawing at the wall, ravaged by pleasure. Just as she started to catch her breath, he sent her spiraling again.

When she tumbled beside him on the mattress, breathless and trembling, he dragged his forearm across his mouth and moved over her, his cock pressing against her wetness. Her body threw a little party, and he grinned arrogantly. "You're not worn out, are you?"

*God*, she loved him.

"Not even close. I wouldn't want you to forget how good we are together when you're all alone in the Big Apple."

Kane gazed down at her as she wound her arms around him. "I couldn't forget a single thing about you if I tried. Not that sexy challenge in your eyes when you're pissed, the feel of your fingers tracing my tattoos when you're sleepy, or the sweet way you whisper things when you think I'm sleeping."

She thought about all the things she'd whispered over the last few weeks. *How am I going to sleep without you...? I wish I were easier to deal with...I never knew how much I could love someone...I hope I make you as happy as you make me...How did you make me love you so much?* "I have no idea what you're talking about."

"You are the suckiest liar I have ever met, and to answer your most recent whisper, there's not a person on earth who could make you do a damn thing. You love me so much because I'm the wood to your strings."

She laughed. "That's *so* cheesy."

He cocked a brow. "I'm the fret to your board?"

"That's even *worse*." She couldn't stop smiling when he was playful like this.

"The chorus to your melody?"

"Ohmygod, *don't*. Just *don't*." She laughed.

"I just wanted to hear your laugh." His eyes narrowed, and he rocked his hips, pushing the head of his cock inside her, making her body thrum with desire. "I know damn well what I am."

She rocked her hips, but he refused to love her deeper. "What's that?"

"The master to your orgasms."

"You've got that right." She bent her knees, opening wider for him, and his eyes flamed. "Now, get busy earning your title."

# Chapter Thirty-Seven

KANE STOOD BACKSTAGE watching Sable perform. He remembered how she'd blown him away the first time he'd seen her play at that little pub in Oak Falls. She'd owned the stage with the same fierce determination and over-the-top passion as she did everything else in her life. He'd never tire of watching her perform or hearing her sing, whether onstage, in the shower, in the car, or anywhere else.

Johnny sidled up to him as she sang the last note, and the crowd went wild. "The world's going to be missing out when Sable goes back to Oak Falls. I can't say I blame her, though. This life isn't for everyone."

"They'll be missing out as you slow down, too, John." He watched Sable strut across the stage. "Look at her out there. She's fucking amazing. You think her fans know how strong she is to have given up her life these last few months so her friends could live out their dreams?" Hell, she'd given up her privacy for much longer than that. She'd be talked about for years. The unforgettable musician who chose family over fame.

"No, but the ones who care enough to see it know how strong she is to have dealt with all that awful press. There are only two people who matter, and that's you and her. Did you have any idea when you first met Sable that you'd end up madly in love?"

Kane thought back to their first encounter on the side of the road, when she'd climbed out of that cherry-red truck in baggy, paint-speckled overalls, her hair pinned up in a messy bun. He could still feel the impact of her sea-green eyes when their gazes collided and the way her sweet, rough whiskey voice had done him in. "I had no idea about that or the many other ways that spectacular, stubborn woman would change my life."

Johnny laughed. "I bet she thinks the same thing about you, which is why I have to fire you, bro."

Kane scoffed. "Yeah, right."

"I'm serious. This was never supposed to take over your life. You saved my ass in more ways than one. Now it's your turn to be happy. I've been talking with Victory, and she's lined up a few management candidates for the band."

"John, I'm all set to go on the international tour. I'm good."

"And you will." Johnny clapped a hand on his shoulder. "As Sable's arm candy."

Kane laughed. "*Shit.*"

"Prepare to be humbled, my friend."

"John, really."

"It's a done deal, so, in the words of the Beatles, *Let it be.*"

The crowd erupted into applause and cheers, drawing his attention to Sable. Less work and more time for her? *Sign me up.* "If you're serious, I want to check out anyone you're considering."

"I wouldn't have it any other way. Brett's doing background investigations before Victory recommends anyone. They're copying you on all the reports, and I'd really appreciate it if you could be the first to interview them, because if they don't pass you, they're not getting to me."

"All right, but promise me you won't hire anyone until we're both sure it's the right person, even if it takes a year."

"I wouldn't dare." Johnny nodded toward the stage as the crowd quieted.

"I'd like to dedicate our last song to the man who gave me a safe place to fall into," Sable announced, and as they started playing the intro to "In Too Deep," excitement roared through the stadium, and his love's whiskey voice sailed into his ears.

> *"You can run but you can't hide*
> *From the people or the lights*
> *You can mask the pain, go along for the ride*
> *But the walls close in, and you scramble up the sides*
> *Losing your grip*
> *Losing your mind*
> *Losing your life, one flash at a time"*

Memories of that rooftop night came rushing back. He remembered the sweet sound of her voice on the balcony below his, which had drawn him to her hotel room, and her frustration when she'd answered the door.

> *"All those years mapping it out*
> *It slips away and I want to shout*
> *Come back, fucking stay*
> *I want to breathe another day"*

The anguish he'd seen in her eyes that night appeared before him, bringing with it that bone-deep ache to help her through the pain.

*"Where do I go*
*When does it end*
*How do I leave this land of pretend"*

The lyrics hit differently after all these months. She wasn't just strong.

She was a fucking warrior.

*"Invincible onstage*
*The music takes over*
*I fade away like night to day*
*A voice in the lights*
*Only fingers working strings*
*It's a wonder I'm anything"*

*"There it is*
*I see the door*
*But these legs won't carry me anymore*
*I crave the lights, the music, too.*
*I'm lost but I'm found*
*I'm so damn confused*
*I need a safe place*
*A place to live, a place to breathe*
*A place to just fucking be me*
*I need a place to start anew*
*A safe place to fall into…"*

When she sang the last note, the crowd went wild, and Kane filled with pride. "I can hardly believe that's *my* girl."

Johnny nudged him with his elbow. "That's her best song.

She told me you helped her write it."

"Nah. It was all her, but she got it wrong. It's not a wonder she's anything at all. She's *everything*."

"You're so gone, dude." Johnny laughed as Sable led her bandmates off the stage and she headed straight for Kane.

"I sure am, and I wouldn't want it any other way." He drew Sable into his arms. "You were fucking phenomenal, babe." He kissed the ever-loving daylights out of her as her bandmates and Johnny whistled and whooped.

She beamed at him. "Now I'm really all yours."

"I can't ask for more than that." As Johnny and his band headed up to the stage, Kane said, "Fuck it. *Yes, I can.* I want an encore."

With the roar of the crowd competing with their thundering hearts, he took her in another soul-searing kiss.

KANE SAT ON a couch in the green room with his arm around Sable, watching the rest of the concert on a big screen with her bandmates.

"This is my favorite set," Tuck said, bobbing his head to the beat and mouthing the lyrics. "He always saves the best few songs for the end."

Kane patted Sable's arm. "Sounds familiar."

"Our last song or my last guy?"

"Both." He kissed her.

"I will not miss watching you two make out," JP said.

Sable looked thoughtfully at him. "I never thought I'd say this, but even with all the shit we've gone through, I'm glad we did the tour, and there's nobody I'd rather have done it with than all of you."

"Even though you had to put up with me being an ass for a while?" JP asked.

"Are you implying that you're no longer an ass?" Lee asked, and they all laughed.

"What's the first thing you're going to do when you get home?" Tuck asked the group.

"Kiss my kids and make love to my wife," Chris said.

"What about after that five minutes of wifely torture?" JP ribbed him.

Chris swatted the back of his head.

"I'm going to sleep for a week," Lee said.

"Not me," JP said. "I'm going to hit JJ's and give the Oak Falls ladies a shot at getting all this." He motioned to himself.

"In other words, you're going to do what you did before the tour, and go home alone?" Sable teased.

"*Yup.*" JP laughed. "I don't know why groupies love me and girls back home don't."

"Groupies want a piece of the famous guy regardless of who comes before or after them. Pun intended," Kane said. "And from what I know about Oak Falls women, they prefer quality over quantity and loyalty over ego." He squeezed Sable's shoulder. "Right, babe?"

"Absolutely." She leaned forward and lowered her voice as if sharing a secret with the other guys. "I'm only in it for the money and the Big Daddy equipment, but don't tell him that."

The guys chuckled.

"Like I said, *quality.*" Kane kissed her.

"Tuck, what are you going to do when you get home?" Lee asked.

Tuck took a swig of his beer. "Look for a new place for us to practice. What about you, Bell?"

"I'm going to bathe in motor oil and sleep on my deck." She clinked her beer bottle with Tuck's. "If you guys are into it, maybe we can find a place to share for practices and split the rent."

"Sounds good to me," Tuck said, and the guys agreed. He looked at Kane. "I guess we'll be seeing a lot more of you in Oak Falls?"

Tuck had pulled him aside last week and said, *Sable's my best friend. Please don't fuck her over.* Kane respected the hell out of him for it. "For sure. We don't know what our schedules will look like yet, but you can count on seeing me."

"I plan on going to New York to see him, too," Sable said.

"Really?" JP said. "I thought after the tour it would take an act of God to get you out of Oak Falls."

Kane had basically said the same thing when she'd offered to travel to see him, but his stubborn girl had insisted their relationship had to be equitable.

"Sable being in a long-term relationship *is* an act of God," Tuck said, earning more laughter and agreement.

"Hey, you guys want us to play at your wedding?" Lee joked.

Kane felt Sable stiffen against him.

"What planet do you live on? We're not rushing into that. We're good just like we are." She looked at Kane, brow furrowed. "We *are* good, right?"

He'd marry her tomorrow if she'd go for it, but after that reaction, he wasn't about to offer it up. "We're good, babe. No worries." His phone rang, and Sable moved so he could pull it from his pocket. "It's Zoey. Excuse me a minute." He got up and answered it on his way out the door. "Hey, kid. How are you?"

"Great! Jilly's in labor!"

He stopped in his tracks. Jillian wasn't due until next month. "What? Are you sure?"

"*Yes!*" she hollered, and he heard the same in the background through the phone. "That was Jilly and Grandma Lily. Grandma says the twins are just anxious to meet me and their new baby cousin." Jillian's brother Beau and his wife, Charlotte, recently had a baby girl they named Briar Rose Sterling-Braden. "Jilly needs Dad. Can you bring him home?"

"He's onstage, but I'll get him there. Let me talk to Lily." He waited as she handed Jillian's mother the phone.

"Hi, Kane," Lily said.

"Hi. Are Jilly and the babies okay?"

"Jilly's fine, just a little nervous, as is to be expected, and twins are usually early, so hopefully they'll be fine, too. Clint is on his way to take us to the hospital." Clint was Jillian's father.

He took down the name of the hospital and called his cousin Brett to arrange for a security team to watch over Jillian and another detail to be waiting for him, Sable, and Johnny when they arrived. He called his assistant and had her arrange private flights to Maryland for them and for his family members and headed back into the green room as he texted the tour manager to meet them by the stage. "Tuck, do you know the lyrics to the rest of the songs in this set?"

Tuck nodded. "Every one of them, why?"

"Jilly's in labor. We've got to get Johnny off the stage. You're going to fill in."

Sable pushed to her feet, worry written in her pinched brows. "She's not due for almost a month."

"I know. Her mother said twins are usually early. Hopefully everyone will be fine. Will you come with us?"

"Of course."

Tom met them by the stage, and when Bad Intentions finished the song they were playing, he filled Johnny in. Johnny turned to the crowd, announcing, "My fiancée is in labor, and if I don't get my ass home, she'll never let me play again. Please welcome the amazing Tuck Wilder, who's going to finish out this set. *I love you, Pittsburgh!*"

As the audience cheered, Johnny ran off the stage, his face sheet white. "Is she okay? Are the babies okay?"

"Yes." Kane prayed they would be. Sable's hand slid into his, and he took his brother by the arm, heading for the exit. "Let's go."

# Chapter Thirty-Eight

KANE HAD NO idea how fathers-to-be got through waiting for their children to be born. They'd been at the hospital for nearly two hours and hadn't heard anything. He was a nervous wreck and beyond thankful that the hospital had made special accommodations for their families to wait in a private room in an administrative area that required key card access. His family should be there soon, and the security team was ready to escort them in. Not that they had to worry about paparazzi in the small town of Pleasant Hill, Maryland, but word had spread quickly after Johnny's announcement at the concert, and there were dozens of well-meaning fans out front with balloons, congratulatory signs, and cell phones at the ready.

He tried to focus on the conversations taking place around him and not the worries peppering his mind. He didn't want to worry Zoey. She was chatting excitedly with Sable and Jillian's parents and two of Jillian's brothers, Nick and Jax, and their wives, Trixie and Jordan.

"How many sisters and brothers do you have?" Zoey asked Sable.

"Five sisters and one brother," Sable said.

"Wow. I hope I get that many," Zoey said.

Kane threw more silent prayers out to the powers that be, hoping Jillian and the babies would be okay. Too anxious to sit still, he gave Sable's hand a squeeze and got up to pace.

Sable fell into step beside him a minute later. "There's a liquor store around the corner. Do I need to make a run?"

"No. I'm just anxious to hear something."

As he pulled her into his arms, Nick walked over and said, "I feel ya, man. I can't sit still, either."

"I'm glad I'm not the only one losing my mind," Jax said as he got up. "This is taking far too long, isn't it?"

Kane and Nick agreed.

"Relax, boys," Lily said. "Having babies takes time, and this is Jilly's first labor and delivery."

"Labor can take forever," Zoey chimed in. "Jilly and I read a bunch of books about it. She told me not to worry no matter how long it takes."

"That was good advice," Lily said. "Come on, Zoey. Let's go get a soda." She guided Zoey out of the room.

"They're right," Jordan said. "One of my friends at work was in labor for eight hours."

"Lily was in labor for twelve hours with Beau," Clint added. "And when she had Jax and Jillian, she was in labor for six hours. So it really hasn't been that long."

"Yes, but Jilly was already in labor when we got here," Kane pointed out.

"I say we go in there and see what the hell's going on," Nick said gruffly.

"Or at least find someone who can check on them for us. Let's go hunt down a nurse," Kane said.

"That's not a good idea, boys," Clint said.

"What if something went wrong?" Nick barked.

Sable put her hands up. "Stop. We're *not* going to think that way. Jilly and the babies are in good hands, and the last thing she and Johnny need is you two charging through the halls creating unnecessary chaos. On the off chance that something does go wrong, they'll be well taken care of by doctors who do this every day. And if that does happen, they'll need our support more than ever, and so will Zoey. So pace if you have to pace, and grumble to yourself if you have to grumble, because Zoey doesn't need to see her uncles lose their shit."

"I can see Sable's going to fit into our family just fine."

They all turned at the sound of Kane's mother's voice. There was a flurry of activity as everyone greeted his family.

"Girl, that was badass," Harlow said, hugging Sable. "I knew I liked you."

"Johnny wasn't kidding when he said you were like a female Kane," Aria said, hugging her.

As Kane hugged his mother, he caught Sable's grin over Aria's shoulder.

"The babies will be okay, honey," his mother reassured him. "Don't worry until there's a reason to worry."

"Easier said than done," he said as his father moved in for a hug.

"You definitely met your match, son," his father said.

"Yes, I have." He reached for Sable's hand, pulling her into the fold as his sisters went to talk with the Bradens.

"Hi," Sable said warmly. "It's so nice to finally meet you in person."

"For us, too, honey. Our hug is long overdue." His mother sounded a little choked up as she drew Sable into her arms.

"Mom, are you okay?" Kane asked.

"More than okay," she said. "All I ever wanted was to see my kids happy on all fronts, and I didn't know if I'd get that chance. I know you said you were happy before you met Sable, but a mother knows when something is missing. Now one son is having babies, and the other is madly in love with a wonderful woman. We're halfway there."

He'd known she'd worried about surviving cancer, but to hear her say it brought a wave of sadness *and* a heap of gratitude, because she was here to see those milestones, and hopefully she would be around for many more.

"The girls were making bets about Kane screwing things up with you before we had a chance to meet," his father said as he embraced Sable.

Sable looked at Kane with so much love, she wouldn't have had to say a word to make her point. "I'm afraid he's as stuck with me as I am with him."

"I wouldn't want it any other way." He kissed her.

"The babies are here!" Zoey squealed as she ran into the room, followed by her grandmother and Johnny, both of whom were in tears. "I have a sister *and* a brother!"

Everyone cheered, and Johnny said, "Jilly's tired, but she was a trooper, and she's elated. The babies will be in the Special Baby Care Unit for a while, but the doctor said they should be fine. We named them Lyric and Lennon."

As everyone "*Awwed*," Zoey exclaimed, "I named Lyric, and Dad and Jilly named Lennon because Grandma Jan loves the Beatles."

Tears slid down his mother's cheeks. "Oh, Johnny."

"At least that's better than Ringo," Nick said.

As the others converged on Johnny and Zoey with hugs and congratulations, Kane, bowled over with relief, drew Sable into his arms, and hell if he wasn't as teary-eyed as his brother.

"Congratulations, Uncle Kane," she said softly. "You *really* do love kids, don't you?"

"Mm-hm." He nuzzled against her neck, relief and love stacking up inside him. "These babies will change Zoey's world for the better, and Johnny and Jillian are already great parents."

"Well, don't get your hopes up for any anytime soon, but play your cards right and maybe one day you'll drop the Big and just be Daddy for a whole new reason."

"Just when I didn't think I could be any happier, you go and hand me the icing on the cake." As he lowered his lips to hers, he said, "I'd wait a lifetime for that with you."

# Chapter Thirty-Nine

SABLE SANG ALONG to the radio as she finished replacing the brakes on a customer's car. "Bloody Valentine" came on, and her mind zipped back to the Valentine's Day Festival. She'd been falling for Kane even then. It had been a week since she'd seen him, and she missed him more than she imagined possible. They'd been doing the long-distance thing for two months, and it was like being on separate buses all over again, only worse. They talked on the phone and video chatted between visits, but there were no stolen kisses or glances across the room. When they were together, they were better than ever, but when they were apart, they were like teenagers longing to sneak out and reconnect.

Tuck's voice sailed into her ears as he sang along to the radio. She looked at him two bays down, working on an old truck. Her heart hurt. Tuck, JP, and Lee were moving to LA after they finished the fall tour. They'd signed on with Shea, and she had a slew of promotional opportunities lined up for them. Sable would miss all of them, but her life and Tuck's had been interwoven for so long, she couldn't imagine what it was going to be like not seeing him every day.

"You've got a pretty good voice," she called over to him.

"You could be a professional singer."

"And give up all this?" He motioned around him. "For what? Women at my beck and call? Free drinks?"

"The best tables in restaurants," Buddy chimed in.

"Who wants all that?" Tuck said.

"I wouldn't mind it for a few weeks," Eli said as he walked into the shop from the office. "Especially the girls."

"You know, Tuck, if you end up hating LA, you'll always have a job here," she said.

"I'll keep that in mind." His eyes twinkled as his lips curved up. "You know I'm not going to hate LA, right?"

"Yeah, I know. But you won't find a cooler best friend no matter where you go."

"You got that right."

Their gazes held, a world of memories passing between them. "Thea would be proud of you, so don't fuck it up."

He nodded, looking a little choked up.

That made two of them.

Sable's phone chimed, and she pulled it from her pocket. Her pulse quickened at the sight of a text from Kane.

"Lover boy?" Eli teased.

"Don't you have work to do?" Sable said, opening the text.

Kane: *Hey babe. Hope you're having a good day. I'm in a meeting wishing you were on your knees under the table.*

The phone rang in the office, and Eli hollered, "I've got it."

Sable: *That's funny. I was just thinking that this brake job would be more fun if your mouth was between my legs.*

A devil emoji popped up, and she smiled.

Kane: *Tomorrow can't get here soon enough.*

He was coming tomorrow night for the grand opening of Grace's play.

"Sable, someone needs a tow out on Route 85," Eli said.

Buddy and Tuck were elbow-deep in their current repairs. "I'll go. Who is it?"

Eli's brow wrinkled. "Shoot. I forgot to ask."

"A'right. What kind of car? Where on 85?"

"Um, I *think* they said a blue car, and I forgot to ask where on 85."

"*Eli.*" She called out, "Eli's no longer allowed to answer the phones."

Tuck laughed.

"Aw, come on, Sable," Eli complained as she headed into the office to get the keys to the tow truck. "I'll be more careful next time."

She left without answering, letting him sweat it out, hoping he'd learn.

With the windows down and the warm August air kissing her skin, she drove out to Route 85. She saw a black—not blue—sedan with its hood up and pulled over behind it. She climbed out of her truck, and her heart nearly stopped as Kane walked out from behind the hood, looking even more delicious than the first time she'd seen him, wearing the same dark slacks and crisp white dress shirt, sleeves rolled up to his elbows.

"Need a hand, city slicker?" She sauntered over to him, wondering what the heck he was doing there.

"I think I might." He rubbed his jaw, his gaze raking slowly down the length of her. "I just bought a house in town, and I'm looking for a woman who's good with her hands to move in with me."

"You bought a house in town." She scoffed. "As if that would ever happen. What are you really doing here?"

His brows knitted. "Do you always call men liars?"

"Only when they fuck with me." She put a hand on her hip.

A slow grin slid across his handsome face. "I'd like to be fucking with you. I'd like to be doing a lot of things with you." He drew her into his arms. "I miss you, baby, and I couldn't wait another second to see you. I'm tired of the back-and-forth. I want to wake up with your hair strewn across my chest and have breakfast at your parents' house. I want to fall asleep with you in my arms and have dinner together every night of the week." He kissed her softly. "I want to make love when and where we feel like it."

"That sounds like a dream come true, but we live hundreds of miles apart."

"I want to live here, with you."

Her heart raced. "But you hate small towns."

"I love you, and your family, and this rinky-dink town with its nosy neighbors and silly festivals has grown on me. This is where your heart is, baby, which means it's where my heart belongs."

"Kane...?" Tears welled in her eyes.

"What do you say, babe? Will you move in with me?"

"You..." Her voice cracked. "You're serious? You bought a place? *Here?*"

"Yes, with lots of land so you'll never feel confined, and if you don't like it, I'll sell it and we'll live in your apartment above the shop. I don't give a damn where we live as long as we're under the same roof."

She was stunned speechless.

"*Or* I could live there by myself, and you could stay in your apartment...?"

Nervous laughter bubbled out. "*No.* I want to live with you. I'm just shocked. You're moving *here?* For *me?* You're changing your whole life because you love me?"

"Baby, I told you months ago I'd do anything for you, and I meant it. Remember when you asked me why I decided to expand my business internationally and I said I felt like I was missing something?"

"Yeah."

"Well, now I know it wasn't another business venture that I was missing. It was you. *Us.* We're so good together, baby. Nothing could ever replace what we have. I'd have given you a ring today, but I thought it would scare you off, so I went with the house."

Her heart stumbled. "Are you serious? You would have asked me to marry you?"

"In a heartbeat," he insisted.

"I guess that shows you how much you know. I love you, Kane. You're the man I want to spend the rest of my life with. I wouldn't have gotten scared off."

"Well, *hell.* In that case..." He sank down on one knee and pulled out the most gorgeous ring with a big, square black diamond surrounded by three leaf-shaped white diamonds on either side.

The breath rushed from her lungs.

"Baby, I'm pretty sure I've been falling in love with you since the first time I saw you climbing out of your truck in those paint-speckled overalls, and I've fallen deeper in love with you with every passing day. I didn't know it was possible to love someone so much, it feels like we're two halves of the same person. I love your honesty and your resilience. I love the way you *fight* for the people you love and the way you stand up for yourself, and I love the way you love me with everything you have." Tears slid down her cheeks as he said, "There is nothing that I want more in this world than to be the one who stands up for *you*, who pampers you even when you fight me on it, and who loves you every minute of every day, whether or not we're arguing, until the day they bury me six feet under." He pushed to his feet, gazing deeply into her eyes. "Sable Eloise Montgomery, will you do me the honor of marrying me and becoming Mrs. Big Daddy Bad?"

Laughter burst from her lungs, and through a blur of tears, she said, "Yes, you ridiculous, beautiful fool. *Yes*, I'll marry you!" She threw her arms around him, and he lifted her off her feet, spinning her as they kissed, both of them murmuring "I love you" between kisses.

When he set her down, he took her hand, and as he slid the ring on her finger, he said, "I've never seen you wearing a ring. If you don't like this one, I'll buy you one you do like, and if you can't wear a ring because of work, then I'll have Aria tattoo my name on your finger."

She laughed. "Oh, Kane. I love this ring. It's perfect for me, just like you are." More tears spilled down her cheeks as she went up on her toes and kissed him.

"I love you, too, baby. Let's go for a ride, and I'll show you our new digs. We'll come back for the tow truck."

Sable was on cloud nine. She couldn't stop looking at Kane, or the beautiful ring, as they drove through town. He'd not only changed her world, but he'd changed the way she saw herself. Seven months ago, she didn't know she'd only been skimming the surface of life. Kane made her want for herself the love and joy she'd spent a lifetime wanting for her siblings. When he turned onto the long stretch of road that led to Deloris's house, she said, "Are you sure this is the right street? This is Deloris's road."

"It was." He reached for her hand. "Now it's ours."

There were no other houses on the street. "*How?* They sold it two months ago."

"I know. I was there signing papers."

She was stunned silent again.

"It took me a while to wrap up things in New York, and then I had to design your ring."

"You designed it?" Would he ever stop finding ways to surprise her?

"Yes, with my jeweler friend. I wanted it to be perfect for you. Then he had to make it, and it took me a while for me to figure out if I should lead with the house or lead with the ring."

"And you say *I* overthink?" She was in awe.

Dozens of familiar cars and trucks lined the street. Grace, Pepper, Harlow, Aria, and Zoey held up a massive WELCOME HOME banner, and the rest of their families were waving and cheering. Even Jillian and Johnny were there with their babies, and Tuck, JP, Lee, Eli, and Buddy, too. Balloons danced from long strings tied to the porch railing, there were streamers wrapped around the columns, and the gardens were overflowing with colorful flowers.

Sable's heart swelled to near bursting. "*Kane.* What have you done?"

"I fell in love with a small-town girl and wanted to give her the world."

Everyone cheered as they climbed out of the car. Kane's smile was bigger than the sun as he came to Sable's side, holding up his hand, and made a turnaround motion, calling out, "She said yes!"

Gasps, squeals, and more cheers rang out as, Grace, Pepper, Harlow, Aria, and Zoey flipped the banner over, changing the message from WELCOME HOME to CONGRATULATIONS.

As their families converged on them and they were passed from one set of loving arms to the next, Sable looked at the man who had become her best friend and hadn't just given her the world but had become it and said, "I hope you know I would have said yes without a house or a ring."

"I do," he said as he embraced his mother. "That's how I knew you were *the one*."

Axsel shouted, "Because she was after his Big Daddy, not his bank account."

As laughter erupted around them, Pepper called out, "And she was so busy falling for Mr. Bad, he snuck his heart in there, too."

Kane pulled Sable into his arms as more laughter rang out and said, for her ears only, "Snuck nothing. I had to beat you over the head with it."

"I never said I was easy."

"I wouldn't have it any other way. You, my stubborn, challenging girl, are anything but easy." As he lowered his lips to hers, he said, "But loving you is the easiest thing I've ever done."

# READY FOR MORE?
## MEET THE HOT, WEALTHY, WICKEDLY NAUGHTY BRADENS AT RIDGEPORT!

Follow Pepper Montgomery to her happily ever after with Clay Braden in **PLAYING MR. PERFECT**, the first book in the fun, sexy, spin-off series The Bradens at Ridgeport! Now you can pre-order and buy ebooks, paperbacks, and audiobooks, directly from my bookstore and save on pre-orders, books, and bundles. Follow the link below to shop and save!

Scientist Pepper Montgomery is all about work and no play. As a quarterback, Clay "Mr. Perfect" Braden plays for a living. When Clay needs Pepper's help to get his head back in the game, sparks fly. But while he's determined to teach her the benefits of hands-on research, it's her heart that takes the hit, and she wonders if he's just been *playing* Mr. Perfect all along.

Buy direct and save: **shop.melissafoster.com**

Love loyal cowboys and hot bikers?

Meet The Whiskeys: Dark Knights at Redemption Ranch

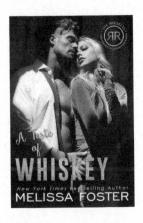

Sasha Whiskey is done with always doing the right thing. She's ready to wrangle in the one man not looking to be caught and give him a taste of Whiskey. With any luck, one taste won't be nearly enough. Come along for the steamy, emotional ride in this friends-to-lovers, forbidden romance.

Buy direct and save: **shop.melissafoster.com**

## Have you met the Steeles?

Kick off your shoes on the sandy shore and enjoy the sweet small towns of Silver Island, home to coffee shops, boat races, midnight rendezvous, and the sexy, sharp-witted Steeles. They have a penchant for pranks, a passion for loyalty, and a trunk full of secrets.

**Pro:** *Stuck sharing a bed with my hot, broody boss*
**Con:** *He's trying to get me fired*

*World Discovery Hour* reporter Sutton Steele spends her days trying to keep her job, while her insanely hot, infuriating boss, Flynn Braden, would love nothing more than to see her gone. When their assignment goes awry and they're stuck in a remote location with only one bed, the only thing hotter than their emotions is their explosive chemistry. Come along for the fun, sexy ride as Sutton and Flynn discover there's a fine line between love and hate.

Buy direct and save: **shop.melissafoster.com**

# New to the Love in Bloom series?

If this is your first Love in Bloom book, there are many more love stories featuring loyal, sassy, and sexy heroes and heroines waiting for you. The Bradens & Montgomerys is just one of the series in the Love in Bloom big-family romance collection. Each Love in Bloom book is written to be enjoyed as a stand-alone novel or as part of the larger series. There are no cliffhangers and no unresolved issues. Characters from each series make appearances in future books, so you never miss an engagement, wedding, or birth. You might enjoy my other series within the Love in Bloom big-family romance collection. Find one that looks fun and dive in, or download the reading order and start with the very first book in the entire Love in Bloom series, SISTERS IN LOVE.

### See the Entire Love in Bloom Collection
www.MelissaFoster.com/love-bloom-series

### Download Free First-in-Series eBooks
www.MelissaFoster.com/free-ebooks

### Download Series Checklists, Family Trees, and Publication Schedules
www.MelissaFoster.com/reader-goodies

# More Books By Melissa Foster

## STANDALONE ROMANTIC COMEDY
*Hot Mess Summer*

## LOVE IN BLOOM BIG-FAMILY ROMANCE COLLECTION

### SNOW SISTERS
*Sisters in Love*
*Sisters in Bloom*
*Sisters in White*

### THE BRADENS at Weston
*Lovers at Heart, Reimagined*
*Destined for Love*
*Friendship on Fire*
*Sea of Love*
*Bursting with Love*
*Hearts at Play*

### THE BRADENS at Trusty
*Taken by Love*
*Fated for Love*
*Romancing My Love*
*Flirting with Love*
*Dreaming of Love*
*Crashing into Love*

### THE BRADENS at Peaceful Harbor
*Healed by Love*
*Surrender My Love*
*River of Love*
*Crushing on Love*
*Whisper of Love*
*Thrill of Love*

**THE BRADENS & MONTGOMERYS at Pleasant Hill – Oak Falls**

*Embracing Her Heart*
*Anything for Love*
*Trails of Love*
*Wild Crazy Hearts*
*Making You Mine*
*Searching for Love*
*Hot for Love*
*Sweet Sexy Heart*
*Then Came Love*
*Rocked by Love*
*Falling For Mr. Bad* (Previously *Our Wicked Hearts*)
*Claiming Her Heart*

**THE BRADENS at Ridgeport**

*Playing Mr. Perfect*
*Sincerely, Mr. Braden*

**THE BRADEN NOVELLAS**

*Promise My Love*
*Our New Love*
*Daring Her Love*
*Story of Love*
*Love at Last*
*A Very Braden Christmas*

**THE REMINGTONS**

*Game of Love*
*Stroke of Love*
*Flames of Love*
*Slope of Love*
*Read, Write, Love*
*Touched by Love*

**SEASIDE SUMMERS**

*Seaside Dreams*
*Seaside Hearts*

*Seaside Sunsets*
*Seaside Secrets*
*Seaside Nights*
*Seaside Embrace*
*Seaside Lovers*
*Seaside Whispers*
*Seaside Serenade*

**BAYSIDE SUMMERS**
*Bayside Desires*
*Bayside Passions*
*Bayside Heat*
*Bayside Escape*
*Bayside Romance*
*Bayside Fantasies*

**THE STEELES AT SILVER ISLAND**
*Tempted by Love*
*My True Love*
*Caught by Love*
*Always Her Love*
*Wild Island Love*
*Enticing Her Love*

**THE RYDERS**
*Seized by Love*
*Claimed by Love*
*Chased by Love*
*Rescued by Love*
*Swept Into Love*

**THE WHISKEYS: DARK KNIGHTS AT PEACEFUL HARBOR**
*Tru Blue*
*Truly, Madly, Whiskey*
*Driving Whiskey Wild*
*Wicked Whiskey Love*
*Mad About Moon*

**WILD BOYS AFTER DARK**
*Logan*
*Heath*
*Jackson*
*Cooper*

**BAD BOYS AFTER DARK**
*Mick*
*Dylan*
*Carson*
*Brett*

**<u>HARBORSIDE NIGHTS SERIES</u>**
Includes characters from the Love in Bloom series
*Catching Cassidy*
*Discovering Delilah*
*Tempting Tristan*

**More Books by Melissa**
*Chasing Amanda* (mystery/suspense)
*Come Back to Me* (mystery/suspense)
*Have No Shame* (historical fiction/romance)
*Love, Lies & Mystery* (3-book bundle)
*Megan's Way* (literary fiction)
*Traces of Kara* (psychological thriller)
*Where Petals Fall* (suspense)

# *Acknowledgments*

Writing a book is never a solo process. I am grateful to my friends and family for their time and patience and would like to specifically thank my son Jake, aka musician Blue Foster, for helping me with musical elements in this story, and my daily sounding boards and shoulders to lean on, Lisa Filipe, Sharon Martin, Amy Manemann, Natasha Brown, and Sue Pettazzoni. I continue to be inspired by my fans, many of whom are in my fan club on Facebook. If you haven't yet joined my fan club, please do. We have a great time chatting about the Love in Bloom hunky heroes and sassy heroines. You never know when you'll inspire a story or a character and end up in one of my books, as several fan club members have already discovered. www.Facebook.com/groups/MelissaFosterFans

To stay abreast of what's going on in our fictional boyfriends' worlds and sales, like and follow my Facebook fan page. www.Facebook.com/MelissaFosterAuthor

Sign up for my newsletter to keep up to date with new releases and special promotions and events and to receive an exclusive short story featuring Jack Remington and Savannah Braden. www.MelissaFoster.com/Newsletter

And don't forget to download your free Reader Goodies. For free ebooks, family trees, publication schedules, series checklists, and more, please visit the special Reader Goodies page that I've

set up for you!
www.MelissaFoster.com/Reader-Goodies

As always, loads of gratitude to my incredible team of editors and proofreaders: Kristen Weber, Penina Lopez, Elaini Caruso, Juliette Hill, Lynn Mullan, and Justinn Harrison and my *last set of eagle eyes*, Lee Fisher.

# Meet Melissa

www.MelissaFoster.com

Melissa Foster is a *New York Times, Wall Street Journal,* and *USA Today* bestselling and award-winning author. Her books have been recommended by *USA Today*'s book blog, *Hagerstown* magazine, *The Patriot,* and several other print venues. Melissa has painted and donated several murals to the Hospital for Sick Children in Washington, DC.

Visit Melissa on her website or chat with her on social media. Melissa enjoys discussing her books with book clubs and reader groups and welcomes an invitation to your event. Melissa's books are available through most online retailers in paperback, digital, and audio formats.

Shop Melissa's store for exclusive discounts, bundles, and more. shop.melissafoster.com